ST. MARTIN'S

MINOTAUR
MYSTERIES

PRAISE FOR JOYCE KRIEG'S MURDER OFF MIKE

"An intriguing, behind-the-scenes look at contemporary talk radio in Krieg's superior debut, featuring fresh, smart, and feisty sleuth Shauna J. Bogart. . . . This riveting mystery will leave readers eager for the sequel."

—*Publishers Weekly*

"Krieg's debut reads like the work of a seasoned mystery writer—in many ways, in fact, it reads better than the work of many genre veterans."

—*Booklist starred review*

"Krieg hasn't missed a trick in plotting and fleshing out her novel with memorable characters."

—*Carmel Pine Cone*

"Krieg is a skilled and smooth writer who keeps up the excitement and a sense of lurking danger through the whole book. . . . [A] highly satisfying book. *Murder Off Mike* won the 2002 St. Martin's prize for best first traditional mystery, and I can see why."

—*Cozies, Capers, and Crimes*

"Shauna J. Bogart is a funny and likable first-person narrator; the background of the radio, musical, and political scene of the California capital is vividly realized."

—*Ellery Queen*

"Joyce Krieg's writing strength is her background in radio. She's comfortable with the equipment. She gives the reader a working knowledge of the tools of the trade and uses them skillfully to advance the plot. . . . Shauna Bogart is an interesting amateur sleuth and *Murder Off Mike* shows a lot of promise."

—*Mystery News*

"Readers will quickly comprehend why *Murder Off Mike* won the St. Martin's first novel contest."

—Harriet Klausner

"Krieg has all the right skills and a terrific backdrop in the world of talk radio."

—*The Poisoned Pen*

MURDER OFF MIKE

JOYCE KRIEG

St. Martin's Paperbacks

Library of Congress Catalog Card Number: 2002035389

ISBN: 0-312-98760-9

Printed in the United States of America

St. Martin's Press hardcover edition / April 2003
St. Martin's Paperbacks edition / May 2004

St. Martin's Paperbacks are published by St. Martin's Press, 175 Fifth Avenue, New York, NY 10010.

10 9 8 7 6 5 4 3 2 1

ACKNOWLEDGMENTS

Murder Off Mike would not exist if not for the best first Traditional Mystery Novel contest sponsored by St. Martin's Minotaur and Malice Domestic, that most wonderful mystery fan organization. A thousand thanks to the volunteer readers (that's you, Jane Platino!) and to St. Martin's "First Lady of Mysteries," Ruth Cavin, who chose my manuscript from the field of finalists and whose eye for detail and helpful suggestions made it a far better book than I could ever have done on my own. Words will never be adequate to convey the gratitude I feel toward Ms. Cavin, St. Martin's Press, and Malice Domestic for making a lifelong dream come true.

The background for *Murder Off Mike* comes from my experiences working at two Sacramento radio stations. To the old gang at Earth Radio 102 and KFBK NewsTalk 1530: Hope I got it right! Mark Stennett and Curtis Carroll vetted the manuscript for technical accuracy, and Allen Chamberlin made sure I had Sacramento's one-way streets running in the right direction. The Monterey writing gang—Hugo Gerstl, Paul Karrer, Mickey Nowicki, Marilyn Tully, Arlen Grossman, Dennis Alexander, Alan Irwin, Claudia Ward—slogged through early versions of the manuscript with great patience. For unflagging support, my thanks to Steve Krieg, Maxine Carlin, Penny Spar, Susan Goldbeck, and Harry Warren. I am most grateful to my agent, Jimmy Vines, for his early enthusiasm for my work. A toast to Roger Krum, executive director of the Sacramento Jazz Jubilee, for throwing one helluva party every Memorial Day weekend—and for all those free drink tickets.

"Hi, you're on the air with Shauna J. Bogart."

On Line One, Lenny from Rio Linda wants to talk about the black helicopters landing at Beale Air Force Base.

Liz from Carmichael holds on Line Two. She's planning to share her theory connecting Roswell with the JFK assassination.

One of the regulars, Ferretman Bob, hovers on Line Three. Today he wants to challenge the candidates for governor to take a stand on the legalization of ownership of guess which member of the weasel family.

Tiffany on a cell phone is waiting on Line Four. She thinks she has the lucky numbers to win a thousand bucks in the Gold Rush Giveaway.

On Line Five, Rudy from West Sacramento says something "most peculiar" is happening in an apartment building across the street from the State Capitol.

Welcome to talk radio.

My name isn't really—thank God—Shauna J. Bogart. But that's what they used when all this got on TV and in the papers. In less than a month, I'll celebrate the last birthday in which I can legitimately put a three at the start of my age. A couple of long-term live-in relationships under my belt, one quickie marriage, no kids. I happen to think I'm better looking than my publicity pictures would lead you to believe, without all that makeup and mousse the stylist at the photo studio gooped on me. When I got my first job in radio twenty years ago, I was the token female. Today, I'm still the only employee pulling down a permanent, full-time air shift who uses the restroom with the Tampax machine.

We've got the requisite right-wing blowhard on the air in the morning. Middays you'll hear a shrink for a couple of hours, then a regular doc, an investment guy, even a cooking feature at noon. Early evenings, Sacramento Talk Radio lines up a sports show, then Dr. Hipster from eight to eleven. More about him in a minute.

My show is the afternoon news and talk block. I consider myself the station's voice of reason and moderation. Most listeners think otherwise. "Feisty," "outrageous," and "in your face" are the descriptions I like. I don't even mind the "b" word. "Shrill" and "strident" I can do without.

The next segment in the show was supposed to be the Gold Rush Giveaway, according to the program log, which meant I should put Tiffany on Line Four on the air and get the contest out of the way, but Rudy from West Sacramento piqued my curiosity. Tiffany could hang on and rack up a few more minutes on her cell phone. She could always pay for the extra airtime with the one thousand smackers she was about to win.

I punched up Line Five. "Rudy from West Sacramento, you're on the air. What's this most peculiar thing happening down by the Capitol?"

"This is Miz Bogart, yes?" Hesitation and a heavy accent. Not German, not French, but definitely European. Hungarian? Polish?

"First-time caller?"

"I am from that, Miz Bogart."

"Just plain Shauna J. is fine. Welcome aboard."

My producer made a motion with both hands as if snapping an imaginary stick. Break. As in, time to break for the 4:20 commercial segment. I scowled, waved the kid away, and returned my attention to the caller. Josh Friedman was only an intern from Sacramento State University, pathetically eager to please. I could see his chin start to tremble from behind the glass that separates my talk studio from his call screener booth.

"Two men in brown uniforms come into this man's apartment. They looked like police, but not."

Who does this guy think he is with the phony Iron Curtain accent? Boris Badenov? "Go on," I said.

"I heard loud voices."

"What does this have to do with this 'most peculiar' thing you say you witnessed?"

"I saw the man who lives in the apartment lying on the floor. He was not moving and his head, it was bleeding."

"Whoa. When did all this happen?"

"This morning."

I'm five minutes late going into the commercial break. No way can I blow off the sponsors, the political spots stacked up like planes circling O'Hare. Not to mention Tiffany, the contest winner on Line Four.

"Rudy, I've got to take a break, but I definitely want to hear the rest of your story. You stay on the line, okay?"

I slid a tape cartridge into the playback machine and punched the PLAY button. The gravelly voice of Dr. Hipster, plugging tonight's show. I pictured him recording the promotional announcement while sitting behind the control board in the production room, scraggly gray ponytail hanging down his back, scrawny fingers of one hand clutched around the mike, those of the other hand around a joint.

"Killer show tonight . . . biggest thing since this so-called election for governor . . . gonna blow this town sky-high . . . don't touch that dial . . . The Hipster's tipsters have the score, the skinny, and the straight dope . . ."

I listened with one ear to Dr. Hipster's revved-up patter while I prepped Tiffany for her moment of fame. The Doc's taped announcement flamed to a climax. "Trippin' with the Hipster . . . we've got your prescription . . . tonight, eight to eleven."

Next, the Gold Rush Giveaway, Tiffany spewing squeals of delight over the air for thirty seconds or so, then back to Rudy from West Sacramento on Line Five.

The heavily accented caller didn't even wait for me to finish giving the time and temperature. "Dr. Hipster, he is a good man with a good show. I will miss him, yes."

"What's that?"

"Dr. Hipster, his apartment is by the State Capitol, is it not?"

"Rudy, if you're suggesting what I think, that is so not funny."

"I knew you would not be from understanding."

My finger was poised over the button that controlled a tape cartridge with the sound effect of a World War II torpedo. "Why are you calling a talk show with your story? Why don't you call the police?"

Silence. Rudy from West Sacramento was dead air.

I hit the "caller torpedo" tape. The show was so far off schedule, it was already time for the four-thirty news and traffic break. I punched up another tape cartridge with my theme jingle.

"You're listening to the Shauna J. Bogart Show, the only talk program in the capital city not suffering from an overdose of testosterone. We'll be right back after this."

Another commercial in the endless volley of attacks and counterattacks in the election for governor. I called Josh on the intercom connecting the talk studio with the screener booth. "Get Dr. Hipster on the line."

The usual headlines: Earthquake in Japan, car bombing in the Middle East, one gubernatorial candidate accusing the other of something heinous. The usual weather: hot and hotter. The usual traffic update from Captain Mikey in the chopper: tie-ups on 80 and 50, a jackknifed big rig on I-5.

"You're back with Shauna J. Bogart. We'll get on to your calls in a minute, but first, let's clear up that last call from Rudy from West Sacramento." I hit the blinking studio hotline, where Josh had lined up Dr. Hipster to go on the air.

"Hello, you've reached the Hipster Hotline. You know the score. Leave a message at the tone and I'll get back to ya." I shot another evil eye at my call screener. Why did the kid let me put an answering machine on the air? Do I have to teach these interns everything? I'm not that picky, really. I'd given Josh practically no restrictions. Just don't let anyone on the show who's boring. And no ladies named after months or flowers.

I adjusted the mike and took a deep breath. "Dr. Hipster

must be out working on that big scoop about the election." I slammed a public service announcement from Smokey Bear into the tape deck, just to buy time.

Another summons to Josh on the intercom. "Phone the cop shop and have them check out Dr. Hipster's apartment. Just to be sure."

Josh picked up the phone and began tapping numbers.

I poked the intercom button. "One more thing. Send out a news car."

Josh flashed his first smile of the afternoon.

"I already did."

I may whine a lot, but the truth is, the Shauna J. Bogart Show is the best radio gig I've ever had. The reason this was the best job a gal could ever wish for strutted down the hall to the newsroom, all five feet six inches and seventy years of him. Conservative business suit sandwiched between a cowboy hat and a pair of hand-tooled Tony Lamas. He carried a fishing pole in his good right hand. His not-so-good left hand consisted of a silver hook, courtesy of a land mine in Korea. He clutched an unlit Camel—no filter—in the hook. I loved him to pieces, and not just because he rescued me from ever again having to play Twelve Hits in a Row on Your No Repeat Workday.

Top of the hour, time for the six-minute hourly network newscast. This is usually the only chance I have to use the john. But today, I wanted to hover in the newsroom to monitor the police scanners.

I caught up with the boss next to a wall-sized Rand McNally map of the world. T. R. O'Brien's cowboy hat barely touched the equator. He tipped his hat with the hook, winked, and put a finger to his lips. "Don't tell." With his redneck twang, it came out more like "Don' tay-ell." Talking with the boss always made me feel like I was having a conversation with the kid in those old Shake 'n Bake commercials. "An' ah hay-elped."

I made the requisite gushy noises over T. R.'s new fishing pole. "All ready for Alaska?"

"Thought I could sneak out the back door and head out to Folsom Lake an' try 'er out without nobody seein' me."

T. R. O'Brien hardly ever took a day off. But he did allow himself a week at the National Association of Broadcasters convention every fall, and a long weekend in May for a fishing orgy in Alaska. One of those deals where they fly you in to some island lodge with just the guys, your bait, and your beer.

"Did you happen to catch that caller about a half hour ago?"

"The fellah with the accent who says he saw a body in the apartment building down by the Capitol? Yep. Thought you handled it right fine, if that's what you're frettin' about. But for God's sake, do something about that new intern of yours."

"Do you think there's anything to it?"

O'Brien was about to reply when the police scanner squawked to life. "Fourteenth and N. 187."

Fourteenth and N Streets. Dr. Hipster's apartment building. California Penal Code 187. Murder.

My ears caught the last commercial in the network newscast. Learn Spanish in thirty days or get your dinero back. Sixty seconds to showtime. T. R. followed me into the air studio as I donned headphones and placed my theme music into the cart deck. "You sent out a news car, of course," O'Brien said.

I held up my hand to prevent him from saying anything more as I opened the mike. But the boss had to get in the last word. "One thing I respect about Dr. Hipster, he brings in the ratings. I just don't understand why you two have never gotten together."

"Get real!" I shouldn't have snapped. Especially at the man whose good hand signs my not unsubstantial paycheck every two weeks. Plus, he had a point.

Dr. Hipster had been bopping around the airwaves since the sixties. He was that peculiar breed of aging hippie/renegade/survivalist who seemed to thrive in northern California. Pro-gun. Anti-government and anti-big business. Believed in stockpiling food, growing your own dope, and birthing your own babies. Actually believed there were black helicopters landing at Beale Air Force Base.

I liked Dr. Hipster because he was the first person to give this gal a break in a tough, male-dominated industry. He had the honor of sticking me with Shauna J. Bogart as an air name when he offered me my first full-time DJ gig. But I forgave him. I knew the truth: Dr. Hipster was ninety percent shtick. Inside lived a soft-hearted, sentimental sweetheart.

Every few years, our paths would cross at a radio station, a rock concert, or an industry convention. We liked the same foods (deep-dish pizza, Szechuan Chinese), the same movies (Marx Brothers, Mel Brooks), and we shared the same attitude toward authority (amused contempt). He was my mentor. He was the big brother I never had. Dr. Hipster had been many things to me. But one thing he wasn't and had never been: my lover.

Ferretman Bob finally got his turn on the air. "... these lovable animals aren't fish or game, so why does the Department of Fish and Game claim jurisdiction ..." I closed the mike and let him harangue while I fiddled with the two-way and tried to raise Gloria Louise Montalvo.

"Glory Lou? It's Shauna J. What's your ten twenty?"

Field reporters love it when you talk cop lingo to them.

"Fifteenth and L. I'll be there any minute, sugar." Glory Lou's southern accent was so sweet and pure you'd swear you were listening to a member of the homecoming court at Ole Miss.

"Copy. I'm going to monitor the two-way on my headphones. As soon as you get to the scene, I'm putting you on the air. Over?"

I've been inside a slew of radio stations around the country. Mostly dumps, but a lot of mahogany-and-marble corporate palaces as well. But no matter how fancy the trappings, they're all rabbit warrens. Lots of tiny rooms and narrow corridors. And the air-conditioning never works. Here it was not even Memorial Day, and already well into the nineties.

I'd stashed T. R. O'Brien, still clutching his fishing pole

and unlit Camel, in the corner. The promotion director popped in to remind me to keep plugging the Gold Rush Giveaway. The sportscaster got wind that something interesting was developing and dropped in to check things out. A couple of guys from the sales department crept in. At least, T. R. didn't have any live bait with him.

Before I had the chance to shoo everyone out, Glory Lou called in a report from the news car. "Sacramento police are investigating a death at an apartment building across the street from the State Capitol. Authorities have not issued a statement, but homicide investigators and the coroner are gathering on the ninth floor."

Dr. Hipster lived in number 904.

"We will keep you updated as soon as more developments are available. Reporting live from downtown Sacramento, this is Gloria Louise Montalvo for Sacramento Talk Radio. Back to you, Shauna J."

Through the headset, Glory Lou continued to fill me in. "You wouldn't believe all the cops around this place. Not just Sac PeeDee, but CHP too. Channel 3 just pulled up. How'd they find out so fast?"

Listened in on our two-way, of course.

More callers, more traffic reports, more local news updates. Glory Lou hailed me on the two-way during a commercial break. "They're bringing out a body bag. Lordy, ten years in this business and that's one of the things you just never get used to seeing."

O'Brien turned to me. "Just say the word. I'll get someone else to take the show for the rest of the afternoon."

Every muscle in my body ached to run. Grab the keys to a news car, rush to Fourteenth and N, climb those stairs to the ninth floor, and break down Dr. Hipster's door. Track down a cop, grab him by the lapels, and demand he tell me what's going on. At the very least, find the nearest bar, hand over my AmEx card to the bartender, and tell him to keep pouring until I'd maxed out my credit line.

But I had a show to finish.

2

"So it's already been bulked and stripped."

"I was only doing what you told me to do." Josh turned to me from behind the wheel of News Unit Four. With his eager blue eyes, blond frizz, and nervous energy, he was a twenty-first-century version of Gene Wilder playing Leo Bloom in *The Producers*.

"I know. I just don't know why I would have put a fresh promo in the pile of outdated carts," I said from the passenger seat.

"Could happen to anyone."

"I suppose." One of the first things I did earlier this afternoon, once I realized this was not turning out to be just another day in talk radio, was to attempt to rescue the tape cartridge with the last promotional announcement Dr. Hipster would ever record. I always keep two stacks of carts in the control room, one for announcements, commercials, and sound effects that will air repeatedly, and the other for tapes that can be erased and the labels peeled off—bulked and stripped—and used for something new. It's possible I could have put Dr. Hipster's promo in the wrong pile. But not likely.

Josh maneuvered the Ford Taurus onto the freeway in the last of the rush-hour traffic. He wasn't supposed to be driving the news car, being only an intern. Insurance. But he beat me to it when we'd both scrambled for the last remaining news car in the station parking lot the second my show ended.

"Why is it so important?" Josh steered the news car around

a stalled RT bus on the 29–30th Street Freeway.

"I'm not sure. Something was off. I just can't put my finger on it."

"He sounded the same as always to me. The usual rant and rave."

"Damn, I wish I'd paid more attention." But why should I have? I'd been focused on psyching up the latest contest winner to put her on the air, plus juggling the rest of the commercials in the stop-set, to pay more than passing heed to Dr. Hipster's usual spiel.

"And I should have double-checked before I bulked and stripped all those carts."

"Not your fault. But you're sure you didn't hear anything out of character?" I knew I was reaching, but I couldn't help it. "Something in his tone of voice, or the words he used?"

"To be honest, I wasn't paying that much attention either."

"I hear you. Well, there's always the logger tape."

I slouched in the passenger seat, turned down the chatter on the police scanner, the two-way, and the on-air monitor, cranked up the air conditioner, and tried to dredge up an instant replay of Dr. Hipster's promotional announcement from my memory bank. "Killer show tonight . . . something-something election for governor . . . gonna blow this town sky-high . . . blah, blah, blah . . . the skinny, and the straight dope . . ."

We drove in silence past Sutter's Fort, an Old West anachronism surrounded by freeways, apartments, Sutter Hospital, and the ubiquitous state office buildings. Josh finally said something. "The coroner might have made a mistake."

"Yeah, right." And Jim Morrison isn't really lying in a coffin in that Paris cemetery.

"No, really. They've been known to make mistakes identifying bodies. It could happen."

"Yeah, right." They probably got Dr. Hipster mixed up with that other tall, skinny guy with the gray braid hanging halfway down his back who lives on the ninth floor at Fourteenth and N.

"I was just trying to help."

I didn't say anything, just swallowed and blinked. Never cry in front of the help.

Josh circled the news car around the lush green of Capitol Park, then turned east on N Street. On the left, the white marble State Capitol, a Victorian jewel tucked away in a vault of steel-and-glass high-rise bureaucracy. On the right, Dr. Hipster's apartment building, another fifties-era soulless slab. A sign next to the door promised wall-to-wall carpeting, central air, and coin-ops. This particular night, it boasted features they don't mention in the rental listings. Cop cars on the sidewalk, doors flung open, light bars flashing, and two-ways crackling. Yellow crime-scene tape crisscrossing the doors. Live satellite trucks from the three network affiliates and the two indies, their dishes poised for action. The reporter from KFBK reciting into a cell phone and the *Sacramento Bee* photographer threading her way through the maze of TV cable. Rubberneckers creeping along N Street, pedestrians peering over the police tape.

Josh double-parked News Unit Four next to the matching news vehicle Glory Lou had been driving. I climbed out and a blanket of hot air dropped over me. Almost six-thirty and it still must have been at least ninety-five. I don't know how those guys on the TV news do it, what with their suits, heavy makeup, and hot lights.

Glory Lou rushed up and gave me a quick embrace. "Hon, I'm so sorry." She was cool and crisp as usual, in a raspberry linen suit and dove-gray silk blouse, size twenty-two from the Macy Woman shop. Her river of shiny black hair was caught neatly in a silver clasp. Here I was, a wilted mess in one hundred percent cotton, bangs plastered to my forehead.

A young woman wearing a Sacramento 'Talk Radio T-shirt and one of those skort things bustled next to Glory Lou. What the hell was the station promotion director doing here? Did Mimi Blitzer honestly think she could turn this scene into some sort of contest? Name Dr. Hipster's killer and win the backstage passes?

"Everything's under control," Blitzer said. "Don't forget, I have a degree in public relations."

T. R. O'Brien stepped in front of Blitzer. Minus the fishing

gear and plus a lit cigarette, deep lines carved into his weathered face. He put his good arm around my shoulders. "I'll take
care of everything. Don't worry about them." He indicated the
TV vans with his hook.

I wouldn't have minded talking to the TV guys if they'd
called in to my show. Where I could have fielded their questions in the protective womb of the studio. But not here. Not
out in public.

As if on cue, the Channel 3 reporter jammed a mike in my
face and his sidekick focused a minicam.

T. R. grabbed the mike and pointed it at himself. "Understand one thing, young fellah. If you're going to stick that
thing anywhere, you can just shove it my way, okay? We're
family at my radio station, and anything that involves one of
mine, you kin talk to me about it."

The Channel 3 guy was a good fifty pounds heavier, six
inches taller, and four decades younger than my boss. The
reporter considered the odds and chose wisely. T. R. repeated
his comments about family for the camera and added, "All of
us at the station extend our deepest sympathies to Dr. Hipster's
son and daughter, Marc and Melissa."

I marveled at T. R.'s incredible memory and intimate
knowledge of each and every one of his forty employees.
Spouses, kids, pets, make of car they drove, make of car they
fantasized about driving, favorite team, amount of spousal support payments: T. R. had it filed away in his memory bank
and could dredge it up on command.

The Channel 3 duo slunk away. "Thanks for rescuing me,"
I told T. R. "But the only thing that will make me feel better
would be for them to catch the guy who did this. Any leads?"

O'Brien and Glory Lou exchanged glances.

"What gives?"

The lines deepened on T. R.'s forehead. "Didn't you and
that kid monitor the station when you were driving over?"

"Josh and I wanted to talk, so we turned down the speakers."

Another exchange of glum looks. O'Brien took a big drag
on his Camel.

"If you won't tell me, I'll go ask our friends at Channel 3."

Glory Lou broke the silence. "The cops are saying they think it might be a suicide. Off the record, of course."

"No way!"

"I'm so sorry, hon, but not according to my sources." Glory Lou flipped open her notebook. "Preliminary investigation shows death likely to have been caused by a single gunshot wound to the head. And they found a note."

Dr. Hipster had everything he could possibly want: money in the bank, friends, two terrific kids. Not to mention a job he loved. "He lived for the show, couldn't wait to go on the air every night. I don't believe it," I said.

Glory Lou patted my arm. "Girlfriend, you never know."

T. R. nodded in agreement. "Seventy-plus years on this planet have taught me, you never know for sure what's going on inside someone else's head."

"What about that phone call from Rudy in West Sacramento?"

Glory Lou consulted her notes. "Cops say they're following up."

The four of us—T. R., Glory Lou, Josh, and me—stood in a grim cluster on the sidewalk in front of the apartment building. The police weren't letting anyone in or out except tenants, and then only with an escort. A couple of men wearing brown uniforms and forest ranger hats ducked under the tape.

"Who are those guys?" Josh wanted to know.

"Private security," Glory Lou said.

"Wonder what they're doing here?" I asked.

Glory Lou wasn't sure. "Sac PeeDee has jurisdiction as far as I know. But there are a couple of assemblymen and senators who live in this building, along with some press corps people and lobbyists. Maybe they're beefing up security for them."

She glanced down the sidewalk. "Speaking of sources, look who's coming to pay us a call."

He was fortyish, tall, and highly Nordic. Brooks Brothers blazer, gray slacks, and loafers. "Lieutenant Larry Gunderson." He flashed his badge. "You Shauna J. Bogart?"

I nodded and shook hands as Gunderson continued, "I've

heard you on the radio. Listen to the show whenever I can."

Here it comes. It never fails.

"You don't look anything like I pictured you."

I faked a smile. "Sorry to disappoint you."

Gunderson pushed a strand of hair into place. "Mind if I talk to you for a few moments over there?" He indicated three police cars on the Fourteenth Street side of the building. "We've got a command post set up."

"Only if I come along," T. R. said.

"You're the station owner, correct? I guess that's okay."

"What a minute," I said. "Glory Lou and Josh are with me. They're coming too."

Gunderson rolled his eyes, but didn't say no.

This was not going to be good news. The meeting with the homicide investigator was going to rank right up with the doctor wanting you to come in to his office right away to talk about your test results. My stomach was doing high jumps by the time we turned the corner onto Fourteenth Street.

"I hope you guys aren't planning to arrest me," I wise-cracked weakly as we passed the media encampment. "I mean, of all the people in Sacramento I have the perfect alibi. I was on the air the whole time."

Gunderson said nothing.

Dr. Hipster's son leaned against one of the police cars at the command post, shock and grief etched on his twenty-two-year-old face. I'd met Marc once before, at the station Christmas party. Like a lot of children of hippie parents, he turned out to be a straight arrow. First-year law student at McGeorge. The Doc's daughter, Melissa, was still in high school, lived with the ex in San Jose. Marc would probably have to take charge of the funeral arrangements. My heart went out to him.

Gunderson spoke to me. "I suppose you've heard this looks like a possible suicide."

I could feel my anger rise, stronger even than grief. "Dammit, why aren't you following up on the Rudy from West Sacramento angle? Here I have someone on my show saying he saw a commotion in this very apartment building this morning. And the Sac PeeDee is doing squat."

"Ms. Bogart, we are following up. I've got officers searching for this Rudy from West Sacramento. We want to find him as badly as you do."

"Try harder."

T. R. lit another cigarette. "Shoot, I'm with Shauna J. I just don't buy this suicide thing. I'd just signed Dr. Hipster to a three-year contract with a hefty pay raise. Just about broke my business manager's heart. So he wasn't hurtin' for money."

Gunderson nodded.

"We're in the middle of a juicy election for governor," T. R. continued in his high-pitched twang. "The Doc loved stuff like that. And he wasn't having personal problems that I know of. It's been a good five years now since he and Donna split up."

"It was the most civilized divorce I'd ever seen," I put in. "They were even decent about dividing up the cats."

"The decedent left a note," Gunderson said. "We've taken the original to the crime lab for analysis, but I've got a copy." He turned to me and pulled a sheet of white paper from his pocket. "I'm not supposed to let you know about this."

I tensed.

"But you seem like a nice lady and I like your show."

Gunderson unfolded the paper.

"He said he did it because of you."

3

Click-click-whir, click-click-whir, click-click-whir.

I tightened the pressure knob on the exercise bike. Get the knees pumping, the heart pounding, those endorphins kicking in.

"He said he did it because of you."

Click-click-whir, click-click-whir.

Crank up the volume on the Walkman. The Stones, "Sympathy for the Devil."

"Killer show tonight."

Pump harder, faster.

"The decedent left a note."

Harder. Faster. Louder.

"Dear Trippin' Sister, I did my own thing. I lit my own fire. I walked on my own golden road to eternal enlightenment. All is meaningless without your love. Thanks for listening. Dr. Hipster."

I was alone in the exercise room at my hideously overpriced "luxury" apartment complex. Working out usually makes me feel better. But not tonight.

No one believed me, dammit. Not the cops, not Glory Lou, not T. R., not even Josh.

Oh, they'd all been so concerned, so careful of my feelings, back at the scene of the crime.

"Something wasn't right in that last promo from Dr. Hipster this afternoon," I'd said to anyone who would listen.

"Of course, hon," Glory Lou said with a sympathetic hug.

"Why don't you go home, get away from all these people, and pour yourself a tall, cool one?"

"The police chief and I go way back," T. R. told me. "I'll make sure he puts his best people on the case."

Josh was no help, other than to drop apologies for erasing the tape cartridge.

I'm not used to not being taken seriously, and I don't like it. Maybe that's why I gravitated to a career where people are forced to listen to my opinions, as long as they keep those fingers off that dial.

"All is meaningless without your love."

My feet flew from the pedals. I tore the headphones from my ears and threw a sweat-soaked towel against the wall. So help me, Dr. Hipster had never given me the slightest indication he had anything but friendship on his mind. No gooey glances, no phone calls late at night "just to talk." A couple of weeks ago, he confessed a yearning for one of his son's professors at McGeorge. "Think she'd go for a worn-out old freak like me?" he asked me.

I gathered up my towel, Walkman, and keys and called for security to escort me back to my apartment. Victor Pahoa tipped the brim of a Smokey Bear hat when he opened the door into the exercise room.

"I didn't think you worked nights," I said after we'd exchanged greetings.

Pahoa punched the second-floor button of the elevator. "Don't usually. Two of the guys on night called in sick today." He yawned and stretched, the uniform buttons straining against his slab of a chest. "It's okay. I can use the overtime."

The elevator door slid open. Victor and I began the walk down the outdoor corridor to my apartment. I nodded greetings to several of my neighbors. An aide to the Assembly Ways and Means Committee on his way to the exercise room. Senator Fred Tanaka (D-San Jose), hoisting a half-dozen shirts in dry cleaner's plastic bags. Diane George, the Capitol reporter for the all-news radio station, right arm straining with the weight of a hefty briefcase. Each accompanied by one of Pahoa's coworkers on the private security force.

I said good night and unlocked my door.

A ball of orange fur growled, hissed, and sank a claw into my ankle.

Another reason this was turning out to be the worst day of my life.

It's not that I don't like cats. I just haven't been around them much. Same as babies. Nothing against 'em. I just haven't a clue what I'm supposed to do when someone plops one in my lap. Bialystock and Bloom, those were the names Dr. Hipster and his then-wife chose for the twin tabbies when they adopted them eight years ago. His ex took custody of Bloom; Dr. Hipster kept Bialystock. Whenever I'd visit the Doc's pad, Bialystock would usually skitter under the bed and cower until I left.

But the cops threatened to take Bialystock to the pound unless someone volunteered to care for him, so what could I do?

Glory Lou would have gladly given "the poor sweet thing" a good home, but her apartment complex had a firm no pets policy. Josh had not one but two allergic housemates. And T. R. had Cora and her Yorkies to consider.

I have no roommates, allergic or otherwise. Obviously no other pets. And at an upscale joint like Capital Square, no one cares if you keep Shamu in your bathtub, as long as you cough up the security deposit.

Like I said, what could I do? I let one of Lieutenant Gunderson's minions put a squirming, writhing feline into a plastic kennel carrier. The officer placed the box in the backseat of the news car. "I found some cat food in the decedent's apartment and put it in the car for you, lady. Also the litter box. Good luck."

I gingerly detached Bialystock's claws from my bare leg and flicked on the lights. Three rooms plus bath. Four, if you count the dining nook as a separate room. The furniture came with the apartment, and since it had been designed by and for the suit-and-tie crowd, lobbyists and legislators taking advantage of the short-term rentals, it was heavy on chrome, glass, and dark leathers. I didn't help things by filling half the living room with an elaborate stereo system, all glowing lights, flickering needles, digital gizmos, and speakers on steroids. Guys love it. Once I've actually lured a man into my pad, he usually ends up spending more time fiddling with the stereo than he does fooling around with me.

The red light on my answering machine pulsated in staccato. I rolled back the message tape, only half listening. Two TV stations, wanting a comment. One of Dr. Hipster's old radio cronies from San Francisco who had just heard the news. A kid's voice, muffled: "Tune me in, tonight at midnight, AM 1620." Some telemarketer trying to convince me to change long-distance carriers. The *Sacramento Bee*, wondering if I had a photograph of Dr. Hipster they could use.

Screw 'em. I didn't even bother to write down the messages. I picked up the remote, flicked on the TV, and caught a tease for the ten o'clock news. "Local radio personality dead in apparent suicide. Details at ten . . ." Like they say, if it bleeds, it leads. I aimed the remote at the TV and pushed the OFF button.

The person I ached to talk to was the one person who'd never again be there for me. Not only had Dr. Hipster been my counselor and coach, but I realized—too late—he'd also been my best friend.

It was Dr. Hipster who helped me get over my early bouts of mike fright. "Forget all those thousands of listeners out in radio-land," he told me. "Just picture talking to your best friend, or your boyfriend. Hell, make someone up; it doesn't matter. Pretend that one person is in the studio with you. Don't ever, ever let go of that one listener."

Dr. Hipster helped me tap into radio's unique ability to communicate intimately and personally. He coached me on how to smooth over mistakes, and how to slip cue from one record to the next without even a second of dead air between. And when I made the big leap from music to talk radio, it was the good Doctor who told me to watch out for callers named after months or flowers.

As for tonight? He'd probably give me the lecture about how any publicity is good publicity, just so long as they pronounce your name right and mention the call letters. Then he'd grin demoniacally, shrug his skinny shoulders, and quote Bette Midler: "Fuck 'em if they can't take a joke."

I'd known I was going to miss Dr. Hipster like crazy. Up 'til this moment, I hadn't realized exactly how much.

I headed for the kitchen, fixed a gin and tonic in one of my collection of radio station coffee mugs, slid open the glass door to the balcony. The temperature had finally cooled to the seventies. Still, I left the sliding door open only a couple of inches. No sense letting the refrigerated air out and the hot air in.

I settled into a molded plastic lawn chair, put my feet up on the railing, and raised my cup in a silent toast to the all-night truckers two stories below and a block away on I-5.

The booze slipped past my throat and straight to my head. Cool, crisp escape. The events of the day played back, like a reel of tape slowly unspooling.

Rudy from West Sacramento: "I knew you would not be from understanding."

Dr. Hipster: "Killer show tonight."

Glory Lou's honey-sweet voice metallic on the two-way: "They're bringing out a body bag."

Lieutenant Gunderson: "He said he did it because of you."

Dr. Hipster again. "Biggest thing since this so-called election for governor . . . gonna blow this town sky-high . . . don't touch that dial . . . The Hipster's tipsters have the score . . ."

Don't touch that dial?

No way!

I took another swallow and gazed down at the freeway. Mostly trucks this time of night, a hypnotic ebb and flow of white and red lights. In the distance I could make out the letters on a green-and-white Caltrans directional sign: Los Angeles, San Francisco, Lake Tahoe. Even though I wasn't going anywhere tonight, I liked having the choices at my doorstep.

Beyond the twin lines of freeway lights, the Sacramento River snaked its way from Mt. Shasta to San Pablo Bay and the Pacific Ocean. On the far bank, I could make out the lights of West Sacramento.

Rudy. Who the hell are you? Call me!

I took my feet from the rail and drained my drink. I almost choked on an ice cube as something warm and furry rubbed my ankle. Bialystock. I scratched the cat under the chin the way I used to see Dr. Hipster doing.

The animal backed away and hissed. "Look, I'm sorry." I felt like an idiot talking to a cat. "I miss him too. But you gotta help me. You were there. What did you see?"

The orange tabby turned and slipped through the door back into the cool dark of the apartment.

The green LED numerals on the face of the clock radio next to my bed showed straight-up midnight. That message on my answering machine. Something about tuning in AM 1620 at midnight? A blues station I'd not heard before. Bessie Smith, Johnny Lee Hooker. Perfect. Helen Hudson, with her version of "Stormy Weather." Helen Hudson? How the hell did this brand-new station latch on to one of *her* recordings? They'd been out of print for at least forty years.

I was just drifting off when the announcer came on. Young, green. Trying to sound old, hip. "You're listening to, uh, non-commercial, charisma-free blues radio for the Sacramento Valley and the universe. Tonight, we pay tribute to one of our own: the late, the great Dr. Hipster."

Then came the familiar singsong of the *Jeopardy!* theme.

The juvenile announcer was back. "Alex, the answer is, what is off mike and out of sight?"

I slept fitfully 'til just before dawn. That Thursday morning, like every weekday morning, my bedside clock radio woke me up, the radio still tuned to the station I'd been listening to when I finally drifted off to sleep. AM 1620, noncommercial, charisma-free blues. All I could hear was the static hiss of a station that had signed off the air.

Dead air.

I yawned, forced my eyes open, and snaked my arm out from under the covers, fumbling for the push button to tune back to Sacramento Talk Radio. My sleep-drugged imagination took over, and I could swear I heard the one-toke-over-the-line voice of Dr. Hipster, chiding me with gentle sarcasm.

Don't touch that dial!

A shaft of sunlight shot through a gap in the bedroom curtains as I bolted from the covers and rushed through my morning routine. The sooner I got to the station, the sooner I could begin searching the one place where I might find the truth. The logger tapes.

4

"Sweet baby Jesus." I sagged against the back of the swivel chair in the production room and stared at the fat reel of logger tape.

And at the inch of splicing tape, a slash of white against brown, marking the spot where one hour of yesterday's show—the hour in which Dr. Hipster's last promotional announcement aired—had been neatly sliced away.

Few things are sacred in live radio, but the logger tape is definitely one of them. A continuously rotating reel recording everything that goes out over the air during a twenty-four-hour period, it's the only tangible evidence a station has as to exactly what was broadcast. The logger tape is an essential tool when a client questions whether his commercial aired as scheduled, or when defense attorneys subpoena our records as they gather evidence to request a change of venue due to pretrial publicity. Not to mention when VIPs call to complain about something a friend of a friend thought they heard on the Shauna J. Bogart Show.

If someone needed a snippet of programming from the logger tape, he'd dub it onto cassette. But no one, not even T. R. O'Brien, would dare mess with the original. Certainly not to the extent of excising an hour's worth of programming.

I sat alone in the news production room, surrounded by mikes, the reel-to-reel machine, a cassette recorder, tape cartridge recording decks, tape erasers, splice finders, speakers. Plus one of the few typewriters left in the building, for making labels. Reporters use the room for putting "wraps" together: their voice wrapped around a sound bite they'd gathered in the field or over the phone.

With my hands on the hubs of the tape and the take-up reel, I backed up a few inches on the pizza-size reel just past the splice, hit the STOP button, then PLAY, just to make sure I hadn't heard it wrong the first time. First came the sign-on of the network newscast at 4:00 P.M. An almost-imperceptible blip from the splice. Then the opening fanfare of the network newscast at 5:00 P.M.

The entire four o'clock hour of yesterday's show—gone.

Just like the cartridge holding Dr. Hipster's last promotional announcement, somehow ending up in the pile of out-of-date carts to be bulked and stripped.

The killer, or one of his pals, could have been sitting in this very chair yesterday evening or earlier this morning, slicing the logger tape with an X-Acto knife. Had anyone peeked in the tiny window in the production-room door, he or she would not have noticed anything out of the ordinary.

Only someone working at the station would have the skill and access to pull off a stunt like this. And it had to tie in to the death of Dr. Hipster, it just had to. It was just too much of a coincidence that first the tape cartridge would "accidentally" disappear, then the entire hour in which I broadcast the first news of his death—and his last promotional announcement—would turn up missing on the logger reel.

Someone wanted to make sure there was no permanent record of Dr. Hipster's last public words.

The sportscaster? He'd been hanging around the newsroom yesterday afternoon and he for sure had the technical know-how. But what motive? As far as I knew, Steve Garland's big ambition was to get on TV, where they make real money.

T. R. O'Brien? The boss and his fishing pole had been lurking around the newsroom. And he prided himself on being able to actually operate every piece of equipment in his radio station. But whoever did this must be Dr. Hipster's killer. And why would T. R. want to permanently silence one of his most popular hosts?

Gloria Louise Montalvo? The reporter was supposedly out

making her beat checks when Josh dispatched her to the Fourteenth and N Street apartments. Glory Lou made no secret about desperately wanting a show of her own. But still. No one committed murder over a late-night radio show in Sacramento, California. Morning drive, maybe.

Mimi Blitzer? I recalled seeing the promotion director lurking around the air studio yesterday afternoon. Motive? I had no idea why she would want to involve herself in the snuffing of one of the station's most promotable personalities. Did she have the smarts to splice tape? Debatable.

That left Josh. I was pretty sure the kid had the technical skill, and he certainly had the opportunity. But, again, what motive? As far as I knew, his only ambition was to survive an internship with yours truly.

Of course, money always works.

I've never figured out exactly what ethnic group Gloria Louise Montalvo represents. I do know she picked up the Scarlett O'Hara accent when her dad was stationed at Biloxi. She must be at least six feet tall and weigh in at two hundred pounds, minimum. Samoan maybe? She's talked about a father who was born in "The Islands" and a mother who claims African and Cherokee ancestry. It must take her all day to fill out those "diversity in the workplace" surveys.

"Getting a head start on today's show?" Glory Lou's bulk filled the open door to the production room.

"Just putting together a retrospective. Dr. Hipster's greatest bits." I hated keeping secrets from someone who'd been a pal, but right now I just didn't trust anyone from the station.

"Hon, that must be hard, listening to his old shows."

I spotted a familiar frizzy head quivering behind Glory Lou. "Aren't you supposed to be in class?" I said to Josh Friedman.

"Just try to keep me away, today of all days."

"Good, because I've got a project for you." I stood, hoping my body would block the rack holding yesterday's logger tape, the date emblazoned in thick black felt pen across the label. "Do you happen to remember Dr. Hipster having a personal security expert as a guest on his show recently?"

Josh shook his head, while Glory Lou said, "Sure, I remember that show. I'm thinking it was two, three weeks ago."

"What are we waiting for?" I said. "It's gotta be on a logger tape somewhere."

"What's gotta be on a logger tape?" Glory Lou said.

"The show with the personal security expert. I have this feeling Dr. Hipster was trying to send a message in his last promo announcement. The tapes from yesterday are missing, but I'll bet whoever's doing this never thought to dig back and find that interview with the security guy."

Glory Lou gave me a shoulders-raised, palms-up puzzled gesture.

"I know it's a stretch that a piece of advice this security expert gave Dr. Hipster several weeks ago could have ended up on the air yesterday," I said. "But at this point, what else do we have to go on?"

The Happy Mandarin Palace has three things going for it. One, it's right around the corner from the radio station. Two, the food's cheap. Ambiance is not the third thing. Formica and plastic, no waitperson service. You don't even get a plate, just a foam container.

A beer and wine license, however, is the third thing. Bottles of Corona Light and Sutter Home White Zin nestled in a tub of ice next to plastic packets of soy sauce and Chinese mustard. Only in California.

I unwrapped my chopsticks while Glory Lou dove into her broccoli beef and Josh chomped on an egg roll. No background music, just a steady chop-chop of the cleaver and sizzle of oil in a hot wok from the kitchen.

"I hear Country 101 is going satellite." Glory Lou tore off the corner of a packet of mustard and dabbed the contents on her egg roll. "My sources tell me they're getting bought by Federated Communications. They're going to fire the entire air staff, even the morning team."

"What's Federated Communications?" Josh asked.

I made the sign of the cross with my chopsticks to ward off evil. "They own over a thousand radio stations around the country. Federated controls the airwaves in virtually every major market."

"And now it looks like the vultures are invading Sacramento," Glory Lou said.

"You guys hear of a new station in town?" I asked. "Plays blues music late at night, comes in at AM 1620?"

Josh shrugged and reached for the soy sauce. "Probably just some guys at the student station at UC Davis having fun."

The glass door to the Happy Mandarin swung open, letting in a squall of fiery air along with a familiar figure. Mimi Blitzer waved a hello toward our table. We had room for a fourth, but our returning gestures must have been lukewarm, because the promotion director plopped her tote bag at a table for two in the corner.

Glory Lou rested her chopsticks on the edge of the white foam clamshell. "Run that business about the personal security expert by me again."

"Jack Krueger, retired FBI agent, wrote a book about personal security, how to keep your family safe in an unsafe world, something like that. Guest on the Hipster show a couple of weeks ago, just like you remembered."

"He must have been a perfect fit for all those paranoid Hipster-heads."

"He kept the phone lines lit all three hours. The next day, Dr. Hipster corners me in the lunchroom. Did I listen to last night's show, and wasn't Krueger right on. He's telling me I should be more concerned about my personal security. I'm about to brush it off as more of his usual survivalist b.s."

I searched my memory bank trying to recall whether anyone might have wandered into the lunchroom and overheard that conversation. Someone was always hanging around waiting for the coffee to perk or for the microwave to finish nuking their lunch. So chances were good one or more people from the station heard what Dr. Hipster next told me.

"That security expert had one idea that I thought made sense," I said to Josh and Glory Lou.

"The concept is that families and close friends should make up a secret code phrase, something that sounds innocent, but when you say it, the others will know that you're in trouble. Say you're being held hostage and forced to make a statement to the media. Like Patty Hearst."

"Who?" This from Josh.

"Dr. Hipster and I decided on our own code phrase, right there in the lunchroom," I said, ignoring Josh. " 'Don't touch that dial.' It's something neither of us would ever say unless we were in some sort of trouble."

" 'Don't touch that dial'?" Josh said. "What's wrong with that?"

"It's such a cliché, so trite. Kinda like you never, ever hear a professional musician using the phrase, 'and all that jazz.' "

"Besides," Glory Lou said, "in case you haven't noticed, radios haven't had dials since Great-Grandpa was tuning in *The Shadow* on his Atwater-Kent."

"The point is," I continued, "do either of you recall Dr. Hipster saying 'don't touch that dial' in that promo we aired during the four o'clock hour yesterday?"

Josh gave a mournful shake of his head. "Sorry. I was chatting up the callers waiting on hold."

"And I was out in the field," Glory Lou said. "The mayor was just finishing up a news conference at City Hall when Josh radioed to check out the possible 187 at Dr. Hipster's apartment building. Hon, why don't you just check the logger tape?"

God, I wanted to tell them. I looked at Josh, then Glory Lou, and saw only curiosity and compassion. It couldn't be either of them, could it? Glory Lou, the closest thing I've got to a best girlfriend in Sacramento. And Josh—could the heart of a calculating killer beat inside that lovable nerd exterior?

I gazed at a wall calendar showing the Chinese zodiac in bold red characters and wondered if anyone outside of the station might have recorded yesterday's show. One likely source came to mind. It went against all of my more rational instincts to pursue it. But I couldn't think of an alternative.

I turned to Josh. "When we get back to the station, see if you can track down Ferretman Bob for me."

Mimi Blitzer returned to her table with a white foam box of food. Today the station cheerleader wore a peach-colored polo shirt embroidered with the Sacramento Talk Radio logo over a plaid miniskirt. She pulled a bridal magazine the size of the Sacramento yellow pages out of her tote bag, opened the steaming lunch container, and began to fork down rice and chicken while studying up on honeymoon destinations.

"What gets to me is the suicide note. It just doesn't feel right," I said to Josh and Glory Lou. "You guys take a look and let me know what you think." I pulled the photocopy Gunderson had given me from my backpack, unfolded the single white sheet, and passed it to Glory Lou.

"I mean, what is this garbage 'All is meaningless without your love,' " I said when she finished reading. "The Doc and I both hated all that touchy-feely, let's-all-have-a-group-hug crap. He would never write something like that."

"Hon, you just never know."

Josh peered over the padded shoulder of Glory Lou's jade-green raw silk suit. I out-aged her by at least five years, but Glory Lou managed to look like the grown-up while I was still the unkempt teenager.

"I'll grant, a guy who's about to end it all may not act logically," I said. "But try to picture this: He composes a su-icide note on his word processor, even types his name under where his signature will go, runs it through the laser printer on station letterhead, signs his name, seals it up in an envelope with my name typed on it, then picks up the gun? I don't think so."

"Girlfriend, people do crazy things. There's no figuring, sometimes." Glory Lou folded the note and passed it back to me.

Josh practically raised his hand to be called on. "I've got it! Why don't we see if Dr. Hipster left a copy of the note on his hard drive?"

"Hon, Glory Lou's got an even better idea." She patted his shoulder. "How about you put your college education to work figuring out how we can find Rudy from West Sacramento?"

Josh deflated. "I can't."

"What do you mean, you can't? A smart young fellow like you, surely you keep records of all the callers in that big ol' computer of yours."

I came to Josh's rescue. "He's only following my orders. I don't want people who call my show to feel threatened or intimidated, like they're going to end up in Big Brother's data bank or something. They only have to give us their first name and the city they're calling from. They don't even have to give us their real name."

Josh did have a file set up in the computer to keep track of the regulars, just to make sure they don't get on the air more often than every two weeks. He also kept a file with names and addresses of contest winners. "I already checked," he told Glory Lou. "So did the police. There's no Rudy from West Sacramento in either file. During the show this afternoon, why don't you make a public appeal for Rudy to come forward? If he was listening yesterday, he might be listening today."

"Absolutely. I was thinking the same thing."

I could see a worry line forming between Glory Lou's coal-black eyes. "This is still under investigation by the police. Maybe you should run it by T. R. O'Brien first."

"O'Brien doesn't care what I do as long as I bring in the ratings." But I wondered.

Glory Lou was already out the door of the restaurant, Josh at her heels, while I still fussed with my leftovers. Josh hesitated, then turned back to me.

"There's something I didn't tell the police about Rudy from West Sacramento."

5

"Jeez, why keep it a secret?" I asked when Josh finished.

"The cops pissed me off so much with their questions that I decided not to tell them anything more than I absolutely had to. All this bogus crap about 'doesn't the FCC require us to keep records of everyone who calls in to our talk shows' and all."

So Josh decided not to tell Lieutenant Gunderson about the music playing in the background when Rudy from West Sacramento called the show. A party? Josh asked, just making idle chitchat with the callers waiting their turn to go on the air. Some band practicing in the background, according to our mystery man. By the time Rudy got on the air with me, the musicians had taken a break.

"I don't suppose you recognized the music, or noticed anything else useful that might help us track him down?" I asked Josh as we walked across the searing heat of the asphalt parking lot to the station.

"Stop treating me like just another kid. Of course, I recognized the music. Dixieland, 'Sweet Georgia Brown.'"

"How's a kid—okay, a college student—like you know anything about that corny old music?"

"Everyone knows the jazz festival's coming up at the end of the month. Everyone knows it's a big deal for this city. Even a kid like me."

I saw the flowers on my desk and recoiled.

A large, cheery bouquet, bright and sunny daisies, carnations, and roses, topped with a giant yellow smiley face button. Which sickhead fan had been tasteless enough to send such a monstrosity less than twenty-four hours after the death of Dr. Hipster? I resisted the urge to chuck the whole thing in the trash, and tore open the plain white envelope taped to the smiley face button. If the sender urged me to "have a nice day," I swear, I was going to retch.

We hope you enjoyed last night's show. Tune us in again tonight! Your friends at AM 1620.

I hefted the basket of pink and yellow blossoms and went in search of T. R. O'Brien's secretary, who doubled as the receptionist during the lunch hour. Mrs. Yanamoto had been working for T. R. since around the time of the Beatles' first appearance on the Sullivan show, typed at least a bazillion words a minute on an IBM Selectric, and refused to learn how to use a word processor. Most of us figured Mrs. Yanamoto and T. R. had worked so well together for so long because she was the only person at the station tinier and tougher than the boss.

"Did you happen to see the person who delivered these?" I unloaded the bouquet onto Mrs. Yanamoto's desk.

"Indeed, my dear. I thought it was unusual because he wasn't with one of the regular floral delivery services and he didn't ask me to sign for them."

"Do you remember what he looked like?"

"He seemed like a nice young man. Tall, brown hair, wearing jeans and a T-shirt, but neat and clean. Except for one of those dreadful tattoos."

"A tattoo? Did you get a look?"

Mrs. Yanamoto frowned in thought. "I believe it had something to do with snowboarding. 'Amped on Snowboarding' perhaps."

A description that would fit roughly ninety percent of the young male population of Sacramento.

I returned to my desk, unearthed the voluminous press kit the Sacramento Traditional Jazz Society had sent me, and pulled out the schedule of band performances leading up to the

Memorial Day weekend festival. Something called the New
Bohemia Jazz Orchestra had a gig at the West Sacramento
Raley's supermarket yesterday afternoon from three-thirty,
then moved on to the Raley's on Freeport Boulevard at five-
thirty.

The timing fit. The New Bohemians would have had to
break at around four-twenty—when Rudy got on the air with
me—to make a five-thirty date on Freeport Boulevard.

I know it usually sounds like we're making it up as we go
along, but good talk radio takes a certain degree of prep. Study
the newspapers and the latest news magazines. Bone up on
whatever author is in town flogging a new book. At least read
the dust jacket and the table of contents. Set up some fun
sound effects: shrieks, groans, belches, barks. I usually tape
the Letterman and Leno shows and the hot sitcoms the night
before and pull off the best one-liners. I know it's a violation
of copyright. So sue me. They should be grateful for the publicity.

But today, my instincts told me to forget planning any topics and to blow off the interviews I'd set up. Just open up the
phone lines and let the listeners pour out their sorrow, their
disbelief, their memories, and their theories. It's therapy and
it's damn compelling radio.

Another lesson from Dr. Hipster.

"I've got a present for you, doll." Monty Rio handed me a
cassette tape. "Highlights of Dr. Hipster's shows from the past
few weeks. I pulled them off the logger tape and put them
together in a montage. I thought you might be able to use it
if you need to fill time."

Monty Rio, operations manager at Sacramento Talk Radio.
A possible suspect?

At most stations, he'd be a big deal. The operations manager controls the entire on-air sound, from hiring a morning
team to deciding who gets stuck working Christmas. But at
our shop, T. R. O'Brien made all of the important decisions,

leaving Monty Rio with the nitpicky details and an endless mound of paperwork.

Most of the staff treated Monty Rio with condescending scorn, but I thought he was okay. One of my earliest childhood memories is hearing him on the Sherwood show on the old KSFO out of San Francisco, reading the news when Chet Casselman wasn't around. Monty Rio had been somebody once, back in the days when radio announcers were major local celebrities.

But still. He'd been in the newsroom yesterday afternoon. He knew how to run all the equipment. No one would have noticed anything out of the ordinary if they'd happened upon Monty fiddling around with the logger tape. Shoot, he'd just told me he'd pulled Dr. Hipster's sound cuts off the logger tape and spliced them together.

"Thanks, Monty," I said, placing the cassette on my desk. I wondered, though, if I'd have the heart to play it.

I've already made it clear I had no romantic interest in Dr. Hipster. I looked up as the guy who did make my heart beat a little faster walked into the newsroom. And headed straight for *my* desk!

T. R. O'Brien's wife Number One—B.C., Before Cora—had a career as a fashion model. Vivi starred in a series of newspaper ads for I. Magnin back in the fifties, elegant as all get-out in Christian Dior and Balenciaga. The product of their six-year marriage inherited his mother's height and dark good looks. And her good taste in clothes.

Normally, I wouldn't have had anything to do with the guys who sell radio time. I find them demanding, obnoxious, slippery, and definitely not to be trusted. But for Terrence O'Brien Jr., general sales manager at Sacramento Talk Radio, I made an exception, and not just because he was drop-dead gorgeous. Or the boss's son. He was easygoing, considerate, and showed at least a degree of empathy with the on-air staff. While most sales managers decorate their offices with plaques from the Million-Dollar Club and posters illustrating smarmy slogans like "What Is Hustle?" and "Attitude Makes the Difference,"

Terrence O'Brien Jr. covered his office walls with autographed publicity stills of legendary DJs: Cousin Brucie, Alan Freed, Larry Lujack, Dr. Don Rose, Humble Harv. I sensed a kindred spirit.

Terrence patted his hundred-dollar haircut into shape and smiled, showing off the result of years of orthodontia. His Armani-ed butt was perched on the edge of my desk. Any other guy, I would have asked him if that was a cell phone in his pocket, or was he just glad to see me. But like a teenager with a crush, I turned awkward and tongue-tied. So I just nodded hello.

"I've been looking for you all day. I just want you to know how terribly sorry I am. The whole family is."

I tried to think of an appropriate response.

"All of us—Father, Cora, and I—have nothing but respect for how you've handled this terrible situation."

"Yeah."

"I know it must have been an incredible strain. You deserve a break."

Terrence handed me a business card. The Monterey Pavilion—Another Fine CalFac Property!—in elegant script. "I've booked a suite for you for this Friday, Saturday, and Sunday night. You can leave as soon as you finish your show and be there in time to watch the sunset from your room. It's a double, so if you'd like to bring a friend, be our guest."

The only person with whom I'd like to share a double bed in a fancy hotel at the coast leaned against my desk. Single (divorced, no kids). He dated, he was straight. I'm single, I date, I like men. My mug does not scare horses or small children. So what was his problem?

"What about my show on Monday?"

"Don't worry about that. You rest up, walk on the beach, get a massage. We'll just play some 'best of' tapes."

A weekend on the coast. I knew the station had trade with the hotel in Monterey—they get advertising, we get rooms—so it wasn't costing Terrence anything. But still, with trade, it's usually just management types and clients who land the goodies and we on-air drones get squat. I hadn't been to Monterey in years, not since the days when I ditched high school

to hang out on Cannery Row. The bluebird of happiness didn't
necessarily start trilling in my heart, but the vulture of gloom
did loosen her talons just a tad.

Almost every afternoon, I give Mimi Blitzer a ring to see if
she has any goodies in the prize closet for me to give away
on the air. I keep hoping for a P.T. Cruiser or a week in Tahiti.
And usually get stuck with free oil changes and dinners for
two at The Olive Garden.

Blitzer answered her extension on the second ring. She
didn't have the keys to a Porsche or plane tickets to Paris for
me to give away. Big surprise. She did have a trip to Disneyland, but she was hoarding it for the morning show. They
always get the good stuff.

What she had left for me was a pair of tickets to the Sacramento Jazz Jubilee.

It would figure. A town like Sacramento, the hottest event
of the year would have to be a Dixieland festival. "Oh, joy.
Pizza parlor music."

Mimi chided me over the interoffice phone line. "What kind
of attitude is that? Just you wait. The instant you announce
you've got a pair of Jubilee badges to give away, the phones
will ring off the hook."

I was silent.

"What if I also throw in dinner for two at The Olive Garden?"

"Do I have a choice?"

"Don't forget the Gold Rush Giveaway."

"If only I could."

I used to get excited about things like elections for governor.
But somewhere between Watergate and Whitewater, the flame
died. I still vote—in honor of my father's one term in the
State Senate, if for no other reason—but when it's just me
inside the voting booth, I keep hearing a tiny voice whispering,
"Who cares?"

This year's election pitted a veteran pol against a younger

techno millionaire. Nadine Bostwick: sixtyish, feisty career
politician from San Diego. Worked her way up the ranks, from
precinct captain to Speaker of the Assembly. Jeff Greene:
forty-something, rugged good looks, Harrison Ford in one of
his white-collar action hero roles. Founder and CEO of a
multimillion-dollar Silicon Valley start-up that actually had a
sensible business plan and managed not to tank. He held my
father's old seat in the State Senate. Married, three kids.

T. R. O'Brien swaggered through the newsroom and stopped
at my little corner. "Mrs. Yanamoto told me she just saw Junior at your desk. I thought I'd better check 'n' see the kid
wasn't botherin' you."

Terrence O'Brien Jr. could bother me anytime he wanted,
but I didn't feel like sharing that information with his father
and my boss. "Thanks for the weekend in Monterey," I said.
"It sounds like just what I need. Grab a six-pack, lie on the
beach, and listen to the waves."

"That's the spirit!" O'Brien settled back in an empty chair
next to my desk, his cowboy-booted feet resting on the desktop, one hand and one hook behind his head. T. R.'s honest
green eyes and creased, weathered face appraised me with a
combination of concern, respect, and affection. Swear to God,
if Junior ever looked at me like that, I'd marry him in a minute.

"Can I tell you"—kin ah tayl yeeuu—"you're handling this
thing like a real trooper. I know lot of other gals—guys too—
would have fallen apart under the pressure. But not our Shauna
J. You're the best."

Partly to deflect the subject away from me, and partly because I really did want to know, I asked O'Brien if he'd heard
anything about services for Dr. Hipster. "Last I heard, the family was going to do something back home in San Jose.

"I got a call from one of Dr. Hipster's fans this morning,"
T. R. said. "They're putting together a memorial service. Tomorrow morning at ten at Cesar Chavez Plaza."

"That sounds like a scene Dr. Hipster would have appre-
ciated."

"I'd be honored if you'd ride over and sit with me and
Cora."

I felt another rush of affection for my cantankerous boss.
He knew it would be an awkward, difficult moment for me.
Questions, prying eyes, whispers. He knew the strength of his
power and personality was the best protection I could have.

The hell with the age difference. If it weren't for Cora, I'd
marry T. R. O'Brien in a minute. And have his children.

"Have you heard anything about a new station in the market?" I asked. "Plays the blues, located at the far right on the
AM dial?"

"Negatory on all of the above."

"I could have sworn I picked up something last night. And
then this showed up today." I gestured to the bouquet and the
smiley face balloon bobbing on my desk.

"You sure it wasn't one of those big stations from Salt Lake
City or somewhere that you pull in late at night with the skip?"

The skip: the physical property of radio signals to bounce
off the surface of the earth, fly into the stratosphere, then
carom back to ground, often hundreds or thousands of miles
away, especially at night. The world map on the newsroom
wall, covered with pins on Guam, Finland, Montana, Alaska,
and dozens of others, are sites where listeners have picked up
our station and sent us a postcard. Our chief engineer sends a
card in return, verifying their receipt of our signal. DXers, the
serious hobbyists are called.

"I don't think so. No fading or static. I'm pretty sure it was
local."

You don't get to be as crafty—or successful—as T. R.
O'Brien without knowing your competitors and every move
they're making. Plus, he was president of the Capital City
Broadcasters Association. If there was a station playing the
blues at midnight at the far right end of the AM band, T. R.
O'Brien would know about it.

But still, I'd heard it.

Had I been totally unhinged by the death of my friend?
Had one gin and tonic gone to my head? Could it have been
a dream?

O'Brien hauled himself out of the visitor's chair next to my

desk. "Say listen"—T. R. turned to me before walking away—
"you plannin' on sayin' anything about the Hipster thing on
your show this afternoon?"

"You mean like inviting listeners to call in with memories
and stories and tributes to Dr. Hipster? Like putting out an
appeal for Rudy from West Sacramento to call in again?"

"Yup."

"Well, yeah. Do you have a problem with that?"

O'Brien pointed his silver hook at me. "Only if you *don't*
do it."

My ears caught the opening notes of the top-of-the-hour network newscast jingle. Six minutes to showtime. I grabbed my
folder full of clippings and the program log, and hurried to
the control room.

Adjust the mike upward and shove the chair into the corner.
I like to stand, to pace when things get really hot. Keeps my
energy level up. Folder with news clippings on the counter
directly in front. Program log to the right, sound effects and
commercial carts stacked to the left. At eye level, the meters
and indicator lights bounce to the electronic beat.

No engineer. I fly solo. Tighter that way. More control. Just
me, the microphone, a computer terminal, and the control
board. And the listeners.

The monitor screen connecting me to the computer in
Josh's call-screener booth was already filled with names of
callers waiting to go on the air with me. Sandy in Placerville.
Louis in Lodi. Morris in downtown Sac, and Tom on a car
phone.

Twenty-some years of being Shauna J. Bogart and I still
needed a minute or two before each show to slip into character. I shut my eyes, took several deep breaths, and pictured
the on-air persona I'd created: taller, makeup more vibrant,
hair wilder and redder. Sparkly earrings and clanky bracelets.
Bright silk dresses. Where that image came from, I have no
idea. But it worked.

Today, I heard the voice of Dr. Hipster, with the advice he
gave me the first time I hosted a talk show: "Just remember,

this isn't journalism. Hell, this ain't even yellow journalism. It's showbiz, and don't ever forget it."

As I breathed deeply, I filled with the essence of Shauna J. Bogart's brash, bright, and passionate personality. She'd be running the show for the next three hours. A momentary rush of electricity as I flipped the mike switch to the ON position.

"Ladies and gentlemen, put your radio in its upright, locked position, because Shauna J. Bogart is on the air! First an hour of open line, then stay tuned during the four o'clock hour for a very special guest. Live in our studio, direct from his gig at the homicide division at the Sacramento Police Department, Lieutenant Larry Gunderson."

He showed up right on time, in the middle of the network newscast at 4:00 P.M. Today, the preppie homicide detective's button-down had a faint yellow stripe. In deference to the heat, he draped his blazer over the back of the chair in front of the guest mike.

Gunderson and I exchanged the ritual pleasantries. "Thanks for coming on such short notice."

"Glad to do it. Your boss and the chief are old friends. And it's like I told you yesterday. I'm a fan."

He brought me and my listeners up-to-date on the investigation. "We're still awaiting more tests from the coroner, but the preliminary evidence is not inconsistent with a suicide. One shot was fired at close range. The gun was found in Dr. Hipster's hand."

"Don't you think it's odd none of his neighbors heard anything?"

"Most of them weren't home on a weekday morning. And the incident occurred in the room Dr. Hipster apparently used as a home recording studio. Soundproof."

Gunderson fiddled with the mike cord. "As I mentioned, it will take several more days for all of the test results to come in. But the condition of the body at the time of discovery was not inconsistent with a self-inflicted gunshot wound occurring four to eight hours previously."

"And I suppose you checked the gun for fingerprints."

"Just one set. The decedent's."

I glanced at the program log and shuddered. At the 4:20 break in the log, the traffic coordinator—the gal who puts the logs together—had whited out the line indicating Dr. Hipster's promo.

No matter what T. R. decided to do to fill the void, it would never be the same.

I hadn't really planned what I'd do with the show once I was finished interviewing Gunderson, but I needn't have worried.

JEFF GREENE ON LINE ONE! Josh messaged on the call-screener computer.

THE SENATOR? I tapped into the keyboard.

Josh responded by holding two thumbs up from his call-screener booth.

I messaged back: HE'S NEXT AFTER THE BREAK. SEE IF YOU CAN LINE UP BOSTWICK TOO.

An all-too-familiar figure burst through the control-room door. Jeez, not Mimi Blitzer!

"This is a closed studio," I said.

Blitzer leaned over the console, forcing me to look at her pinched features. Her head quivered and she clenched her lips in a pout.

"This is a closed studio," I repeated.

"I wouldn't put that caller on the air yet if I were you."

"I beg your pardon?"

Blitzer eased off the console, placed her hands on her flat hips, and favored me with a smirk. "Aren't you forgetting something?"

Cripes! Not the damn contest.

You could be a big winner in the fabulous Sacramento Talk Radio Gold Rush Giveaway! Watch your mailbox for your contest announcement with your lucky prize number. Then, keep it tuned to Sacramento Talk Radio. If you hear us announce your lucky number and call us within fifteen minutes, you could win one thousand, five thousand, even ten thousand dollars!

I mean, isn't it enough that we give our listeners interesting, thought-provoking programming? Round-the-clock news updates? A bit of companionship on that lonely commute? Do we have to resort to bribery to win your loyalty?

"You were supposed to do the contest five minutes ago," Blitzer said. "You keep this up and you're going to be in trouble. Big trouble."

"Yeah, yeah, yeah." I snatched the three-by-five card that had appeared in her fingers. Where had she been hiding it? Not in her cleavage, that's for sure.

It was easier to cave than to endure another Mimi Blitzer lecture. For sure, she'd try to remind me about how competitive this market is, with two other news/talk stations, plus sports talk. Didn't I know how important the spring Arbitron ratings period is for information-based programming? Mimi Blitzer loved to throw around hotshot MBA marketing terms like "information-based programming." What's wrong with just plain talk radio?

But Blitzer had a point. That's what this game is all about, in the end. The Arbitron ratings. High numbers allow a station to charge more for commercial advertising time. Killer ratings equal big profits.

So I announced the damn lucky numbers from Mimi Blitzer's three-by-five card and rattled off the names of the sponsors. "But I'm not going to put the winner on the air if they call in during the interview with Jeff Greene," I warned a retreating Blitzer.

"I didn't agree with everything Dr. Hipster stood for," the governor wannabe said when I finally got him on the air, "but I listened to his show whenever I had the chance. And I always will cherish the memory of the experiences we shared on The Farm Team."

"The Farm Team?" I knew Jeff Greene was a graduate of the political think tank, but I hadn't realized Dr. Hipster had ever participated.

"Several members of the media are invited to attend each year. I was lucky enough to go through the program with Dr. Hipster eight years ago."

Eight years past, I would have been far from the Sacramento

scene, spinning disks on a Lite Rock station in Seattle.

All right! I grinned and returned the two thumbs-up to Josh through the glass. According to the message he'd just flashed on the monitor, Nadine Bostwick was parked on Line Three.

But the Speaker of the Assembly would have to wait.

Rudy from West Sacramento was holding on Line One.

6

The boss never calls you into his office to deliver bad news before your show.

Not because he fears you'll engage in tearful on-air good-byes, or attempt to recruit your listeners to start a letter-writing campaign to save your gig, though that's been known to happen. What really causes radio station bosses to shiver in their pinstripes is the threat of sabotage. A favorite stunt is for the about-to-be-fired DJ to bulk-erase all of the tape cartridges: the promotional announcements, the jingles, the commercials.

These days, the boss usually hands you your severance check, someone from HR watches you clean out your desk or your locker in the jock lounge, and security escorts you out of the building. Sometimes they even change the locks.

They always do it after your show.

T. R. O'Brien is a good guy. But I still keep a current résumé and aircheck, telescoped down to edit out the commercials and fluff, showcasing my best bits, in my safe-deposit box. In this business, you never know.

If I'd had the foresight to aircheck today's show and 'scope it down, it would have sounded something like this:

". . . Assembly Speaker Nadine Bostwick, you're on the air with Shauna J. Bogart . . .

". . . Rudy from West Sacramento, glad you called back. Got some serious questions for you, but first, what's this business about 'I vahnt to vahrn you'? Who are you channeling today? Bela Lugosi? . . .

". . . Congratulations, Meredith Mulchick of Citrus Heights! You just won five thousand dollars in the Sacramento Talk Radio Gold Rush Giveaway. Way to go, Meredith! . . ."

I crossed and recrossed my legs, trying to get comfortable on the hard wooden chair outside the boss's closed office door. Nothing I'd said or done, as far as I could tell, would have caused T. R. O'Brien to order me to report to his office before I went home.

"Good night, dear." Mrs. Yanamoto locked her desk drawer. "I'll see you tomorrow."

"Same here." If I'm not reporting to work at station K-EDD, otherwise known as the Employment Development Department, waiting in line to file for unemployment insurance.

I leaned toward the closed door sealing off T. R.'s inner sanctum. I could hear his rough-edged twang, but couldn't distinguish any words. I barely made out a fast-paced female voice.

A consultant? A new program director? Someone with a briefcase full of research? T. R. would study the spiral-bound report, shake his head slowly. "Sorry, Shauna J., especially in light of what happened yesterday. But these focus group results don't look good. I'm gonna have to cut my losses, buy out your contract. . . ."

T. R. stuck his weather-beaten face out the door. "Dammit, I told Mrs. Yanamoto to call me as soon as you showed up. I hope you ain't been waitin' long."

A thick stack of computer printouts held center court on T. R.'s massive mahogany desk. Tiny Mimi Blitzer, a smirk on her face, rose halfway from a brown leather guest chair. Okay, I'd been a little late reading the contest numbers this afternoon, but still.

"Gosh, I'm really sorry about getting into the contest so late," I said as I seated myself in the second guest chair. "I promise it will never happen again." Never let them even begin to take control of the conversation. Always be the one who lobs the first shot. Another lesson from Dr. Hipster.

"Aw, shoot." T. R. waved his good hand at me. The silver hook rested on the printouts. "I'm not worried about that. You're in the middle of a breaking news story and a personal crisis. You're doing a terrific job, by the way."

I returned Mimi Blitzer's smirk with one of my own.

"But this is about the contest," T. R. continued. He shuffled the stack of tractor-fed paper with the hook. "You know how important this contest is to the station. We've put all our resources behind it. Not just the cash prizes, but print advertising, billboards, TV."

Like I've said, T. R. O'Brien is basically a good guy in an industry peopled by some sleazy types. So I refrained from responding with comments about "buying a ratings book" or "trying to hypo the ratings." Instead, I returned what I hoped was a thoughtful nod and said, "We're competing against two other news/talks, plus an all-sports station, in a market with advertising revenue that can support only two of us. The spring ratings period is crucial to the success of this station for the next six months."

"I've bet my desk with my partners that the Gold Rush Giveaway will deliver the ratings for us," T. R. said. "We can't have anyone threatening the credibility of the contest. If word got out on the street, it would destroy us."

This time, I didn't bother to watch my tongue. "Hold on a minute! Shauna J. Bogart earns her ratings. I don't have to bribe my listeners."

"It's not you I'm worried about." T. R. continued to draw figure eights with the hook on the stack of printouts.

"Didn't that winner you had this afternoon sound a little young?" Mimi Blitzer raised her hand to tuck a hank of her brown pageboy 'do behind one ear. I caught a glimpse of the glitzy chips that made up her engagement ring.

"Meredith what's-her-name? I wasn't paying that much attention. And so what? Not all of my listeners are 55–death."

Fifty-five–death: radio slang for the 55-and-over demographic age group. The category most advertisers ignore.

It's not enough in this crazy business to have huge numbers of people tuning in to your show. They have to represent the right demographic group if the station's going to make any money. Most ad agency media buyers lust after the 25–54 age bracket, with women 24–34 being considered pure gold when it comes to buying power. News and talk radio tends to draw an older crowd, the 55–death listener.

Blitzer consulted the legal pad on her lap. "I had a nice little chat with Miss Meredith Mulchick after she won five thousand of our dollars this afternoon. Would you believe, she's nineteen years old, a sophomore at Sac State?"

What happened to the days when the promotion director's only role was to hang banners and pass out bumper stickers? I resisted the urge to pick at a hangnail and wished I'd brought along a prop, like Blitzer's handy legal pad. She'd also toted along a ballpoint pen and one of those yellow highlighters. T. R., I was sure, desperately wished it was still okay to light up indoors. I could see the outline of a pack of cigarettes in his shirt pocket. "So Meredith gets to pay next semester's tuition, maybe goes on a shopping spree at Tower Records," I said. "What's the big deal?"

T. R. flipped a couple pages of the stack of printouts and squinted to read the type. "It wasn't Meredith Mulchick's numbers you were supposed to read today. According to the plan, this afternoon's winning numbers were supposed to belong to Wanda Livingston of Carmichael."

"A thirty-seven-year-old supervisor at Caltrans," Blitzer added.

"Hey, I just read the numbers you guys hand me on the little cards," I told O'Brien and Blitzer.

"Shoot, I know that," the boss said. "Like I said before, we know you're clean."

"Then why drag me in here after my show and tell me all this?"

"We'd like you to keep an eye on that intern of yours."

"Don't you ever drive?" I asked Josh as he relaxed in the air-conditioned splendor of my late seventies Datsun 240Z, a high school graduation present from my old man.

"My roommate borrowed my wheels." Josh cranked up the radio. More political advertising. Clean for Greene. Nadine Bostwick: a choice for a change.

Even growing up with a political gadfly like my father, I

never could dig the obsession for holding political office. Seems to me for the same amount of money, time, and energy, you could do something epic. Like buying a baseball team, or going to Burning Man. Or owning your own radio station.

Still, I guess it would be kind of cool to be governor of California. You get a state car and bodyguards, the office has thick carpets and a massive desk, and you never have to pay for a meal. I once read if California were a separate nation, we'd be something like ninth in the world in terms of wealth and productivity. Which I guess puts the governor on the level of a prime minister or king or emir. Without, thankfully, access to nuclear weapons.

On the considerable other hand, it means committing yourself to living in Sacramento for four years.

"Guess what I just found out," I said to Josh in what I hoped was an offhand voice. "That contest winner we had this afternoon? She goes to Sac State."

"Meredith Mulchick? For real?"

"You have any classes with her?"

"I don't think so. It's a big school, twenty-five thousand students."

"Bet she'll be real popular now, winning all that loot." The traffic pace picked up as we cruised over the American River and onto the 29–30th Street Freeway, and I could only steal a quick glance at Josh. His face reflected only casual curiosity.

"I'm thinking about changing my name when I go on the air," Josh said after a long moment of silence.

"No way. Joshua Friedman is a terrific radio name. Ethnic is in."

"You changed your name."

"That was different."

"Give me one good reason."

I can still remember the night I became Shauna J. Bogart. I'd been working as the engineer for Dr. Hipster's show at the top FM rock station in San Francisco. Picture a year between the Bicentennial and *Saturday Night Fever*, in a converted Victorian a couple of blocks from the intersection of Haight and Ashbury Streets.

Dr. Hipster had convinced the station to hire me as a

button-pusher over several older, more qualified men. Up 'til
then, my career as a budding radio personality had two major
handicaps: I was a teenager. And I was a girl. But I did have
a First Class Radio-Telephone License from the Federal Communications Commission.

Years later, Dr. Hipster told me, "I went to the boss man
and told him if I had to look at the same person over the
console for four hours every day, why can't it be a foxy chick
instead of a gray-haired old fart with a pocket protector?"

So I got the gig.

The night I earned my air name, the DJs had gathered for
our weekly staff meeting in what had once been the front
parlor. A half-dozen hairy, tie-dyed, jeans-clad guys. And me.
The past six months or so, Dr. Hipster had been working me
into his show as a sidekick. Now, I was getting a chance at
my very own show. Sunday nights, but it was a start.

"Just don't call me anything slutty," I said from my corner
of a ratty couch that looked like it'd been with the house since
the Quake of '06.

Dr. Hipster fiddled with the roach clip. "Why don't you
just use your real name? Maybe you'll get people tuning in
curious to hear what Senator Berg's kid sounds like."

"Forget it. I want to make it on my own, not because I'm
some big-shot politician's daughter."

We settled on Bogart for the last name right off. The Baby
Boom generation had recently discovered the films of Hum-
phrey Bogart and turned him into a cult hero. And we mustn't
forget "Don't Bogart that joint."

The "J." part was easy too. It's one of those middle initials
that sounds good rolling off the tongue with just about any
combination of first and last name.

"Shauna," Dr. Hipster said. "Shauna J. Bogart."

"Forget it," I replied.

"Brandi, then. With an 'I.' "

"Lacey?" the morning man suggested. "Paisley? Blaze?"

"No, no, and no!"

The program director cast the deciding vote for Shauna J.
Bogart. Jeez. Why didn't they just call me Sleazy J. Bogart
and be done with it? But the PD paid my salary every Friday.

In cash. And he'd been the one to approve Dr. Hipster's rec-ommendation that I be given a chance at my own air shift.

So I said okay.

That's why, twenty-plus years later, I'm doing my best to be taken seriously as an educated, thoughtful, professional woman. While stuck with a name that belongs to a Laker Girl.

I'd begged T. R. O'Brien to let me use a new air name when he hired me, but he said absolutely not. "Hell, that's why you got the job. Radio listeners all over northern Cali-fornia grew up with Shauna J. Bogart. They already know you and like you. Think I'm going to mess with that?"

Josh turned to me from the black leather bucket seat of the Z-car and repeated his question. "Give me one good reason why it was okay for you to change your name, but not for me."

"Things were different back then, that's all."

I would have recognized Ferretman Bob even without the T-shirt. He lurked in the background at most of our remote broadcasts and personal appearances, slowly working up the courage to sidle forward and request whatever goodie we were giving away: refrigerator magnet, window sticker, Official Captain Mikey Commuter Club key ring. He was about my age, not much taller, with fair skin that always seemed to sport a sunburn peel and a belly that was just starting to congeal with middle-age fat. This evening he wore chinos, a Sacra-mento River Cats baseball cap covering what I knew was a rapidly receding hairline, and a T-shirt with a cartoon of a furry, pointy-nosed creature dressed in striped prison garb. The T-shirt's slogan: Ferret Liberation Now!

Normally, I try to keep as much distance as possible be-tween my bod and fans like Ferretman Bob. Most radio hosts feel the same. The chances of crushing disappointment are just too high when imagination comes face-to-face with off-mike reality. "You don't look anything like you sound." Plus, those hardcore talk radio fans, the regular callers whose lives revolve around the show, can be downright scary.

But I couldn't think of anyone other than Ferretman Bob

who might have recorded yesterday's show. I needed that tape badly enough to set aside my better judgment.

Josh had tracked him down, confirmed that he'd recorded yesterday's four o'clock hour in anticipation of hearing himself on the air, and set up the meet at seven at the Tower Café. I pushed in the door of the restaurant almost fifteen minutes late after the meeting in T. R.'s office and after dropping Josh off at home. Josh! How could anyone accuse that kid of rigging a contest? Just because a student at the college he happens to attend is lucky enough to call in and win!

Ferretman Bob was already settled in at a table for two underneath a potted palm and next to a rattan shelf holding Buddha statues and native carvings. A ghetto blaster the size of a carry-on bag took up most of the space on the table.

I ordered a lemonade and made up for my tardiness by being nice about answering Ferretman Bob's questions. Yes, it's a shame and a shock about Dr. Hipster. Yes, there really is a seven-second delay and a "censor" button that we use on occasion. No, it's not true that certain telephone exchanges have an advantage in getting through for contests. Yes, this is my real hair color, and no, I've never met Dr. Laura nor do I care to.

"I guess this is what you came for." He gave the boom box a gentle push in my direction.

I punched the FAST FORWARD button on the cassette tape, trying not to appear too eager. Years of working with tape had given me a sixth sense about how much ribbon to allow to fly by to reach the exact spot I was looking for. I hit STOP, then PLAY. "The lady told me to call in and win . . ." Tiffany, yesterday's contest winner. I'd overshot by five minutes or so. I rewound, then tried the PLAY button again.

"Killer show tonight . . . biggest thing since this so-called election for governor . . . gonna blow this town sky-high . . . don't touch that dial . . . The Hipster's tipsters have the score, the skinny, and the straight dope . . ."

Don't touch that dial!

So Dr. Hipster did sense something big was about to go down. He knew as early as the previous evening, when he would have recorded the promotional announcement. He tried to send me a message for help.

Or a warning.

I forced my voice to remain steady. "Mind if I make a copy of this?"

"It's all yours." He waved a hand in dismissal, as if he met with media celebrities and treated them to tapes of their shows every day. "I already made a copy for myself."

"Thanks. I owe you." I popped the EJECT button, snatched the cassette, and slipped it into my backpack.

Bob's eyes wore the same expression of adoring innocence as those of the cartoon critter on his T-shirt. He ached to find out what this was all about, I could just tell. I wasn't about to tell anyone, especially a listener, my suspicions. But I felt like I had to offer him something for his trouble and loyalty. Money would have been tacky, and the obvious other thing went way against my standards.

"This is going to be a big help on a story we're working on," I said. "When it breaks, I'll make sure you get credit. Anytime you want to come on the show, just let my producer know it's Ferretman Bob and I'll make sure he puts you at the head of the line. And that rule about waiting two weeks before you can go back on the air? We'll waive it just for you for the next three months."

Bob took a swallow of Sudwerk Pilsner, the local brew he'd been sipping, to hide his emotion. "I can't begin to thank you. I won't abuse the privilege, I promise."

I emerged from the "Midnight at the Oasis" ambiance of the Tower Café and paused under the neon sign marking the location of the original Tower Records, bobby-soxers jitterbugging to a spinning record. The flagship music, video, and bookstore had moved to the other side of the street years ago, and the Tower Café now occupies the drugstore where a teenage Ross Solomon had sold 78s from a single record rack back in the forties. Rather than go home to an empty apartment with only Chinese restaurant leftovers and a cranky cat for companionship, I dodged the cars across Sixteenth Street to engage in some serious hanging out and browsing.

It must have been the influence of those acres of books, the collective thoughts, theories, and ramblings of thousands of creative souls. That, plus the B. B. King music playing on the Tower Books sound system. My mind began to free-associate: that blues station on the radio the night before. A tribute to Dr. Hipster. "Alex, the answer is, what is off mike and out of sight?"

Off Mike and Outta Sight by David Sequoia Morgan. It came to me. A slender tome full of hippie-dippy peace-love-groovy poetry, it came out right about the same time as *Jonathan Livingston Seagull, Fear of Flying*, and all those Carlos Castaneda books.

Sure enough, there it was, still in print. One of those "perennial classics" editions. By now, David Sequoia Morgan had probably ditched the New Age name, put on a pin-striped suit, and was making big bucks on Wall Street. I plucked the paperback from the shelf, turned to the last page, and gave a little squeal of victory. Line for line, word for word from Dr. Hipster's supposed suicide note. A smooching couple a few feet away relaxed their clinch for a moment and looked at me in annoyance.

I felt like I ought to put a paper bag over my head before I walked up to the cashier to actually spend money on something so sappy. At least it wasn't a cat calendar.

"My kid needs this for a book report," I said to the clerk. She had a buzz cut and a pierced eyebrow. I realized she hadn't even been born when *Off Mike and Outta Sight* had been a cult hit on college campuses.

"Hon, guess what!" Glory Lou's voice positively gushed out of the receiver.

"Macy's is having a sale on Wonderbras?"

"I'm just getting back to the station from my beat checks. T. R. is working late and calls me into his office. As I live and breathe, that man never sleeps. So he tells me he's trying to figure out what to do about filling Dr. Hipster's show."

"Yeah, we can't run satellite programming from the network forever." I kicked off my sport sandals and sank into the couch. "Not with the election coming up."

"Those are almost his exact words. T. R. tells me he needs to find someone right away, what with the election right around the corner and us still being in the spring book. T. R. tells me he needs to find someone who already has a reputation and a following in the market, and someone who's already familiar with local folks and local issues, and someone he won't have to break in."

"So he offered you the gig," I interrupted.

"Can you believe it, hon? I start on Monday."

We exchanged congratulatory squeals. "Now let me tell you my news." I flipped to the last page of *Off Mike and Outta Sight* and quoted the verse.

"He did his own thing.
He lit his own fire.
He walked on his own golden road to eternal
*   enlightenment.*
All is meaningless without your love."

"Dr. Hipster copied his suicide note from a poem in an old book?" Glory Lou said after a moment of silence.

"Yeah. And you know what?"

"What?"

"It still makes absolutely no sense."

7

T. R. O'Brien steered the Lincoln west on I Street, Sacramento's midtown residential district transitioning into downtown government offices. I spotted spiky tops of palm trees, then the block of grass that made up Cesar Chavez Plaza.

Father and son rode in the front seat while Cora and I shared the back, just like two old married couples. I didn't mind having the chance to visit with T. R.'s wife, a ballsy redhead with a Carol Channing voice and a post-diet Liz Taylor body.

I scoped out the scene on the green rectangle across the street from City Hall.

Hippie vans, Harleys, cop cars, land yachts with State Assembly and Senate plates, TV remote vans. Pickup trucks with gun racks and bumper stickers. T. R. parked the Lincoln in the media zone in front of City Hall and slapped a press placard on the dash.

A typical Dr. Hipster crowd. A little tie-dye, a lot of redneck, cops both on duty and off, clerks and aides from the State Capitol and City Hall, moms with baby strollers, nuns, reporters galore, bikers, and a couple of shopping-cart people who'd wandered over to see if there was any free food. I saw the communications manager from the Greene for Governor campaign as well as several staffers from Nadine Bostwick's office. Mimi Blitzer had set up a folding table with a guest book and display of memorabilia from Dr. Hipster's career.

At least, she had the good taste not to be passing out entry blanks for the Gold Rush Giveaway.

Was anyone in this crowd of oddballs, politicos, and law officers capable of holding a gun to Dr. Hipster's head and pulling the trigger?

Someone had reserved the front row seats for the "immediate family," i.e. T. R., Terrence, Cora, and me, the alleged widow. I seated myself gingerly on the metal folding chair, scorching in the ninety-degree heat. People keep telling me about Sacramento, "But it's a dry heat." To which I reply, "Yeah, but it's still hot."

I don't own anything black that's suitable for the tropics, so I'd put on the nearest thing to "appropriate attire" I could find in my closet: a light wool navy-blue suit an image consultant at a station I'd worked at in San Diego coerced me into buying. The consultant said it would give the air team a more "professional" look when we went out on remotes and personal appearances. I did hang on to the thing when I left San Diego, figuring it would come in handy if I ever wanted to go underground as a flight attendant. Or funerals. I just worried about which would finish first: the service, or my armpits.

Josh Friedman hovered on the edge of the hippie contingent, looking lost. I waved and patted the empty folding chair next to me.

"Did you see this?" Josh handed me a clipping from this morning's *Bee*.

DJS FIRED AT COUNTRY 101 AS STATION GOES SATELLITE.

I skimmed enough of the article to confirm the rumor Glory Lou had dropped at lunch yesterday. Another local station bites the dust. Eight more jocks frantically sending out tapes and résumés to the dwindling number of stations around the country actually employing live, local air talent.

A young tie-dye couple sang a Van Morrison medley. The mayor issued a proclamation, one of the bikers read a poem, and T. R. announced the station was setting up a scholarship in Dr. Hipster's memory. The president of the local chapter

of Vietnam Veterans of America told how Dr. Hipster orga-
nized a platoon of listeners to stand vigil when some sickhead
threatened to blow up the Vietnam War Memorial in Capitol
Park. The guy who runs the Loaves and Fishes soup kitchen
talked about how Dr. Hipster came in to help out—anony-
mously—every Friday afternoon.

I knew about the vigil at the Vietnam War Memorial, but
this was the first I heard about the soup kitchen thing. What
did T. R. say the afternoon we found out Dr. Hipster was
gone? You never really know for sure what's going on inside
someone else's head.

The story I chose to share when it was my turn to mount
the podium went pretty well, all things considered.

Sacramento, a summer evening in the early seventies. I was
around ten. My old man had dragged me up to the capital city
for yet another political meeting. After taking me to dinner in
the Senator Hotel restaurant, Dad decided it was time to continue his daughter's political education.

We piled into a cab and rode past the State Capitol, deserted
government office buildings, Weinstock's, Bruener's Furniture
Store.

Over a brand-new freeway, a sharp right, and into a scene
that up 'til now had existed for me only in the pages of history
books and *Life* magazine.

Crumbling piles of brick buildings, ancient, empty hulks.
Broken windows staring bleakly onto dark streets. I shivered
in the evening heat, reminded of photographs I'd seen of San
Francisco after the 1906 earthquake. Or London during the
Blitz.

"This, my dear, is an example of what happens without
sound urban planning," my father intoned after paying the cab-
driver to wait for us. "First they decide to build the damn
freeway. Then they start evicting the jobless and the elderly,
and knock down all the historic buildings. Some of these have
been around since the Gold Rush days."

I could tell the old man was about to launch into yet another
speech about the fate of the urban poor. I searched the blasted
landscape for anything that might provide a diversion,
glimpsed a flicker of light as a door opened on a second-story

balcony. Music wafted onto the deserted street. Moody Blues, "Nights in White Satin."

A shadowy figure appeared on the balcony. "Hey, kid, c'mon up. The party's just starting." He tossed a key from the balcony.

I gazed up at my dad, silently pleading.

"Fifteen minutes," he said. "If you're not back down here in exactly fifteen minutes, I'm coming up after you. And calling the cops."

I plucked the key from the potholed asphalt of Second Street, let myself through a battered wooden door bearing a radio station logo in faded paint, and picked my way up a rotting staircase. I looked up to the landing and saw the same figure from the balcony, skinny, bearded, with thoughtful brown eyes.

"What a dump," I said. God, I felt so sophisticated quoting a line from a Bette Davis movie.

Dr. Hipster put on a long record (*Alice's Restaurant*, as I recall) and invited me to join his "old lady" out on the balcony for a spot of refreshments. A joint and a fifth of tequila. I told him I was trying to cut back, and settled for a paper cup of ice water. When I think of what people put into their bodies back in those days, I'm amazed any of them are still alive. And a few years later I was just as bad.

The empty tequila bottle was perched on the balcony railing. I made a move to clear it away.

"Whoa, are you trippin'?" Dr. Hipster grabbed the bottle. "What happens if the janitor finds an empty in the trash?"

Ah, the flower-child era. Peace, love, and paranoia.

Dr. Hipster pried up a loose board from the balcony floor, revealing an empty space of four or five inches between the floor and the subfloor. He slid the empty tequila bottle into the space. I heard the tinkle of glass hitting glass. This wasn't the first time a dead soldier had found its final resting place in the floor of the radio station balcony.

"I think of those days every now and then," I said as I squinted in the Sacramento sun from the podium at Cesar Chavez Park three decades later. "Sometimes I wonder about what happened to those kids. Sometimes I wonder if things could have turned out any differently for us."

I paused and scanned the sea of upturned faces.

"But mostly, I wonder if anyone ever found all those empty tequila bottles in the balcony floor of that old brick building in Old Sacramento."

That last line drew some chuckles, and I decided to quit while I was ahead. Always leave 'em laughing. And wanting more.

"Shauna J.? Shauna J. Bogart?"

I turned from the sidewalk as I made my way back to O'Brien's Lincoln.

"Hi, it's Lucille Benson."

She was pushing fifty, tall, slender. Thick brown hair styled in a smooth, chin-length flip. Either she hadn't started to go gray yet, or she knew a really good colorist. Lucille Benson—who the hell was she, anyway?—was dressed in a slim black skirt, a navy silk blouse, a single strand of pearls, and expensive black pumps with gold trim. I've always envied women who can pull off that simple, understated look. Me, in a getup like that, I'd look like a nun.

"I just wanted to let you know I really enjoyed your comments about Dr. Hipster," she said, shaking my hand. "I know you don't remember me, but I was on the balcony at the old radio station that same night you were talking about. I was Lucy LeMoyne back then. Dr. Hipster's girlfriend."

Hair swinging to the waist. Halter-top minidress made from a cut-up American flag. No bra, legs for days. She and Dr. Hipster soul-kissing on the balcony during that long record. Sure, I remembered Juicy Lucy.

She continued, "You're right about everything."

I really wasn't in the mood to get chummy with this woman, but neither did I want to be rude. "Right about what?"

"Oh, just how we've all changed a lot since those days. Look at me: married, three kids. My youngest just went off to college, can you believe it? And here I am, working for The Establishment, quote-unquote."

God help me, she even made little quote marks with the index and middle fingers of both hands. "Didn't you know? I'm managing the Sacramento office for the Greene for Governor campaign."

"Gee, Lucille, that's real nice."

She placed a hand on my forearm, smiled, and dropped her voice into a conspiratorial, just-between-us-girls whisper. "Of course, it wouldn't do for The Establishment types to find out about our notorious past, would it?"

"Lucille, as far as I'm concerned, none of us inhaled."

She laughed and her eyes crinkled into a network of fine lines. "I'm so glad we had this chance to catch up on old times." She pulled a business card from her Coach bag and wrote a number on the back with a slim gold pen. "This is my private line. Have you heard of the Professional Women's Network? I'd love to have you come to the next luncheon as my guest."

"Gee, thanks, Lucille. I'll keep it in mind." I fumbled in my pockets until I found a business card that wasn't too dog-eared. I didn't write down my private number.

It wouldn't be a funeral without food, so T. R. O'Brien invited the staff to lunch after the service. I ended up sharing a table on a small patio at Le Jazz Bistro with T. R., Cora, Terrence, Mimi Blitzer, and a pale man whom she introduced as her fiancé, Alvin something. I would have preferred to sit indoors, in the air-conditioned pink-and-black art deco comfort of one of downtown Sacramento's favorite eateries. But T. R. and Cora had been real good about not smoking during the service. They deserved a break.

"Alvin's graduating from law school next month," Blitzer said as she made introductions. "King Hall, UC Davis. He's already gotten a job offer from the Department of Consumer Affairs."

I doffed the jacket of the navy-blue suit and draped it over my chair. I was tempted to strip off my panty hose under the cover of the heavy pink tablecloth. Probably would have had Terrence not been sitting next to me.

I was trying to decide between the swordfish and the pasta special when T. R. folded his menu and lit a Camel. "I'm going to memo the staff this afternoon. But I might's well tell y'all now. Before you hear rumors out on the street."

Now what?

"Now what, Father?"

T. R. O'Brien and Terrence O'Brien Jr. Now there was a classic collision of personal style. The father: all angles, rough edges, rude noises. With his freckled, weather-beaten face, gap-toothed grin, and ears sticking out from underneath his cowboy hat, he always reminded me of Alfred E. Neuman on Social Security. The son: smooth, suave, sophisticated, a thirties movie matinee idol transported to the new millennium. Tyrone Power with a BMW and a cell phone.

"Now what, Father?"

My best friend was dead. Supposedly put a bullet through his head because of unrequited love for me, leaving a note copied word for word from a sappy Me-Decade bestseller. Someone—who?—from the radio station tried to destroy all the recorded evidence of Dr. Hipster's last broadcast. A pirate radio station was sending out strange messages at midnight. Dr. Hipster had said in his last promo that he was working on a big exposé about the election for governor. An ex-girlfriend pops out of the past. Who happens to be working for one of the candidates.

Now what, indeed?

"It looks like another talk station is about to go on the air," T. R. said.

Great. We already had one other all-talk station to compete with, plus a news/talk combo and sports talk. Could a market the size of Sacramento support yet another talk station? Could Shauna J. Bogart hold her own against a new competitor?

"What makes you say that, Father?"

T. R. stubbed out his cigarette and leaned forward. "For one thing, someone's doing a helluva lot of telephone research. What tipped me off is, Cora got a phone call from their people about a week ago." T. R. paused, and squeezed his wife's shoulder with his one good hand. "She played along, answered all of their questions. What's her favorite radio station, what kind of talk show does she like to listen to, would she listen to another talk station if there was an alternative."

"The usual," Junior said.

"Their methodology sounded downright familiar. So I made a phone call to Triple R, made like I was interested in hiring them to do a research project for my radio station. They were so sorry. They already had a client in Sacramento and, of course, they have a no-compete policy."

I pushed away the rest of my salad. Triple R. Ratings, Revenue, and Research, Inc. Their m.o.: conduct a research project for the radio station that had hired them, usually telephone out-calls or focus groups, then convince station management their local air personalities were a bunch of losers. Clean house, save big bucks. Sign up with satellite programmers and syndicators, make big bucks.

Ratings, Revenue, and Research. The name could not be more brilliant. Ratings, the standard by which talk hosts, newscasters, and DJs live and die. Revenue, the advertising sales money machine, fueled by high ratings. Research, the magic ring that marries ratings to revenue. Triple R, the most influential and feared of all the radio consultants. The three-headed god—or demon—of radio.

T. R. pushed his cowboy hat back with his hook. "I made a few phone calls to folks I know in the syndication business. Pretended I was interested in signing their personalities for my station. They're so sorry. There's another talk station in the market that's just now got 'em under contract. We know it's not us. We know it's not the other news and talk stations in the market. Stands to reason, there must be another station coming into the market."

T. R. touched the lighter's flame to another cigarette. "You know those syndicated personalities that are suddenly all under contract here in Sacramento? It's all the right-wingers, the ultra-conservatives."

I groaned aloud. "*Sieg Heil* on your dial."

"Don't you worry none," T. R. said. "Soon's I get back from Alaska, we'll make the first strike. We're all set to roll with a new TV campaign and double our usual showing of bus backs, just in time for the election. You know what I keep promising you guys, one more killer ratings book and ad revenue keeping pace, and we can afford to go digital."

"That'll be the day." I said it with a smile, but secretly I mourned the impending death of analog, the hands-on manipulation of tape. Not to mention vinyl.

"Good thing we're in the middle of the Gold Rush Giveaway, then," Mimi Blitzer said. "Didn't I tell you, Alvin, that contest was just what this station needed?"

"Brilliant, baby, brilliant." Alvin paused from buttering a sourdough roll and tapped Blitzer on the nose with his index finger.

That lovey-dovey gesture brought out the devil in me. "How come, if that contest is such a great idea, you always make me read the winning numbers right in the middle of a breaking news story?"

"Don't give me a lecture about the ethics of broadcast journalism," Blitzer pouted.

"The news biz lost its virginity the day William Randolph Hearst told that photographer, 'You supply the pictures, I'll supply the war,' " T. R. said. "But I get what you're saying."

"If we could just spend a fraction of that prize money on new equipment, and better jingle packages, and decent pay for the support staff, the ratings would take care of themselves," I said.

I twirled my fork in a scoop of seafood pasta. Yesterday, I was supposed to have read the winning numbers belonging to a Caltrans clerk, not some coed from Sac State. "You know in advance whose numbers you're going to read over the air. You're not picking them at random. The contest is rigged, isn't it?"

Blitzer patted her lips with a pink linen napkin. "Rigged. That's such a loaded term. We prefer to consider it prearranged."

"Lighten up, kiddo," T. R. said to me. "You've been in this business long enough to know the ropes."

"Okay, I admit I don't always give the concert tickets to the ninth caller. I'll pick the one who sounds the most excited, or who hasn't won before. But, jeez, we're talking about thousands of dollars here."

"The stakes are just too damn high," T. R. said. "We're the only family-owned station left in the market. You have no idea what an uphill battle I'm fighting." He let out another plume of smoke. "No idea at all."

"T. R. O'Brien, you old fart!"

We'd just started on coffee (for all) and desserts (for some). In other words, Cora and I were splitting a chocolate mousse.

T. R. leaped out of his chair. "Neil Vermont, late as usual!" Lots of hugging, backslapping, and male bonding.

The Neil Vermont?

I'd never met Neil Vermont, but I saw his name every day, carved on a brass plaque in the lobby of the station. T. R. O'Brien, Neil Vermont, Grant Simmerhorn, and Wallace W. Wilson III. Founding partners of Golden Empire Broadcasting. Four buddies just out of the army who decided to pool their resources and invest in a radio station. So the legend went, they drew cards to decide who actually got to run the station. T. R. picked the ace of spades with his hook.

"I feel terrible about missing the service," Vermont said after T. R. had finished introductions. "But I just plumb got a late start from Pebble. Soon as I hit town, I called Mrs. Yanamoto on the cell phone. She told me I could find you here."

Pebble Beach. Neil Vermont's share of the profits of the radio station must be even bigger than I'd guessed for him to be able to afford such a choice piece of real estate.

Vermont pulled up a chair between the elder and younger O'Brien men. If Terrence was Sean Connery in his 007 days, then Neil Vermont was Sean Connery in *The Last Crusade*. Tall, tanned, and a shiny dome utterly devoid of hair.

"You've got quite an election for governor going," Vermont said. "I monitored the station and the competition for most of the ride up here. The election is the hottest topic, no question."

"It's good for business," T. R. said. "Listeners tune in to find out the latest and to call in with their opinions. And I make money hand over hook selling advertising."

Vermont laughed. "Just so long as you insist on cash in advance."

I let the two of them talk of their upcoming trip to Alaska, lures and Coors, and turned my attention back to the chocolate mousse. One o'clock bonged on the bells of the Church of the Blessed Sacrament just across the street. A light rail train slipped silently down K Street, past bright banners promoting the Jazz Jubilee hanging limply in the shimmering heat. Volunteers from the Nadine Bostwick for Governor campaign stuffed leaflets into the hands of state workers heading back to the hive after lunch.

"Shauna J. Bogart? Excuse me, but there's a phone call waiting for you."

The waiter led me into the air-conditioning and to a telephone at the maître d's podium.

"Shauna J.! Lordy, I'm so glad I found you!" Glory Lou, flustered for once in her career. "You've got to meet me at the PeeDee right away."

"Why?" I could feel chocolate mousse rising in my throat.

"They just found Rudy from West Sacramento."

8

He sat behind a table in the press room at the police station, a clump of media microphones duct-taped in front of him. Rudy from West Sacramento, sandwiched between two suits: Lieutenant Gunderson and some guy who identified himself as the attorney for CalFac, parent company of the Capital City Ventures apartment complexes.

Gunderson spoke first. "Mr. Rudolf Wolinsky came voluntarily to us this morning at the advice of his attorney. Mr. Wolinsky immigrated to the United States from Poland five years ago and gained employment with the maintenance staff for Capital City Ventures for an apartment complex at Fourteenth and L. He was afraid to come forward until now because he thought it might jeopardize his status as a resident alien. Is that right, Counselor?"

The attorney nodded. "Mr. Wolinsky told his wife what happened, and she insisted he come forward. We promised Mr. Wolinsky no one will take away his work permit. In return, he's agreed to tell his story."

The caller who had haunted my show the past two days addressed the microphones. A meaty, thirty-something Fred Flintstone type wearing jeans, work boots, a Sacramento Kings tank top, and a loutish grin.

In heavily accented English, Rudy from West Sacramento told of a Wednesday morning assignment to check out a leaky faucet at a ninth-floor apartment. "Over and over did I knock on his door. He did not answer. I used my passkey to let in myself. Dr. Hipster came out of his bedroom. At me he waved a gun. To me he says to leave. I did that."

Rudy glanced at his attorney for reassurance. "I told my boss I was not good feeling. I asked to take the rest of the day off. I drove around and at the Raley's in West Sacramento I arrived."

"You saw him wave a gun around. But did you see any shooting?" the attorney asked.

"No, sir. That I did not."

"Then tell us why you called a radio talk show and told a story of seeing a murder."

Rudy ducked his head and shrugged. "I have nothing good to say. I was angry at the man for pointing a gun at me when I just wanted his faucet to fix. I was feeling like up things stirring."

I understood the feeling. Some days, I felt like up things stirring too.

"You thought you were just having fun?" the lawyer prompted.

"Yes, that is so."

The attorney turned to the reporters and cops. "Mr. Wolinsky certainly made an error in judgment. It was a stupid thing to do. He hopes this clears up any confusion that may surround this unfortunate incident."

My best friend is dead. An unfortunate incident?

Josh turned to me and whispered, "Aren't you going to ask him?"

"Kid, it's your story. You ask." I felt like Rosalind Russell in *His Girl Friday*.

Josh did me proud. He stood tall and spoke boldly. "Joshua Friedman, Sacramento Talk Radio. Mr. Wolinsky, you called Shauna J. Bogart's show from a pay phone at the Raley's supermarket in West Sacramento. There was a Dixieland band playing in the parking lot, correct?"

"Yes, sir."

"What was the name of the song that the band was playing while you waited on hold?"

Rudy glanced at the attorney. The suit gave a slight nod.

C'mon, Wolinsky. Don't be the real Rudy from West Sac-

ramento. Say you don't remember. Say you never heard any music. Please don't say it was "Sweet Georgia Brown."

"It was that Georgia song," Rudy said. "The song called 'Sweet Georgia Brown.' "

So that was that.

I opened the show that afternoon by reading the poem from *Off Mike and Outta Sight.* The poem Dr. Hipster copied into the suicide note. "All is meaningless without your love."

Jane from Davis was the first caller. "This business about *Off Mike and Outta Sight.* Can you quote-unquote believe it?"

Quote-unquote. Who kept using that phrase? I wondered if Lucille Benson made the little quote marks with her fingers as she talked to me on the phone. There's no rule about using your real name when you call a radio talk show. If Jeff Greene's Sacramento campaign coordinator wanted to be Jane from Davis, it was okay with me. As long as she contributed something of interest to the general audience.

"Go ahead."

"I just want to set the record straight. You're on the right track with the book thing. *Off Mike and Outta Sight* was where Dr. Hipster hid his quote-unquote personal stuff. You know what I'm getting at."

"He hid his stash inside a book?" It would figure.

"He hollowed out a copy of *Off Mike and Outta Sight* and used it to hide his dope." She paused to laugh. "I remember he told me this was the most appropriate use he could find for such a piece of drivel."

"How do you know all this?"

Jane from Davis paused. "Everyone knew. All of Dr. Hipster's close friends from back then, I mean."

Meaning I hadn't been part of the Doctor's inner circle as defined by the former Juicy Lucy. B.F.D., but still.

Jane from Davis continued, "So now we've set the record straight, right?"

"We have?"

"We have."

• • •

Yellow letters glowing against the black screen of the computer terminal spelled out a familiar name. No way! I almost let the traffic jingle run out before I composed myself.

I punched Line Two.

"Rudy from West Sacramento. You're on the air with Shauna J. Bogart."

"Good afternoon, Ms. Bogart."

"Welcome back to the show. And speaking of shows, that was quite a performance you put on at the police station this afternoon."

"I am very happy that you enjoyed it."

My fingers tapped out a desperate message to Josh on the computer: DON'T LOSE HIM! CALL THE COPS. HAVE THEM TRACE THE CALL. SEND GLORY LOU DOWN TO THE PAY PHONE AT RALEY'S IN WEST SAC!

I glanced over at Josh through the glass in the screener's booth. He already had the phone receiver in his hand.

"Rudy from West Sacramento, to what do we owe the pleasure of your call today?"

"Ms. Bogart, I just have one thing I desire to tell you. Do not believe everything you may see at the police department. What you hear on the radio, it is the truth."

Click.

Monty Rio, all gold chains and cheap cologne, blew into the control room just as another "Go with Greene" commercial started. "Doll, might this be what you're looking for?"

I stared at the tattered paperback the operations manager held in his right hand. "Where'd you get that?"

"Dr. Hipster's desk."

It wasn't the "perennial classics" edition I'd picked up at Tower Books the previous evening.

But it was still a copy of *Off Mike and Outta Sight*.

I hadn't planned on playing the highlights tape Glory Lou put together from Dr. Hipster's memorial service. Once, live and in person, was enough, thank you very much. But it would fill ten minutes of airtime. So I ad-libbed an intro ("For all of you who couldn't get off work this morning and missed it . . ."), let the cassette run, and followed Monty back to the newsroom.

He pulled open the top drawer of the desk Dr. Hipster shared with the hosts of the weekend gardening show and the Sunday morning religious hour. "T.R. asked me to clean out Dr. Hipster's drawer, pack up anything that wasn't station property, and ship it down to the kids in San Jose." He demonstrated finding a paperback book in the drawer.

Off Mike and Outta Sight.

Monty lobbed the paperback into a cardboard box on the adjacent desk.

"Mind if I take a look?" I gestured toward the box.

"No problem, babe."

I flipped through the pages of the skimpy paperback. Only a quarter-century old, and the pages were already browned and crumbling. Someone had marked several sections with a yellow highlighter. Including the last poem.

"Hey, Monty, do you mind taking the board for a few minutes?" I glanced at the newsroom clock. The Dr. Hipster tribute tape would run out in roughly three minutes. "Get us into the next traffic report and commercial break."

"Sure thing, doll."

I waited for the ops manager to leave the room, then reopened Dr. Hipster's desk drawer and pulled out the front file folder. Dr. Hipster's fan mail, a dozen or so handwritten notes and cards. And his replies, laser printed on station letterhead, signed and inserted between each piece of fan mail. The replies bore last Tuesday's date—Dr. Hipster's last day of life. I figured he must have spent an hour or so that evening catching up on correspondence, planning to pop them in the mail the following day. Then death intervened.

One fan letter was missing a matching reply. I opened an Ansel Adams card depicting Half Dome in winter and read the sweeping black felt pen handwriting inside. "Your mention of *Off Mike and Outta Sight* the other night brought back a lot of memories. David Sequoia Morgan and I had a little thing going for a few months right after Woodstock. Did you know

I was the inspiration for the last poem in the book? I'll be mighty impressed if you can remember how it went."

It was signed Janice, followed by a post office box number in Placerville.

I sank slowly into the swivel chair in front of the desk. Could it be that Dr. Hipster never composed a suicide note, just a routine reply to a fan letter? The "Trippin' Sister" he referred to in the salutation wasn't me, but some former hippie listener named Janice up in Placerville?

"Everything okay, babe?"

I looked up to see the tanned face of Monty Rio back in the newsroom.

"Going through Dr. Hipster's stuff is hard, that's all." I rose and tried to appear calm while my mind reeled with possibilities. Someone kills Dr. Hipster—accidentally? on purpose?—then goes through Dr. Hipster's desk drawer looking for something, anything, that might help with a cover-up. He or she finds a piece of correspondence that could be construed as a love letter, snatches it from a file folder, seals it up in an envelope with my name typed on it, and places it on or near the body where the cops will find it.

All indicators pointed to someone from the station. Someone I worked with, joked with, and hung out with on a daily basis.

I watched Monty place old airchecks, a coffee mug with a broken handle, and a half-eaten bag of sunflower seeds into a corrugated cardboard box. I put Dr. Hipster's copy of *Off Mike and Outta Sight* and the file folder of fan mail on top. Monty reached for a roll of sealing tape.

"I've got a great idea," I told Monty. "I'm going to be driving through San Jose on Monday, on my way back from Monterey. Why don't I drop this off at Dr. Hipster's kids' place?" I lifted the box from the floor before Monty could respond. "It would save you a schlep to UPS."

Terrence O'Brien lied.

I didn't get to the coast in time to watch the sunset from the balcony of my room at the Monterey Pavilion.

Not that I was complaining. My suite was bigger and classier than my apartment, all muted southwestern colors and blond woods. Chocolate on the pillow, and a key to the minibar. I clutched a cold gin and tonic and opened the French doors to the balcony.

Sharp, crisp scent of the ocean. Barking sea lions and twinkling lights from the restaurants on Fisherman's Wharf and the boats in the Monterey yacht harbor. Someone was playing jazz saxophone at a nearby nightclub. In the distance, a foghorn sounded a mournful counterpoint.

It didn't have the charm of watching the truckers on I-5, but I could get used to this.

I could also get used to not being Shauna J. Bogart. It was a relief, just for a long weekend, to escape to a place where no one has heard of Shauna J. Bogart, where no one has his mind made up how she should look or behave.

I just wondered how long it would take before I started missing Shauna J. Bogart like crazy.

I'd left Shauna J. behind at the station on the first note of the jingle for the 6:00 P.M. network newscast. Once home, I stuffed a few things into an overnight bag. What do you need for the coast, anyway? Swimsuit, beach towel, shorts, couple of T-shirts. Of course, clean undies, toothbrush, blow dryer, and all that stuff. At the last minute, I remembered how the fog rolls in at night and tossed in a sweater.

On my way to the parking garage to retrieve the Z-car, I stopped by the security office and slipped Victor Pahoa a twenty to feed Bialystock over the weekend. Remembered cleaning out the litter box and threw in another twenty.

There are few things in life more relaxing than barreling down I-5 in a sports car on a warm evening in late spring. I let the wind and the highway noise blow the events of the past three days from my mind: Rudy from West Sacramento, "He did it because of you," the missing tape, *Off Mike and Outta Sight*, Juicy Lucy, Rudy's press conference. Just zero in on that white line, groove to the cracks in the asphalt, crank up the radio, and drive.

Crank up the radio.

Another night, another car, another late spring evening, another highway. Another campaign for governor. My father and I were heading north on old Highway 99, to a political rally in Redding. The routine on our road trips was always the same: backseat piled with suitcases, campaign signs, and pamphlets, Dad driving and me riding shotgun. I was in charge of the maps and the radio.

Mornings we laughed with Don Sherwood on KSFO out of San Francisco, along with everyone else in northern California. Afternoons and early evenings, it was Russ Hodges and Lon Simmons calling the Giants games.

Late nights brought an extra dose of magic. I'd carefully ease the dial on the Motorola. If it were a good night, I'd pull in KSL from Salt Lake City, WLS out of Chicago, KJR in Seattle, KFI in Los Angeles, or Wolfman Jack on one of those "X" stations booming from just across the Mexico border.

Thanks to the magic of the skip—the physical property of AM radio waves to bounce across the continent—I bopped up and down California's highways, cozy and snug inside the Cadillac. Red taillights and an occasional lighted billboard punctuated the inky black out the windshield. Inside, only the green glow of the radio dial. Rock 'n' roll, jingles, dedications, news bulletins. But most of all, the patter of the jocks: Larry Lujack, B. Mitchell Reed, Dick Biondi, Pat O'Day, Russ "The Moose" Syracuse.

If I couldn't snag a distant station, it was always fun to try out the small-town stations on the road. Visalia, or Yuba City, or Paso Robles, you'd be sure to hear some kid on his very first air shift, all stammers, fumbles, and dead air. Or one of the veterans from one of the big markets, down on his luck.

Today, the magic has all but vaporized. Sure, the skip still works. Those big powerhouse stations are still around, still booming across the hemisphere.

But they all sound the same.

Good old fun-lovin' rock 'n' roll Top 40 radio was dead by the end of the seventies. Most AM stations are doing news,

talk, or sports, or they're simulcasting with their FM sister
stations. Maybe they've gone Spanish. Flip around the AM
dial in the evening, you'll pick out a ton of stations. All airing
the same syndicated talk show.

It's even sadder on the small-town stations. With satellites
and computer technology, they can run syndicated shows all
day long. Not just talk, but music too. That DJ who sounds
like he's from your hometown is probably broadcasting from
a studio in Hollywood or Nashville or New York. Thanks to
sound drops—pre-recorded local material—you'll swear the
jock is right across the street.

I just wondered where the radio talent of the future will
come from, now that those five-thousand-watt stations in Ba-
kersfield are all airing canned programming. When the Rush
Limbaughs and Casey Kasems and Dr. Lauras sign off the
logs for the last time, who will be waiting in the wings,
prepped and ready to take their places?

Oh, well. Maybe by then we'll all be tuning in to the
Internet.

Thank God for broadcasters like T. R. O'Brien, who still
believe in local programming and community service.

And in the magic of radio.

I gave up finding anything interesting to listen to on the
radio, popped a Jimmy Buffett tape into my Walkman, and
slipped on the headphones as I steered off Highway 156 onto
101. Yeah, I know it's illegal. But there's never a cop around
when you need one.

One last crazy thought.

If the skip works on the earth, then it should also work in
space. Theoretically, if one of those AM radio waves were to
pop through a hole in the ozone layer, it should keep flying,
bouncing off distant planets, asteroids, and stars. I pictured
alien beings tuning in their receivers and hearing a Larry Lujack bit, or a Wolfman Jack howl, just as fresh and pure and
magical as it had been three decades ago.

Or even picking up the Shauna J. Bogart Show.

9

I pulled one of those pink "while you were out" phone message slips off my door at the Monterey Pavilion when I returned from my morning walk to Fisherman's Wharf and back. Someone named Jock Freeman wanted me to return his call. At least, the front desk did get the hotline number to the newsroom right. And they didn't mangle the area code too badly.

They'd also checked the URGENT box.

"What brings you to the station on a Saturday morning?" I asked Josh when I had him on the line.

"The call screener for the gardening show called in sick at the last minute. Mr. Green Thumb is all offering to pay me if I'll come in and produce his show."

"Gee, Josh, that's great!" For this you called me long distance on my day off?

"The fax in the newsroom ran out of paper and I'm all what am I going to do? I knew Monty Rio keeps the extra paper locked up in his office. I'm all . . ."

Since when did "all" become the official conversation filler? What was wrong with "like" and "you know"?

"So, like, you broke into Monty Rio's office."

"I got this ladder out of the engineering shop, and then I'm all—"

"Better that I don't know the details. Just tell me what you found."

"Mr. Rio keeps the paper in a box right under his personal

fax machine in his office. So I couldn't help looking at a fax that came in for him this morning, could I?"

I sat on the bed and undid the Velcro straps on my Tevas. "Go on."

"Remember yesterday afternoon, when T. R. told us about that research company coming into Sacramento? And how they're probably setting up a talk station to compete with us?"

"Triple R?"

"That's who Mr. Rio got a fax from! They're coming to Sacramento on Monday."

The kid was practically hyperventilating.

"They've got a meeting set up with Monty Rio at nine o'clock Monday morning at the Hyatt."

So Triple R is courting our own Monty Rio to work for their new station in the market. Interesting gossip, but hardly urgent. Still, I didn't want to dampen Josh's enthusiasm. "That's a great piece of detective work. But let's keep this to ourselves, okay?"

I sank back into the feather pillows, the phone stuffed between my chin and shoulder. The new station could be a good career move for Monty, especially if they offered to make him the general manager. More money, more status, and more chances to spend long lunches with his cronies at Paragary's Bar and Oven.

"It was a good thing I got more fax paper when I did, because Mr. Green Thumb is doing this contest where listeners fax in recipes using homegrown zucchini," Josh continued. "I'm all swamped! Oh, yeah. Remember that lady from the Greene for Governor campaign? The one who you think called your show yesterday and called herself Jane from Davis?"

"Lucille Benson?" I sat up.

"She shows up at the station and she's looking for Terrence O'Brien, like it's real important. But all she's doing is dropping off a reel with a new spot for the campaign. She says it's important that it starts Monday morning. I took her tape and told her I'd turn it over to traffic and they'd get it on the log. Is that okay?"

"Good work, kid. Listen, do you have classes Monday morning?"

"Nothing I can't skip."

"Terrific. Better grab a pen and some paper. You're going to want to take notes."

Cannery Row had pretty much stopped being a stink, a poem, a grating noise, and all that Steinbeck jazz long before I made the scene. When I was a kid and my dad had a campaign stop in Monterey, I used to ditch the meeting and pick my way along the abandoned Del Monte Express tracks to explore the ghostly ruins of the old sardine processing plants and the decaying red-light district. I knew things wouldn't be the same after more than a quarter century. But still, I wasn't prepared for the onslaught of saltwater taffy shops, T-shirt stores, and theme restaurants that had replaced the funky bohemian atmosphere of the old row.

They hadn't exactly paved paradise and put up a parking lot, but it sure as hell didn't feel right.

A tiny storefront shoehorned between a cinnamon roll place and a sunglasses emporium caught my eye. Final Vinyl Used Records.

I browsed idly through bins of discs. Carole King's *Tapestry. Sergeant Pepper, Disraeli Gears, The Doors,* that Mamas and Papas album where they're sitting on top of each other in the bathtub. The soundtrack of a generation gathering dust in crates.

"Bargains! Three for $10." Weird old stuff. Perry Como, Teresa Brewer, some guy named Joe "Fingers" Carr. Helen Hudson, *Live at The Blue Door.*

Helen Hudson?

As far as I knew my mother had recorded just one album and it sure as hell wasn't *Live at The Blue Door.*

I stared at the faded color photograph of a red-haired singer in a blue sequined dress, leaning against an upright piano, the background a smoky indigo haze. I flipped it over to devour the liner notes.

Gone.

Or, rather, lost behind a red sticker emblazoned in seventy-two-point bold type with the warning: DJ PROMOTIONAL COPY!

NOT FOR RESALE! I clawed my nails into the back of the sticker, trying to peel it off, but four-plus decades had left it permanently bonded to the LP jacket. Along with the sticker, I was pulling off most of the cardboard and all of the type.

"Can I help you?" A fiftyish Jerry Garcia type wearing a Monterey Jazz Festival T-shirt turned down the Mario Lanza record he'd been listening to and looked up from behind the counter.

"I'll take this," I said, placing the Helen Hudson album in his paw.

"That bin's three for ten dollars. You can't buy just one."

"It's okay. You'll get your ten bucks." I pulled my wallet out of my backpack and drew out an Abe Lincoln.

The teddy bear looked at the figure on the album cover, then at me. He fiddled with some figures on an invoice pad, then said, "It's okay, lady. You can have it for five."

Whatever happened to hotels with coffee shops? These days, they're all tarted up with wallpaper and plants, bearing cute "theme" names like The Greenhouse or The Gazebo. The Atrium, here at the Monterey Pavilion. Where does a gal go these days to get a decent tuna melt?

The Atrium turned out to be a glass-domed faux-Victorian conservatory roughly the size of an Olympic skating rink and dripping with greenery, wicker, and chintz. The only other tourists having breakfast this particular Sunday morning was a stern-faced couple wearing his'n'her Alcatraz sweatshirts. They did not appear to be having fun yet.

I treated myself to an artery-clogging cheese omelet with home fries and opened the file folder filled with news clippings and Internet downloads I'd brought from the station, catching up on the political news. I popped a strip of extra-crispy bacon in my mouth and tackled the first clip in the file, a full-page article from the *San Jose Mercury-News*. "Down on The Farm: A Look Inside California's Premiere Political Think Tank."

As a privately funded, unincorporated group, little is known about the inside workings of The Farm Team, according to the *Mercury-News* article. Unnamed sources described how a core group of philanthropists, Hollywood liberal types, and the few computer millionaires who had managed to avoid the dot-com dot-bomb had provided the seed money for a campus to train promising young leadership talent, "The Farm Team." They settled in an old farmhouse and outlying buildings near the University of California-Davis campus and offered a series of weekend workshops, week-long seminars, and semester-long college courses. Enrollment was by invitation only. It was rapidly becoming not only a badge of honor, but a requirement for an aspiring politician courting the environmental and ethnic vote to claim membership on The Farm Team.

Well, la dee dah. So my home state, notorious for its wacky politics, had finally crafted the equivalent of the East Coast political machine under the guise of self-improvement. By invitation only. If you'd once succumbed to the lure of a Double Whopper, or forgot to recycle your bottles of designer water, were you automatically disqualified? I wondered if free massages were part of the program, along with naked deal-making in the hot tub.

Still, it might make an interesting topic for the show, especially since Davis was within our listening area. I stuffed the clipping back into the folder and dipped a triangle of toast into a blob of melted Jack cheese.

That afternoon I spread a towel I'd pirated from the hotel's health club onto the fine white sand of Asilomar Beach, popped the top off one of the beers I'd scored on yet another raid on the minibar, and opened the *Carmel Pine Cone*. The front page featured a full-color photo of a deserted cove in Big Sur, a classic picture postcard scene of crashing waves, golden brown hills, Monterey cypress, and dazzling sky. "CalFac to donate Big Sur property to State Parks system." I skimmed the story only because I recognized CalFac as the same company that owned the hotel where I was spending the weekend. The hotel chain had offered to donate thousands of acres of pristine land to the state in return for permission to build a resort and golf course on the southernmost portion. The local environmental groups and politicians would have preferred to see the entire property remain undeveloped, but given the task of raising the millions to purchase the property, the locals figured part of a park was better than none.

I idly flipped the pages, searching for my favorite feature in small-town newspapers, the police log, when an all-too-familiar headline caught my eye.

"Classical station to air satellite programming; morning, afternoon announcers lose jobs."

It seemed to be happening everywhere. On the one hand, I was pleasantly surprised a market the size of Monterey—what, a hundred thousand people?—had the advertising base to support a classical music station. On the other hand, two more announcers were on the street, pitching tapes and résumés.

The Social Spotlight page featured my boss's fishing pal, Neil Vermont, at a swank bash at The Lodge at Pebble Beach, his arm around a stunning, expensively dressed older woman named Vivienne Kostantin, according to the cutline.

I pulled a fistful of staff photos from my backpack and scribbled my autograph repeatedly, hoping Mimi Blitzer wouldn't mind a little sand between the pages. And that she'd appreciate my effort to please the listeners on my day off.

By late afternoon, a stiff offshore breeze had picked up, threatening to whirl the newspaper and my "homework" into the surf. I stuffed the papers into my backpack. I was just gathering up the empties when I spotted a figure in a brown uniform and Smokey Bear hat watching me from just a few yards away. One of the rangers from the Asilomar State Conference Grounds across the street.

Great. All I need is for this to turn out to be a no-alcohol beach. I shoved the cans to the bottom of the backpack, shook the worst of the sand out of the Monterey Pavilion's towel, and gave a smart salute to the ranger as I slogged back to the Z-car. He ignored me.

I'd just phoned in my dinner order to room service—fettuccine, salad with blue cheese dressing, chocolate mousse—when the bedside phone beeped.

"Shauna J.! It's Terrence O'Brien."

"Oh, hi," I involuntarily dragged the word out to three syllables and hit a high C.

"Just checking in to see how you're doing on your weekend in paradise."

"It's been great." I did my best to sound breezy, casual. "I found this cool used record store and spent the afternoon at the beach."

"I'm so glad you're having a good time. Listen, if you want to spend another day, go ahead. Just put it on the station's account."

"Thanks, but I really need to be heading home. I already made arrangements to deliver Dr. Hipster's stuff from the station to his kids in San Jose Monday afternoon."

"That's very kind of you to do that. But the important thing is for you to just relax and enjoy your weekend, you hear?"

"That's great advice, but I've just got too much on my mind."

"Of course. Dr. Hipster was a good friend. It'll take time for a loss like that to heal."

"It's not just that." I paused, not knowing what to say without coming across as deranged and deluded as many of Dr. Hipster's listeners. "I just can't help but think—"

"Go on." Terrence spoke in a soothing tone.

"It's gotta be someone from the station," I blurted.

I expected more calming platitudes, but Terrence surprised me by saying, "That's interesting. I've been having those same thoughts myself."

"Go figure," I said, excited that someone finally agreed with me. "It has to be someone who has access to our logger tape, and who knows how to splice tape. And someone who got into the control room the afternoon they found Dr. Hipster, and who switched that tape cartridge with his promotional announcement into the stack to be erased."

"That's just what I've been saying to myself. But of course, I don't have the technical knowledge you do to put it all together. I'm proud of you. Damn proud."

Terrence's voice dropped to a throaty whisper. "I've been thinking about you a lot lately."

Stop! In the name of love!

He took my silence as a cue to continue. "We really should get to know each other better. Let me take you to lunch next week. No, wait. Dinner. Even better. Does Tuesday night work for you?"

I willed my voice to sound casual and allowed as how my datebook was pretty full, but I could probably squeeze him in Tuesday evening.

"Tuesday evening it is, then."

If this had been the old *Mary Tyler Moore Show*, I'd have tossed my beret into the air. Instead, I picked up the phone, called room service, and changed my dinner order. Chef's salad, dressing on the side, whole wheat bread, no butter. Cancel dessert.

If I was going to lose ten pounds by Tuesday evening, I'd have to diet like crazy.

10

"Go away!"

She looked something like the way I remembered Donna, Dr. Hipster's ex-wife, from the last time I'd seen her around five years ago. But tougher, beefier. She stared me down from the porch of an Eisenhower-era tract home in San Jose. A large, Y-shaped crack snaked across the faded pink stucco over a warped and scratched door. The Monday afternoon traffic on I-280 thundered in the background.

I tried again. "I'm Shauna J.—"

The woman wore purple Bermuda shorts over a set of thighs sculpted by Sara Lee. Her T-shirt proclaimed: "It's not a hot flash, it's a power surge." I was glad I'd opted to dress conservative: white canvas slacks and a navy-blue T-shirt, sans slogans.

A blur of orange fur scuttled into the darkness of the back hallway. Bloom, I assumed, the litter-mate of Dr. Hipster's cat. The woman squinted against the Silicon Valley smog and folded ham-sized arms across her chest. "Yeah, yeah. I know who you are. One of those radio people."

"—Dr. Hipster's belongings from the station—"

"My sister had a good thing going. That lowlife husband of hers had finally cleaned up his act. Making good money at the ad agency. They had a nice house in Mill Valley—not like this piece of crap—and the kids were doing great in school. Then he got hooked up with you radio people again."

"—drove all the way from Sacramento—"

"Don't you get it? We don't want you here. Get out of our lives."

"—box in the trunk of my car—"

"Get off my sister's property before I have to call the cops!" The woman slammed the door in my face. A chunk of stucco clunked to my feet.

Fine. I know when I'm not wanted. The hell with Dr. Hipster's stuff. I was just opening the door of the Z-car when Marc beckoned to me from the carport. Tall like his dad, but not so stringy. Marc had obviously consumed more vitamins, pumped more iron, and indulged in far fewer controlled substances than the old man.

"What was that all about?" I asked when I was within conversational distance.

Marc shushed me and directed me to the far side of a decade-old Honda Civic. "She can't see us from here. No sense getting her more riled up than she is already."

"Who the hell is she, anyway?"

"Aunt Connie. Mom's sister. She's the oldest and has always been real protective of Mom. Me and Melissa too."

"They ever make a movie of the story of her life, Kathy Bates would be a real natural."

"Lucky for us, I'm putting her on the bus to go back home to Fresno tomorrow morning. Aunt Connie never married and never had much of a life for herself. We're the only family she's got. She took it real hard when Mom and Dad split up."

"And blamed 'us radio people' for the breakup."

Marc nodded and indicated for me to stay put behind the Honda Civic. He ventured to the front yard for a peek through the front window. "The coast is clear."

We maneuvered the cardboard box into the carport without any explosions from inside the house. "I really appreciate everything you've done." Marc placed the box on the dusty cement floor.

"No problem. Wish I could do more. Listen, you and your dad used to get together every Sunday morning, right?"

Marc smiled at the memory. "Sure, ever since I moved up to Sacramento to go to law school. Every chance we had, we'd get together for Sunday brunch."

"So you saw him last Sunday," I said.

"Yeah."

"Did your old man mention working on a big story about the election? Or going on the air with an exposé of one of the candidates?"

"You know Dad. Every show was going to be big, blowin' the town sky-high."

"But nothing specific."

"He talked a little bit about The Farm Team, just wondering aloud if it might make a good topic for a future show, what with Jeff Greene being a product of the program. Dad could do a show about those weekends he spent there doing seminars on media relations. Then he decided as a topic it wasn't all that hot."

"A bunch of buttoned-down policy wonks," I agreed.

Marc paused to chew on his lower lip. "He did ask me about contracts. Wanted to know about the statute of limitations and whether a contract signed like forty, fifty years ago was still valid. I reminded him I was only a first-year law student, but I promised to do some research. I never had the chance to get back to him."

"Do you recall whether he ever used the phrase 'Don't touch that dial' while you were talking during brunch?"

"His danger code? He told me and Melissa about that around a month ago, but no, I don't remember him saying that on Sunday. I would have picked up on it."

"I'm still trying to get my head around the idea of your dad killing himself. It just doesn't make sense."

"Tell me about it."

"Can you remember anything else he said, a story he might have been working on? Something that was weighing on his mind? Anything at all that might shed some light?"

"Mostly we talked family stuff, nothing important, just catching up. I told him some stories about law school, and like I said, he wanted to know all about contracts and the statute of limitations." Marc's forehead furrowed in thought. "Oh, yeah. He said something funny in connection with this contract. Something about a blue door."

I felt a startle of emotion. Fear? Anticipation? Just a flutter, gone in a second. That Helen Hudson album from the used record store. "You mean *Live at The Blue Door*? Like a title of something? Maybe an LP?"

"No, he didn't say it like that. He was looking at his notes while we were discussing contracts, and I just remember him reading aloud about 'that contract from the blue door' or something like that." I must have looked puzzled, because he added, "Do you think that was important?"

"I have no idea."

I changed the subject, asking Marc if he'd given any thought to cleaning out Dr. Hipster's apartment. "I'd be glad to help if I can. I'm not much good with heavy lifting, but I can always wrap dishes or pack up books."

Marc leaned against the Honda. "It's almost overwhelming. I've got finals coming up and Mom 'n' Melissa can't deal with it by themselves. I'll probably just hire professional movers and have them put everything in storage until we figure out what to do. Maybe we'll have a big yard sale. Or give it all to the Salvation Army or something."

"Jeez, you can't be serious!"

Dr. Hipster didn't leave much in the way of an estate. But what there was of it was top choice. Mostly gifts from grateful artists after Dr. Hipster had been one of the first DJs in the country to give them airplay. Janis Joplin's tambourine from the Monterey Pop Music Festival. The tablecloth John Lennon doodled on backstage at that last concert at Candlestick. A charred piece of one of Hendrix's guitars, Jim Morrison's autograph on the cover of the first Doors album, and an entire set of original silkscreen posters from the Fillmore. We're talking an auction at Sotheby's here.

We made a deal, Marc and I. I'd do some checking, find out how much Dr. Hipster's rock memorabilia was really worth. Marc would hold off on the yard sale until I came back with the facts and figures.

"Look at it this way," he said. "If it were Aunt Connie instead of me making the arrangements, she'd probably just make a big bonfire out of all of Dad's stuff."

"Not when she finds out how much loot she could make putting his collection on eBay."

• • •

I barely beat the early afternoon commuter traffic out of Silicon Valley. The back of a Valley Transit Authority bus on 280 urged me to listen to "Imus in the Morning" on a San Francisco FM. Last time I gave it a listen, that station was airing a local morning news block. Not again.

The 240Z's radio picked up Sacramento Talk Radio around Fairfield. Surprise: I'd expected to hear Monty Rio breaking in to The Best of Shauna J. with the live spots and the current time and temperature checks. But instead, I heard the voice of the man of my dreams telling me it was ninety-seven degrees at 3:40 P.M. "Stay tuned as we reveal this hour's lucky numbers in the Gold Rush Giveaway!"

Terrence O'Brien wasn't half-bad on the air. He definitely had the pipes. But, like many amateurs, he tried way too hard to sound like Your Big-Time Radio Announcer. He'd be a natural if he'd just relax and be himself. Terrence O'Brien wants to be on the radio. I want to get closer to Terrence O'Brien. Let's just say I happen to offer my services as a coach. I could just see the two of us, cozy in the tight confines of the production room. Me at the controls, me in charge, Terrence O'Brien following my orders, Terrence O'Brien taking my direction. I grinned wickedly.

I mean, I don't want to marry the guy. But a fling would be nice. A good, old-fashioned summer romance. It would be fun to show up at the State Fair media party in August with someone drop-dead gorgeous at my side.

The inevitable commercials for the candidates for governor kicked in. Jeff Greene, already congratulating himself for engineering the deal where CalFac donated a chunk of the Big Sur ranch to the State Parks system. I suppose this was the tape Lucille Benson delivered to the station Saturday morning. I turned down the sound.

Let's say it wasn't suicide. Someone killed Dr. Hipster. Why?

They say when in doubt, follow the money. Who profits?

Marc and Melissa, as Dr. Hipster's heirs, for starters. Marc had been in Sacramento the afternoon of his father's death, supposedly in class at McGeorge. Easy enough to check out.

But I didn't see Marc as a likely suspect. For one thing, he seemed clueless as to the potential worth of his father's collection of rock memorabilia.

Donna, the ex-wife scorned? The cops found the former Mrs. Hipster working her shift at the ICU at O'Connor Hospital in San Jose last Wednesday afternoon. Motive, maybe, but no opportunity. The sister seemed a likelier culprit. That woman definitely wasn't recording on all eight tracks.

Don't forget, someone at the radio station had to be part of it. If not the actual killer.

Gloria Louise Montalvo? I guess you could say she profited, since she was tagged to take over Dr. Hipster's old-time slot. But she was a pal. It couldn't be.

Josh Friedman? Nah. Much too high-strung to pull off a capital crime.

Monty Rio? Last Wednesday afternoon, like most afternoons, he was holed up in his office. He liked to make us think he was working on a Peabody Award–winning feature. More likely, all he was working on was a fifth of Jack Daniel's. I didn't see the operations manager in the role of a killer. But he definitely had the opportunity and skill to slice up the logger tape.

Mimi Blitzer? She'd shown up in the control room when the story of Dr. Hipster's death was breaking. But how would she profit?

Marc had mentioned his dad asking for advice about a contract. Could it have had anything to do with Jeff Greene, Nadine Bostwick, and the election for governor? But Marc had alluded to a contract written some fifty years ago. About the time Nadine Bostwick was celebrating her bat mitzvah. Jeff Greene, if he were around at all, would probably have been *in utero*.

The Sacramento afternoon commute was grinding full-on by the time I crossed the Yolo Causeway. Captain Mikey in the traffic chopper advised using surface streets. I took the Harbor Boulevard exit and turned onto West Capitol Avenue.

West Sacramento.

Separated from the capital city by the river and the county

line, West Sacramento had at one time been the proud gateway to the city. Back forty, fifty years ago, West Capitol Avenue gleamed and vibrated with neon-lit motels, coffee shops, and nightclubs. Then the interstate went in, turning the motel strip into a tired and tawdry home of welfare families, hookers, and hustlers. Still, the Raley's supermarket looked prosperous enough. I pulled into the supermarket parking lot, cruising until I spotted the pay phone at one corner of the store.

The telephone where Rudy from West Sacramento supposedly called my show last Wednesday afternoon.

I knew it was pointless. But I couldn't help it. I parked the Z-car and emerged into the relentless Sacramento heat.

No phone booth. Just a pay phone framed by plastic and steel, bolted to the cement wall of the store. No intriguing phone numbers scrawled onto the wall. No phone book. Just a cord dangling forlornly. Not even any interesting footprints. Just an empty box of Tic Tacs and a couple of stamped-out cigarette butts.

I tried to picture the scene last Wednesday afternoon: loutish Rudy clutching the receiver, waiting for his turn to go on the air. A Dixieland band playing "Sweet Georgia Brown" from a makeshift stage in front of the store.

Nothing. No clues. No flashes of divine inspiration.

What had I expected?

I got back into the car and swung back onto West Capitol Avenue for the short ride into downtown Sacramento.

If I'd known what was waiting for me at home, I'd have boogied right back onto I-80 and kept driving. Not stopping until I reached, say, Chicago.

11

I dropped my overnight bag on the landing to my apartment and turned the key in the lock, planning nothing more strenuous than fixing a gin and tonic and calling Josh to see how he had fared on his "homework" assignment. I pushed open the door.

I noticed the records first. Someone had pulled all of my records off the floor-to-ceiling shelves. Even my mother's old jazz collection. I could see the orange, blue, and black cover of *Aloha and Ole!* lying on top of a jumble of record jackets. My books were heaped in a corner, and my collection of sixties-vintage *Mad* magazines had been flung across the couch. The contents of my desk drawers lay in mounds on the floor.

Victor Pahoa arrived within two minutes after I placed the call to security.

"Man, I don't believe this." Pahoa shook his head as he surveyed the damage.

I ventured through the rest of the apartment. It was pretty much a repeat of the living room: drawers opened, contents dumped, clothing pockets turned inside out, books and papers strewn about. I almost gagged when I pictured strange fingers—nasty fingers—pawing through my underwear drawer.

But nothing, as far as I could see, had been deliberately broken. Nothing was missing. My small collection of semi-valuable jewelry (mostly silver and turquoise Native American stuff) had been dumped on the bedroom floor, next to the magazines that had once been neatly piled on my night table. My stereo and TV were intact, although they'd pulled my videos off the shelf. Just as long as they hadn't messed with my copy of *Young Frankenstein* or *The Blues Brothers*.

A real policeman arrived about fifteen minutes later. He didn't look much older than Josh Friedman, but he did earn points with me by listening and taking lots of notes. They probably have a seminar at the academy on dealing with media celebs.

"Been a lot of apartment break-ins in this neighborhood lately," he said after I told my story. "You might want to talk to your landlord about getting better locks."

"Is it burglary if the lock wasn't forced or the windows weren't broken? And if nothing was taken?" I asked.

"Ma'am, did anyone besides yourself have a key to your apartment?" the officer asked.

"Just the apartment manager and the security staff."

"And you say nothing appears to be missing."

"As far as I can tell. They overlooked the obvious stuff anyway, the TV and the stereo and my jewelry."

The young policeman snapped shut his notebook. "Maybe they wanted to scare you."

"Man, I just don't believe this," Victor Pahoa repeated after the officer had left. "Your place was fine when I came in to feed your cat this morning."

Bialystock!

I'd forgotten all about the cat.

I began calling his name in a high-pitched singsong voice, just like I'd heard Dr. Hipster using when he talked to Bialy. Even tried making little cooing and kissy noises.

Scritch-scratch from inside the front hall closet.

I yanked open the door and braced myself as I peered into a dark tumble of coats, umbrellas, and mops. The scum had even slit open the vacuum cleaner bag. Bialystock's kennel box lay on its side in a corner. The cat crept from the darkness behind the plastic container and began tentatively rubbing my ankles.

"Bialystock!" I scooped up the orange tabby and cradled him. I waited for the cat to tense and leap from my arms.

Instead, he relaxed, purred, and nuzzled my chin.

"You poor thing. I'm so sorry." I buried my face in his fur. I was crying now. I couldn't help it.

The phone rang just as I'd finished putting the last record back on the shelf. Josh, wanting me to come over so he could tell me how his morning went. I'd been so upset about the burglary, I'd all but forgotten about the assignment I'd asked him to carry out.

"Can't you tell me over the phone?"

"We've got to show you. Please?"

Oh, well. I could use a break from cleaning.

I found the address Josh had given me, a Craftsman-era bungalow along the Twenty-first Street frat row in Sacramento's Midtown district. The letters D and X cut out of three-foot-high red-painted plywood hung over the door. Delta Chi? Somehow I hadn't pictured Josh as a frat boy. I happened to glance up as I walked the cracked cement sidewalk to the front porch. A copper wire snaked from an upstairs window to the roof, where it draped over a rickety TV antenna. That cinched it. This was no frat house. DX in radio lingo stands for Distance Transmission. These boys were some serious radio fanatics.

The inside was about what you'd expect. Bookcases made of bricks and boards, milk crates overflowing with magazines and videos, empty pizza box on the coffee table, dusty stuffed moosehead, complete with the requisite pair of black lace panties dangling from one antler above the fireplace, pyramid of empty beer cans in one corner. But there were some decent pieces of furniture too: a couple of leather easy chairs and one of those armoire/cabinet things hiding the TV and VCR.

"Nice couch," I said as I sank into a brown leather eight-footer.

"Josh's dad owns a furniture store." This from the guy Josh had introduced as Android. A sweet-faced kid who would have been right at home on the set of *The Brady Bunch*, if it hadn't been for the spiky haircut and earring. "Friedman's Fine Furniture. You know, tell them . . ."

"Hey, put a lid on it," Josh said.

My eyes adjusted to the dim light of the living room. "Nice 'do," I said to Josh.

Where there'd once been a halo of fine yellow frizz hung limp straight locks. Shiny black.

"That's part of what I wanted to show you. You know how you wanted me to hang out at the lobby of the Hyatt, just to see if Monty Rio really showed up for the meeting with the research consultants?"

"That's why I'm here, isn't it?"

"I did even better. I infiltrated the meeting. Android works at the Hyatt on weekends, banquet setup. So I'm all borrowing his uniform—"

"He only had to hem up the pants legs about ten inches," Android interrupted.

"—and I got some hair straightener and some of that spray-on hair color. Don't worry, it will all wash out. I pretended like I'm part of the hotel staff, and I needed to go into their conference room and empty the wastebasket and check on supplies."

"What if Monty Rio had recognized you?" I felt a duty to scold, even though I secretly admired the kid's ingenuity.

"But he didn't."

I leaned back and put my feet up on the coffee table. "Find out anything interesting?"

"One of the suits from Triple R was making a presentation about a television commercial. 'Talk radio for the new millennium'! "

" 'Talk radio for the new millennium'? How lame," Android contributed.

"I couldn't stick around to see anything else without looking suspicious." Josh waved a plastic bag above his head like a trophy. "But I did get their trash."

One teabag. Three empty containers of nondairy creamer. Five empty wrappers of sugar substitute. One wad of gum. Yuck. Two used tissues. Double yuck.

One piece of Triple R letterhead, covered with type. One corner was badly wrinkled, crushed in a briefcase, maybe, or mangled by the copier. At any rate, it ended up in the trash.

I smoothed the paper and studied the printing. A daily broadcast schedule, apparently for the new talk radio station. Like T. R. O'Brien had predicted, it was mostly syndicated right-wingers, G. Gordon Liddy and his ilk.

"What's this 'Obie in the A.M.'?" I said, pointing to the morning drive section of the schedule. "I never heard of any syndicated morning show hosted by anyone named Obie."

"Could be worse," the Android kid said. "At least it's not B.O. in the A.M."

Before I left the frat house for home, I made a quick trip to the upstairs loo. After hovering a few minutes and actually flushing the john, I turned the tap in the sink and left the water running to cover my tracks.

I found the room with a copper wire hanging from the window on the second try. The wire originated in a set of gray metal industrial shelves holding a shortwave receiver, a ham radio transmitter, amplifiers, mixing console, mike, turntable, cart machine, even a Gentner phone mixer. A poster-size map of the world, dotted with pushpins, covered the adjoining wall. Postcards too: La Voz Del Cid, The Voice of Laryngitis, Texas Free Radio, Radio Caroline. A tape cartridge labeled "Jeopardy Theme" rested on top of the cart machine.

I have a soft spot in my heart for techno-nerds, the shy, geeky guys with the slide rules who grow up to be Steve Wozniak. And pirate radio is way cool. Anne Frank huddling around a clandestine radio in the Secret Annex, listening to Winston Churchill talk about blood, sweat, toil, and tears. A teenage John Lennon reeling in American rock 'n' roll from a pirate ship anchored in international waters off the British coast.

But still. Josh and his housemates had hassled me on the night my best friend died. Not to mention risking a ten-thousand-dollar fine and a year behind bars if they got nabbed by the Federal Communications Commission.

Footsteps in the hallway behind me. I could hear Josh's worried whisper and Android, loud, nervous, as he turned the faucet handle. "Doesn't she know Sacramento has a water shortage?"

I turned and faced the guilty pair. "The game is over, kids. This isn't your science project. It's a pirate radio station. You two put the message on my answering machine last Wednesday night. You sent the flowers."

I turned my attention to Android. "I knew you looked familiar. You're the local kid who aced the *Jeopardy!* teen tournament last season."

The two stood silently.

I folded my arms.

"Young men, in the immortal words of Ricky Ricardo, you've got some 'splainin' to do."

12

"The Blue Door, the west end's swingin'-est night spot, proudly presents Miss Helen Hudson."

Applause and cheers as the unknown announcer's voice faded. Then the contra-alto tones that had haunted my childhood launched into the opening bars of "St. James Infirmary Blues."

I put the LP on the turntable as soon as I arrived back home from my visit to Josh's house. The stage announcer's introduction at the start of Side One, Band One, was the only reference to The Blue Door. Helen Hudson, in her inane between-song patter, didn't drop a clue. What West End? Where?

Dammit, Mother!

I flipped on the radio to catch Glory Lou's first time out of the box as a talk show host. Caught her just as she was congratulating Seth Torkelson of Rancho Cordova for winning five grand in the Gold Rush Giveaway. I sipped a gin and tonic, listened to Glory Lou's show with one ear and my mother's record with the other, and mentally replayed the scene earlier this evening at Josh's place.

Josh Friedman and Andrew Stoller met three years ago at a *Star Trek* convention. Josh had been seventeen and Andrew fifteen. Despite the age difference, they struck up a friendship through a mutual fascination with radio in general and DXing in specific. DXers—shorthand for Distance Transmission—get their kicks by pulling in far-off stations. Finland, or American

Samoa. When they discover a new station, they write to the chief engineer noting the date and time the broadcast was received, plus a description of the signal strength, interference, noise, propagation fading, and overall merit. SINPO, to the hobbyists. The chief engineer sends a postcard and puts another pushpin in his map.

A subcult of the DX enthusiast collects pirate radio stations, the unlicensed broadcasters who face jail or worse to put across their message. Some are motivated by politics. Others feel disenfranchised by commercial radio and are driven to present alternative music and views. Some do it just because it's incredibly cool.

By the time Josh had finished two years of college and Andrew had won the *Jeopardy!* teen tournaments, simply receiving pirate broadcasts hadn't been enough. They took some of Andrew's prize money, made several forays to local swap meets, bought some good gear out of the Harris Allied catalog, and cobbled together their own radio station. They schemed the maiden voyage of their pirate station for weeks. Josh formatted the music, while Andrew wrote most of the bits. Three nights of broadcasts, with three sets of teases sent to me: first the message on my answering machine, then the flowers. The next night, a pizza was supposed to arrive with instructions on when to tune in that evening.

"We didn't mean to harass you, honest," Josh said. "We just wanted to get your attention and show you how good we sounded. We were hoping maybe you'd tell Mr. O'Brien about us and we could get a show on a real radio station. Just on the weekends or something to start."

But in the middle of their hijinks, Dr. Hipster turns up with a bullet in his head.

They'd already left the message on my machine, and it was too late to cancel the flowers. By the next day, when they realized how bad their timing had been, they were too scared to 'fess up.

"It was all my idea," Andrew told me. "Don't blame Josh. And please don't take his internship away from him."

What could I do? Of course, I forgave them. I mean, if Dr.

Hipster hadn't given me my first big break, I would have been doing the same thing when I was their age.

Before I slipped under the sheets, I made one last phone call, to Victor Pahoa at the Capital Square security desk. Just to see if he happened to tell anyone he'd be taking care of my cat over the weekend.

The weathercaster on the Tuesday morning news promised a cooling trend. Highs "only" in the upper eighties. I scrounged through the mound of clothing still dumped on the closet floor. Found an oversize green T-shirt that wasn't too badly creased and a broomstick skirt that was supposed to look wrinkled anyway. Sport sandals and my blue canvas backpack completed the ensemble.

I didn't want to go back to Dr. Hipster's apartment. But after my conversation with his son in San Jose the previous day, I needed to make sure Dr. Hipster's collection of rock memorabilia was safe. I walked the seven blocks to the apartment complex across the street from the State Capitol, turned my key in the lock, and slowly pushed open the door.

Less than a week since Dr. Hipster had died, and already the place had a deserted, empty feel to it. Stale air, spider plant drooping in a macramé hanger, a *Sacramento Bee* from two Sundays ago turning yellow on the kitchen table, a thin coat of dust on the glass-topped stereo system.

The good stuff was present and accounted for: Janis Joplin's tambourine, the Jimi Hendrix guitar, John Lennon's doodles, the autographed Doors album cover, the Fillmore posters.

I wasn't sure what I expected to find. Dr. Hipster had been an indifferent housekeeper, so it was hard to separate his typical messiness from a deliberate search-and-destroy mission. Not to mention the disarray left by the EMTs and the cops. I worried about whether the police had discovered Dr. Hipster's stash, then remembered we'd smoked the last of it the previous weekend, while watching *Ferris Bueller's Day Off* for the umpteenth time. We'd lit up just as the Ben "Bueller" Stein scene began.

The residue of what I assumed was fingerprint powder still clung to the doorknob leading to the recording studio that Dr. Hipster had set up in the spare bedroom. The scene of the crime. I assumed the apartment maintenance people had cleaned up, but I wasn't about to check and make sure.

I found Dr. Hipster's laptop and printer where he'd left it on the dining table, flicked it on, and scrolled through the files until I found the last time he'd logged on: last Wednesday morning at eight-thirty, a Word document titled Inventory. The document turned out to be a catalog of Dr. Hipster's rock music collectibles. Inventory. I had to admit, it was a project a man contemplating suicide might undertake. Getting his affairs in order and all that. Nonetheless, the list would come in handy if I were to keep my promise to Dr. Hipster's family to have the collection appraised. I hit Control-P and waited for the printer to spit out four pages of text.

Dr. Hipster's desktop seemed uncharacteristically tidy, but considering the circumstances, who knew? Just a pencil cup, one of those "page a day" *Far Side* calendars (still showing last Wednesday's cartoon), and a small spiral-bound notebook. New, never used. I tucked it in my backpack.

I opened the bottom file drawer and began thumbing through the manila folders. Taxes, insurance, divorce decree, birth certificate, pink slip to the van. Nothing that struck me as out of the ordinary. One folder with "Farm Team" printed on the tab in Dr. Hipster's wispy hand. I pulled that one out of the drawer and spread the contents on the desktop.

One certificate, dated eight years ago, acknowledging Dr. Hipster's expertise in leading the workshop on media relations. A program on folded cardstock already turning brown around the edges, listing the events at the weekend seminar: How to Write a Press Release that Won't Get Tossed, Timing Your Press Conference for Maximum Impact, Managing a Hostile Media Person. One session title made me laugh out loud: WordStar or WordPerfect: Which Word Processing Program Is Best for P.R. in the Nineties?

A single sheet of notepaper contained just three lines of handwritten text.

The Farm Team=Foundation for Progressive Public Policy
FPPP=CalFac
CalFac=Greene?

Unlike the certificate and program, the notepaper looked new, no discoloration around the edges, the penned lettering unfaded. Recent enough to be notes related to that really big story he was working on about the election? Possibly. Had he managed to unearth something new about The Farm Team in those few days he had left after he told his son the topic was a yawner?

I reassembled the folder and its contents, and stuffed it inside my backpack.

A curled brown leaf from the spider plant crunched under my foot as I entered the kitchen. I felt another pang of loss when I spotted the postcard I sent to Dr. Hipster during my last trip to Hawaii in the middle of a jumble of Chinese take-out menus, pizza coupons, and business cards on the refrigerator. I carefully slid the card from underneath the magnet and read in my own hand, "Having a time here. Wish you were wonderful." I smiled, but my hand shook as I reverently placed it back under the magnet. When would I stop missing him?

Two business cards fell to the floor. Clumsy me. One I recognized. Capital City Ventures. Dr. Hipster's landlord, as well as mine and half the renters in downtown Sacramento. I retrieved the other card and read in a Jetson-esque typeface:

RETRO ALLEY

R. Peter Kovacs, Prop.
Cool Stuff from the '50s '60s '70s

A local phone number and address in Old Sacramento followed.

This Kovacs person could be useful in getting an appraisal of Dr. Hipster's collection. I slipped the card into my pocket.

I poured a generous glass of water—no leak in the faucet—
for the spider plant, locked the door behind me, and walked
out into the morning sun.

I climbed into the front passenger seat of the station news car
and struggled to tuck the seatbelt around my wrinkled skirt.
Glory Lou was impeccable as usual in cream linen pants and
a teal-blue silk blouse. The top of her head almost scraped the
ceiling of the Ford Taurus. She'd pushed the seat back so far
my feet barely reached the floor mat.

Glory Lou had been more than a good sport when I called
her to suggest a drive out to Davis to check out The Farm
Team and its connection to the Jeff Greene campaign. The big
story about the election that Dr. Hipster may or may not have
been working on. I'm sure she secretly viewed the trip as the
mother of all wild-goose chases. Shoot, all I had to go on were
three lines on a scrap of notepaper. That, and a hunch.

"I'm with you, girlfriend." I could tell Glory Lou was trying hard not to sound patronizing. "Dr. Hipster must have been
sitting on a really, really big story about the election for governor."

"He was probably going to break the story on his show last
Wednesday night," I said.

"And you think the Greene people decided to silence him
permanently."

"We'll never know for sure unless we check it out. The
cops sure aren't doing squat."

"Aren't you forgetting something, hon? The cops found
your Rudy from West Sacramento."

"Course I haven't forgotten. I just don't believe it was really him."

"But you do believe the Rudy from West Sacramento who
keeps calling your show."

Glory Lou signaled to pass a moving van on the Yolo
Causeway. In the winter, I-80 spans a temporary lake created
when the Sacramento River bursts over its banks. In spring,
the waters recede, revealing nutrient-rich soil. I gazed out
across vast yellow acres of safflower stretching to the horizon,

pulsating in the heat on both sides of the freeway.

"Let's say someone killed Dr. Hipster to silence him," Glory Lou continued. "What does that have to do with your apartment being burglarized?"

I turned up the air conditioner. "I'm not sure. Unless they were looking for something in Dr. Hipster's apartment, couldn't find it, and thought I might have it."

"I follow you, girlfriend."

"Whoever searched my apartment must have known I was going to be gone for the weekend. They also knew that the security guy was going to be coming in to feed the cat. They waited 'til after Victor fed Bialy for the last time—Monday morning—before they broke in and messed with my stuff."

Glory Lou nodded at me to continue.

"I called Victor last night and asked him if he let anyone know I was going to be out of town this weekend."

"And?"

"His girlfriend. And his boss."

I turned the topic of conversation around to Jeff Greene, comparing notes with what Glory Lou and I knew about the candidate for governor.

For more than half a century, the orchards owned by Jeff Greene's parents and grandparents in what would become Silicon Valley produced crate after crate of the nation's finest cherries and apricots. Then, in the fifties, the Greene family planted their final, and most profitable, harvest: tract houses. Malvina Reynolds's little boxes made of ticky-tacky. Dr. Hipster's ex and kids could very well be living in one of them.

The Greene family took the loot and moved to a millionaire's rancho in the foothills above Cupertino. Young Jeff Greene attended Stanford and fell in with a pair of engineering students who had designed a primitive computer game. Greene had no interest in bits, bytes, or yellow stick figures gobbling up dots on a screen, but he did recognize a hot business opportunity.

By the mid-eighties, the cyber millionaire needed a new challenge. Santa Clara County Board of Supervisors came first, then the State Senate. From there to governor seemed a stretch at first. But now it looked like if he could beat Nadine Bostwick, he could add it to his résumé.

Married to his college sweetheart. Three kids, one in high school, two still young enough to qualify for the kid's plate at Denny's.

"Not to mention, yummy to look at," Glory Lou said.

"Big-time," I agreed.

Glory Lou steered the news car onto the Highway 113 off-ramp of I-80, then left on Russell Boulevard, heading away from town and deep into farm country. Flat fields of tomatoes and rice, bisected by a grid of two-lane county roads. This is the part of California the travel magazines never write about, the agricultural empire east of the Coast Range, far from the Hollywood sign and the Golden Gate Bridge. We might as well have been driving across Iowa.

After traveling perhaps five miles west on Russell Boulevard, Glory Lou slowed and signaled a left turn. "This has got to be the place."

At first glance, it was a duplicate of every other farm we'd passed since exiting I-80. White, two-story wood frame house from the turn of the last century. Water tower, barn, white picket fence. But neater, glossier. No rusted hulks of discarded farm equipment, manure piles, or stench of ag chemicals. Just a Martha Stewart vision of what a farm ought to look like, right down to the designer scarecrow planted in the middle of the plot of organic veggies. Next to the barn, where you'd expect to see a row of farm labor cottages, stood a cluster of low-slung buildings, each painted a different bright primary color, solar panels positioned on the roofs. In a center courtyard, under the shade of a eucalyptus tree, a dozen or so students lounged on the grass and focused on the words of a bearded, jeans-clad man who sat cross-legged on a bench in front of them.

The tires of News Unit 5 crunched over gravel as Glory Lou pulled through the gate and up to a faux Victorian gazebo. Cute, for sure, but I still knew a guardhouse when I saw one. A young woman popped out of the wooden structure and leaned into the driver's side window. She bubbled with athletic enthusiasm, was deeply tanned, with sun-streaked brown curls caught up in a scrunchie. She wore the uniform of resort staff the world over: polo shirt with embroidered logo and brass name tag, khaki shorts, blazing white sneakers.

She looked at the Sacramento Talk Radio logo emblazoned on the side of the news car and consulted a clipboard. Her perkiness visibly sagged. "Gosh, I don't see you on the schedule anywhere. Are you sure you made an appointment?"

"Positive, honey," Glory Lou lied. Appointment? We'd only just decided to trek over to Davis and find The Farm Team campus about an hour ago.

The young woman retreated to the guardhouse and picked up a telephone. I couldn't hear what she was saying, but I could see her face harden into a mask of authority when she reemerged a few moments later. "Sorry, but everyone on our media relations staff is in a meeting. You'll have to come back some other time."

"Sorry won't cut it. We have an appointment. This is simply unacceptable after we drove all the way out here." Glory Lou matched her icy tone. "At least let us come in and look around."

"Absolutely not. Our students and faculty have a right to their privacy. It isn't fair to them to interrupt their studies every time someone from the news media decides to show up."

I leaned forward and turned toward the driver's side window. "Will they be out of their meeting this afternoon?"

"You still can't come back without an appointment."

"I know." I handed my business card to the guard. "I was thinking maybe your media relations person could meet me at my office this afternoon. Anytime between three and six o'clock."

13

"Bucolic" is a word that comes to mind in describing the town of Davis. As in: "A bucolic university town some ten miles west of Sacramento . . ." Parents like Davis because it feels like a safe haven when compared to the social and political intensity of the UC campuses in Los Angeles and Berkeley. But even bucolic Davis leans far enough to the left for Rush Limbaugh to have dubbed it "The People's Republic of Davis" during his Sacramento radio days. And it has a decent daily newspaper that I hoped might cover the goings-on of The Farm Team on a regular basis.

Glory Lou parked in front of a squat, cinder-block building on the edge of the downtown district. Ersatz California mission, down to the red tile roof and arch over the front door. A wooden sign hanging from the arch announced the home of the *Davis Daily Delineator*. "Serving Davisites Since 1893."

Newspaper city rooms lost most of their romance when the reporters traded in their typewriters for word processors. News deserves to be accompanied by the ka-chunk and zing of a Royal or Remington, not the tippy-tap of hands scurrying over a keyboard, like hamsters scrabbling in their cages. Still, the city room of the *Davis Daily Delineator* had its moments: crackle of police scanners, publicity posters for the candidates for governor with teeth blacked out and mustaches drawn in, framed front pages of one hundred years' worth of newsmaking disasters, from the San Francisco earthquake and fire to the World Trade Center attack.

The receptionist led the two of us, Glory Lou armed with her tape deck and me with Dr. Hipster's notebook, through the city room and out a side door for our meeting with the *Davis Daily Delineator* managing editor.

Outside?

A blue pop-up canopy stood on a concrete pad on the north side of the *Delineator* building. Parked under the canopy was a battle-scarred wooden desk, a worn leather executive chair, and two white molded plastic patio chairs. A bright orange extension cord snaking from the building powered a fan and laptop computer. More lines hooked up the telephone and an intercom box. One of those Lung Association signs that thanked you for not smoking was duct-taped to one of the aluminum canopy legs. Someone had whited out the word "not."

A gnarled gnome of a woman rose from behind the desk.

"Yeah, yeah, I know who you are." She gestured toward the chairs with a claw clutching a burning cigarette.

"Don't blame me for the hospitality. I run the friggin' newspaper. But those granola-crunching, tree-hugging lib-ruls on the City Council say I can't smoke in my own office. So here I am. Helluva deal when it's raining."

Dark brown hair, salted with gray, styled in a severe chin-length bob. She was an inch or two shorter than me, which would definitely make her a candidate for the petite department at Macy's. But I bet she had a hard time finding clothes that fit. Unlike most women whose bodies sag to pear-shape as they age, Aggie Tarbell was all top. Below the waist, her figure tapered to nothing hips and a flat bottom. A loose white blouse over black stirrup pants accentuated the inverted pyramid.

Aggie Tarbell seated herself behind the desk, took a long slow drag on her Virginia Slim, and stared at Glory Lou and me for a long moment.

"Thanks for seeing us at the last minute," I said.

"Always glad to shoot the breeze with a couple of sisters from the fourth estate." She paused for a chuckle that turned into a cackle and ended with a hacking cough. "To what do I owe the pleasure?"

"We're gathering background information on The Farm Team for an upcoming special about the election. Our story won't be complete without reviewing the coverage in your newspaper. I'm sure it's extensive."

She took a long, slow drag and contemplated the underside of the blue canopy. "Why didn't you ask me something easy?"

"I'm not sure if I understand."

"Take a look at this burg. What do you see? A university and a bunch of mom 'n' pop businesses. No shopping mall, no major industry since the Hunt-Wesson cannery closed a couple of years ago."

"So?"

"No advertising, get it? No way there's the advertising base in a town like this to support a daily newspaper." She shoved a copy of today's edition across the desk. "Take a look at the back page of the front section."

A full-page ad, do-gooder public service copy. Clever Ways with Compost! After scanning tips on more than I ever wanted to know about making good use of eggshells, coffee grounds, and old pizza boxes, I found the line of text at the bottom of the page: Sponsored by the Foundation for Progressive Public Policy.

I folded the paper and handed it back to Tarbell. "So your boss, the owner of the paper or whoever, won't let you write about The Farm Team."

"Not unless it's a puff piece."

"Still, I'd think you'd be curious. You must have done some digging on your own, talked to people, took notes. Maybe someday you'll sell your story to CNN, write a book even."

Aggie Tarbell studied Glory Lou and me like a crafty old poker player at one of the seedier casinos in Reno.

"Tell you what," I said. "You help us out, I'll make it worth your while. You share your notes with me, and I'll arrange for you to be the guest host of my show the next time I go on vacation. Three hours of airtime a day for an entire week. You book the guests, you talk about whatever you want. Repealing the antismoking ordinance, I don't care."

"Anything I want?"

"Anything."

Our hostess rewarded us with a grin that revealed gray, brown-streaked teeth. "You're on." It works every time. No one can resist the lure of having their very own forum.

"You mentioned puff pieces," I continued. "I imagine your paper does things like write up graduations and award ceremonies out at The Farm."

"I swear, if I have to cover one more of those things, I'll heave."

"So there might be a story or two about the year Jeff Greene spent at The Farm."

"Let me show you the morgue."

Aggie Tarbell led us back into the *Delineator* building, stopping at the door to crush out her cigarette in a coffee can filled with sand. The *Davis Daily Delineator* morgue—stuffier corporate papers prefer to call it the library or even, God help us, the archives—was located in a musty, windowless cave just off the city room. Thankfully, the paper's budget covered air-conditioning. Dozens of oversize binders the size of a newspaper page lined the shelves on two walls. Tarbell found the one labeled "April–June" for a year in the early nineties, pulled it from the shelf, and placed it on a long wooden table.

We endured several moments of phlegm-riddled hacking while Tarbell flipped through the yellowing pages. "There." She turned the book toward Glory Lou and me.

A group photo, thirty or so young men and women wearing Farm Team polo shirts and holding certificates. "Another fresh crop of future leaders," according to the cutline.

"That's Jeff Greene." Aggie Tarbell tapped a ragged, yellowed nail against a younger version of the gubernatorial candidate in the second row.

Glory Lou pulled the binder closer and made a stab with a manicured, pink nail. "Could that be Marvella Kent?"

"The city councilwoman? Lemme see." I studied the image of a striking African-American woman in the first row, then read the small type under the photo. "You're right."

I turned to Aggie Tarbell. She'd been watching us from the doorway, a patient old lizard eyeing the trail of a couple of spiders. "What would it cost for you to make a copy of this photograph for us?" I asked.

"Normally we charge thirty for photo reprints. But I'll give you the industry discount. You can have it for twenty." She knocked on an adjoining darkroom door. A brawny Latino emerged. "Julio, got time to go through your files and find a negative, make a copy?"

"Give me fifteen minutes or so." Julio disappeared behind the darkroom door.

Tarbell turned her attention back to Glory Lou and me. "I'm due at the Chamber of Commerce luncheon in another ten minutes. You can leave the money for the photo with the receptionist. And give me your fax number. I'll send you what I can from my notes this afternoon. I'll trust you'll use the information wisely."

"You have my word."

The crone looked positively wistful. "All I ask is that if you break an interesting story, you think of Aggie Tarbell and give her a piece of the action."

"Of course." I thanked Tarbell and took a closer look at the newspaper coverage of The Farm Team graduation. "Is that Terrence O'Brien? Standing right there next to Jeff Greene?"

Glory Lou followed my finger. "Hon, you've got to get that man off your mind."

I gave Glory Lou what I hoped was a puzzled look.

"Don't look at me like that, sugar. I can always tell. Shauna J.'s got a crush. But don't worry none. I think he's interested in you too."

I turned the binder in Glory Lou's direction and continued pointing. "Would you just shut up and look at the picture? Doesn't this guy look like Terrence O'Brien? Or what Terrence O'Brien would have looked like around eight or so years ago?"

She pushed her hair behind her ears and studied the photograph. "As I live and breathe. What do you suppose he was doing there?"

"Attending seminars, I guess. Maybe at one time he thought

he might go into politics, before he decided to follow in his father's footsteps."

Someone had left another bound file on the table. 1958. I began riffling the pages, just to kill time until the print had finished developing and drying.

A small ad on the page with the theater and club listings stopped me cold.

"Sweet baby Jesus. Glory Lou, you've got to take a look at this." I tugged her away from the darkroom door and back to the book of fifties-era newspapers.

Glory Lou followed my pointed figure and gave me a blank look.

"Don't you get it?" I said. "It's The Blue Door."

"Sorry, but I still don't get it."

"Dr. Hipster's son told me his dad was asking about the legality of a contract signed forty or fifty years ago. A contract having something to do with a blue door. Here it is in black-and-white, Sacramento, 1958—"

Glory Lou interrupted before I could finish. "And a night-club named The Blue Door. As I live and breathe."

14

"You really think something went down out at The Farm back when Jeff Greene was going through leadership training, and he's been covering his ass ever since?" Glory Lou said. "I mean, at the time he was just planning to run for some local office in Silicon Valley."

We were back in the news car, retracing our steps on I-80, eastbound, back to Sacramento.

I allowed as how maybe I was reaching. "But now the stakes are higher. Greene's running for governor. And Dr. Hipster was on the faculty for a weekend seminar on media relations the same time Greene was attending classes out there. Something might have happened. Something Dr. Hipster witnessed."

Glory Lou eased her foot from the gas and downshifted. "Cop car on my tail."

"What's the worry? They never pull over media vehicles."

"Then why's he following so closely?"

I peered into the rearview mirror.

The car behind us changed lanes without signaling. The driver floored it. All I saw was a cream-colored sedan, no marking, cell phone antenna and a red light on the roof. I didn't catch the license number, but I did register that the plates didn't have a diamond or hexagonal symbol indicating a government vehicle. "Looks like some sort of private patrol," I said as Glory Lou eased her size ten pump from the clutch.

We rode in silence across the Yolo Causeway. Then I said,

"What makes you think Terrence O'Brien is interested in me?"

"Sugar, I can always tell. For one thing, he asked me about you a couple of weeks ago. He cornered me in the lunchroom and asked, all casual-like, whether I knew if Shauna J. Bogart was involved with anyone."

"No way!"

"For real. Then he wanted to know whether it was true what he'd heard about you and Dr. Hipster."

"What'd you tell him?"

"The truth, as far as I knew it. The two of you were good friends, old friends, but whether you had exchanged bodily fluids, I didn't think so."

Glory Lou took her eyes off the traffic for a moment and looked at me. "Listen, girlfriend, a handsome, eligible male like Terrence O'Brien doesn't ask those kinds of questions unless he's interested."

We crossed the Pioneer Bridge arching over the river into downtown Sacramento. "Where to?" Glory Lou said. "We could stop at City Hall and see if Marvella Kent is in."

"We're closer to Old Sacramento. Let's look for The Blue Door."

I opened my backpack and pulled out the photocopy of the fifties-era ad the receptionist had made for me back at the *Delineator* office. Three columns by five inches filled with a line drawing of a partially open door with musical notes pouring out. The text proclaimed:

The Blue Door

Jazz • Be-bop • Blues
Cocktails
215 K Street
Sacramento

"The West End's Swingin'est Night Spot"

Even though I live only a couple of blocks away from Old Sacramento, I don't spend a lot of time there. It's like how the native San Franciscan never goes to Fisherman's Wharf, or how L.A. locals avoid Hollywood and Vine. Too touristy.

Forty or so years ago, Sacramento's West End was among the most notorious red-light districts on the West Coast. Then in the late sixties, I–5 bulldozed its way through downtown, isolating eight square blocks of the West End from the rest of the city.

Someone got the idea to turn what was left of the slum into a historic district, a Wild West version of New Orleans's French Quarter. The city and state joined forces, pushed the bums across the river into West Sacramento, rehabbed the derelict buildings back to their Gold Rush splendor, stripped the asphalt streets down to their original cobblestones, and added wooden sidewalks and reproduction gaslights. The old whore never looked so good.

News Unit 5 bounced along the cobblestones. Glory Lou swung into a parking spot in a fifteen-minute zone in front of Fat City at the intersection of Front and J Streets. She placed a Working Media placard on the dash and opened the door.

We walked along the wooden boardwalk of Front Street, restaurants and souvenir shops to our left, the Sacramento River across the street to our right. In the open space in front of the California Railroad Museum, a crew pounded stakes for a giant blue-and-yellow striped tent. Getting ready for the Jazz Jubilee just three days later.

Left turn on K Street. The odd numbers were on our side of the street. Evangeline's, 113 K Street, Round Table Pizza at 127, Chinese take-out place holding down the 131 spot near the corner. Next block had to be The Blue Door at 215 K Street. Or whatever occupied 215 K Street fifty years later. I was so excited I almost started running.

Across Second, K Street narrowed, passed under an arch, and plunged into a dank pedestrian tunnel under I–5. I supposed the street numbering would pick up on the other side of the tunnel. We entered the tunnel.

Places like this give me the creeps. I'm always imagining muggers lurking in the shadows. But if you have to walk in a tunnel under a freeway, this one wasn't bad, piped-in music and a mural depicting significant Sacramentans through history, Maidu Indians to Eleanor McClatchy. The closest we came to being assaulted was by a kid on an out-of-control skateboard. And it was shady and cool.

An uphill climb brought us to a landscaped pedestrian mall on the east side of the freeway, the downtown Holiday Inn the first building on the odd-numbered side of the street. I peered anxiously at the gold letters above the door: 301.

"How could we have missed the two hundreds?" This from Glory Lou.

"I don't know, but I have a bad feeling about this."

We retraced our path under the pedestrian tunnel, my hopes plummeting with each step. On the other side, I ran to the first building facing K Street on the odd-numbered side. 131, the Chinese take-out place.

"I'm going back to the tunnel," I declared.

"Hon, what's the use? Anyway, my dogs are killing me."

"Suit yourself. I'm going back."

Glory Lou caught up with me a couple of minutes later. She found me standing toward the west entrance to the tunnel, facing the left side, shaking my head slowly. A chain-link fence separated the tunnel from a parking lot under the elevated freeway.

This is where 215 K Street should have been, this bleak, empty concrete slab. The Blue Door. If they hadn't knocked it down years ago to put in the freeway.

"Dammit, Glory Lou, I'm sorry I was a bitch. But we were so close."

"Hon, I'm sorry too. But what did you expect to find, even if this Blue Door place was still here?"

"I don't know." I scuffed my sandals aimlessly on the dusty cement floor of the tunnel. The name of Dr. Hipster's killer scrawled on the wall of the women's john? That contract Dr. Hipster had asked his son about written on a cocktail napkin? The ghost of Helen Hudson?

I took one last look at the dark, empty hole that had once held The West End's Swingin'est Night Spot. "Let's get out of here."

. . .

A red helium balloon bobbed in the sky above Old Sacramento, tethered above one of the buildings on Second Street. "Retro Alley" was printed in bold black letters on the side of the balloon.

Retro Alley. I fished into my pocket and pulled out the business card I'd pilfered from Dr. Hipster's refrigerator this morning. R. Peter Kovacs, Prop. Dealer in collectibles. We followed the balloon to a two-story brick building next to an ice-cream parlor on the east side of Second Street.

A pair of sawhorses supported a hollow-core door in front of the building. The door, in turn, held boxes of paperback books, mostly recent thrillers and mysteries. A sign handlettered in black felt pen on a manila file folder told us "Your choice. Two for a dollar. Great summer reading!"

A larger version of the business card was painted on the window, in the same sixties-era type:

RETRO ALLEY

R. Peter Kovacs, Prop.
Cool Stuff from the '50s '60s '70s

A gaudy poster promoting the Jazz Jubilee ("A Hot Time in the Old Town Tonight!") covered the lower right corner of the window.

Inside: Lava Lites, revolving mirrored disco balls, racks of bowling shirts and polyester leisure suits, pink flamingoes, fuzzy dice, a transistor radio that had probably been new when Sputnik was launched, Rickie Tickie Stickies (still in their original packaging), shelves of troll dolls and sno-globes, a painting of Elvis on velvet.

This was, indeed, cool stuff.

The expensive goodies were in the back. A locked case housed a collection of first editions. *Carrie*, *A Is for Alibi*, *Interview with the Vampire*, a full set of Travis McGee novels.

Fat black binders were lined up neatly on a shelf above the glass case: Vintage Hollywood, Current Movie Stars, Star Trek, Jazz/Big Band, Country Music, Vintage Rock, Current Pop Music, Sports. One of the binders lay open on top of the glass case, revealing an autographed eight-by-ten photograph of Diana Rigg as Emma Peel. Twenty bucks.

A man stood behind the glass case, his back to us, a telephone receiver held to his ear. R. Peter Kovacs, Prop., I assumed.

"The band needs one more rehearsal before the Jubilee."

Pause.

"I know. But it's still rough getting in and out of my solo on 'Sweet Georgia Brown.'"

Pause.

"Tonight works for me. Herman's garage at seven?"

I stood next to an upright piano and studied a framed autographed poster from the Bobby Kennedy presidential campaign with a "Not For Sale" sticker. Kovacs, or whoever he was, finished the phone call.

His eyes were green, intelligent, with a hint of mischief. When he smiled, I noticed one of his front teeth was chipped, and his nose looked like it had been busted once. He had hippie hair, black flecked with gray, curling past his ears and flowing over his collar.

He caught up with me in front of the framed autographed RFK campaign poster.

"Bobby signed that for me when I was a kid just a couple of days before the California primary. My older sister brought me along to one of her Young Democrats rallies, and I just happened to be in the right place at the right time. I would never part with it. Perhaps I can interest you in something else?"

Glory Lou and I introduced ourselves and did the business card/handshake ritual.

"Call me Pete." He was almost a head taller than me, which would have put him just under six feet. Well-worn jeans fit trimly and were topped by a black T-shirt bearing the logo of The Hot Times Dixieland Jazz Band.

Pete Kovacs slid my business card into the back pocket of

his jeans. "I listen to your show every day. You know what?"

Here it comes.

His smile faded. "Never mind. It wasn't important. How can I help you?"

Oh, well, what did I expect? There I was, the media celebrity with limp, matted hair stuck to my forehead, a sloppy T-shirt, and a shapeless cotton skirt more wrinkled than crinkled. For once in my life, I wished I had learned how to use makeup.

I told Kovacs about my mission for Dr. Hipster's heirs: to arrange an appraisal of the rock memorabilia collection and possibly find a buyer.

"Dr. Hipster. What a tragedy. I didn't agree with all of what he had to say, but I always enjoyed the trip."

I was about to get into my backpack and pull out the inventory list I'd printed from Dr. Hipster's computer, but Kovacs beat me to it, producing an identical list from the IN basket on his desktop.

"Dr. Hipster had me over to his apartment recently to look at his collection," he said. "He needed an updated appraisal for insurance. I told him before I could be of any assistance, I needed a list of what he had. Then I got busy practicing for the Jazz Jubilee and never had a chance to start pricing anything."

"Would you be interested in doing the appraisal for Dr. Hipster's kids?"

"I'd be honored. And if the family decides to sell the collection, I could steer you in the right direction."

"That'd be terrific."

There was no particular reason to stick around. I thanked Kovacs and began edging toward the door. Then I turned back. "You've got my card. I guess you'll call me when you have the appraisal done?"

Kovacs looked up from a shelf where he'd been straightening the troll dolls. "Absolutely. And you feel free to call me, just to check on my progress."

"Sure thing."

"Well. Nice meeting you."

"See ya."

• • •

Glory Lou squeezed my hand as we walked along the wooden sidewalk. "He's adorable!"

"Who, Kovacs?"

"Of course Kovacs. Who else?"

"He's okay."

Glory Lou unlocked News Unit 5. We stood on the boardwalk, leaving the doors open to let the hot air escape. "As I live and breathe, I don't believe you sometimes. He's cute, he's a Democrat, he has his own business, he's the right age for you, and he wasn't wearing a wedding ring."

I fanned myself with my notebook. "The right age for me? What the hell does that mean?"

"Old enough to remember Bobby Kennedy, but not old enough to have actually voted for him. Perfect for you."

I slid tentatively into the passenger seat. Still hot, but no longer capable of producing first-degree burns. "He's a musician in a Dixieland band. What if he's plays the banjo?"

Glory Lou started the engine. "He likes you."

"Get outta here!"

"No, really. He likes you."

She pulled out onto the cobblestone street. "I can always tell."

15

Mimi Blitzer beckoned me into the radio station lunchroom. I almost gagged on the aroma of Blitzer's fruit-scented shampoo mixed with the odor of burnt popcorn from the microwave. "I need to talk to you about the Gold Rush Giveaway," she said in a low voice.

"Jeez, not the contest again. I just got here. At least let me check my voice mail."

"Last night, we gave away one thousand dollars to another Sac State student. Twenty years old, lives in the dorms."

"Let me guess." I placed the back of my hand on my forehead in imitation of Johnny Carson's Great Karnak bit. "The winner was supposed to be a forty-year-old court clerk. Her husband works for the state, something with computers, between the two of them they make seventy-five grand a year and, oh yeah, they just bought a new tract house in Folsom."

"This isn't a joke." Blitzer placed both hands on her narrow hips. "The right card with the right lucky numbers left my office. The wrong card with the wrong numbers got read on the air. Someone is opening the envelopes and tampering with the cards."

"It happened on Glory Lou's air shift. Why bother me about it?"

"Sac State students? Your intern?" Blitzer thrust out her neck, almost touching my nose with hers.

"Oh, for God's sake. Josh wasn't even in the station last night. Get a grip."

"I want that kid out of here."

"Forget it. No one has the power to hire and fire except T. R. O'Brien."

"T. R. put me in charge of the contest while he's on vacation."

"I'm impressed." I turned on the linoleum floor and took a step out of the tiny lunchroom. "The kid stays. And that's final."

"Epic!" Josh Friedman flourished a sheaf of fax paper as I approached my desk in the newsroom.

Aggie Tarbell had come through, just as she'd promised. I snatched the fax sheets from Josh's hands and cleared a space on the desk. Gone only three days and already my work space was a jumble of mail, interoffice memos, press releases, old newspapers, and discarded fast-food containers.

I pressed the curl out of the flimsy sheets and squinted to skim the tiny print. The sales department gets a fancy new plain paper fax machine. The newsroom limps along with an antique that spews rolls of waxy paper. T. R. justifies his parsimony by pointing out a good ninety percent of the press releases that get faxed into the newsroom go directly into the trash. But still.

The telephone on my desk interrupted my reading. Terrence O'Brien, calling to confirm our dinner date. Morton's, reservations at eight. "I'll pick you up quarter 'til . . ."

"Don't be silly. I live only a couple of blocks from Morton's. I'll meet you there."

"Are you sure? I don't want you taking any chances if there's some nut out there stalking local media personalities."

"Not to worry. I feel all but certain now this is an inside job, someone from the station."

"That's amazing. What makes you so sure?"

"Remember the other night, when I mentioned to you about the missing tapes? Get this: Dr. Hipster was trying to send a coded message that he was in danger, or that something big was about to break. Whoever destroyed the tapes had to be from the station and he—or she—is trying damn hard to make sure no one hears that message."

Terrence whistled in amazement through the interoffice phone line.

"I'm on the air in less than five minutes," I said. "We'll talk about it more this evening."

I popped into the production studio and grabbed a CD from the rack.

Captain Mikey was just finishing his first traffic report of the afternoon as I signed on the log, donned headphones, stacked the carts for the first commercial break, and placed the CD in the playback machine in the control room. The final chords of the theme jingle faded. I flipped open the mike.

"Welcome to the Shauna J. Bogart Show. I'll take your calls in a minute. But first, presenting the First Annual Shauna J. Bogart Award for the most boring, overrated annual event in Sacramento. And the winner is . . ."

I punched up a sound effect of a drumroll.

"The Sacramento Jazz Jubilee!"

Then I started the CD player. It didn't matter which cut came up. With a title like "All-Time Dixieland Favorites," I knew they'd all feature that perky toe-tappin' sound.

"I ask you, is this how we want to represent the culture of the capital city of the great state of California to the world? Rinky-tinky, razzmatazz music that should have been given a decent burial at least fifty years ago? Even Cleveland—Cleveland, of all places—gets the Rock and Roll Hall of Fame. Sacramento gets a Dixieland festival!"

Every phone line blinked hysterically.

"I know what you're going to say," I continued. "The Jazz Jubilee is the biggest event of its type in the country, if not the world. It's good for the local economy. It draws thousands of tourists."

I grabbed the mike and paced around the control room, as far as the cord tethering me to the control board would let me go. "Have you actually listened to any of the lyrics to these allegedly wholesome, all-American Dixieland tunes? Happy, contented darkies shuffling on the levee, waiting for the *Robert E. Lee*? Or some man who done her wrong and she's still willing to take him back, even though he beat her black and blue? Give me a break!

"You know how the pizza delivery business got started? Those Dixieland bands in the pizza parlors. They drove everybody out!"

The phone calls were predictable. The head of the Visitors and Convention Bureau reminded me of the hundreds of thousands of dollars the Jazz Jubilee pumps into the local economy. "Did you know, the Sacramento Jazz Jubilee consistently ranks in the top five annual events in California when it comes to attracting tourists from out of state? Right up there with the Tournament of Roses Parade."

Tom from Rancho Cordova challenged me to defend the lyrics of hip-hop against any tune published before 1950. The publicity director for the Jazz Jubilee called in. "Every year we bring together one hundred thousand people for a four-day music festival. There are no riots, no bad trips, and practically no arrests. There's plenty of food and drink and no one has to sit in the mud. Can you say the same about Woodstock?"

I hadn't had so much fun in a long time.

Mimi Blitzer came boiling into the control room. I started the 3:20 commercial break a couple of minutes early, just to keep her from going into a core meltdown.

"Do you have any idea what you're doing?" she seethed as soon as the ON AIR light went dark. "Don't you know about the remote?"

"What remote?"

"The entire station is broadcasting live all day Friday from Old Sacramento. Morning drive all the way 'til Glory Lou's show ends at eleven. Including *your* show. The station has a float in the parade and I expect *you* to be on it along with everyone else. Didn't you read my memo?"

"Gee, Mimi, I must have missed it. What's the big deal?"

She all but stamped her tiny foot. "This is a major station promotion. I've placed an ad in the Jazz Jubilee program inviting everyone to stop by and meet the air talent. We're giving away free sun visors. And we have a guaranteed winner every hour in the Gold Rush Giveaway!"

The final commercial in the stop-set warned me about a substantial interest penalty for early withdrawal. I shrugged my shoulders and raised my hands palms up. Innocent little me.

"You're back with the Shauna J. Bogart Show. I've just been informed by our esteemed Director of Marketing and Promotion that the Sacramento Jazz Jubilee is an officially sanctioned station event. This same Director of Marketing and Promotion informs me that the Shauna J. Bogart Show will be broadcasting live from Old Sacramento this Friday afternoon. Just to show this entire event the respect and dignity it deserves, I pledge to burn a banjo, live and on the air. Anyone interested in helping in this worthy cause, c'mon down!"

I could see Mimi Blitzer through the control-room glass running down the hall. Probably on her way to the ladies' room to toss her cookies. For once she wouldn't have to stick her finger down her throat.

Josh typed a new name into the call-screener terminal. LINE THREE. PETE FROM OLD SACRAMENTO. R. Peter Kovacs, Prop. of Retro Alley. Well!

Other callers had been waiting longer. But I punched up Line Three.

"I'm a musician in a Dixieland band, okay? But I understand where you're coming from."

"You do?"

"I'll bet your first exposure to traditional jazz was *The Lawrence Welk Show* or Ed Sullivan. Joann Castle. Big Tiny Little, Joe 'Fingers' Carr, and Dorothy Provine. Am I right?"

"Well, yeah. I mean, it's so corny."

"Joann Castle and Big Tiny Little kept ragtime alive in the fifties and sixties when hardly anyone was playing or recording it," Pete from Old Sacramento continued. "Unfortunately, their style managed to thoroughly turn off anyone who wasn't already collecting Social Security."

"You ain't just whistling 'Dixie.' "

"That cornball style that you denigrate is not how those songs were originally written, or how the composers meant them to be played. Pop music from the early part of the last century was elegant, masterful, worthy of respect."

"If you say so."

"I'll grant you, the lyrics were hardly politically correct. But they reflected the context of the times: drugs, racism, domestic violence. And overriding all that, the search for contentment, happiness, and love. What I find fascinating is that the issues really haven't changed all that much in a hundred years."

"The more things change, the more they stay the same." Was I actually agreeing with this guy?

"But that's not why I called."

"Oh?"

"I want to invite you to be my guest at the Jazz Band Ball this Thursday night."

"You called my show to ask me out?"

"Sure. Why not?" Pete from Old Sacramento sounded way too smug and sure of himself.

"What's the Jazz Band Ball?"

"Does that mean you'll accept?"

"Just answer the question."

"It's a party and a jam session for all of the people working to set up the Jazz Jubilee, plus VIPs and any musicians who are already in town. Thursday night at eight at The Firehouse."

"Okay . . ."

"Does that mean yes?"

"No! I mean, I guess so. Sure. Why not?"

"There's one more thing you should know about the Jazz Band Ball."

"What's that?"

"It's a costume party."

"What, like Elvira? In your dreams, mister!"

I could almost see the mischief in Pete Kovacs's eyes. "You're supposed to come in a costume representing a musical era covered by the Sacramento Jazz Jubilee. Roughly 1895 to 1955. Ragtime to swing."

"I can't wait."

"Put me on hold," Pete from Old Sacramento said. "I'll talk

to your producer and work out all the details, like when and where I should pick you up."

My fingers put Line Three on hold. Then I typed a message to Josh:

DO NOT—REPEAT, DO NOT—GIVE HIM MY HOME ADDRESS!

A few moments later, Josh messaged back:

I TOLD PETE YOU'D MEET HIM THURSDAY NIGHT AT 8 AT THE FIREHOUSE. HE SOUNDED PRETTY DISAPPOINTED HE COULDN'T PICK YOU UP AT HOME.

I gave Josh a two-word reply.

And it wasn't TOO BAD.

Glory Lou called me on the two-way from City Hall. "I got Marvella Kent! She's agreed to come on your show tomorrow afternoon, in the four o'clock hour."

"Good work!"

"One more thing."

"What's that?"

"I told you he liked you."

I hadn't really expected anyone from The Farm Team to take me up on my request to send a representative to my "office" this afternoon, so I was surprised when Mrs. Yanamoto called me during the four o'clock network newscast to say that two women from "some farm thing" waited for me in the lobby. Surprised, and glad I had planned to do only open line the rest of the afternoon and didn't have to bump a guest. I sent Josh to the lobby to escort the pair to the control room, help them don headphones, and settle in behind the mikes, while I speed-read the press kit they'd brought with them. I felt another jolt of surprise.

This wasn't just a couple of dweebs from the media relations staff. One of the women turned out to be Arliss Drach, chairman of the board and general manager of The Farm Team.

She was mid-forties, tall and bony, shoulder-length brown hair streaked with gray held in place at the nape of her neck by a silver clip shaped like a dolphin. Smaller versions of the silver dolphins dangled from her earlobes. She wore Birkenstocks, a khaki wraparound skirt, and a denim blouse embroidered with The Farm Team logo, row of sunflowers with cartoon happy faces in a rainbow coalition of colors: brown, red, yellow, pink, white, and black. All she lacked was a PBS tote bag to complete the liberal do-gooder ensemble.

The other half of the team looked familiar. She was dressed in an identical getup, except that her Farm Team blouse was ironed. She identified herself as director of media relations. As soon as she gave her name—Tricia Nakamura—I placed her. Up until six months ago, she'd been a reporter for one of the local TV stations. Then she lost her job in one of the periodic shake-ups endemic to the industry. Public relations is the job of last resort for most displaced journalists, especially in a city like Sacramento, where PIO—public information officer— posts with state agencies abound. On the one hand, I could understand the lure of PR: regular hours, decent pay, no fighting over who gets stuck working on Christmas, and freedom from the tyranny of ratings, consultants, and focus groups.

On the other hand, I'd sooner put on a paper hat and make a career out of supersizing your order.

"We're always happy to share The Farm Team story with the media," Arliss Drach said into the mike after I'd introduced the guests and set up the topic. Her whiny monotone made it sound as if she wished she were anywhere but here. Undergoing her annual pelvic exam, perhaps. "Thank you for inviting us to appear on your show."

I consulted the notes Aggie Tarbell had faxed to me. "You're welcome. Just curious—are you any relation to Sievers-Drach?"

"Benjamin Drach was my great-grandfather. He formed the company to help San Francisco rebuild after the Great Quake and Fire."

Sievers-Drach was one of the state's major construction and engineering firms. Whether your project involved repairing a cracked driveway in front of your house or drilling for oil in the Santa Barbara Channel, chances are you'd be dealing with Sievers-Drach or one of its subsidiaries.

Before I had the chance to make a comment, Drach continued, "My father started The Farm Team in 1978. He was

disturbed at the disillusionment and cynicism everyone felt
toward politicians and the political process in the wake of the
Watergate scandal." She spoke like she had rehearsed and re-
cited the story many times over, honing it to perfection. "My
father believed that service to one's city, state, or nation in a
democratic society should be a noble calling. He founded The
Farm Team to restore that sense of honor among upcoming
generations of political leaders."

"What, exactly, do you people do out there?"

"We offer a full curriculum of political leadership training,
from weekend seminars to semester courses. Our programs
cover topics like successful grassroots organizational skills,
public speaking techniques, creative public policy, understanding the state budget process, just to name a few."

"What about this business about it being 'invitation only'
to participate in your training program? That doesn't sound
very democratic to me."

Nakamura shifted in the swivel chair and acted as if she
was about to make a comment, but Drach persisted in the same
monotone, "We're very proud of our recruiting program. We
literally scour the state looking for the best and brightest, not
just from our universities, but from community colleges, grassroots neighborhood groups, local councils and boards, environmental organizations, minority advocacy groups, and the
like. The Farm Team wants to nurture political leadership,
wherever it may come from."

"As long as they toe the liberal line."

"If you're insinuating that The Farm Team has a political
agenda, you're absolutely right. We believe in fiscal respon-
sibility in handling taxpayer money, stewardship of our state's
magnificent environmental resources, and equal opportunity
for all, regardless of ethnic background, religious belief, or
sexual preference. We've never kept our core values a secret,
and quite frankly, never understood why those positions
should be considered controversial."

Indeed, by California standards, they were about as middle-
of-the-road as you could find.

Nakamura finally managed to jump in. "That's why The
Farm Team never filed with the Secretary of State to be in-

corporated as a nonprofit. We want to maintain our ability to take an active part in the political process."

And to make sure your books aren't open to inspection by the public.

I glanced down to the console, where I'd spread out the sheets of fax paper. "The Farm Team gets its funding from the Foundation for Progressive Public Policy, right?"

"That's correct," Drach said.

"And let's just see who contributes to the Foundation for Progressive Public Policy." I paused for drama and plucked a sheet of fax paper from the console, smoothed out the curl. I read aloud the names of a tobacco company, two oil firms, a big manufacturer of agricultural chemicals, Amalgamated Beverages, the CalFac hotel chain. "And, of course, Sievers-Drach."

Nakamura leaned toward Drach, who lifted one side of her headphones so the media relations manager could whisper something.

I used the hesitation to continue. "Those hardly sound like folks who would be interested in supporting a liberal think tank. Tell me, for example, why a big construction company like Sievers-Drach would want to donate five million dollars on an annual basis to provide leadership training to the very people who want to control growth?"

"Are you familiar with the concept of checks and balances?" Drach's tone of voice didn't sound annoyed any longer. More like anger just barely at the simmer level.

"I got a passing grade in eighth-grade civics."

"Then you know what happens in countries where the system of checks and balances doesn't work, where certain classes of people are continually disenfranchised from the political and economic process."

"Eventually, they rise up, revolt, and overthrow their oppressors. So what you're saying is," I kept going, before Drach could pose another rhetorical question, "these big corporations figure it pays off in the long run to encourage participation in politics by people of all viewpoints and persuasions. Even people and groups that may oppose everything that big business stands for."

"All we're trying to do is keep the playing field level."

"Better a leftie gets elected to the State Assembly than sets fire to the Bank of America."

"I would hardly put it in such Machiavellian terms."

So big tobacco, oil, and construction launched the political career of Jeff Greene and dozens of liberals like him. Gave them access to a certain degree of power, but never let them forget who pulls the strings. And Dr. Hipster discovered—what? And he was silenced by—whom? Greene? The Farm Team? The Foundation for Progressive Public Policy?

I needed time to think, to sort out the conflicting theories racing through my mind. Time to do more research, more background digging. But time is one commodity that doesn't exist in live radio. Not with callers lined up, commercials hovering on the program log, and the clock ticking relentlessly toward the next news break.

Rather than let Arliss Drach continue to score points while I foundered, I cut off the interview and thanked the two Farm Teamers for taking time out in their busy schedule to come on the show.

"It was our pleasure," Nakamura said. "You know, you should really think about joining us for one of our weekend seminars. The Farm Team is always on the lookout for experts from the news media who can help educate the newsmakers of the future."

"You'd be perfect," Drach said just before I shut off the guest mike. "Just like Dr. Hipster."

16

If I could get away with it, I'd wear jeans and a sweatshirt every day. Luckily, I chose a career where no one can see me or care what I'm wearing. But jeans and sweats don't work in a city where the temperature hits ninety and beyond approximately five months out of the year. Since moving to Sacramento, I've invested in the first sundresses I've owned since the sixth grade, plus lots of skirt/top outfits in loose, gauzy, one hundred percent cotton. The Lawrence of Arabia look.

I zipped myself into a blue-and-yellow sundress and decided it might make it for a dinner date with Junior at Morton's, especially if I classed it up with one of my Native American silver necklaces and a matching bracelet. I tossed a crocheted shawl around my shoulders in case it cooled off after sundown and donned a pair of flats. No stockings. The backpack would hardly do, but I don't own an evening bag. So I shortened the strap on an old fanny pack and figured I could get away with carrying it as an impromptu purse.

Not bad. Not great, but not bad, I decided as I checked myself out in the full-length mirror on my closet door. If Janis Joplin had survived that last bad trip at the Landmark Motel in Hollywood and lived to the far end of her thirties, she'd probably have looked something like this.

I scooped out some meat by-products into a bowl for Bialystock and made a quick phone call to Victor Pahoa down at the security office, just to ask him to keep an eye on things in case I came home late. Or not until the next morning.

• • •

Morton's is supposed to be one of the capital city's hot power dining spots. But until this evening, I'd never stepped inside the imposing door on the Downtown Plaza. I'd heard it was expensive and heavy on the red meat, which tended to scare off the crowd I hang out with.

Classic steakhouse decor: dark wood, thick green carpet, hefty furniture. My eyes adjusted to the dim light and I searched the dining room for a handsome man, seated alone.

I spotted a familiar figure slicing into a slab of grilled meat at a table near the door. Not Terrence O'Brien Jr., but Lieutenant Gunderson of the Sacramento Police Department. His dinner companion was around fifteen or so years older, tiny eyes set in a pear-shaped head, all jowls. He was dressed in civvies, but something about him shouted cop. The man rose to pull a pager off his belt, revealing a matching avocado-shaped physique, all gut and butt.

I didn't have a chance to say hello to Gunderson and his beefy companion. Junior materialized out of the gloom, gave me a hug, and steered me toward his table. "You look stunning!"

Truth was, my date was way more stunning than I could ever hope to be. Elegant light gray suit, cream-colored shirt, silk tie just slightly loosened. Dark hair perfectly styled, brown eyes, dazzling smile, dimple. An aging but still hunky soap opera star.

The waiter pulled out my chair and performed the napkin-in-the-lap ritual. Terrence and I studied the menus and placed our orders. The twenty-four-ounce porterhouse for Junior and the filet mignon at a mere sixteen ounces for me. By the time this date was over, I was going to consume my allowance of fat and cholesterol for a good month. Terrence ordered what must have been his second Dewar's on the rocks, while I asked for my usual gin and tonic. We agreed to split an appetizer of sautéed mushrooms. Good. Now we'd both have garlic breath.

I stirred my drink. "So . . . placing any bets on who's going to win the election?"

Junior lifted his shoulders slightly and smiled, flashing the dimple. "I don't get involved in politics. I'm just glad it's a close race and both candidates are spending a lot of money on advertising. I'll make my budget for May and then some."

I took another sip of my drink to stop myself from plunging into my usual diatribe about all the political advertising cluttering up my show. Sure, it brings in the moolah, but it drives away listeners. Every time a spot for one of the candidates comes on, you can almost hear the collective punching of car radio buttons on every freeway in Sacramento.

"I'd think you'd be taking a personal interest, seeing as how you went through The Farm Team with Jeff Greene," I said.

"Oh, that. The Farm Team was Father's idea. He thought I ought to do something with my life besides hanging around the radio station all day. So he pulled strings with his contacts and got me in. As it turned out, I got a lot more out of the experience than I thought I would."

"Did they offer any seminars on contracts?" I couldn't stop thinking about that comment Dr. Hipster made to his son, about the legality of a contract from forty or fifty or so years ago. A contract that had something to do with a blue door.

"Not that I recall. They didn't get into that law school stuff."

"What makes you say you got a lot more out of it than you thought you would?"

"Oh, just building up my confidence, and making contacts of my own, and learning more about the community, and how the political process works and all that." He waved his hand, as if to dismiss the topic, and took a hefty gulp of his drink. "I want to congratulate you on a terrific job of detective work. Figuring out that Dr. Hipster left a coded message for help in that last promotional announcement he recorded."

"Thanks. It was no big deal."

"Nonsense. You were brilliant. Lieutenant Gunderson was really impressed too. I passed along your tip to him, and he told me he's reopened the investigation. He asked me not to tell anyone, but, well . . ." Junior leaned across the table and lowered his voice. "The police think Dr. Hipster may have been killed by a deranged fan."

As if on cue, the preppie homicide dick materialized at our

table, his dinner companion towering in the background. We exchanged handshakes and pleasantries. Gunderson introduced his pal as Edward Glott. Gunderson and Glott. Could have been the morning team at a polka station in Milwaukee.

Gunderson pulled up a stray chair. "You find out anything else that would shed any light on the case, you be sure to call us." He pulled a business card out of his pocket, wrote something on it, and placed it in my hand. "This is a direct line into my office. Also my pager, and my cell phone number. Call me anytime, day or night. We want to solve this as badly as you do."

With that, Gunderson and Glott returned to their table.

"You should go on the air with all this," Junior said.

"You think?"

"But of course." Terrence shifted into his Big-time Radio Announcer voice. "Police reopen Dr. Hipster death case, now say it's murder. Details on the Shauna J. Bogart Show. Stay tuned."

"Maybe."

Junior leaned in closer. "So, what's your theory?"

Where do I even begin? "You mean, like what big story Dr. Hipster was working on that got him killed?"

"That, and why he left that coded message that only you would pick up on in that promotional announcement."

"I've wondered about that too. He usually recorded the promo right after he finished his show. That would mean around eleven o'clock at night, at least ten hours before he died. He would have had plenty of time to make a run for it if he thought he was in danger."

"Unless he was already being held captive, or knew he was being watched."

Now there was an angle I hadn't considered. Had Dr. Hipster spent his last hours in some unknown location, under armed guard, tied up, perhaps drugged, and then dragged back to his apartment for the final, fatal confrontation?

"It just seems odd to me," Junior said, "that if he had the chance to put a coded message in a promotional announcement, that he didn't also have the chance to call the cops."

"Maybe he did, and the cops brushed it off as some sort of media stunt. Or maybe . . ."

"Yes?"

I gulped my drink and decided to keep that last thought to myself. "Maybe nothing, really."

Or maybe, I had been about to say, the cops were in league with the killers.

Junior drained his drink. "Let's talk about something less depressing. Tell me about yourself. Did you always want to be a talk radio host?"

I gave him the edited version of The Shauna J. Bogart Story: the lonely teenager with her favorite DJs as her only real friends, the advisor of the high school audiovisual club encouraging her to take the test for an FCC license, getting hired as an engineer at San Francisco's hot FM rock station, Dr. Hipster giving her a chance at a show. Bouncing around the country from one rock station to the next. "I figured I'd be spinning records and reading liner cards until the day they carted me off to the old DJs' home. Then your father called me."

Junior ordered yet another drink. I shook my head and mouthed "I'm fine, thanks," pointing to my almost-full glass, when the waiter asked if I'd like another round. I'd actually consumed about half the gin and tonic, but I'd been busy spooning ice from my water glass into my drink tumbler whenever Junior looked away, so the glass appeared full. An old trick I'd learned to keep my wits about me when it was clear my date wanted to drink himself blotto.

Our main course arrived, and we lost ourselves in our own private red meat orgies. I'm not a big steak eater (more a reflection of budget and cooking skills than eco-politics), but this was one special hunk of meat, all delicate smoky flavor and buttery texture. Now I know why men take up cigars.

I put down my knife and fork. "How about you? Were you born with a contract in one hand and a rate card in the other?"

"I was always fascinated by radio. Runs in the family, I would suppose."

"When you were a kid, did you think there were itsy-bitsy people inside the radio?"

There went the dimple again. "I remember thinking there was a tiny orchestra inside the dashboard of Father's Lincoln."

We both laughed, our eyes locked for a second, and I felt a momentary rush of kinship and rapport. Then the dimple vanished and Junior took another slug of scotch.

"So what happened?" I prompted.

Junior rattled the ice cubes in his empty glass and didn't answer immediately. "I did on-air work for a couple years, had a few laughs. Then I looked around the station parking lot one day and realized all the Mercedes and Porsches belonged to the sales staff."

"You are so right. And the air staff's driving around in the beat-up Hondas and Toyotas."

"See? Everything works out the way it's supposed to work out, eventually."

We never did get around to an official dessert. Junior ordered a brandy and I nursed an Irish coffee. When Junior offered to drive me home, I didn't make any protests about how easily I could walk the few blocks separating Morton's and the Capital Square complex. If the man of my dreams planned a lingering good-bye on my doorstep—or beyond—I was not about to object. He piloted his BMW out of the Downtown Plaza underground garage, made a right on J Street, and drove straight through Seventh instead of turning right at the giant guitar in front of the Hard Rock Café. I started to squeak an objection when Junior said, "Hey, the evening's still young and I've got something I'd really like to show you."

He turned wide onto Sixteenth Street, and floored it as Sixteenth merged into Highway 160, heading out of the downtown core. I began to wonder if I should have been paying more attention to the amount of alcohol Junior had consumed, and less attention to my libido. I knew Junior lived in a condo complex off American River Drive, because I looked up his address in the staff directory and drove out there once to scope it out when I knew he was stuck in a sales meeting. Oh, the shame! Could that be our destination? And what was the "something" he was planning to show me? A waterbed and a basket of party favors from Goldie's Adult Bookstore?

Junior torqued the BMW across two lanes of traffic, exited

the freeway, and lurched onto an all-too-familiar frontage road.

A straight shot to the radio station. Hardly the romantic rendezvous I'd lusted after.

Junior placed a hand between my shoulder blades and guided me along the deserted corridors of the business wing to his corner office. He dropped into a leather chair behind the desk, opened the top drawer, and pulled out a black plastic object the size of a cigarette case.

A cassette tape.

"You're the first person who's heard this in a long time." He placed the cassette into the boom box on top of his desk and pressed the PLAY button.

The final notes of the Donna Summer version of "MacArthur Park," then a young male voice shouting at breathless speed. "Another fabulous Friday on the home of the hot hits with Terry Tiger, the radio host who loves ya the most!"

"You?" I said to Junior.

"The one and only."

He let the aircheck run a few more minutes, more inane patter, more intros and closings from tunes that had been hits in the disco era. "I worked weekends and filled in for vacations while I was going to high school and college," Junior said when the tape ran out. "So what do you think? Do I have what it takes or not?"

That was the whole point of this evening? So I could critique an aircheck from twenty-plus years ago? "I think you showed a lot of promise." I studied the framed photos on the off-white plaster wall of his office: Cousin Brucie, Dr. Don Rose, The Real Don Steele, Larry Lujack. The legends of Top 40 radio. "With a little more seasoning and the right opportunity, you could have been killer."

"Thanks. That means a lot, coming from you." Junior pulled open the bottom desk drawer and lifted out a bottle of cognac and two brandy snifters. "A toast," he said as he began pouring. "To what might have been and never was."

I took a ceremonial sip, just to be polite, then tucked the glass behind a potted jade plant on the credenza.

"And to what is still to come," Junior said just before swallowing two fingers' worth of booze.

I excused myself to use the loo, tracked down Glory Lou in the control room, and waited for the next commercial break. "Think you could help me out of a jam when your show is over?"

"That depends. What's up?"

I told her about my date with Terrence O'Brien Jr.

"As I live and breathe. First you get asked out by Pete Kovacs, then you have dinner with Junior. All in the same day. I'm impressed!"

"Yeah, well, my date is sitting in his office getting shit-faced. I don't want him driving in the condition he's in. Can you help me get him home?"

Glory Lou made a snorting noise. "Anyone else but you asking and I'd call the CHP to have him pulled over for DUI. Why don't you just let him sleep it off in his office?"

"And have it hit the rumor mill? No way." All I needed was for Mrs. Yanamoto to discover Junior sprawled in his office chair, bleary-eyed and stubble-faced, when she showed up for work the next morning. Before the morning was out, everyone from Captain Mikey to the fellow who comes by to hose down the news cars and grub out the fast-food wrappers from the backseats would know that the boss's son was found passed out in his office after a date with yours truly.

As soon as Glory Lou signed off, we poured Junior into the passenger seat of the same news car we'd driven to Davis that morning. Glory Lou took off for Junior's condo while I followed in his BMW.

I tailed News Unit 5 through the gates of the condo complex. We helped Junior stumble through the door of his end unit and dropped him like a sack of cement on the brown-and-green plaid living-room couch. His decor was almost a duplicate of Morton's, all leather, dark wood, and deep greens and rusts. The stuffy men's club look, via Ralph Lauren.

"You gals didn't have to go to all this trouble," Junior said with a thick tongue. "I could have gotten home by myself just fine."

"Of course. But it's awfully easy to get yourself over point-zero-eight these days. Glory Lou and I would have hated to see you get nailed."

"It was no trouble at all," Glory Lou chimed in. "Tomorrow, we'll just forget all of this ever happened, sweetie."

Junior had already passed out on the couch, his head falling back on a pillow appliquéd with a mallard paddling through cattails.

Glory Lou was halfway out the door, but I beckoned her back. "Check this out," I whispered. I led her into Junior's study and flicked on a desk lamp. What I really wanted to do was snoop through his bedroom. See if he had a stash of porno tapes, or a supply of exotic paraphernalia. Or even worse, smelly, rumpled sheets. But there would be no way to explain our presence in Junior's bedroom, should he come to and find us. In the study, we could claim we were looking for something innocuous, like the telephone.

The lamp illuminated three expensively framed photographs atop Junior's desk. One was a color magazine advertisement for I. Magnin, featuring a tall, dark-haired model in a haute couture ball gown. "Vivi Models the New Look for the 1957 Social Season," according to the headline.

"Junior's mother. T. R.'s first wife," I explained to Glory Lou in a soft voice.

The second was a more recent photograph of the same woman. The years had been kind to Vivi. Not to mention the services of an expensive health spa and expert plastic surgeon. Still slender, still elegant, dark hair now a shimmery silver.

"I hear she's loaded," I continued. "Her second husband was Stas Kostantin."

"The big developer?"

"The same. When the Big C caught up with him a couple of years ago, she inherited everything. T. R. told me the whole story. I hear she owns half the real estate in downtown Sacramento."

"The half the state doesn't own." Glory Lou shifted her attention to the third frame on Junior's desk. "Do you believe this?"

I put my hand over my mouth so I wouldn't snicker and wake up Junior.

It was a black-and-white eight-by-ten publicity still. A young Junior, paisley shirt and muttonchop sideburns, seated in front of a radio microphone. Printing at the bottom of the photograph announced: "The T.O. Show! Saturdays and Sundays, Midnight to 6! Starring Terry Tiger!"

"The Terrence O'Brien Show," Glory Lou said.

"Don't be too sure. Could just as easily stand for Terrible Outrage. Or Tritely Offensive."

As soon as I'd mocked Terry Tiger, I was sorry. I'd listened to his aircheck, so I knew trite and offensive weren't too far off the mark. But he'd had the dream and given it his best shot. If I hadn't had some lucky breaks and dogged determination, I might have suffered the same fate.

A quarter century later, Terry Tiger's flame still burned brightly in the jungle of Terrence O'Brien's soul.

I felt closer to him than I'd ever felt before. And I wanted nothing more than to turn out the desk lamp and get the hell out.

It seemed like I'd spent most of the day riding around in News Unit 5 with Glory Lou. She pulled onto U.S. 50, heading back toward the downtown high-rises. "Have you heard the latest about E-Z 1240?"

"Just that they're getting bought by Federated Communications, but everyone knows that," I said. E-Z 1240 was owned by a local family and had been playing that syrupy, stringy elevator/dentist office music since before Lowell Thomas was a cub reporter.

"The Federated people are going to go syndicated Spanish as soon as they take over."

Another Spanish station. Nothing personal against my amigos from south of the border. But here we go again, another local, independent broadcaster bites the big one. I wondered if Bill Clinton had any idea of the monster he was creating in 1996 when he signed the Telecommunications Act, allowing corporations to own pretty much as many radio stations as they wanted. I also wondered what Happy Hal Harper, the veteran

E-Z 1240 morning man, was doing this evening. Brushing up on his *Español*, probably.

"I did some checking up on your new boyfriend," Glory Lou said, changing lanes as deftly as she changed subjects.

"What new boyfriend? Junior?"

"No, silly. Pete Kovacs. Who else?"

"One date does not a boyfriend make."

We sped past the headquarters of the Sacramento Municipal Utility District—SMUD, my favorite local acronym—and the Sac State campus. "I'll bite. What did you find out about Pete Kovacs?"

"It's just like I told you this afternoon. He's perfect for you."

Two years older than me. Registered Democrat. Moderate drinker. No smoking, no gambling. Divorced, one kid just finishing her first year of college.

"How'd you find all this out?" I asked as Glory Lou took the Sixteenth Street exit off the W–X.

"You know me, I never reveal my sources. Oh, yeah. I also asked one of my contacts at the sheriff's department to run Kovacs through NCIC. His record's clean. Not even an unpaid parking ticket. He's a keeper."

"Do you think you could do any checking up on Lieutenant Gunderson?" I asked.

"Sweetie, I didn't know you went for those straight-laced, pure-Aryan-race types. Anyway, he's married."

"Not like that. I just want to know if he's clean."

"I'll see what I can do." Glory Lou stopped at a traffic signal and gave my outfit a once-over. "I hope you're not planning to wear that on your date with Pete Kovacs."

"What's the big deal?"

"I know you don't pay attention, but the Jazz Band Ball happens to be one of the hottest social events of the year. It's very exclusive, invitation-only. You have to know the right people to get on the guest list."

"I'll figure something out."

"Tell you what, hon. The media coordinator at the Music Circus owes me a favor. What size do you wear, a ten?"

More like an eight above the waist and a twelve below. I guess that averaged out to a ten.

"You don't have to do that, really. You've done plenty already," I told Glory Lou. "Schlepping me to Davis this morning, and then all over Old Sacramento. Checking out Pete Kovacs on top of that. Thanks. I mean it."

"Girlfriend, it was no trouble at all. I didn't want Pete Kovacs to turn out to be N-A-F-L-E."

"N-A-F-L-E?"

"Sweetie, don't you ever read the personals? N-A-F-L-E stands for 'Not another fucking learning experience.' "

I looked for Victor Pahoa on the Capital Square grounds when Glory Lou dropped me off, but I didn't see anything of the young security guard.

But I did see someone on the short walk back to my apartment. A tall, bulky figure with a pear-shaped head lurked at the far end of the hallway.

He was wearing a forest ranger hat. I glimpsed the shine of a badge on his lapel when he passed by one of the security lamps. I didn't need to get close enough to read the name on the badge. Or to see the tiny, narrow eyes.

I would have recognized that ovoid silhouette anywhere.

Lieutenant Gunderson's friend from dinner. Edward Glott.

17

The Gold Rush Giveaway woke me with a blare of trumpets and an agitated announcer from my bedside clock radio. "Stay tuned and if we read your lucky numbers, call us within fifteen minutes and you could win one thousand, five thousand, even ten thousand dollars!"

I rolled out of bed, brushed my teeth, showered, and shuffled into the kitchen to switch on the coffeepot. While I waited for the brew to perk, I sifted through a pile of bills, take-out menus, and coupons on my dining table until I found what I was looking for.

Obviously, I was not supposed to be sent a lucky number for the Gold Rush Giveaway. As an employee of the station, I'm not eligible to win a penny. But all of my personal records are in my real name, and that's what I have listed in the phone book. So guess who got a Gold Rush Giveaway entry form in the mail? I scanned past the garish colors, exclamation points, and starbursts until I found the tiny type at the bottom. Copyright Price Marketing, followed by a phone number with a 314 area code. I checked the front of the phone book. St. Louis.

"Price Marketing. Mel Price speaking."

Bingo! I figured rightly that Price Marketing would be a one-man shop, with the big guy himself answering the phone when he wasn't on the road selling contests to radio stations. He probably contracted out for design services for the cheesy flyers and hired a couple of high school geeks to create the database of potential winners.

I identified myself as Mindy Balzac, promotions gal for a brand-new station in Seattle.

"Mimi Blitzer down in Sacramento is a friend of mine. She tells me the Gold Rush Giveaway is going like gangbusters. Think it would work for us?"

"It'll work anywhere." Price's hearty midwestern accent reverberated through the phone. I yawned and watched the morning sun peek through the curtains while he talked. "We can create a concept for any market. You're in Seattle, right? Let's see: It's Raining Greenbacks. Whaddya think?"

More like, it's raining b.s. But I kept my opinions to myself and made the appropriate enthusiastic response. "Mimi gave me the basics on how the contest works, the direct mail piece with the lucky numbers printed on it. Just wondering, no big deal, but what's your security like? Could anyone tamper with the contest?"

"We've got the best security this side of the Israeli army. My wife and kid do all the data entry and pick all the winning numbers. No way they're going to mess with their meal ticket."

"All in the family."

"You bet."

"How about your printer?"

"We do all of our printing overseas. Cheaper that way. And we use a mail house here in St. Louis to affix the labels and do the actual mailing. They're another small family operation, been around since 1946."

"And I suppose you FedEx the liner cards and printout of the lucky numbers directly to the general manager of the station running the contest."

"From my office to his signature in less than twenty-four hours."

"That's terrific." I couldn't think of anything else to ask that might shed light on who—besides Josh—might be tampering with the Gold Rush Giveaway, so I told Mel Price I'd think about it and get back to him.

I should have been working out.

After contemplating the sorry sight of my upper arms in a

sundress yesterday evening, I should have been in the Capital Square weight room, doing some serious biceps curls. Instead, I swam a few lazy laps, then relaxed in the hot tub before heading down to the station to prep for the show.

I waved to Victor Pahoa as he patrolled the edge of the pool area. "Take a load off." I indicated the teak deck chair next to the hot tub. No cheap aluminum patio chairs with plastic webbing at a classy joint like Capital Square. I hauled myself out of the bubbling water, sat on the cement edge with my lower legs still submerged, and wrapped a beach towel around my shoulders. "Working days for a change?"

"Something like that. Glott came by last night and sent me home early. He's sayin' he'll finish my shift, so's I could get some sleep and come back in the morning. He's changing everyone's schedule for the rest of the week."

Pahoa sighed and leaned back in the deck chair. "It's making a mess out of my school schedule, for sure."

"Glott? Who is he, anyway?"

"Captain Glott? You never met him?"

"Not that I recall."

"He's the boss. Chief of security."

I didn't say anything, so Pahoa kept talking. "He's mostly locked up all day in his office, talking on the phone with his old buddies at the cops."

"Edward Glott used to be in the Sacramento Police Department?" I shouldn't have been surprised. Lots of retired cops work in private security.

"Yes, ma'am. He retired about five years ago. But he still wants all of us to refer to him as *Captain* Edward Glott."

I studied the swirling, steaming water. "Did Glott give you any reason why he was changing everyone's work schedule?"

"Just some lame story about Wolinsky needing to take the rest of the week off."

"Wolinsky? Rudy Wolinsky?"

"Yeah. You know him?"

"I'm not sure. Big Polish guy, kind of reminds you of Fred Flintstone?"

Pahoa chuckled and nodded his head slowly. "Fred Flintstone. I'll have to remember that."

"I thought he was in maintenance for the Capital City Ventures complex over at Fourteenth and N."

"Not unless he's got a twin. Rudy Wolinsky is in security right here. Graveyard."

From Gunderson to Glott to Rudy from West Sacramento. An evil Tinkers-to-Evers-to-Chance, with Dr. Hipster tagged out of the game. Permanently.

I pulled the towel closer around my shoulders.

Nowhere to go for help or advice. The local cops couldn't be trusted. I couldn't rely on the rent-a-cops who guarded my own home. Not with Captain Edward Glott in charge. Someone at the station had to be involved. I didn't dare share all of my suspicions—and fears—with anyone. Not even Josh and Glory Lou. Nor Junior.

T. R. O'Brien? One of the most honorable men I'd dealt with in an industry known for its sleaze factor. He was due to arrive at the Alaska Airlines terminal at Sacramento International this evening. I could trust T. R. O'Brien. I just wondered if I could wait long enough for him to arrive home.

Mrs. Yanamoto greeted my arrival at the station with a cheery wave. Two sales assistants gave each other high-fives at the mail slots, and even Mimi Blitzer favored me with a smile.

I pulled the memo out of my mailbox.

To: Entire Staff
From: Terrence O'Brien Jr.
Subject: Day Off

Congratulations! The latest ArbiTrends put us Number One in adults 25–49 and we're showing significant improvement in Time Spent Listening in all dayparts. The sales department has reached budget for May with five days to go. Father and I appreciate the efforts each and every one of you has put in to achieve these goals. Therefore, I am declaring a staff holiday with pay for this Friday, the start of the Memorial Day weekend. For those of you who must work due to your airshifts or other duties, we will, of course, pay time-and-a-half. Again, congratulations, and enjoy your four-day weekend!

I reread the memo and slowly placed the paper back in my mail slot. Something was off. Junior wasn't one for wild, generous gestures. T. R., for sure. But T. R. couldn't have had anything to do with the decision to grant a staff holiday, Junior's references to "Father and I" notwithstanding. The ArbiTrends came out only yesterday, and T. R. was still in Alaska.

Gil Loomis, the chief engineer, materialized next to the mail slots. His face wore an expression that was half pleased, half puzzled.

"What's up?" I asked.

"To be honest, I'm not sure. Junior just gave me this."

Gil showed me a card confirming a reservation for Gil Loomis and guest for four nights lodging and two hundred dollars in food and beverage credits at the Monterey Pavilion. Starting this Thursday evening.

"That's terrific, Gil! I was just there last weekend. You'll have a wonderful time!"

"I guess. I'm just worried about the remote on Friday."

"The live broadcast from the jazz festival?"

"Yeah. But Junior told me not to worry. He said Brandon could handle it."

Brandon Nguyen was the station's engineering assistant. Not much older than Josh, he'd been with the station only since the first of the year.

"Brandon will be fine. You just have a good time and don't worry about us." Mimi Blitzer would have her knickers in a knot when she found out about her precious remote, but that was her problem.

Gil's worry lines eased. "I guess you're right. Norma and I could use a holiday."

"We'll compare tan lines when you get back."

• • •

Monty Rio had clearly never gotten the message about the ozone layer. Skin the color of well-oiled teak peeked out from a souvenir polo shirt from the Sacramento Ad Club golf tournament. The operations manager hovered at my desk and brandished Junior's memo. "Hey, babe! A four-day weekend!"

"Hi, Monty."

"I don't know about you, babe, but Monty Rio's going to blow this joint. Gonna head up to Reno for the weekend."

"That's terrific."

"Say, I've got an idea."

Normally, I enjoyed bantering with Monty Rio. But now he just gave me the creeps. Plus, I needed to review my notes for my upcoming interview with Marvella Kent.

Monty seated himself, facing me at eye level. "Why don't you come along with me, babe? We could play some slots, catch the Kenny Rogers show, have some fun, you know. . . ."

"Great idea!" I picked up the phone and pretended to punch in a number. "Let me just call Lois and make sure it's okay with her." It was a running gag between Monty and me. Though he liked to play the rake, the man-about-town, Monty was all talk. In reality, he was devoted to his wife of thirty-plus years. As far as I knew, he never strayed.

"Seriously." Monty scooted his chair closer and fixed me with a look devoid of the trademark Monty Rio b.s. "I've got something I need to talk to you about. But not here at the station. Can you meet me someplace after your show? The Salt Shaker?"

"Sure thing."

I checked my phone and e-mail messages. The usual: publicists trying to wheedle me into booking the latest diet doctor, fading movie star, or relationship counselor on the show. Assorted cranks. The mother's club president at the Little Lamb Christian Pre-school wanting to know if I'd sit in a dunk tank at their school carnival. Yeah, right.

One message worth saving. Lisa Roberts, reporter from *Ra-*

dio and Records, looking for a quote to include in an obituary she was preparing on Dr. Hipster. The L.A.-based weekly newspaper is one of the most influential trades in the radio business. Calls from *Radio and Records*, you always return.

Lisa Roberts's voice mail informed me that she'd stepped away from her desk for a moment or was tied up on another call. I left the studio hotline number.

I sent a message to Josh on the call-screener computer during the network newscast at the start of the show.

IF A LISA ROBERTS FROM RADIO AND RECORDS CALLS, PUT HER CALL THROUGH TO THE SHOW. EVEN IF I'M IN THE MIDDLE OF SOMETHING ELSE. ALSO CALL PETE KOVACS AND GIVE HIM MY HOME ADDRESS. TELL HIM IT'S OKAY TO PICK ME UP AT HOME TOMORROW NIGHT.

P.S. WIPE THAT SMIRK OFF YOUR FACE.

I made my usual trip to the women's john during the network newscast at four. T. R. O'Brien's secretary occupied the stall next to mine. I'd recognize those size four Ferragamos anywhere.

"Mrs. Yanamoto, it's Shauna J. Have you heard anything from T. R.?"

"Not a thing, and I'm a little concerned," Mrs. Yanamoto's clipped, high-pitched voice came from the adjoining stall. "He had a two-hour layover at noon at the Seattle Airport."

"And you never heard from him?"

"Not a word. It's not like him not to call in for messages." I could hear her sigh from the other stall. "I don't want to be there when he reads that memo Junior made me type about giving everyone a day off with pay on Friday."

"For real."

"Not that I'm complaining. I believe I'll leave early to spend the weekend with my grandchildren in Cupertino."

"I'm sure T. R.'s flight was just delayed." Yeah, right. That's what everyone says, just before the airline officials start calling the relatives with the bad news.

"I suppose you're right."

"Do me a favor, okay? When he does call in for messages,

be sure to tell him I need to speak to him as soon as he gets home. Tell him it's urgent."

"Of course, dear."

Glory Lou called me on the newsroom hotline at the end of the network newscast, just as I was making the segue into Captain Mikey's traffic report. "I did some checking up on Lieutenant Gunderson. He's basically clean."

"Basically."

"There was one incident, back when he was a rookie. He and another officer got into a shootout with some suspected drug dealers. A fifteen-year-old kid was killed. Gunderson's sergeant managed to smooth things over with Internal Affairs."

I didn't need to ask Glory Lou the name of the sergeant who saved Gunderson's rookie career. But I did anyway, just for the record.

"Some fellow named Edward Glott."

Marvella Kent was fifteen minutes late, but I didn't panic. Politicians are always late. I used the time to fill in my listeners on the connection between the Sacramento City Council member and The Farm Team. I reviewed her record on the council, her election six years ago representing the Oak Park neighborhood. Her impressive achievements in revitalizing Sacramento's historic African-American community: day-care centers, small businesses, parks, recreation programs. Her service as a delegate at the last national political party convention. And her endorsement of Nadine Bostwick for governor.

As if on cue, Marvella Kent swept into the studio, nominally escorted by Josh. A tall, majestic woman in a brightly colored dashiki, long beaded earrings, and a 'fro slightly grayer than the one she wore in the *Davis Daily Delineator* photo eight years ago.

I introduced the councilwoman as she slowly and with great ceremony arranged herself in front of the guest mike. A head of state of an emerging African nation making an appearance before the United Nations could not have conducted herself with more presence and dignity.

"Councilwoman Kent, you're a graduate of the political leadership training program known as The Farm Team. Tell us how you managed to land an invitation to participate in the program."

"I was in my second year of law school at McGeorge when I got a call from Arliss Drach. She'd heard about me through one of my fellow volunteers in the Peace Corps who was already enrolled in The Farm Team program."

"And then you ran for City Council."

"I could never have done it without The Farm Team."

"What do you consider the most important thing you learned during your time with The Farm Team?"

"Just generally building my self-confidence, especially in public speaking. As well as all the invaluable contacts I made. The Farm Team was a wonderful experience. But now it's time to move on."

A message from Josh flashed on my monitor.

LISA ROBERTS FROM RADIO AND RECORDS HOLDING ON THE HOTLINE.

Damn! Of all the bad timing. Anyone else, I would have taken a message, called back later. But you never, ever, blow off a call from *Radio and Records*. "We'll be back with more from Sacramento City Councilwoman Marvella Kent on the Shauna J. Bogart Show. Stay with us now for a special guest, Lisa Roberts from the weekly radio industry magazine *Radio and Records*. Lisa, is it alright if we talk on the air?"

"Works for me."

I gave *Radio and Records* basically the same comment I'd been giving the local press. "Dr. Hipster taught me everything I know about radio. I wouldn't be where I am today if it hadn't been for his generous help and guidance." I repeated the tale about hiding the tequila bottles under the radio station balcony in the derelict neighborhood that would become Old Sacramento back in the early seventies.

"This is great stuff," Lisa Roberts said when I'd finished. "Can I talk to you a minute off the air?"

It was half past the hour, so I introduced Monty Rio with the local headlines. *L.A. Times* poll shows Nadine Bostwick pulling ahead of Jeff Greene. Jazz Jubilee officials predict record crowds. Temperatures creeping back to the nineties by the end of the week. Captain Mikey in the traffic chopper warned us about a backup on the Marconi Curve. I monitored the air sound through one headphone and held the telephone receiver to my other ear.

"Off the record, okay?" Lisa Roberts said. "Word's out on the street that your station's changing format."

"No way."

"From what I hear, your GM has hired Ratings, Research, and Revenue to consult on a format change to syndicated talk."

"Oh, that." I didn't know I'd been holding in tension until I released it in a small laugh. "Someone in the market has hired Triple R, and they're about to go on the air with syndicated talk, but it's not us."

"That's not what my source tells me. I got it straight from Judith Lowenthal, the senior vice president at Triple R. She used to be my GM when I did on-air work in Miami. Once in a while, she tosses a tip my way."

"Thanks, but I don't think it's anything. My GM is coming back to town this evening. I'll run it by him and see what he says." I tried to sound light, but doubt dragged me down. T. R. will fix everything when he gets home. I swept doubt aside and opened the mike.

"At 4:35 on a Wednesday afternoon, you're tuned to the Shauna J. Bogart Show with my guest, Sacramento City Councilwoman Marvella Kent. Ms. Kent, before the break, you mentioned something about it being time to move on from The Farm Team. Could you elaborate?"

"I listened to your show yesterday. So I take it you understand all about where The Farm Team gets its money to put on seminars and workshops, to provide a free political education to a poor girl from the 'hood like me, and help her get elected to the City Council."

"Sure, all those big corporations, the liquor and tobacco and oil industries, CalFac and Sievers-Drach."

"For years, I looked the other way when Amalgamated Beverages put up billboards in my district, with their targeted messages to young African-American men to buy their fortified beverages. After all, the Foundation for Progressive Public

Policy fronted most of the money for the after-school drop-in center in Oak Park, and for beautification of Martin Luther King Boulevard."

"And as we revealed yesterday on this show, Amalgamated Beverages is one of the big donors to the Foundation," I said, thinking of Arliss Drach and her comment about checks and balances.

"But when CalFac came in and wanted to put in a card club in the old Del Prado Ballroom, I had to take a stand against those who would prey upon and profit from the weaknesses of the most vulnerable members of our community. I held the swing vote that would have changed the city charter to allow gambling, and I voted no."

"I remember that. Big controversy a year ago, as I recall. And I suppose ever since then, the donations from the Foundation for Progressive Public Policy have trickled to a halt." I made a mental note to make sure the Oak Park after-school drop-in center got prominent play in our rotation of public service announcements.

"Not yet, but it wouldn't surprise me."

RUDY FROM WEST SACRAMENTO ON LINE TWO.

I felt my scalp prickle underneath my headphones. "Councilwoman Kent, hold that thought while we take a call. Rudy, welcome back. We haven't talked since Friday afternoon."

"This is so." His broken English was starting to sound like a regular part of the show. Just like Captain Mikey in the traffic chopper and Monty Rio with the local headlines.

"I've missed you," I said.

"I have nothing for the radio to say until this very afternoon, yes."

"So tell me, Rudy, aren't you a little tired?"

"I am not from understanding."

"Working all those night shifts as a rent-a-cop, I figured you'd be catching up on your sleep instead of calling talk shows."

A pause. "I do not know from how you speak." Rudy sounded genuinely puzzled.

Then he was gone. Dead air on Line Two. Maybe he was just a nut case after all.

I segued into a commercial break and continued to chat with Marvella Kent off mike. "What was Jeff Greene like, back when you and he attended class together at The Farm Team?"

She pushed her chair away from the console, backing off from the guest mike, apparently not totally convinced she wasn't still on the air. "He was one of the golden boys, no doubt about that."

"What do you mean, golden boy?"

"Off the record?"

"Of course."

Kent paused for a moment to study the silver curlicue rings decorating the long fingers of both of her hands. "It was just understood that certain students were being handpicked for bigger things than just local politics. You take an ambitious young man with money and looks and the right connections."

"And a willingness to make deals?"

"I don't know for certain. I just remember there was a handful of students who were always going off to dinner parties with Arliss Drach and her inner circle, or being invited to golf weekends at Pebble Beach with the big corporate donors."

"And one of those students would be—" I nodded my head in the direction of the studio speaker, where a Greene for Governor commercial was playing. ". . . his many accomplishments include California's newest state park on the spectacular Big Sur coast . . ."

"The golden boy himself," Kent said.

I waited to hear the announcer tell me the commercial was paid for by the Greene for Governor Committee, opened the mike, gave the time and temperature, and reintroduced Councilwoman Kent. "The Foundation for Progressive Public Policy has been very generous to the Oak Park neighborhood," I said. "I'm just curious, were these unfettered donations, no strings attached?"

Kent answered with a sarcastic smirk that my listeners couldn't see. "You know the answer to that as well as I."

"I'm not sure if I do." Of course I did, but I wanted to continue the discussion. "You'll have to spell it out for me."

"Rule number one in politics: There's no such thing as 'no

strings attached.' You may not have to return the favor today, tomorrow, or even this year, but someday you'll be expected to pay in full. With interest."

I pushed open the glass doors leading to the parking lot shortly after six and headed for the Z-car, on my way to meet Monty Rio at The Salt Shaker.

"Ms. Bogart?"

I turned from the half-opened car door to face the speaker.

She was mid-forties, short blond curls, maybe twenty pounds over her fighting weight, dressed in a lime-green pant-suit and strappy white sandals, and wearing secretary glasses with rhinestones at the corners. It took a minute, and then I placed her. Lily McGovern, lobbyist for one of the state's big environmental organizations, Earth Guardians.

"I just got back into town after a meeting in San Francisco. I listened to your show for most of the drive," she said. "You're on the right track with your questions about The Farm Team."

"That's good to know." I leaned against the car door and forgot all about Monty Rio and The Salt Shaker.

"You know that new state park down in Big Sur? The one Jeff Greene is taking credit for?"

"Sure."

"There's more to it than just CalFac donating the land because they're good guys. A whole lot more. Are you interested?"

"Of course." Like, duh! I only wished she'd arrived back in town an hour earlier so I could have put her on the air.

McGovern raised her right hand to shade her eyes against the late afternoon sunlight. "This is just for background, you understand."

Damn! Still, I'd take what I could get. "If that's the way it has to be."

"Here's how the deal went down. Two years ago, CalFac arranged to turn over most of that ranch they owned in Big Sur to the Foundation for Progressive Public Policy. FPPP then deeded it over to the state. The original deal, when CalFac donated the land to FPPP, is the dirty one. Follow me so far?"

"CalFac? You mean the company that owns that hotel chain on the coast? The Monterey Pavilion and all the others?"

"The hotels are just part of it. The real money is in high-rise office buildings and major apartment complexes. CalFac is one of the biggest landlords in the state," McGovern said.

"CalFac to the Foundation for Progressive Public Policy to the state parks system. So far, so good."

"See, CalFac held back some of the Big Sur land for its own use, enough and then some to put up a hotel and a golf course. It'll be the biggest resort between Santa Barbara and Monterey."

"Oh." I felt my interest flag. This was McGovern's big scoop? The resort was common knowledge, at least in the local Monterey press.

I must have let my disappointment show, because McGovern gave me one of those "I know something you don't know" smiles. "CalFac made private deals with all of the major environmental groups in the region. The organizations agreed not to stand in CalFac's way when it comes to building the resort. You know, petitions, protests, lobbying the county supervisors and the state Coastal Commission. In return, CalFac donated a portion of the land to the Foundation for Progressive Public Policy, and made substantial financial gifts to the organizations that would have tried to stop them."

"If these groups are so dedicated to protecting the environment, why didn't they tell CalFac to take their money and stuff it?"

McGovern dug around in a woven straw shoulder bag and pulled out a cigarette case and lighter. She glanced around as if to make sure no one saw her, then lit up. "Yeah, I know I'm polluting my own environment," she said after the first puff. "But old habits die hard. To answer your question, have you ever spent much time with one of those little community grassroots organizations? You're looking at a half dozen or so volunteers operating out of someone's kitchen table. Out of the blue, someone's tossing literally hundreds of thousands of dollars their way."

"In return for their willingness to shut their eyes when it

comes to the interests of the guy with the moneybags."

"Hey, I didn't say I thought it was right. But consider the position these little environmental groups are in. This is more money than they could ever hope to raise on their own, and look at all the good they can do with it, like busing inner city kids to the Monterey Bay Aquarium, or rescuing stranded sea otters."

"You're looking at a lot of bake sales," I conceded.

I paused to wave good night to Mrs. Yanamoto as she locked the front door to the station and trotted across the parking lot to her late-model Honda Accord. "Someone had to have put the deal together," I said to McGovern. "Someone who knows his way around the corporate world, but who also has an impeccable record with the eco community, someone they would trust." I felt a leap of inspiration and answered the question I was about to ask. "The golden boy of The Farm Team."

"He tried to get Earth Guardians to buy into the deal and accept the payoff. I've got a paper trail like you wouldn't believe, letters, e-mails, legal briefs. And yes, Senator Greene's name is all over it."

"What happened?"

"We were between the proverbial rock and a hard place. Obviously, the deal stunk up the place, but no one can afford to permanently slam the door on someone as powerful as CalFac. So, Earth Guardians decided to sit this one out." She took another drag, and her pink-lipsticked mouth turned up in a smile. "But I kept all the paper."

A Raley's delivery truck rumbled off Highway 160 onto the frontage road. I waited for the roar to fade, then said, "Will you come on the show tomorrow and bring all that paperwork with you?"

"You know I can't do that."

Damn!

"But I am willing to make copies of the documentation and let you use it for background. Just as long as you keep me and Earth Guardians out of it."

I experienced another one of those intuitive flashes, when two seemingly unrelated facts come together and make sense.

"I'm not the first media person you've talked to about this, am I?"

"Dr. Hipster came to see me in my office two days before his death. He'd apparently overheard something during those weekend seminars he did out at The Farm. When it looked like Jeff Greene might actually have a serious chance to become our next governor, Dr. Hipster thought it was worth checking out those old rumors."

"Did he say anything about a contract? A contract that had something about a blue door in the title?"

McGovern gave me a puzzled look and shook her head.

"Just a sec." I reached for my backpack from the front seat of the Z-car. "Our fax number is on my business card. The sooner you can shoot your documentation my way the better."

McGovern stamped out the cigarette with her sandaled foot on the asphalt surface of the parking lot, then stooped to retrieve the butt. She placed her thumb and index finger on the butt, and squeezed and turned the remnants of the cigarette so that the remaining tobacco fell to the ground. I stared, fascinated, as she stuck the filter into her jacket pocket, presumably for disposal in an ecologically responsible manner later on. You don't see a gal field-stripping a cigarette very often. At least no one could accuse the lobbyist for the state's leading environmental organization of littering.

"No faxes, no phone calls, no e-mail," McGovern said. "I'll meet you here same time tomorrow."

Isn't this how Woodward and Bernstein got their start, meeting up with Deep Throat inside a deserted parking garage somewhere in the nation's capital?

McGovern took a step back, as if to leave, then turned back to me. "If I have even the slightest suspicion this is going to turn out like it did for Dr. Hipster, I won't show."

18

The Salt Shaker was definitely a Monty Rio kind of place.

Cocktail waitresses oozing out of Vegas showgirl outfits. Mirror squares and gold leaf. Fake waterfall with phony flames leaping from the pool at the foot of the cascade.

Our operations manager fit right in. Then again, so would Wayne Newton.

I slid into a booth opposite Monty Rio in the twilight of the bar. We ordered our first round: scotch and soda for Monty, and the usual g-and-t for Shauna J. I made a vow that this evening would not turn into a rerun of last night: no late hours, no red meat, no rescuing a tipsy date.

"That was quite a show you did this afternoon," Monty said after our waitress sashayed away with our drink orders.

"I'm glad you enjoyed it."

Monty Rio smiled, showing a row of perfect capped teeth. "You're a smart one, babe. I knew that from the day you did your first show with us."

"This little get-together was your idea, Monty. What did you want to see me about?"

Monty swallowed a handful of peanuts. "You're not one for small talk, doll, I can see that. But you're good. You could be working in New York or L.A."

"Get outta here." I still couldn't figure out what Monty Rio was leading up to.

"Don't put yourself down, doll-face. You've got talent. The Shauna J. Bogart Show is starting to get attention from the big markets. I've been getting calls about you."

"What kind of calls?"

"The usual. Program directors wondering when your contract is up, consultants wanting to know if all the street talk they've heard about our afternoon show is true."

I popped a peanut in my mouth and nodded at Monty to continue.

"I got a call about you just this past Monday from the program director at KFI in Los Angeles. It's a big station in a big market. You should check it out."

I shrugged. "Sacramento's not exactly my idea of paradise on earth, but T. R. O'Brien is a great boss."

The waitress reappeared with our drinks. I took a sip, while Monty toyed with his swizzle stick. "Listen, doll, what I'm saying is, if I were you and had a chance to get out of here, I'd grab at it."

I ran my finger around the rim of my glass a few times. "This has something to do with Dr. Hipster, doesn't it?"

Monty Rio gazed down at his cocktail napkin. He folded and unfolded it four times with trembling fingers. When he finally raised his head, his skin tone had turned from tan to gray and the lines had carved new territory on his forehead and around his mouth. The gold chain around his neck clashed grimly with the pale skin peeking out from the V-neck of his knit shirt.

A minute ago, I'd been bantering with an aging George Hamilton. Now I stared into the eyes of an old man.

"So help me, I had no idea what they were up to," Monty whispered at last. "So help me God."

I restrained the urge to grab Monty Rio by his pink polo-shirted shoulders and shake the truth out of him. I concentrated on keeping my voice steady and even. "You spliced the logger tape to remove Dr. Hipster's last promotional announcement, and you made sure the carted version ended up in the stack to be erased."

I'll bet he also faked the suicide note. Probably searched Dr. Hipster's desk drawer, found the file of fan mail and realized the reply to Janice in Placerville, quoting the poem from *Off Mike and Outta Sight,* could be construed as a love letter.

Type my name on an envelope, stuff and seal the letter inside, and you've got a plausible suicide note. After all, who but the operations manager could get away with tossing newsroom desk drawers with no one paying attention? Except maybe T. R. O'Brien.

Monty looked at me helplessly. "I had no idea. You've got to believe me."

"Who's they?"

Monty said nothing. Just squeezed his eyes shut and shook his head repeatedly.

Our waitress hovered, waiting to see if we wanted another round. I shooed her away.

Monty took a generous swallow of his scotch and soda. "Babe, you've got to understand. I was just following orders."

Jesus. How much grief had that phrase caused in the last seventy-five years?

"I know, Monty. It's okay." I paused to collect my thoughts. I mean, I was about to accuse the man I had a crush on for months with being involved in the worst crime there is. "Terrence O'Brien told you to edit the logger tape and erase the cart, didn't he?"

"Junior?" Monty dismissed the younger O'Brien with a shake of his head. "He wouldn't have had the brains, or the guts. It was the old man."

"T. R.?"

Monty nodded.

Over at the bar, two men wearing green blazers with the logo of a local real estate office played liar's dice with a clatter-clunk of dice and cup. At a nearby table a fiftyish man in a business suit had his hand on the thigh of a miniskirted twenty-something. The jukebox pumped out a Village People tune. From the booth in front of me, a foursome waved their arms. Y-M-C-A! How could everything around me be so trivial, so banal, while my soul was exploding?

T. R. O'Brien was behind the murder of Dr. Hipster? For God's sake, why?

When I was finally able to organize my thoughts, I asked Monty, "I didn't know T. R. O'Brien was involved in the Greene for Governor campaign."

"Greene for Governor?"

"Isn't that what this is all about? You know, the big story about the election that Dr. Hipster was supposed to be working on?"

Monty swirled the ice cubes in his glass. "I have no idea. I've already told you more than I should have."

I turned my head toward the door at the sound of familiar voices shouting with glee. Terrence O'Brien and three of the station's sales guys strutted into the cocktail lounge and waved at Monty and me to join them. "We made our May budget, so we're celebrating," one of them said. "Drinks are on us."

Monty slid out of the booth, picked up his drink, and waited for me to follow.

"Look, Monty, I'm going to beg off," I said. The last thing I wanted to do was sit in a bar all night listening to the sales staff swap war stories. "Tell the guys I've got to be somewhere else this evening, okay?"

"Can we talk some more tomorrow?"

"Of course. How about lunch?"

"Sure. And thanks, babe." Monty helped me unfold myself from the booth and strap on my backpack. "Don't forget what I said."

"What's that?"

"You're good, doll-face. Take my advice, call KFI and see what's up. Go for it, and get out while you can." Monty winked at me and was gone.

The American River Parkway is one of Sacramento's better ideas. Twenty-three miles of greenbelt stretching from Old Sacramento along the American River to Folsom Dam. A paved bicycle path runs along the banks of the river through the length of the parkway. It's a miracle the developers didn't manage to put up condos and "view" homesites along every inch of the riverbank.

I was in desperate need of working off nervous energy after the meeting with Monty Rio. I wheeled my bike out of the storage locker in the underground parking garage at Capital Square and picked up the bike trail at Discovery Park, just across the American River from downtown. I pedaled past dense tangles of blackberry bushes and tall grasses, releasing pent-up anxiety with every revolution. A light breeze from the Delta made the cottonwoods dance overhead, and the late evening sun slanted through the branches.

The local papers regularly issue warnings to women not to ride or jog on the bike trail alone, especially the lower stretch where the homeless like to camp. But I'd long ago decided not to live my life in fear.

This evening I encountered maybe a dozen joggers in twos and threes and a like number of cyclists, all in pairs or groups. But mostly I pedaled in solitude, accompanied only by the whistle of the wind, the hum and chirp of assorted insects, and my own rhythmic breathing. The temperature was still in the seventies and I was sweating within ten minutes.

How could T. R. have done such a thing? A man I admired and respected. I mean, I understand the election for governor is a big deal, but is it worth giving up a lifetime of principles? And Monty Rio. Once he realized what was really going on, why didn't he call the cops?

Unless he knew the cops couldn't be trusted. Or unless T. R. had paid him off.

I kept going back to Monty Rio's parting words: "Go for it, and get out while you can." It sounded like an ad for athletic shoes. Then why did it feel so sinister?

Now, more than ever, I needed to talk to T. R. O'Brien.

I turned around at Cal Expo, pedaled back to Discovery Park, and crossed the American River on a steel suspension bridge. The bike and I continued downriver on the banks of the Sacramento, passing under the I Street Bridge and emerging into the gaslight, brick, and cobblestone Gold Rush ambiance of Old Sacramento.

The joint, as they say, was jumpin'. Men and women wearing identical blue-and-white T-shirts scurried around a huge blue-and-yellow striped tent in front of the State Railroad Museum. Sound checks in progress, wood-and-wire mesh snack stands going up, thousands of folding chairs being snapped into neat rows. Overhead, the balloon advertising Pete Kovacs's store bobbed in the twilight. I thought briefly of the

"Prop." of Retro Alley and our date for the Jazz Band Ball. Was he helping the volunteers, I wondered, pounding nails into a hamburger stand or stringing cable from the stage to the speakers? Perhaps he was practicing with his band. I pictured him in jeans and T-shirt, long hair tied back, seated at a battered upright piano, fingers repeating a particularly intricate passage.

I wondered, too, whether he was thinking about me.

The lady's yellow three-speed carried me out of Old Sacramento onto Capitol Mall in the fading sunlight. I rode down Front to O Street, turning left on O, the Crocker Art Museum on my right and Crocker Park on my left. During the day, these streets would be choked with commuters. But like many cities, Sacramento's downtown empties out at five o'clock. The city streets were even more deserted than the bike trail had been.

I could see there was no traffic on Third when I was still several yards away on O Street. So I kept up a steady pace, not slowing at the corner. Then a squirrel darted in front of me. I clamped onto the bike's brake grips and swerved.

Out of nowhere, a car. Slam! The car's front bumper jolted my bike's front fender. I'm flying, thudding onto grass, tumbling. Squeal of tires and roar of engine. Pain. My wrist, my shoulder, my hip, my shin. Papers, magazines, and a water bottle from my backpack scattering into the street. And finally the squirrel, skittering safely into Crocker Park.

If it hadn't been for that squirrel, the bike and I would have been a tangle of bones, blood, and spokes in the middle of Third Street.

I lay on the grass in front of the Crocker Art Museum, whimpering, then slowly straightened my trembling legs and tried to stand. Everything hurt, but nothing seemed to be broken and the only thing bleeding was the palm of my hand.

A disheveled woman pushing a shopping cart full of plastic garbage bags and aluminum cans began gathering up the papers and magazines that had fallen out of my backpack. She handed the disorganized stack of paper to me without a word. The *Carmel Pine Cone* from last weekend had ended up on top.

"Did you happen to see the car that hit me?" I asked.

She stared at the ground for a good thirty seconds, then spoke slowly, showing brown, broken teeth. "Guy floored it all the way to I-5. He didn't even stop for the sign at P Street. You're lucky, lady."

"Yeah." I dusted the grass clippings off of my knees, dug into my backpack, and pressed a ten into her hand. "Thanks, okay?"

She placed the bill into an inner pocket and began pushing her overloaded cart. "Lady, you know what they say."

"What's that?"

"It's not safe to be out riding your bike here by yourself."

I picked up the battered remains of the bicycle from where it had landed in the gutter. I might be in one piece, but the three-speed would need major surgery. I limped the two blocks to home on foot, pushing the bike.

The lush landscaping and tan stucco of Capital Square had never looked more welcoming.

I returned the remains of the bike to the storage locker next to the Z-car in the underground garage. My legs were still too shaky to attempt the stairs, so I treated myself to an elevator ride. Light and bell announced the second level. The shiny silver doors slid open.

"May I escort you to your apartment, ma'am?"

Edward Glott, wearing the brown uniform and broad-brimmed hat of the Capital Square security force.

"Silly me! I forgot something in the laundry room." I backed into the elevator and jammed the CLOSE DOOR button.

Back to the cavern of the parking garage. I crept up the stairs to the third floor, my ankles, knees, and thighs screaming at every step. On the third level, directly above my apartment, I watched Edward Glott pace in front of my door.

I stood silently at the railing for ten minutes, watching Glott. I don't know what I would have done next had not a woman struggling with a bulging briefcase and overflowing cardboard box emerged from the elevator and walked in my direction. I recognized my upstairs neighbor, Diane George, State Capitol reporter for Sacramento's all-news station. She ducked her head when she drew closer, but not before I took in the smudged eye makeup and trembling chin.

"Jeez, you look even worse than I do. What happened?"

She let the box and briefcase drop to the cement walkway and choked out three words. "I got fired."

"No way!"

Diane George had been covering the State Capitol for at least a quarter century, winning every conceivable local and regional broadcast award. Pols and fellow journalists usually spoke of her in the same reverent tones used when mentioning Helen Thomas, first lady of the White House press corps.

"Laid off, downsized, let go, F-I-R-E-D," came out between sobs. I scrounged around in my backpack and found a wad of tissue. Diane took them from me with a nod of thanks and began dabbing at what was left of her eyeliner.

"So what happened?" I said.

"You heard we got bought by Federated. Well, they came into town today and called a mandatory staff meeting."

"Let me guess, they told you they weren't going to change anything. No one had a thing to worry about."

Diane almost managed a smile at the universal radio management lie. "After all the speeches, they start calling us one by one into the general manager's office. The Federated consultant had the nerve to tell me Sacramento radio listeners don't care what happens at the Capitol. So Federated won't be needing my services any longer."

"Come with me." I hefted Diane's briefcase. "It sounds to me like you could use a good stiff drink."

I escorted Diane George down the elevator to the second level, along the walkway, past a glowering Edward Glott, and into my apartment. I fixed that promised good stiff drink for Diane and one for myself and motioned for her to join me at the kitchen counter.

"I'm sure you'll land on your feet," I told her as we both settled onto the bar stools. "You're good at what you do and have so many connections. Some other station will snap you up in a heartbeat."

Diane gave me a sour look. "You know better than that. I'm pushing fifty and I'm used to making decent money. No one in the industry will touch me when they can get some kid right out of college to do an okay job for half of what I'm making. There's only one option left for someone like me." She began to sniffle again.

"Not—"

"Yes. Public relations."

I slammed the deadbolt to my front door the instant Diane George left. Not that it mattered. As head of the security force, Glott would have access to all the passkeys. I dragged a dining chair over to the door and jammed it under the knob. It was supposed to work, if you believed all the magazine articles about women keeping themselves safe on the road.

The bedroom window. If he wanted to, Glott would be able to pop the flimsy aluminum window frame in a snap. I ran to the kitchen, Bialystock following in my wake, and grabbed pots, pans, bottles, and jars. I arranged them in a jumble on the sill and on the floor under the window. A little surprise for Edward Glott and his boys.

That left the sliding door leading to the balcony. Somehow, I couldn't picture Glott's big butt rappelling up the side of the building. The broomstick that I already kept jammed into the track would surely be enough.

Got to talk to T. R. O'Brien! I dialed his home number, but got only the machine. High-pitched staccato delivery. "Can't come to the phone. Too busy makin' money."

Tried Glory Lou at the station. Out on her beat checks. The producer for the sports talk program that preceded Glory Lou's show promised to have her call me ASAP.

A bandage for my hand, then a shower. I opened a can of kitty vittles for Bialy and picked at a microwave dinner. Tried to watch *Jeopardy!* but couldn't concentrate. Not even when my favorite category, Potent Potables, came up. I gave up, flicked off Alex Trebeck, fixed myself another gin and tonic, slid open the balcony door, and seated myself in a patio chair. I held the cat on my lap and gazed at the traffic on I-5 for a long time.

Glory Lou called just after eleven.

"You're not going to believe what happened! I'm riding my bike home, okay?" I started.

Glory Lou interrupted in a voice devoid of her usual sugar and spice. "Hon, I've got something important to tell you."

I waited.

"Something bad just happened to Monty Rio."

19

"I read about Monty Rio in the *Bee*."

Josh Friedman on the other end of the phone, ringing me up at my apartment the next morning. "He's going to be okay, won't he?"

"I don't know. I checked in with the Med Center about ten minutes ago. He's stable, still critical."

I'd slept no more than fifteen minutes at any one stretch, bolting awake at the slightest noise, convinced Edward Glott had finally figured out how to get into my apartment. Then I'd switch on the bedside lamp, call the hospital to badger them for an update about Monty, leave still another message on T. R.'s answering machine.

I gave up on sleep and staggered out of bed when it started getting light. I paced the apartment, too scared to venture outside. No way was I going anywhere today unless I was with someone I knew and trusted. Which pretty much left me with no one. Maybe Glory Lou and Josh.

At 8:00 A.M. I started calling the station.

"I'm sorry, dear, but T. R. hasn't come in yet," Mrs. Yanamoto told me. "I'll have him call you as soon as I see him.

"Isn't it a terrible thing about Monty Rio?" she added.

My mother didn't leave me much of an inheritance. Just her collection of vintage jazz 78s and LPs. My inheritance from my father is less tangible, but more substantial. After a lifetime of railing against the military-industrial complex, Dad spent his last decade quietly investing in Silicon Valley's then-infant computer industry, getting out well before the dot-com meltdown. I socked away the dividends in CDs and T-bills. It's not enough to make me rich, but it does give me a nice cushion of fuck-you money. You know, whenever a gig or a relationship gets too sticky, you dive into your stash of fuck-you money and hit the road.

It was beginning to look like no amount of fuck-you money would get me out of this jam.

Josh was calling me from a pay phone on campus. "There's this form that you've got to sign if I'm going to be able to continue my internship with you over the summer session. The deadline is today at noon."

"How long have you known about this deadline?" God, I sounded just like my father.

"I asked my independent studies advisor for more time," Josh continued, ignoring my question. Just the way I would have done. "But she's all if she breaks the rules for one student, she has to for everyone."

"It's almost eleven. What do you expect me to do?"

"I could come over right now and you could sign it. I can make it to your place and back to Sac State by noon, easy."

What could I do? He was so eager, so anxious to succeed. And he was turning out to be the best producer I'd ever had.

Another ring. I lunged for the receiver, hoping it was Mrs. Yanamoto, telling me T. R. had just arrived home from Alaska.

"Shauna J.! Have I got an important assignment for you."

Mimi Blitzer. What the hell does the promotion gal want now?

"You live near Old Sacramento, right?" Blitzer continued.

"So?" Whatever I said could and would be used against me, I just knew it.

"I need you to stop by and pick up the media passes for the Jazz Jubilee on your way to the station."

"Why can't you do it?" I know I sounded snotty. But I was

exhausted, worried, and scared. I was beyond social niceties with the likes of Mimi Blitzer.

"I've got more important things to do. I've got a major station event in less than twenty-four hours, in case you've forgotten. Not to mention, a wedding to plan."

Josh arrived in a rush of books, papers, and pens. I put my name on the dotted line and he bolted for the door.

"Mind if I go along?" I asked, reaching for my keys and backpack.

"I guess not. But why?"

"Just need to get out, that's all." I didn't want to tell the kid I was too frightened to leave the four walls of my apartment by myself. Next thing, I'd be turning into one of those old ladies who never leaves the house until her emaciated body is found surrounded by stacks of old newspapers and a couple dozen cats.

"What exactly happened to Monty Rio?" Josh asked as he steered his Geo Metro across the light rail tracks at Twelfth Street. "Besides what was in the paper this morning, I mean."

Even though I'd been hounding the Med Center and the CHP for details, I actually didn't know much more than what was in the short notice in the newspaper. But I didn't want to admit that to Josh.

"From what I've been able to find out, Monty left The Salt Shaker around eight o'clock last night and headed straight home to his condo in South Natomas. He lost control of his car on the Garden Highway."

"The part that runs along the river?"

"Yeah. He ran his car off the levee and hit a tree. I guess he's lucky the tree stopped his car from going into the river."

"Was he drunk?"

"He'd been drinking, yes. He'd had one drink with me, and one with some of the guys in the sales department after I'd left."

Maybe if I'd stayed, this wouldn't have happened.

"But he wasn't drunk," I said. "The hospital says his alcohol level was point-zero-six. He was within the legal limit."

"Did his brakes fail?"

Or did someone tamper with the steering? Rear-end his car?

"Who knows? The highway patrol says it'll take several days before they'll be able to check everything out."

And if the CHP is in league with Lieutenant Gunderson, Edward Glott, and their ilk, we may never know the truth.

I lurked in the hallway at Sac State, idly studying the bulletin board while waiting for Josh. The usual hand-lettered "roommate wanted" flyers, advertisements for term paper ghostwriting services, and posters promoting raves. "Get paid for listening to the radio!" one handbill promised. No 1-800 number, just a number in the 530 area code, and a 756 prefix. Davis.

"You're stuck with me for another three months," Josh announced as he emerged from the independent studies office.

"It goes both ways, kid, when it comes to being stuck."

I promised to treat Josh to a cheeseburger and fries at Tiny's if he'd run a couple of errands with me. One would be to Old Sacramento, to pick up Mimi Blitzer's precious media passes. But first, I needed to check something out in the Fabulous Forties.

Ronald and Nancy Reagan had rented a house in the Fabulous Forties back when he was governor of California. Despite the presence of The Actor, it was a classy neighborhood. A grid of tree-lined streets numbered in the forties just east of downtown, the Fab Forties date to the Roaring Twenties. Old money, by California standards. The neighborhood reeks of daddy's stock portfolio, prep school, the patrons' circle at the symphony, and languid summer afternoons at the Sutter Lawn Tennis Club.

Like I say, they let in Ronnie and Nancy. They also let in T. R. O'Brien, so I guess the scales balanced out.

I directed Josh to park in front of a pseudo English Tudor mansion near the intersection of Forty-fifth and M, the epicenter of the posh district. "I always feel like I should be wearing Bermuda shorts and a polo shirt when I come to this part of town," I whispered to Josh as we trod the flagstone path to the front door.

"With a little crocodile embroidered on it," Josh agreed.

He lifted the heavy knocker and let it drop against the thick oak door several times. Lots of Yorkie noises—yips and scratches and scrambling—but no sign of human habitation.

"Let's try around back." I began walking along the flower-lined driveway to the backyard.

"Looking for someone?"

The voice came straight from the Bronx. I turned from the gate to the backyard and faced the owner. She was probably pushing seventy, though it was hard to be sure. It was a pretty terrific facelift, I had to admit. The hands were a dead give-away, all brown spots and thick, ropy veins. She was turned out in Fila tennis gear, complete with racquet.

"I'm Hildy Meyers. From next door," she said, indicating a pink stucco hacienda with her tennis racquet. "Help you two with anything?"

I introduced Josh and myself. "We're concerned about the O'Briens. T. R. was supposed to come back from vacation last night."

Hildy Meyers remained on guard. "Cora asked me not to talk to anyone."

"We're from the station. It's okay," I bluffed.

"Well, all right." Hildy Meyers relaxed slightly. "Cora came over to my house early yesterday morning. I was just starting my morning power walk. She asked if I'd mind feeding her dogs for a few days. Pick up the mail, that sort of thing. We've been neighbors since 1972. Of course, I said I'd be happy to help."

"Did she say where she was going?"

"Nope. Cora was in a terrific hurry, just had one overnight bag with her. The airport limo picked her up at around six-thirty. I've not heard from her since."

"And she didn't give you any idea when she'd return?"

"Nope."

I wrote out a message to T. R. and Cora on the back of my business card. "Call me ASAP!" I added my home phone number and underlined ASAP three times, just to make sure.

I handed the card to Hildy Meyers with strict instructions to give the card to T. R. or Cora the minute she saw either one.

I drummed my fingers against my knees, fear and doubt gnawing at me to the bone as Josh drove back into the downtown district. Where the hell was T. R.? What's with Cora, fleeing at sunrise? Helping her hubby escape from the law? Running from a killer?

The red Geo Metro continued west on Capitol Mall toward Old Sacramento. A broad avenue with a grassy strip in the center, Capitol Mall is walled on both sides by steel-and-glass office towers. Mostly state office buildings, but some private corporate skyscrapers in the mix. Wells Fargo. Capital Bank of Commerce. CalFac.

"Pull over at the corner," I instructed Josh.

"What for?"

"I'm not sure. Just pull over and let me out. Circle the block a couple of times. I should be out in ten minutes or so."

It was a sheer impulse, dropping in on the headquarters of CalFac. I had not a clue as to what I expected to find. But I knew most of the downtown real estate that wasn't owned by the state government was held by Capital City Ventures, a CalFac subsidiary. Including Capital Square and Dr. Hipster's apartment building. I also knew Capital City Ventures, and thus CalFac, was the employer of Edward Glott and Rudy Wolinsky.

The express elevator whisked me to the twenty-fifth floor. I waited for my stomach to catch up, then stepped into the foyer of CalFac's executive offices.

The view was a showstopper: Old Sacramento, the wide and winding Sacramento River, I-80 arching gracefully over the river and disappearing into the hazy western horizon, the Yolo Causeway shimmering in the distance.

"On a clear day, you must be able to see all the way to San Francisco," I said to no one in particular.

"It is spectacular, isn't it?" I started and turned to see a woman dressed in a prim and proper business suit. Even a blouse with a bow, hadn't seen one of those since the first

Bush administration. She rose from behind the kind of mahogany desk usually reserved for the executive suite. Ms. Weatherstone, according to the nameplate. Beyond an open door behind the desk I could see a windowless room housing a word processor and massive filing cabinet, and I heard the hum-thump of a copier. Ms. Weatherstone, I supposed, spent most of her time slaving away in the cave. I wondered if she had some sort of buzzer alerting her when someone pressed twenty-five on the elevator in the ground-floor lobby.

She was about to go into the "May I help you?" routine when the phone rang and she became embroiled in a lengthy discussion about plane tickets to London. Saved by the bell. I used the opportunity to snoop. And to think of a plausible story.

If the interior designer had wanted to impress me, he succeeded. Green marble walls, the real thing, not faux. An expensive Oriental carpet topped a brightly polished parquet floor. A Wayne Thiebaud original from his slices of pie period graced the wall next to Ms. Weatherstone's desk. I was definitely out of my league in my embroidered blouse from Mexico, cotton gauze pants, canvas backpack, and Tevas.

A massive pair of closed rosewood doors led into the inner sanctum. I imagined hush-hush whispers of deals being made, the *scritch-scratch* of documents being signed with a Mont Blanc pen. A discreet brass plaque next to the door proclaimed the home of CalFac, Inc., and its subsidiaries, which included Capital City Ventures.

CalFac. Maker of deals with impoverished environmental activists, courtesy of chief negotiator Jeff Greene, to make sure nothing stands in their way to developing a mega-resort in Big Sur. Owner of the Pavilion hotel chain. Major financial supporter of The Farm Team. Which leads right back to Greene for Governor.

I felt a queasy twinge in the pit of my stomach that had nothing to do with the elevator ride.

There was more writing on the plaque. Established 1958, Stas Kostantin, Founder. The names of six partners, including Vivienne Kostantin. And Neil Vermont.

I'd figured the widow Kostantin would be one of the key

players. But I hadn't counted on Neil Vermont, T. R. O'Brien's business partner and his fishing buddy. No wonder he could afford a house at Pebble Beach.

"May I help you?" Ms. Weatherstone had finished upgrading the London plane tickets and returned her attention to me.

If you have to lie, pick something as close to the truth as possible. Another piece of advice from Dr. Hipster.

"I'm Shauna J. Bogart, from Sacramento Talk Radio," I said, handing a business card to Ms. Weatherstone. "I'm putting together a series of interviews with Sacramento's most influential women, and I'd very much like to include Vivienne Kostantin. I wonder if I might see her for a few moments?"

Ms. Weatherstone frowned, but maintained her bland, finishing-school tones. "Mrs. Kostantin hardly ever does that kind of thing, but I'll certainly pass along your request when she calls in for messages."

"She's out of town?"

"Mrs. Kostantin is spending most of her time in Pebble Beach these days." She paused, as if carefully choosing her next words. "It's not a secret any longer. She and Neil Vermont announced their engagement last week. They're to be married in September."

"That's terrific!" I didn't really have an opinion one way or another, but I wanted to keep Ms. Weatherstone talking.

"Yes, we're so happy for her. For both of them. After Mr. Kostantin passed on, we were afraid she'd never find true love again." Ms. Weatherstone's plain, serious face positively glowed.

"Tell them both congratulations from me."

"So how was it up there?" Josh asked as I folded myself back into the Geo Metro.

I didn't answer immediately. Instead, I pawed through my canvas backpack until I unearthed the *Carmel Pine Cone* from the last weekend. Vivienne Kostantin and Neil Vermont, smiling for the photographer in the "Social Spotlight" column. So T. R.'s first wife—and Terrence's mother—was hooking up with T. R.'s longtime business partner and fishing buddy. I held the newspaper on my lap and stared at the photo while Josh continued driving west toward Old Sacramento.

"A little rich for my blood," I said, finally answering Josh's question. "Killer view, though."

20

Josh's car dodged a golf cart loaded with beer kegs as he bumped over the cobblestone streets of Old Sacramento. We followed an RV with the bumper sticker: "Please don't tell my mother I'm a lawyer. She thinks I'm a piano player in a whorehouse." Already the cops had blocked off most of the parking spaces to make way for badge sales trailers and Porta Potties. Signs announced a ban on parking and private vehicle traffic in Old Sacramento starting at midnight.

Josh found a parking spot in a loading zone near the Pony Express statue. I put one of my business cards on the dash and hoped it would placate the gods of parking spaces.

They didn't go in for plush in the Jazz Jubilee media trailer: metal table, four folding chairs, one telephone, a boom box, and a portable television. A sign warned that all requests for press credentials had to be made in advance, in writing. Gee, these folks really know how to court us media celebrities.

We introduced ourselves to a cherub-faced man with a halo of white hair seated behind the folding table. "I'm Warren Harriman, Jubilee media relations. I listen to your show all the time. You don't look anything like I thought you would."

Then a frown crossed his cheery face. "Now, young missy. What's this business about burning a banjo on your show tomorrow afternoon?"

Harriman seemed like such a sweet old fellow, I was almost starting to regret the attitude. "It was just a bit," I said. "Shtick. Nothing personal."

"No offense taken." He handed me an oversize brown envelope filled with our allotment of media passes. "Terrible thing about Monty Rio. Any update?"

I shook my head as I inspected the contents of the packet, just to make sure there were no unpleasant surprises for Mimi Blitzer. Which she'd blame on me, of course. Two dozen oversize white buttons bearing the Jazz Jubilee logo and the word MEDIA in two-inch black letters. A ribbon attached to the button also declared MEDIA, just in case anyone hadn't gotten the message. I also found a set of Old Sacramento vehicle access passes and parking stickers, one for each of our three news cars.

"You'll need those even for your marked news vehicles," Harriman warned. "Nobody, but nobody, drives into Old Sacramento the next four days without a sticker."

Great. Maybe I'd have an excuse for not doing the remote tomorrow. "Gee, Mimi, I had no idea you needed all these different passes just to drive into Old Sacramento. I got turned away by a cop."

I thanked Warren Harriman and turned to leave. "One more thing." He placed a long string of blue carnival tickets in my hand.

"What are these?"

"Drink tickets. For the bar." Warren Harriman's blue Santa Claus eyes twinkled. "Have one on us."

I revised my earlier assessment. The Jazz Jubilee press people did know a thing or two about courting us media celebs.

Since I was in Old Sacramento anyway, I figured it would be a good idea to check out the site of tomorrow's remote before Josh and I left the historic district. We found the Sacramento Talk Radio van parked in front of an ice-cream parlor right next door to Pete Kovacs's store. On the second-floor balcony, facing Second Street, Brandon Nguyen attached cables from the mixing board to speakers, cart machines, and computers.

"We're doing a remote from a balcony?" I looked up and shaded my eyes with the packet of media passes.

"Don't you ever listen to our promos?" Josh said. "You know, 'Live and direct from our historic home in Old Sacramento.' "

"What historic home?"

"I can't believe you didn't read the memo." Who did the kid think he was, Mimi Blitzer? "According to the promos we've been running like at least once every hour, this is the original site of T. R. O'Brien's radio station. Back in the fifties, sixties, and seventies, before he moved out to Highway 160."

"Well I'll be damned." I laughed for the first time in twenty-four hours and took my sunglasses out of my backpack for a closer look. Sure enough, it was the very balcony where I'd watched Dr. Hipster and Juicy Lucy share a joint and a fifth of tequila some thirty years ago. Only where there'd once been a derelict wreck of a building now stood a proud brick structure with freshly painted green-and-gold accents, brass trim, even bunting hanging from the balcony.

I should only look so good after thirty years.

Our chief engineer emerged from behind the station van. "Hey, Gil." I crossed the street with Josh in tow. "I thought you and Norma would be on the road to Monterey by now."

"Any minute now," he said. "I just wanted to make sure Pac Bell got all of our phone lines installed. Good thing I checked, too. They almost forgot the most important thing."

"The broadcast loop?"

"Exactly."

Gil and I shook our heads. Without a broadcast-quality phone line, we'd be stuck all day relaying our live programming from Old Sacramento by microwave link atop the van to the transmitter back at the station. Which was okay for a sixty-second newscast, or even an hour-long special report. But definitely a drag for a remote broadcast scheduled for sixteen hours.

I thanked Gil for his diligence and wished him a fabulous weekend in Monterey. "Better hurry and hit the highway before the commute starts."

"Here, take a couple of these for you and a friend. Andrew or whoever." I handed Josh a pair of the Jazz Jubilee media buttons. We were back in his car, driving along Second Street toward the I Street exit.

"You mean it?"

"Of course. You can bet Mimi Blitzer won't be sharing with anyone once we get these things back to the station."

"Better keep one for yourself."

I was about to make a snotty reply about the likelihood of my attending the Jazz Jubilee on a voluntary basis. We drove past the California State Railroad Museum. A figure in jeans, white cotton shirt with the sleeves rolled up, and a Panama hat with a Red Sox logo sewn on the hatband was talking to a state parks ranger. Most men my age have taken to wearing "relaxed fit" jeans, with the ever-popular skosh more room in the seat and thigh. Pete Kovacs still looked terrific in his 501s.

Maybe sometime this weekend, I'd be in the mood to walk over to Old Sacramento and check out The Hot Times Dixieland Band. From the back of the tent, where no one would recognize me. I slipped a media badge into my backpack, next to the wad of drink tickets. Just in case.

Unlike all of the "theme" fifties diners and drive-ins popping up all over, Tiny's is the genuine article, a fixture on Fulton Avenue since 1957. The lunch rush was pretty much over by the time Josh and I arrived, so we were lucky enough to grab a Naugahyde-covered booth. We placed matching orders for cheeseburgers and fries, a Coke for Josh and iced tea for me.

"I've decided to call myself Jeremy Carlin on the air." Josh twirled a french fry in catsup.

"I thought we settled this the other day. Josh Friedman is a terrific radio name."

Josh pushed his wire-rims up the bridge of his nose. "You don't understand. You didn't grow up here."

"What does that have to do with it?"

"My father owns a furniture store."

"Friedman's Fine Furniture," I said. "I knew that."

"Yeah. Well, what you don't know is that Dad used to put me in his TV commercials. At the end of every commercial, I'd come on the screen and say 'Tell 'em Joshie sent you!' It was Friedman's big slogan. 'Tell 'em Joshie sent you!' The commercials were everywhere. Dad even had me up on billboards for a while, when I was around five or six."

"I'll bet you were adorable."

Josh made a face. "It was fun when I was a little kid. But then, when I'm in sixth, seventh grade, it was really embarrassing."

"Why didn't you tell your father you didn't want to do the commercials any longer?"

"I tried. He finally put an end to it when I was around fifteen. When I stopped being cute."

I patted Josh's arm. "You'll always be cute."

"But don't you get it now? I want to work in radio or TV news in Sacramento. But no one's going to take the Friedman's Fine Furniture kid seriously."

"Surely you've figured it out by now how hard it is to break into this industry. You've got to use every advantage you have. Okay, some news director hears the name Josh Friedman and remembers 'Tell 'em Joshie sent you.' At least it might get you a foot in the door. What's wrong with that?"

Josh swallowed the last french fry. "Then why didn't you use your real name when you started out?" He held up his hand. "And no fair telling me things were different when you first got into radio."

Here it comes. Josh is going to remind me that I'm the daughter of some big politician in Silicon Valley and that I could have used his connections to help my career when I was starting out.

"Why didn't you let Helen Hudson help you?"

I put down my iced tea in midswallow. "How do you know about Helen Hudson?" I've told absolutely nobody about Helen Hudson. Not even Dr. Hipster.

"I'm training to be a reporter, remember? I know how to check things out. I know Helen Hudson was your mother and that she was a singer back in the forties and fifties. Not as famous as Peggy Lee or Teresa Brewer, but she still appeared in nightclubs and cut some records."

I was silent, so Josh continued. "She must have known people in the industry. She was on the radio, she did *The*

Arthur Godfrey Show. There'd be people around who would
have remembered Helen Hudson and could have given your
career a boost. I'm just wondering why you didn't call yourself
Shauna J. Hudson or something. Like Shelley and Nanette
Fabares."

*Because Helen Hudson embarrassed me, okay? All those
trite, corny old songs about moon and June that she loved so
much. Songs that were old even in the fifties. And because she
represented everything that I'm against. A vain, manipulative
woman who covered her minimal talent with makeup and man-
nerisms. A pathetic, shallow person who lived only for attention and applause. I'd spent my entire life trying to live down
Helen Hudson.*

"Look, Josh, this conversation is about you, not me. Don't
try to be someone you're not. Just be the best Josh Friedman
you know how to be. Go with your strengths, kid."

Josh wadded up waxed paper and napkins and started to
slide out of the booth. "Then why don't you?"

Mimi Blitzer's office always reminded me of a cross between
a Pic-N-Save and the dorm room of a cheerleader at some
retro-fifties college. An oversize cardboard box, one corner
already caved in, overflowed with station T-shirts. Her desk
was a blizzard of memos, fan mail in various stages of being
answered, phone message slips, and stack of tractor-fed computer paper. A bulletin board covered with snapshots of station
promotional events and clippings from the *Bee* on one wall. I
always imagined pompoms stashed behind the door, waiting
to be trotted out at the next staff meeting.

Blitzer was on the phone when I approached her office to
turn over the Jazz Jubilee media passes.

"Mother, if I told you once, I told you a thousand times,
the chicken dance comes before the money dance. I am not
going to flap my arms when I've got twenty-dollar bills pinned
to a two-thousand-dollar gown."

A long pause.

"I thought we'd settled that." Blitzer's voice bordered on
shrill. "We're serving the chateaubriand as the main course. I

don't care about Great-aunt Priscilla's clogged arteries."

Pause.

"I've already decided, Mother. There is no way we're serving chicken on my wedding day. Everyone knows only cheapskates choose the chicken."

Blitzer spotted me hovering in the hallway and ended the phone conversation. She looked up from her lap, where fingers had been nervously punching what looked like elastic bands into cardboard half circles. I tossed the manila envelope with the media passes onto her overflowing desk. Blitzer pulled another crescent-shaped piece of white cardboard from a box, barely breaking stride. "The sun visors for the Jazz Jubilee just showed up, only they didn't come assembled. C'mon, give me a hand."

"Gee, Mimi, I don't know." I drew up a visitor's chair and sat. "I was never good at artsy-craftsy things."

"It's simple. You just push the clips at the end of the elastic through the holes at either end of the visor. See?" She finished one visor with a flick of the wrist and perched it atop her brown bob.

Good sport that I am, as well as in need of information, I picked up an elastic band and visor and followed Blitzer's instructions. "I just wanted to follow up on the conversation we had with T. R. the other night about the contest. You know, how it was supposed to be some Caltrans supervisor in her late thirties winning the money, not some student from Sac State."

Blitzer pursed her lips as if I couldn't be trusted and continued her frenetic activity on the assembly line.

"Look, you and T. R. asked me to keep an eye on Josh," I said. "How can I do that if I don't know what I'm looking for? Who actually assigns the numbers and does the selection, us or the people in St. Louis?"

"We didn't have to do a thing except supply a color copy of our logo to their printer. The people in St. Louis did all the work, printing, addressing, and bulk mailing. They supplied us with a printout of all the winning numbers and the households they were sent to. They even gave us the three-by-five cards and a schedule of the day and time each one is supposed to be read."

"Less work for Mother."

"And in case you're wondering, T. R. put me in charge while he's in Alaska." Blitzer waved her hand at the stack of green bar paper on her desk. "Mrs. Yanamoto locks up everything in T. R.'s safe when she leaves for the night. All I keep are the cards that the air staff is going to read the next day. Each card . . ."

"I know, I know," I interrupted. "Each card is sealed in a separate envelope and the seal isn't broken until we read the numbers on the air."

"I've been coming in every morning at seven to personally hand the envelope to the morning team," she said. "I give out the other cards to the producers just before the hosts go on the air."

"I suppose you lock up the cards in your desk whenever you're away from the office."

"And lock the door." She stopped fiddling with the sun visors and glared at me through narrowed eyes. "You know what this means, don't you?"

"Why don't you tell me." I returned the stare.

"There's only one way those cards could be tampered with, and it has to happen between the time I hand them to Josh Friedman and the time you read them on the air."

Just for fun, I opened that afternoon's show with the first track on the Helen Hudson album I'd found at the used record store in Monterey. "The Blue Door, the West End's swingin'est night spot, proudly presents Miss Helen Hudson," followed by my mother's voice crooning "St. James Infirmary Blues."

"The first caller who can identify The Blue Door, and tell us why it's significant, wins a pair of one-day passes to the Sacramento Jazz Jubilee," I told my listeners.

Sam from Roseville swore Marilyn Chambers had made a porno flick called *Inside the Blue Door*. Randy from Orange-vale said he had hard evidence that the Helen Hudson LP had a coded message understood only by the U.N. conspirators. Sue from Rancho Cordova was sure the answer could be found in the radio signals she was picking up in her dental work.

I punched up Line Four.

"You don't know nuthin' about bein' inside no blue door." Estelle from Del Paso Heights had a voice aged in booze and smoke. "It be a swingin' place, a be-boppin' place. On K Street, 'bout halfway between Second and Third in the old West End."

"Where I-5 goes through now."

"That be the place."

"Sounds like you spent a lot of time there."

"Honey, I waited tables most every Friday and Saturday night. The tips, they was good, and I got to see some fine acts for free. Dinah Washington, Ella Fitzgerald, Rosemary Clooney, Scatman Crothers, Helen Hudson."

"Helen Hudson?" My voice cracked with excitement. I didn't realize it would mean that much to me to reach back through time and connect with my mother's dreams.

"Indeed, I remember Miss Hudson. A lovely voice. The lady should have been a much bigger star."

"What was she like? To work with, I mean."

"Honey, I wouldn't know. I be much too busy slingin' drinks to ever do more with the talent than just say 'good evening.' "

It was past time for a commercial break, as Josh's signals kept reminding me, and the conversation was of no interest to the rest of my listeners. "Just one more thing, Estelle from Del Paso Heights, and then we'll move on: Do you recall anything about an important contract involving The Blue Door?"

"A contract?" Estelle's voice rose and fell at least two octaves through the phone line. "Honey, you are asking the wrong gal. Shoot, we didn't even have a contract with the Hotel and Restaurant Employees Local when I made that scene."

I went ahead and gave Estelle the pair of passes to the Jazz Jubilee anyway.

I lingered in the station parking lot after the show, strolling back and forth between the lobby doors and the Z-car, as if I kept forgetting something. I knew Glory Lou was waiting for me at home, impatient to start fixing me up for my date with Pete Kovacs this evening. But I didn't want to miss Lily McGovern and the documents she promised to bring, the paper trail that could destroy Greene's ecologically pure image and that could give me the hottest story of my career. I waited twenty minutes, a good fifteen minutes longer than I should have.

Lily McGovern never showed.

21

Ruffles, lace, feathers, beads, and spangles covered the bed. Chiffon scarves and feather boas spilled from a large paper shopping bag. An open fishing tackle box revealed pallets of makeup, pots of paint, pins, and clips. A sewing basket shared space on the pillow with a blow dryer and a set of electric rollers. Nestled next to the curlers, a roll of surgical adhesive, several packages of stockings, and an open shoebox overflowing with junk jewelry. I almost tripped over a cardboard carton crammed with glittery, spiky shoes at the foot of the bed.

Either the entire cast of *La Cage Aux Folles* had set up camp in my bedroom, or Glory Lou was preparing for my makeover for the Jazz Band Ball.

"Jeez, can't I just wear a silk blouse with jeans?"

"Hon, no one's worn a silk blouse and jeans to a party since 1978." Glory Lou steered me toward the shower. "You're going to be the belle of the ball, just you wait."

I emerged, wrapped in a terry-cloth robe, from the bathroom just as a news update came over the clock radio on my nightstand. Nadine Bostwick continued to pull ahead in the polls.

Glory Lou held up a frothy confection of red satin, sequins, and feathers with a neckline plunging to *there*. One of her "finds" from the Music Circus costume shop. "Joann Worley wore this in *Hello, Dolly!* You know, the scene where she comes down the staircase at the Harmonia Gardens? You'll look fabulous."

"It looks like something I might have bought at Tonya Harding's garage sale."

Glory Lou gave me a put-upon sigh as she dove into the pile of fabric on the bed and hefted another gown. "One of Marian the Librarian's costumes from *The Music Man*. Remember when she sat on the footbridge and sang "Til There Was You'?"

I reminded Glory Lou that I'd never actually taken in a Music Circus performance. "It would figure, a town like Sacramento, they'd line up for days to sit in a tent and watch those corny old musicals."

"You should try it sometime. It's lots of fun. But seriously. What do you think?"

The frock was more subdued than the *Hello, Dolly!* extravaganza, but we're still talking major frou-frou, gingham slathered with white lace ruffles. I made a show of holding it up to myself in front of the mirror. "It makes me look like a reject from *Little House on the Prairie*. Didn't you pick up anything sexy but not slutty?"

Glory Lou triumphantly displayed a twenties flapper dress, orange chiffon dripping with black fringe from hip to midthigh. In her other hand, she waved a matching feathered headband. "Mariette Hartley wore this when she did *Mame*. The scene where she teaches her nephew how to mix a martini. Isn't it darling?"

The flapper dress did have possibilities. "I like it, I really do," I told Glory Lou. "But the color's all wrong for me. Let's face it, we redheads shouldn't wear orange."

I didn't want to go into the real reason. Any skirt landing above the knee risked showing off the lovely black-and-purple bruise I'd picked up in my bicycle accident the night before.

At least I wasn't sharing a room in the ICU with Monty Rio. I'd called the hospital just before I left the station. Still no change.

"I understand, hon," Glory Lou said. "I look like roadkill in anything yellow." She lifted another gown from the bed.

It was blue with just a whisper of green, like the color of

the ocean on the first day of summer vacation. The top shimmered with sequins and was cut low enough to suggest without actually trumpeting an invitation. The sequins ended just below the waist, where a swirl of satin extended just past the knee.

This was a dress made for smoke-filled jazz clubs in Harlem in the thirties. A dress for sipping bootleg gin and listening to "The Viper's Drag." In a dress like this, a gal could find herself in the slammer, on a ship headed to Rio, or standing before the Justice of the Peace before the evening was over.

"Nell Carter wore this in *Ain't Misbehavin'*," Glory Lou said.

I fingered the satin skirt. "Isn't it way too big?"

"And you wondered why I brought my sewing kit. I'll take a few tucks in the waist, then let it back out before I have to return this stuff to the Music Circus."

"The waist isn't what I'm worried about." God, this was embarrassing. "I mean, this dress is going to require major cleavage."

"Listen, girlfriend." Glory Lou's black eyes sparkled. "By the time we're finished, you'll have cleavage." She tossed me the roll of surgical tape.

"What's this for?"

"Instant rack, hon. You start at one armpit, put the tape under your boobs and end at the other armpit. Squeeze 'em together as tight as you can. You might need to do it two or three times."

"Good Lord. Where did you learn stuff like this?" I stared down at my naked natural assets.

"My older sister went to beauty school. She did the hair and makeup for the first runner-up in the 1992 Miss Mississippi pageant."

I had to admit, Glory Lou was good.

Best to forget the gory details of the hair-and-makeup session. Let's just say Glory Lou stopped short of turning me into Tammy Faye Bakker, but did glop on me the average daily allowance of foundation, blush, eyeliner, mascara, and lipstick of your typical TV anchorwoman. I mentioned as much to

Glory Lou. "But of course, dahling. All of the stations will be there tonight. After I'm finished, you're going to look as fabulous as those TV babes. Better."

My hair has two personalities, dry and humid. In dry weather, I get limp frizz. On humid days, it's clotted limp frizz. A bazillion bobby pins and an entire can of industrial strength Aqua Net later, Glory Lou had crowned me with a classic French roll. Sleek, chic, and sultry.

"Put these on." She handed me a package of stockings.

"Do I have to?"

"Seamed stockings are guaranteed to drive a man wild. From Victoria's Secret. You owe me ten bucks."

Josh looked up from the living-room couch, where he'd been ensconced for the past hour with my collection of Allan Sherman records. He stood and whistled slowly. Bialystock took one look at me, arched his back, hissed, and scuttled off into the kitchen.

I pirouetted slowly.

"Va-va voom! I'm all, where's my camera when I need it?"

Between Glory Lou's quick tucks with needle and thread and that little trick with the surgical tape, Nell Carter's dress from *Ain't Misbehavin'* fit like it had been made for me. After Glory Lou had finished "accessorizing" me—rhinestone hair clip, matching necklace/bracelet, and black beaded bag to which I'd dumped the essentials from my backpack—I felt positively Uptown. In seamed stockings.

I only wished my feet didn't hurt so bad. Glory Lou had insisted on heels. "No, you can't wear flats with a dress like that. And don't even think about those Jesus sandals of yours. As I live and breathe, it's only for one evening and you'll be sitting most of the time." She found a pair of blue pumps with chunky two-inch heels in my size in the box she'd lugged over from the Music Circus.

I managed to eject Glory Lou and Josh from my apartment without too much of a struggle. "C'mon, you guys. I can't have you hanging around like Rhoda and Lou, checking out good ol' Mar's date."

Before Kovacs showed up, I called down to the security desk, just to see if Victor Pahoa was available to watch my apartment while I was away. An unfamiliar female voice told me that Pahoa was taking a long weekend and wouldn't be back until Tuesday.

And, I tossed my trusty Tevas into my backpack and slung it over one shoulder. I'd either stash it at the coat check at the party or leave it in Kovacs's car. Damned if I was going to suffer in heels all evening.

The doorbell buzzed at precisely seven-thirty. Pete Kovacs stood in the dim yellow light of my porch.

Wearing a broad-brimmed Smokey Bear hat.

I must have gasped, because Kovacs's first words were, "I don't look that bad, do I?"

The rest of his getup consisted of jodhpurs, boots, a dark blue shirt, red suspenders, a yellow bandanna, and a fringed leather jacket. He wore his dark hair loose, curling in thick waves to his shoulders. "What are you supposed to be, the Seventh Cavalry?"

Kovacs doffed his hat, bowed at the waist, and stepped inside. "One of Teddy Roosevelt's Rough Riders. At your service, ma'am."

He gave my costume the once-over. "I feel like I'm stepping out with a movie star from the Late Show. Ava Gardner or Grace Kelly."

"I clean up right purty, don't I." What I really wanted to say was that Pete Kovacs in his Rough Rider outfit looked terrific. Dashing, even.

Kovacs picked up the album cover to *My Son the Folksinger.* "I haven't heard this in years. Did you know Joe 'Fingers' Carr was the musical arranger of 'Hello Muddah, Hello Faddah'?"

"Gosh." Who the hell was Joe "Fingers" Carr?

"This your ride?" I asked when we arrived at the passenger loading zone in front of Capital Square. Two security guards hovered in the twilight shadows.

"You like her?"

"Her" being a red Dodge Prospector van, circa 1988, with "Parnassus" painted on the side in gold Old English script.

"Cool, very cool."

Kovacs, clearly pleased, gave me a demonstration. He slid open the side door, lifted a homemade awning, and pulled down a set of folding bookshelves. "I take Parnassus to book fairs and antique shows all over the state."

"What's with the name? Who's Parnassus?"

He gave me a stern look from underneath the Smokey Bear hat. "You mean to say you've not read *Parnassus on Wheels*? *The Haunted Bookshop*? You have heard of Christopher Morley, haven't you?"

"Let's just say I'm not going to make this one a true daily double, Alex."

"My God, and you call yourself an educated woman!"

The inside of the van was tidy and lovingly cared for. Kovacs had been listening to some sort of old fogey music on the tape deck, but he popped out the tape when the engine turned over. "You pick the tunes, my dear."

I dialed around on the Blaupunkt. Bob Seger, give me that old-time rock and roll. Perfect. I pumped up the volume and beat my hands against my knees in time to the music.

I stole a glance at Kovacs as he hung a "U" on Capitol Mall at Fifth, heading into Old Sacramento. He was shaking his head, but his lips twitched in a smile.

"They're really into security at this joint," I said as Kovacs turned over his invitation at the back-alley entrance to The Firehouse. A Jazz Jubilee volunteer wearing the official blue-and-white T-shirt checked off our names. She looked harmless enough, but two uniformed Sacramento cops flanked the entrance.

"Don't spread the word," Kovacs said into my ear, "but there's a rumor the candidates for governor might put in an appearance tonight."

Whether Jeff Greene or Nadine Bostwick decided to show or not, the power crowd was definitely out in force. I waved at several recent guests from my show: the publisher of the

California Journal, two state assemblymen, even the mayor, who was decked out in a near copy of the Marian the Librarian gown I'd rejected. I also locked eyes and nodded at a couple of people who recently refused to do my show: a major developer and one of the *Bee*'s editorial writers.

The Firehouse restaurant occupies an authentic hook and ladder station from 1853, complete down to the brass pole. It's another oasis of leather, red meat, and cigars, a favorite with the money-power-testosterone crowd. T. R. had taken me there to lunch once or twice, but up 'til tonight, I'd never stepped into the courtyard out back. An open-air square with brick walls dripped with ivy. A fountain gurgled at the center, hurricane lamps flickered atop wrought-iron tables, and a five-piece combo on a makeshift stage played "Do You Know What It Means to Miss New Orleans." Even the weather was obligingly hot and humid.

"I feel like I've stepped inside *Pirates of the Caribbean,*" I told Kovacs.

I was glad I'd settled on the *Ain't Misbehavin'* dress. It set me apart from the herd. Most of the gals sported either the Dolly-Parton-at-a-New-Orleans-bordello look, or the twenties flapper getup. Even one of the TV reporters setting up for a live shot had gussied herself up in a short, beaded gown and glittery headband. The guys favored the speakeasy-gangster look, all Panama hats, white ties, black shirts, and outrageous pin-striped suits. There were a few silent movie cowboys, a passable Clark Gable, even a man in a wheelchair done up as FDR, down to the jaunty upturned cigarette holder.

Kovacs led me to a wrought-iron table and a waiter took our drink orders. "Do you mind if I excuse myself for a minute?" Kovacs rose from his chair before I could answer. "The band's about to take a break."

I sipped a gin and tonic and watched my date mount the stage and talk to a pale young man holding a trombone. Lookin' good in that Rough Rider outfit. Kovacs, I mean. I didn't even mind that my date's hair was more fabulous than mine.

Kovacs returned in less than five minutes. "Sorry 'bout

that," he said, indicating the band. "They're from the Czech Republic. This is their first trip to the U.S."

"So where do you fit in?"

"I speak a little of the language. My father managed to get out just after the Nazis left, but before the Communists took over."

"That's fascinating!" I put my chin into my hand and peered into Kovacs's green eyes. I think it's what's known as hanging on to his every word. Works almost as well as seamed stockings.

"No one in the band speaks much English. I've been trying to help them as much as I can."

"How is it that they learned to play American jazz?" I asked just as the Czechs swung into "Puttin' on the Ritz."

"They're all classically trained. Back in the days of Communist rule, they listened to that decadent American jazz on the Voice of America. At first, they'd copy the arrangements. Later on, they created their own."

"They'd make terrific guests on my show. As long as you're along to translate, of course. Do you think they'd be up for stopping by the remote tomorrow?"

Kovacs grinned and waved his forefinger at me. "And you're the gal who's going to burn a banjo to protest this corny old music festival."

"Pete Kovacs! So you're the lucky devil with the diva of the Sacramento airwaves!" The leprechaun from the media trailer pulled a wrought-iron chair up to our table just as I was scarfing up the last of the Bananas Foster. Warren Harriman wasn't really all that diminutive, but his cheerful, round face and cap of wispy white hair gave him a Mickey Rooneyesque quality.

"Does this mean, missy, that you've joined the ranks of the jazz fans?" Harriman continued. "Or are you going to tell me this is just purely research?"

If Shauna J. Bogart had been on the air, she would have had a snappy comeback. But all these people at the Jazz Band Ball—Harriman especially—were being so just darn nice, I couldn't bring myself to do it.

"Just let me know if there's anything I can do to help with your remote tomorrow," Harriman continued. "I used to work at T. R. O'Brien's radio station."

"I didn't know that."

"I was the original news director. I retired years ago, just before Monty Rio came on board." Harriman rose, shook hands, and continued to table-hop.

The final glow of sunlight faded above The Firehouse. Drinks flowed freely, but there were no ugly, rowdy drunks. A six-piece band poured out megawatt hot jazz. High Sierra, according to the name stitched onto their red-and-white striped shirts. A stiff breeze blew in from the Delta. Pete Kovacs placed his fringed leather jacket around my shoulders and let his arm linger.

A figure appeared in the dim candlelight next to our table. He was wearing a CHP uniform.

"Shauna J. Bogart?" He tipped his broad-brimmed hat.

I swallowed and nodded.

"Senator Greene would like to have a word with you."

22

Limousines are, in my opinion, highly overrated.

I'm always sniffing for vomit and searching for semen stains, leavings from the previous parties of graduates, promgoers, and newlyweds. Plus, I find it almost impossible to get in and out of a limo gracefully, even with the assistance of the driver. I usually end up flashing my crotch or my boobs.

The officer led me out of The Firehouse, down the cobblestone alley (me hobbling in my heels), to Jeff Greene's limo. Sure, I was scared. I was also pissed that I didn't have a tape deck with me.

Pete Kovacs had tried to come along, but I wouldn't let him. "This is my battle, not yours."

The man who hoped to be the next governor of California emerged from the limo and helped me fold myself in. I just prayed my boobs would stay tucked inside their surgical tape harness.

I arranged myself and the blue satin skirt on the burgundy velveteen seat, in the forward position. Jeff Greene, flanked by two aides, rode backward, facing me. Greene introduced the man on his right as his media liaison, Will Tucker. The other was his Sacramento campaign coordinator, Lucille Benson. Juicy Lucy.

Up close, Jeff Greene wasn't quite as movie-star handsome as his campaign posters would lead you to believe. He had enlarged pores on his nose, a slight sag to the jawline, and a shaving cut on his chin. Still, he looked damned good, if you go for the clean-cut, white-collar type.

Greene and Tucker wore suits, while Benson was dressed in a drop-dead-elegant business lady's power ensemble.

I took a stab at lightening the atmosphere. "Hey, didn't you guys get the word? This is supposed to be a costume party."

No one smiled. Lucille Benson said, "I don't think we're going to make it to the Jazz Band Ball this year." Her voice had the chill of a meat locker.

Greene slid open a panel leading to the front seat and whispered a few words to the driver. I caught a quick glimpse of the officer who delivered me riding shotgun. The limo began to move slowly. The ride was so smooth I barely felt the cobblestones.

West on L Street, toward the Capitol Mall exit of the historic district and across the Tower Bridge into West Sacramento. The limo's windows were so heavily tinted I soon lost all sense of direction.

No reason to be afraid, I repeated to myself. Pete Kovacs knows I left with Jeff Greene's people. They won't dare try anything.

Dr. Hipster probably had similar thoughts when he opened his door and invited Edward Glott and his pals into his apartment. Just a couple of harmless fellows in uniform.

"I think it's terrific you're seeing Pete Kovacs," Greene said. "He's been a loyal party member for years and a great guy."

I nodded and smoothed my skirt.

"You know, of course, that Mr. Kovacs was one of Senator Greene's earliest local supporters." Lucille Benson leaned across to my seat and patted my arm, suddenly all girlfriend-chummy. "He even threw a fund-raiser for us at his store."

Greene whispered something to Will Tucker, who reached into the minifridge and pulled out a bottle of white wine. He uncorked it and carefully poured the liquid into four long-stemmed glasses. The limousine continued to glide along the streets of what I assumed was West Sacramento.

"The gold medal chardonnay at the State Fair last year," Tucker said.

Greene passed the glasses carefully as the limo turned a corner onto what felt like a freeway on-ramp. "A toast." Greene, Benson, and Tucker raised their glasses. "To Shauna J. Bogart and Pete Kovacs. May you have many more pleasant evenings together."

I dutifully raised my glass and took a sip. My palate was so coated with fear I might as well have been swilling Thunderbird. I glanced over at the door handle, careful not to move my head and draw the attention of Benson and Tucker. Could I make a lunge for the door and fling myself out before they grabbed me? And leap into what? Oncoming traffic? The river? I'd probably never even clear the rear tires of thé limo. Glory Lou would have a hard time explaining the mess when she returned Nell Carter's dress to her friends at the Music Circus.

My fingers slid down the cool, satiny fabric of the skirt. The soft interior lights of the limousine bounced off the sequined top that armored my torso in a glittery aquamarine shield. I uncrossed my legs and felt the rare sensation of sleek, silky stockings. Pete Kovacs's fringed leather jacket balanced across my shoulders like a cape. If this turned out to be my night to ascend to rock'n'roll heaven, at least I'd arrive in style.

I took a deep breath and pictured myself back in the safety of the broadcast booth. Just make like they're a couple of annoying callers and you're the unflappable Shauna J. Bogart.

"You didn't hire this fancy car and uncork a bottle of expensive wine to talk about my social life. What's this all about really?"

Lucille Benson responded with a ladylike snort, while Greene smiled and took another sip of wine. "They told me you'd be a fighter," he said.

Will Tucker was tall, thirtyish, conservatively dressed, with skin color that matched the expensive brown leather briefcase at his feet. "You're not going to give up on this business about The Farm Team, are you?"

"Not when my best friend is killed over it."

"I believe the police are investigating a deranged fan in the death of Dr. Hipster," Lucille Benson said.

I nodded and took another swallow of wine to buy time.

Then I said, "Dr. Hipster was part of the faculty for a weekend seminar on media relations the year Jeff Greene was a student. Now Greene's running for governor, Monty Rio's in the hospital, and Dr. Hipster's in the ground."

"That has absolutely nothing to do with the senator. Be that as it may, we would like to see if we can come to an understanding," Tucker said.

"Forget it. I can't be bought."

Tucker's face crinkled in amusement. "The senator has decided to tell the whole story about The Farm Team. We've decided we'll do it on your show tomorrow afternoon."

"What's the catch?"

"There is no catch. The senator goes on the air with you tomorrow afternoon and tells his story. You get to ask as many questions as you want. He'll even take calls from the listeners."

"And in return, I back off. Just like all those little environmental groups down in Big Sur. Oh, yeah. I know all about that."

Lucille Benson rolled her eyes, but Tucker remained unperturbed. "You, of course, are free to continue talking about Jeff Greene and The Farm Team, the Foundation for Progressive Public Policy, CalFac, Big Sur, whatever you'd like. We're confident that after we do your show, there won't be any story from which to back off."

"Really, Shauna J.," Benson said, "you must admit this so-called scoop of yours isn't that big of a deal in the scheme of things. It's certainly not worth taking someone's life. Politicians make deals all the time. Negotiation, give-and-take: It's the very essence of the art of politics."

Why hadn't Lily McGovern shown up with her documentation like she'd promised? Of all the times for a source to bail on me! Still, I might be better off winging it. B.S. was, after all, one of my strengths.

"After Monica and Gary Condit, the voters have become so jaded, it's hard to conceive of any political scandal that'll grab anyone's attention," I said. "But still, I have faith the citizens of California will think twice when they find out the self-proclaimed champion of our natural resources, a candidate whose very name symbolizes environmental awareness, has been making backroom deals with the corporations that are working the hardest to pave over paradise."

"That's a beautiful speech," Benson said. "But you still haven't told us whether you're going to take the senator up on his offer to make a guest appearance on your show tomorrow."

I settled back into the soft velveteen cushions and considered my options. The limousine cruised silently without stops. Definitely the freeway. There had to be a catch, there just had to be. But damned if I could figure it out.

Bottom line: I had no options. I had to do it. The O'Briens were right in the thick of this. Neil Vermont, board member of CalFac, was an old pal of my boss. The two of them were probably sucking beers and trading stories about the one that got away at that fishing lodge in Alaska at this very moment. Junior had attended workshops at The Farm Team the same year Jeff Greene was a student. Not to mention T. R.'s ex— Junior's mom—hot and heavy with Neil Vermont. Now there was an entanglement worthy of a soap opera.

Without a show on the radio, I had no forum. And without T. R. O'Brien and his radio station, I had no show. Like I said, I had no choice.

"This would be an exclusive, right?" I finally said.

"That goes without saying," Tucker said. "Of course, you're more than welcome to invite the media to cover your broadcast. It might prove to be newsworthy."

For some reason, the image of Councilwoman Kent popped into my mind. Something she said on my show yesterday afternoon, about CalFac's plans for an abandoned ballroom in her district. Once again, two apparently disconnected facts clicked into place.

"There's more going on down in Big Sur than just another posh resort and golf course for the big spenders, isn't there?"

Lucille Benson practically gave off sparks. "Isn't it time you put a sock in it? We've already done you a big favor by offering to do your show. Don't you understand? By Saturday morning, Senator Greene's appearance on your little radio show will be in every newspaper in the state."

"You're going to let CalFac put in a casino, aren't you?" I said to Greene. "That's why they're putting you up for the governorship. CalFac knows they can count on you to pave the way for legislation that'll allow them to bring Nevada-style gambling into their hotels on the coast. They've got to do something to turn a profit in those big, empty atrium restaurants. Out goes the wicker and hanging plants, in go the slot machines. Oh, yeah, that's going to score a lot of points with the tree-hugger crowd."

Benson was about to reply, but Greene leaned forward and held out both hands, palms forward. "It's okay. I understand where Ms. Bogart is coming from. Personally, I'm opposed to gambling, but I understand how important tourism is to the coastal communities, and how vital it is that they stay competitive with major tourist destinations, not just around the country, but worldwide."

"So you made a deal. Welcome to Vegas-by-the-Sea."

"I would never, ever force anything like that on a beautiful little city like Monterey or Santa Cruz or Santa Barbara if the local governing body opposed it."

"Oh, I imagine that won't be hard to arrange. I mean, if you can buy a governorship, what's so difficult about buying a city councilman or two in a small town?"

A grimace creased Jeff Greene's handsome features. "The point is, Ms. Bogart, I'm willing to appear on your show tomorrow and answer these very same questions. I'm willing to put my faith in the common sense of the voters. When they have the chance to consider the full picture, they'll agree I'm the best candidate to lead the state for the next four years."

I said nothing, turning the options over in my mind. It would be an incredible show, no question about it. One of those interviews that makes a career. And Greene may have a point. Voter apathy being what it is, by the time the election rolls around, they likely will have forgotten all about the CalFac scandal.

"I realize there will always be questions and controversy

surrounding CalFac and the Big Sur land deal," Greene said.
"Therefore, if elected, I pledge to veto any bill that would
legalize gambling in any community in which CalFac owns
commercial real estate for the duration of my term in office.
Unless, of course, I am given a petition with the signatures of
a majority of the voters in that community."

"And you're prepared to say as much on my show."

"You have my word."

The limousine turned in another direction. I just knew I
was being had. But I still couldn't figure out how.

Greene's handlers took my silence for affirmation. Tucker
took a yellow legal pad out of his briefcase, uncapped a
MontBlanc, and said, "It's all settled then. What time do you
want us to arrive, and what's the address?"

I reminded Tucker that tomorrow's show would originate
not from the radio station, but from the remote broadcast site
atop a balcony in Old Sacramento. "Will that work for you
guys?"

"I don't see why not. As long as our security team can
check it out first."

We firmed up details of time, place, number of mikes, and
size of entourage. Jeff Greene finished his wine and settled
back in the limousine seat, his hands clasped behind his head.
"This will be a real treat, doing the Shauna J. Bogart Show. I
used to listen to you on the radio, back when I was working
in Silicon Valley and you were on the air at that FM station
in San Francisco. Funny, you don't look anything like I pictured you."

We shared memories of twenty years ago and I almost
started to like Jeff Greene. Almost.

The car slowed, turned, then came to a stop. The passenger
door opened and I snatched a peek at a sprawling ranch house
with palm trees flanking the driveway. Could have been just
about anywhere in California. The CHP officer helped Benson
exit the limousine. Greene began to climb out, then turned to
shake hands with me. "Until tomorrow. I'm looking forward
to it."

The door closed, the driver retraced a slow-stop-turn route
through suburban streets. Now it was just Will Tucker and

Shauna J. Bogart, separated by several yards of shadows, sharing the burgundy velveteen seats and soft lighting of the passenger compartment. Without being able to see or hear anything outside the steel shell, I could have been gliding across the continent from inside a corporate jet. Or entombed in a hearse.

This is when they do the deed and dump the body, I figured. They'll drive out to some deserted country road, and next fall, some duck hunter will find what is left of the missing local media celebrity floating in some irrigation ditch in a rice field. The only thing that wouldn't have rotted away will be the sequined bodice of Nell Carter's dress.

The next time the car slowed, stopped, or turned, I'd make a run for it.

The limousine picked up speed, drove up what felt like a small hill, and settled into a steady sixty-five MPH.

Will Tucker looked up from his legal pad. "I hope you realize the Greene campaign had nothing to do with the death of Dr. Hipster. If you continue to pursue this fruitless inquiry, all you'll do is destroy your own credibility."

"Thank you for your concern."

I must have sounded more sarcastic than I meant to, because Tucker leaned forward and said, "I realize that scruples are not a highly prized commodity in your line of work. However, I would hope that recklessly making utterly false accusations, especially when it comes to the taking of another life, would be beneath even someone such as you."

My suspicions were held together by the slenderest of threads. A few words jotted on a notepad. Dr. Hipster's meeting with Lily McGovern. Still, if anyone had the means to pull it off, it would be a well-funded political campaign. Let's say a pair of hired goons turned up at the station just as Dr. Hipster was winding up his last show. He realizes he's in danger, but manages to slip a coded message for help into a promotional announcement. The thugs follow him home and try to force him to—what? Agree to stop his investigation? Turn over his notes? When it became apparent he wasn't going to cooperate, they silenced him for good.

Twenty minutes later I peered through the tinted windows

and could barely make out the bright lights of Downtown Plaza. The long car took three more slow, careful turns, back into Old Sacramento. We must have been gone around an hour. Just enough time to drive to Davis and back.

The CHP officer walked me through the alley back to The Firehouse. Two city cops, officers whom I'd not seen before, guarded either side of the vine-covered entryway. One was tall, muscular, white, and female. The other was short, chunky, black, and female.

Back at the party, candles flickered inside hurricane lamps and the band played "Shakin' the Blues Away." The crowd was doing just that, bouncing on the dance floor in one corner and clustering around the bar at the other corner. The ten o'clock news station was in the middle of a live shot, and the local network affiliates had their trucks and cameras in position for their live feeds at eleven.

Pete Kovacs was still seated at the wrought-iron table where I'd left him. Two gals in flashy, feathered whorehouse floozy outfits perched on either side.

"Not so fast, Ms. Bogart." A sweaty hand grabbed my arm roughly.

I turned and faced a pudgy, rumpled man in his fifties. "Lou Houlihan! You had me scared for a minute." Lou Houlihan was a legend around the Capitol, by reputation and actual record the sharpest campaign consultant in the state. He'd guested on my show several times the past few weeks.

"I just need a quick word with you." He led me to a quiet corner surrounded by potted camellia bushes.

"Houlihan and Associates is working for Nadine Bostwick," he told me. "Her people hired us just this past Monday."

"I thought Bostwick was pulling ahead in the polls," I said, shifting from one aching foot to another.

Houlihan ran his chubby fingers through his thinning gray hair. "She's got her work cut out for her, polls or no polls. Sorry, but the voters in this state just aren't ready to elect a female and a Jew. Not without a little help behind the scenes."

The bartenders had stashed some empty liquor boxes in back of the potted plants. I longed to sit, but I didn't want to put myself at a psychological disadvantage to Houlihan's bulk. "What does this have to do with me?"

"We want you to continue talking about Jeff Greene and The Farm Team on your show. Did you notice, Nadine Bostwick started to pull ahead in the polls when you went on the air with the story? Especially after the wire services picked up on it. We also want you to tell us what you and Jeff Greene were talking about just now during your little limousine ride."

"No way!"

Houlihan grunted. "I was afraid you'd take that attitude."

"Just listen to my show tomorrow afternoon. Then you and everything else in the state will know."

"We can't wait that long. See, here's how it works. A story that breaks on Friday afternoon at the start of a three-day weekend isn't going to do us much good. It won't get into the papers until Saturday morning. Most people won't even look at the papers over Memorial Day weekend, unless it's to find out who won the Indy 500."

"That's your tough luck."

"But if you tell me now, I can get it on the wires tonight and into Friday morning's papers. Plus, I can make sure the story gets the right sort of spin. Know what I mean? You and Greene were obviously talking about something big. Else why all the secrecy?"

I suggested Lou Houlihan do something anatomically impossible.

Houlihan reached into an inner pocket of his well-worn tweed jacket. "I was hoping I wouldn't have to do this."

He pulled out a white five-by-seven envelope.

"I've had my people follow Jeff Greene the past several days, hoping for a moment just like this." He gestured to a figure on a second-floor balcony overlooking the courtyard. In the dim shadows I could barely make out the shape of a man standing next to a tripod. I also saw the familiar silhouette of Edward Glott.

Houlihan slipped a photograph out of the envelope. "Here's your choice: You can tell me what we want to know. Or I'll see to it that this is in all the newspapers and on all the TV stations in the state tomorrow morning. 'Jeff Greene slips away into the night with sexy media star.' Cooperate, and the negatives are yours. You call the shots."

The photograph was grainy and poorly lit. But it was unmistakably me, tits flashing, red lips and fingernails, clinging to the arm of Jeff Greene as he helped me into the limousine. I didn't look like I was dressed for a costume party. I just looked cheap.

I felt sick.

"It's amazing what they can do these days at those one-hour photo places, isn't it?" Houlihan said.

23

"You were gone a long time." Pete Kovacs rose from his seat at the wrought-iron table.

"Whatever." I glared at the two bordello gals. One of whom was sitting in *my* chair. She took the hint, giggled, and retreated.

"We were just leaving," her companion simpered from behind a fluttering fan.

Kovacs introduced the retreating pair as the wife and sister of the clarinet player in the Czech band.

"Whatever."

"Is everything okay?" Kovacs asked when we were alone.

"Sorry. I've just got a lot on my mind. Be a sweetheart and get me another drink, okay?"

I swayed gently in time to the two-beat music, watched Kovacs hack a path through the throng in front of the bar, and tried to put my jumbled thoughts in order.

That big story Dr. Hipster was working on—after all this, could it have had something to do with Nadine Bostwick?

What's the real story behind Jeff Greene's sudden eagerness to do my show tomorrow afternoon?

What can I do to stop Lou Houlihan from putting that godawful photograph in the papers? I don't care about Greene's reputation, but I damn well care about mine.

Who the hell is Edward Glott working for, anyway?

And, most important:

What's with Pete Kovacs? Is this date just a setup by the

Greene campaign? Or does he like me for real?

Kovacs placed a gin and tonic in front of me. A double.

"Do you at least want to talk about it? I'm a pretty good listener. For a guy, that is." He grinned, revealing his chipped front tooth.

Sure, you're cute in that Rough Rider outfit. And you've got fabulous hair. But I'm on to you and your ties to the Greene campaign.

But as far as I knew, Pete Kovacs had no connection to Nadine Bostwick. So I told Kovacs about my encounter with Lou Houlihan behind the camellia bushes. The photograph. And the threat: either I talk, or the photo gets in all the papers.

Kovacs nodded, then said, "Okay, this guy snaps a picture of you getting into the limousine with Senator Greene. Wearing a damn hot outfit." His gaze swept over me appreciatively. "But as long as you put the word out that you were dressed for a costume party and your meeting with Greene was strictly business, what's the big deal?"

"Two things. For one, I won't have a chance to tell my side of the story until Friday afternoon, well after this garbage has hit the morning papers. And get this: Houlihan claims to have a friend at one of the wire services who owes him a big favor. This friend is allegedly going to make sure the caption says the photograph was taken in front of the Experience Motel."

"Asshole!" Kovacs slammed down his bottle of Coors. "Where the hell is Houlihan?"

"I already made a deal with him."

"You did what?"

"I got him to agree to give me until midnight to decide what to do. I'm supposed to meet him back in the corner behind the camellia bushes at midnight. Alone," I emphasized.

"What are you planning to do between now and then?"

"Damned if I know."

"You could tell him to go screw himself, I suppose."

"I tried that already. He didn't take the hint."

"You could sue."

I reminded Kovacs that as public figures, Greene and I

would have a hard time proving we'd been libeled. "Anyway, it would take months to sort it out in court."

Kovacs tipped the bottle to his lips, swallowed, and gazed at the bandstand. "As I get it, your basic problem is that Houlihan has this photo of you getting into Jeff Greene's limousine at around nine o'clock this evening. A photo that could be taken the wrong way, depending on what kind of spin this wire service guy puts on it."

"Exactly."

"No one saw you come back. Houlihan tells you no one's seen anything of Jeff Greene for the rest of the evening. The assumption will be that you and Greene spent the night together. What if we can absolutely and positively establish in front of all three network affiliates that you were with me at eleven o'clock this evening."

I drummed my fingernails against my glass. "What do you have in mind?"

Kovacs smiled wickedly. "Just let me find the boys in the band."

The boys in the band would, of course, love the idea. So would Helen Hudson, the has-been-who-never-was cabaret singer. The only person who would have any reservations would be Shauna J. Bogart.

"Guys, guys!" I sat back in the wrought-iron chair, folded my arms, and scowled at the night sky. "I appreciate the thought. But I'm a radio personality. I perform in a closed studio. I don't do live audiences."

Kovacs stood with five men dressed in various interpretations of the Rough Rider costume. "My band is scheduled to play from eleven to midnight. All the TV stations are going to be doing live shots from the Jazz Band Ball for the eleven o'clock news. All you have to do is appear with the band."

"No way you could be makin' whoopie with Jeff Greene if you're boogyin' with the band," the trumpet player said. "Live and direct on the eleven o'clock news."

"I appreciate the thought, but I don't know."

"It's brilliant," Kovacs said. "Don't try to tell me you can't talk before an audience. You're on the radio every day. It's all showbiz."

"She's probably afraid appearing with us will ruin her reputation," the banjo player said. He was around thirty years old and sported a discreet diamond earring. "How's she going to burn a banjo on her show tomorrow afternoon after she's caught hangin' out with the boys of Dixieland tonight?"

I was afraid, that much was true. One of the most painful memories out of my childhood surrounded the summer Helen Hudson decided it might give her sagging career a jump-start if she developed a mother/daughter act. I was supposed to be the cute and precocious daughter. Shirley Temple, I wasn't. Not even Deanna Durbin. I was shy, clumsy, and plain. Even then, my hair clung to my head in limp frizz.

"C'mon, sweetie, at least try," my mother would whisper from backstage. "Project, honey, project. And smile, for God's sake!"

Mother finally gave up the evening I tossed my cookies all over the drummer's shoes right after Helen Hudson and her little daughter finished a duet to "My Heart Belongs to Daddy." To this day, I avoid all commitments that require appearing onstage before a live audience.

Kovacs crouched so his eyes would be level with mine. "We'll take good care of you, I promise. All you need to do is go out there and introduce our numbers. Just pretend you're back in the studio introducing one of your guests. And look at your audience." He swept his arm to indicate the hundreds of cheerful, enthusiastic party-goers. "They'll be with you all the way. And so will I."

So I said I'd do it.

We moved from the table to a roped-off area between the back of the stage and the vine-covered brick wall. The guys in the band fiddled with reeds and oil and all that musician stuff, while Kovacs pulled his dark hair back and secured it with a rubber band. I said, "Channel 3 plans to do their weather live from the Jazz Band Ball, so that'll be around 11:20. I'll bet 10 and 13 will save this for their closing story. It's fluff and it gives them terrific footage for rolling closing credits.

"Just as long as we keep it clean," I added.

"Oh, man!" the banjo player protested.

"No asking me to bake your jellyroll, okay, guys? The local TV stations may not have much in the way of standards, but I do."

Pete Kovacs was right. The audience roared in approval when I walked past the piano on my way to center stage, head up, shoulders back, swinging the cordless mike carelessly. "Break a leg," Kovacs whispered.

I stood at center stage, smiled, and waited for the applause to die down. I used the moment to take a deep breath and focus, just like I do every afternoon at the radio station. Slip into the Shauna J. Bogart character. Me, but vibrant, bright. Me in makeup, upswept and sophisticated hairdo, satin and sequins and glittery, jangly jewelry.

Jeez. All these years, I'd been imagining myself as Helen Hudson, all tarted up for her cabaret act.

The Channel 3 live cam focused full on center stage. "Thanks for coming out here tonight," I spoke confidently into the mike and focused on the cheerful faces below me. "I'm Shauna J. Bogart from Sacramento Talk Radio, your emcee for the next set. Now, let's hear it for the Hot Times Dixieland Band!"

Well done, baby. Well done. I'm proud of you, sweetie.

I don't know where those memories of Helen Hudson came from. Positive, helpful. All I know is, I'm awfully glad she was there when I needed her the most.

The Channel 3 live cam cut away to an interview with the executive director of the Jazz Jubilee just as the rest of the band tossed it to Pete Kovacs on piano.

This was the first chance I'd had to actually hear him play. About a third of the way through his solo, he abandoned the familiar melody of "Sweet Georgia Brown" and segued into something classical. Rachmaninoff, I think. From that, his fingers merged into "The Entertainer," then "Rhapsody in Blue." He even threw in some Jerry Lee Lewis riffs before romping back to "Sweet Georgia Brown."

I know, it's only Dixieland, but I like it. I like it.

Just as I predicted, the other two network affiliates held

their live shots from the Jazz Band Ball to the close of the eleven o'clock newscast. The Channel 10 and Channel 13 live cams were both focused on center stage as I introduced the sentimental old tearjerker, "Rose of Washington Square." I walked slowly to the upright piano and leaned on the side, sultry and provocative. Just like Helen Hudson in her night-club act.

I guess I didn't distract Kovacs, because I didn't hear any clunkers. But when the number ended, he told the audience, "I've always dreamed of performing with a gorgeous gal draped over the piano. Just like in the old movies. Isn't she terrific? Let's hear it for Shauna J. Bogart!"

"And Mom," I said to myself.

The TV stations packed up their gear and departed around 11:45, just as I introduced the band's second set. This time we got to do the good old-fashioned dirty songs: "You've Been a Good Old Wagon (But You Done Broke Down)," "I Got What It Takes (But It Breaks My Heart to Give It Away)," even the one about baking his jellyroll. 'Round midnight, we finished the set with "Ain't Misbehavin'."

I dedicated it to Lou Houlihan.

The party climaxed with a rousing rendition of "When the Saints Go Marching In" at around one in the morning. Kovacs and I decided to walk back to my apartment. He'd left Parnassus in the parking slot he rents by the month in back of the State Railroad Museum. A good two and a half blocks away from the Firehouse. It wasn't much more of a hike back to my place.

"I had a terrific time tonight," Kovacs said as we walked along the grassy median strip running down Capitol Mall. The normally bustling avenue was deserted at this hour of the night. Even the traffic signals had been turned off. The only illumination came from the white wedding-cake dome of the State Capitol at the east end of the mall and the streamlined modern Tower Bridge spanning the Sacramento River at the opposite end.

"Get outta here." I walked barefoot and carried the loathsome heels. I was probably ruining ten bucks' worth of seamed stockings, but at this point, who cared? I longed for my Tevas, but they were stashed in my backpack. Which was, in turn, stashed in Pete Kovacs's van. Oh, well. It would give me an excuse to call him in the morning.

"What 'get out of here'? I had a great time with you." Kovacs draped an arm around my shoulders.

"First I desert you for over an hour to run off with Jeff Greene. Then you have to rescue me from Lou Houlihan. You call that a good time?"

"I don't know when I've had so much fun. You were terrific with the band. We may have to find a place for you as our regular emcee."

"There's something I need to ask you," I said as we stepped onto the sidewalk of Third Street. We were just a block away from the spot where the squirrel had saved my life the previous evening.

"Okay." But Kovacs's voice sounded less confident. Probably thinking I'm going to ask about herpes. Or worse.

"Are you really working for Jeff Greene?"

"Oh, is that it? Sure, I'm supporting Senator Greene. I support a lot of causes I believe in. Just call me the last of the lefties."

"Why Greene?"

"Mostly because he's a liberal who also seems to have some understanding of business and the challenges facing the business community. Especially those of us trying to run a small retail establishment."

He tightened his grip on my shoulder. "I'm not part of his inner circle or anything like that. You've probably seen more of Jeff Greene these past few weeks than I have. Why do you ask?"

"No big deal. Just wondering."

Do I invite him in? I'm not the kind of gal who has sex on the first date. Well, not since the early eighties. So, what's the expected ritual for a first date these days? You like the guy and want to see him again. But it's too early to let him see you naked. Do you let it go with just a kiss good night at the front door and a promise to give you a call?

I was so preoccupied, I almost forgot about Edward Glott.

I detoured Kovacs to the P Street entrance to Capital Square, up to the third-floor walkway. The same vantage point where I'd watched Glott pace in front of my front door the night before.

No Glott. But in his place, the two officers who'd guarded the entrance to The Firehouse earlier this evening. The bulked-up white female. And the chunky black female. Cagney and Lacey. Carrying heat.

Glott would have expected me to return in the same van I departed in. I clutched Kovacs's hand and led him along the third-floor walkway until we overlooked the passenger loading zone on the N Street side of Capital Square. The unmistakable avocado shape leaned against a RENTALS AVAILABLE sign.

Now what was I going to do?

"I'll walk you past those gals at your door and make sure you get safely inside. No problem," Kovacs said in a whisper.

"You don't understand," I whispered back. I could have spit directly onto Glott's Smokey Bear hat. "These guys play for keeps. I think they're the ones who killed Dr. Hipster. They've put Monty Rio in the intensive care unit and they tried to do a number on me last night."

I backed slowly away from Edward Glott, careful not to make any noise.

"What the hell is this all about, really?" Kovacs spoke softly, but I could sense the suspicion in his voice. I didn't blame him. Had the tables been turned, I would have chalked up this evening to another date from hell, one of Glory Lou's NAFLE.

"Let's just get out of here. I'll explain later."

"What are you planning to do if you can't go home?" Kovacs walked on tiptoes in his boots.

"I'm not sure. The Holiday Inn is close. Maybe I'll see if they've got a vacancy."

"You could spend the night at my place."

After the comfortable clutter of the store, Pete Kovacs's "place" was a surprise. Where Retro Alley was chock-a-block with kitsch from the fifties, sixties, and seventies, not to mention the upright piano, his living space was stark and spartan. It was also directly above the store.

Kovacs held the door open for me and switched on the light. A vast, empty space took up almost the entire second floor. Inexpensive, minimalist furniture huddled at the windows overlooking Second Street: futon, chest of drawers, dining table, two director's chairs. Fine decorating by Cost Plus. A small TV perched on the round, blond wood dining table. A nook housed a miniature kitchen with a two-burner stove, a microwave, a small sink, and a fridge big enough to hold a couple of six-packs and maybe some leftover pizza.

I don't know why I'd said yes to Kovacs's invitation. I was tired, tired and scared. And still feeling the buzz from the glass of wine in Jeff Greene's limo and that double gin and tonic. I didn't totally trust Pete Kovacs. But I didn't know where else to turn.

And he did promise me a guest room and a clean toothbrush.

"They let you live above the store?" I walked slowly through the empty, loftlike space, my stockinged feet echoing on bare, hardwood floors.

"It's not zoned residential. But the landlord doesn't care, long as I pay the rent on time."

He led me into the guest room. "I set this up for my daughter when she comes out to visit. Now that Claire's all grown up, she doesn't make the trip very often. She has her own life now." He sounded wistful.

The guest room, at least, showed some signs of life. A real bed, not just a futon, with a cheery madras spread. Framed Ansel Adams posters on the wall and a bowl of potpourri on the nightstand. I picked up an eight-by-ten color photograph from the top of a small student desk. Pete Kovacs, standing next to a petite teenager with long dark hair. It looked like they were on the ferry to Martha's Vineyard.

"Here, you can sleep in this." Kovacs tossed me a T-shirt, size XL, bearing the logo of something called the San Francisco Antiquarian Book Fair. He also handed me a sealed plastic pouch filled with toiletries. Something you'd pick up in first class on an overseas flight. At least, he'd come through on the guest room and the clean toothbrush.

I can't remember the last time I'd felt more awkward or ill at ease.

"You'll find a bathrobe on a hook on the bathroom door. Oh, yeah. There should be a set of clean towels in the cupboard under the sink."

I nodded.

"Look," Kovacs said. "I know this is awkward. I didn't plan for the evening to end like this." He laughed briefly. "Well, maybe once or twice. But you know what I mean."

I laughed too, glad the ice had finally been broken.

I finished up in the bathroom and turned down the madras spread on the guest bed. The Antiquarian Book Fair T-shirt hung well past my hips. The cotton felt blissfully soft and comfortable, a welcome relief from the surgical tape that had lifted and sculpted my boobs all evening.

I heard the sounds of a bathroom faucet being shut off, footsteps heading toward the futon, and the snapping of a light switch.

He seems like a nice guy. Too good to be true?

I lifted the straight-back chair that went with Claire Kovacs's student desk and lugged it to the guest-room door. Careful, so as not to scrape it against the floor. I was about to jam the chair under the doorknob, just in case. Then I remembered something.

I opened the door, leaned against the frame, and gazed across the empty, darkened vastness of Pete Kovacs's living quarters. A faint square of light from Second Street filtered through the curtained window onto the futon.

"You asleep?" I asked.

A grunt, unintelligible, came from the futon.

"I almost forgot to tell you something."

Another grunt, but this time it sounded affirmative.

"Thank you for inviting me. I had a really good time with you tonight."

24

A garbage truck rumbling down Second Street woke me with a jolt. 6:56 A.M., according to the alarm clock on the night-stand.

I sat up, groggy and confused. How did I end up in a strange bed, wearing a T-shirt promoting a festival for eccentric book collectors?

Then I saw the ruddy scab covering the scrape on the palm of my hand and I remembered. Dr. Hipster. The election for governor, Monty Rio, Edward Glott's goons guarding my apartment. T. R. and Terrence O'Brien involved, not sure how. And Pete Kovacs.

Jeff Greene—possibly the next governor of California—is going to be a guest on my show this afternoon. An interview that could be crucial to his career. And to mine. This could turn out to be an interesting day.

I scurried into the bathroom and did the toothbrush/shower routine as quickly and quietly as I could, wrapped my dripping hair in a towel and my bod in a burgundy terry-cloth bathrobe, and tiptoed out of the bathroom.

"Good morning!"

Damn. He was already awake, dressed, and seated at the dining table. All bright and cheery.

I made a show of yawning. "Don't you ever sleep?"

"Not during Jubilee weekend. It only comes once a year and it's way too much fun to waste time sleeping. I can always sleep next week."

He'd already made coffee, bless his heart, and toasted a couple of sourdough bagels from Trader Joe's. He'd also brought in the morning papers.

I dove into the *Bee*, searching for Lou Houlihan's incriminating photograph. Nothing. The only photo relating to the campaign was on the front page, below the fold. A smiling Nadine Bostwick, clasping both hands over her head at a rally at a shopping mall in the San Fernando Valley.

"It might be a little early for that photo of you to hit the papers." Kovacs calmly sipped his coffee. "Midnight's a pretty late deadline for most of the morning papers."

"After this afternoon, it'll be too late," I said. "Jeff Greene's appearance on my show will make Lou Houlihan and his stupid photograph old news."

I seated myself in a director's chair and helped myself to a buttered bagel, while Kovacs picked up the Metro section and resumed his reading. Me in a bathrobe and the old man dressed for work, reading the paper and drinking coffee around the breakfast table, just like an old married couple.

A boom box on the kitchen counter was tuned to Larry and Ron, my station's morning team. Larry Morgan, the loudmouth right-wing jokester and Ron Sebastian, the straight-man sidekick. According to Larry 'n' Ron, we should expect record crowds for the opening day of the Jazz Jubilee. As well as temperatures creeping back into the nineties and a second-stage smog alert, thanks to a big forest fire outside of Placerville. Topping the headlines for this hour, Nadine Bostwick moves up another notch in the polls.

A noise caused me to bolt forward in my director's chair, sloshing coffee onto the front page of the *Bee*. What the hell? A band playing right outside the window?

Kovacs barely raised his eyes from the newspaper. "Why don't you go out to the balcony and check it out?"

I wrapped the bathrobe around myself tighter and double-checked the knot on the sash. Just to make sure I wasn't going to flash any garbagemen who might still be working Second Street. I opened the door leading to the balcony and stepped outside into the hazy morning sunshine.

The lively strains of "Panama" reached hell-raising levels.

The band wasn't on Pete Kovacs's balcony. It was, however, camped out on the balcony belonging to the building next door. Along with Larry 'n' Ron, their producer, the engineer, and two tables full of electronic equipment.

I'd forgotten all about the live broadcast of the morning show.

I leaped back through the door. But not fast enough.

"Wasn't that our own Shauna J. Bogart on the balcony next door?" I heard Ron ask Larry through the tinny speaker on Kovacs's boom box. Larry replied, "I think you're right, Ron. Someone needs to tell her this isn't a pajama party." Yuck, yuck. "And speaking of the cat's pajamas, let's hear it for The Cats and Jammers Dixieland Band. Wasn't it terrific of them to stop by?" Ron said it certainly was terrific. "At 7:36, this is Sacramento Talk Radio, checking in with Captain Mikey in the traffic chopper. Then stay tuned as we read another lucky number in the Gold Rush Giveaway. The next winner could be you . . ."

Kovacs still had his head buried in the newspaper. But I could see him holding back a smile, damn him.

"Cut that out, and help me find something to wear. I'm not going to miss this opportunity to plug the show." I couldn't see zipping myself back into the *Ain't Misbehavin'* dress in the harsh glare of the morning light, like a high-class hooker after a particularly profitable night.

Kovacs loaned me a Celtics sweatshirt and a pair of jeans that didn't fit too badly. A little tight in the hips and loose in the waist, and I had to roll up the cuffs. I would have cheerfully performed the sex act of Kovacs's choice in return for a set of fresh underwear, but I was much too embarrassed to say anything. Anyway, if Pete Kovacs had a collection of ladies' lingerie stashed away someplace, I, for one, did not want to know about it.

He reached under the dining table. "I thought you might be needing this." He handed me my backpack.

"My Tevas!" I grabbed the bag and gleefully pulled out a pair of clunky sandals.

This was turning out to be a very good day indeed.

I could practically have jumped from Kovacs's balcony into

Larry Morgan's lap. The railings on both balconies were only around hip high and a gap of maybe a foot separated the two buildings.

"Are you crazy?" Kovacs said when he caught me with one leg slung over the decorative railing. "You could get hurt doing that."

He escorted me downstairs, through the darkened display space of Retro Alley, then next door, past the radio station van parked in front, up the stairs of the ice-cream parlor. The couple who owned the creamery had already opened, and several early birds scarfed up Larry 'n' Ron specials. Lots of whipped cream and nuts, from what I could see. Kovacs directed me up the stairs to the second floor and into a room filled with brightly colored balloons, streamers, clown posters, and video games. A private room for kids' birthday parties. Mercifully, it was not in use.

The party room led to the balcony, where Larry 'n' Ron were just making the transition out of the eight o'clock network newscast.

"Shauna J. Bogart! Welcome aboard. To what do we owe this honor?" Larry gushed. He was around forty, bearded and blue-jeaned. Ron Sebastian, a dozen years younger, believed in the dignity of the news. As always, he wore a suit, white shirt, and tie.

In addition to shamelessly plugging my show, my impromptu appearance with Larry 'n' Ron gave me a chance to check out the remote. Prep myself on what was in store for me up on the balcony this afternoon.

Two folding tables in an "L" shape. The host and guests faced Second Street, while the engineer and his gear sat on a table facing Pete Kovacs's balcony. Along with the ubiquitous pot of coffee and pink bakery box of donuts, without which no morning show would survive.

Wires, cables, and telephone lines, neatly bunched in conduit connectors, ran along the table legs and over the balcony to the radio station van on Second Street. I was glad to see the engineering staff had installed a cart machine and had brought a box full of tape cartridges containing sounders and theme music. I like to be in control. A printout of the program log showed the times of commercial spots the board operator would be playing back at the station. A laptop computer provided a communications link between the producer and the board op. Either Larry or Ron had fashioned a hood out of a manila file folder to shade the laptop's screen from the already blazing sun.

I'd promised Jeff Greene I wouldn't say anything about our conversation in the limo until this afternoon. But he didn't say I couldn't promote his upcoming appearance. "Senator Greene is coming on my show this afternoon," I said into the guest mike.

"Terrific! What are you planning to talk about?"

"You'll have to tune in and find out."

"Sounds killer!"

Sounds killer. Didn't Dr. Hipster use similar words in his last on-air promo? Plugging a show about the election for governor. A show he never got to do. I shuddered inwardly.

Larry 'n' Ron waited for me to say something. Lord knows, we can't have any dead air. "Yeah. Should be killer." I pushed my chair away from the guest mike.

Then I noticed the message scrolling across the laptop screen.

Rudy from West Sacramento on Line One.

"We have a caller on Line One," I said, interrupting before Larry could move on to the next segment in the show. "Rudy from West Sacramento, I believe."

"Good morning." The phony accent again.

"Rudy, what's on your mind this morning?"

"I am wanting to give you my congratulations. For having Senator Jeff Greene on your show, I mean."

"Gee, thanks, Rudy."

"I am wondering. Will you be talking about Dr. Hipster?"

So far, I'd not actually come out on my show and said I thought there was a connection between the Greene for Governor campaign and the death of Dr. Hipster. I paused for a minute, then said as lightly as I could, "You'll have to tune in and find out."

"That I will do. But this I want you to remember. The blue door."

"*Live at The Blue Door*, you mean? Helen Hudson's record?"

But Rudy from West Sacramento was gone. I might have known.

I retraced my steps through the party room, down to the ice-cream parlor, and along the wooden boardwalk to Retro Alley. Pete Kovacs sat at his desk, counting change in the cash drawer. He'd brought the boom box from upstairs along with him.

Kovacs looked up. "I hate to be a rude host, but I'm going to be pretty busy today. I promised to set up chairs at The Firehouse lot this morning. The band's going to be in the parade, and we've got a set at four at Turntable Junction."

"No problem." I could take a hint. "I'll just go upstairs and get my backpack and stuff and be out of your hair pronto."

The dress I placed on a hanger I'd found in the guest-room closet, while all the other junk—stockings, shoes, jewelry—got shoved in the backpack. I emptied the evening bag of important stuff like my wallet and keys into the backpack.

"I could give you a ride," Pete said.

"Don't worry about me. I know this is a big weekend for you. I'm just wondering, is it okay if I leave the dress behind the counter 'til I can pick it up later?"

"Of course. My assistant will be watching the store for most of the day today. I'll leave her a note."

Larry Morgan gave the eight-thirty time check. The sound on Pete Kovacs's boom box turned to fuzz. Static. Dead air.

I placed my backpack on the glass case housing the first editions. I twirled the dial and heard a collage of competing stations, loud and clear. So the boom box wasn't out of order.

There are few things more serious to a radio station than being off the air. If the listeners can't find their favorite station, even for a few minutes, they'll punch up someone else's station. You may never get them back. Not to mention the advertising revenue that's lost for good for every minute the station is silent. If you're off the air, you're dead.

I grabbed my backpack. "See you later, okay?"

Kovacs looked up from a pile of mail that he'd been sorting. "Listen, if you want to use my place during the Jubilee, feel free. You know, if you need a place to crash for a few hours, or just a clean rest room with no lines."

One minute he's giving me the heave-ho, now he's turning into a glommer. "Sure thing." I was one foot out the door.

"See you 'round this weekend, then."

I was panting by the time I'd run back through the ice-cream parlor and up the stairs to the remote. "Why are we off the air?" I demanded as soon as I saw the engineer.

Brandon Nguyen's young face was creased with concern. "The problem's back at the transmitter, not here at the remote. I called the station. They're working on it."

"Any idea what the problem is?"

Nguyen shook his head. "SMUD's been doing some work out in our neighborhood the past few days. Maybe they cut a cable."

"Wouldn't the backup generator kick in?"

"It should," the engineering assistant agreed.

Nothing I could do. I slung my backpack over one shoulder and hiked back to Capital Square, dodging the tail end of the commute traffic.

Cagney and Lacey were not camped in front of my apartment door. But Edward Glott was. Along with Rudolf Wolinsky, allegedly a.k.a. Rudy from West Sacramento. Both wore the uniform of the Capital Square private security force.

From my aerie on the third-floor walkway, I watched Glott converse briefly with Wolinsky, then turn and walk away. Wolinsky leaned against the door of my apartment.

I didn't know what else to do, so I trudged back to Old Sacramento. CLOSED sign on the door to Kovacs's store. Just to be sure, I tried the lock. Closed, for sure. A smaller sign informed me that Retro Alley would open at ten-thirty, a good hour away.

I crossed Second Street and peered at the balcony over the ice-cream parlor. I could see Brandon Nguyen talking into the telephone linking the remote with the station, and I didn't hear any air sounds coming from the speakers mounted on top of the station van. Not a good sign.

Warren Harriman let me use a telephone in the Jubilee media trailer. I reached Glory Lou at home. "Can you come down to Old Sacramento and pick me up? Oh, yeah. One more thing. Stop by my apartment and check on the cat."

"Consider it done, sugar. I won't even ask why you spent the night in Old Sacramento."

I made three more calls. One to the station, to see if Mrs. Yanamoto had heard anything from T. R. I got a recording in Junior's Big-time Radio Announcer voice informing me the business offices of Sacramento Talk Radio were closed for the Memorial Day weekend.

The second call was to T. R.'s house. I got the same maddening recording I'd been listening to these past three days.

Finally, I called the Med Center and asked about Monty Rio. Still no change.

I sat cross-legged on the grass in the shadow of the Pony Express statue to wait for Glory Lou. A life-size bronze horse and rider, frozen in time, paid tribute to the romance and danger of the Old West. The news car pulled up twenty minutes after I'd called.

Glory Lou held out a section of newspaper between her thumb and index finger as soon as I piled into the car. It was a front page of the *Sacramento Bee* from a week ago Wednesday. "Greene-Bostwick Race Too Close to Call."

"I found this at the bottom of the cat box when I stopped by your apartment to check on Bialystock. He's fine, by the way."

It was the last *Bee* Dr. Hipster would ever read.

"Look inside," Glory Lou said. "Don't worry. These are the bottom layers. It should be clean."

I gingerly opened the newsprint and found a Ziploc plastic bag between two pages of the sports section. The bag contained a manila file folder. On the tab, in Dr. Hipster's unmistakable spidery hand, were three words. The Blue Door.

25

"Not one mention of Jeff Greene?" Glory Lou asked as she piloted the news car down H Street, away from Old Sacramento. "Are you sure?"

"Absolutely." I was back in my usual spot in the front passenger seat. The contents of Dr. Hipster's Blue Door file were spread across my knees and the dash.

An eight-by-ten black-and-white photograph. A three-by-five card with a lucky number from the Gold Rush Giveaway contest. One newspaper clipping. One fax. Three lined sheets torn from a reporter's notebook. Five stapled pages of e-mail printouts, dated two weeks previous, between Dr. Hipster and someone whose signature line was Judith Lowenthal, senior vice president at Ratings, Revenue, and Research.

"The first one's from this Judith Lowenthal to Dr. Hipster," I read aloud to Glory Lou:

" 'Been thinking about you a lot lately and hope all is going well with your show. I want to share some news that I'm sure will be of interest. Officially, you didn't hear it from me, but I just got the final report of a research project Triple R is doing in Sacramento. It involves your station, and it's going to come down within the next two weeks. Can't go into detail, but it means you'll be looking for work. I know of a talk station in New Orleans that's looking for someone just like you. I've already put in a good word and sent them one of your airchecks.' "

"Holy mother of God," Glory Lou said. "T. R. was going to fire Dr. Hipster?"

"Not just him. All of us," I said. "Dig this, what Dr. Hipster wrote back to Judith Lowenthal.

" *'Hey, thanks for thinking of the old Hipster. The Big Easy could be a trip. You sure my station's changing format?'* "

"Did she write anything back?"

"Yep."

" *'You know me. Nothing happens at Triple R without Judith Lowenthal knowing about it. In fact, I just got off the phone with Terrence O'Brien Jr. putting together the final details to sign up the new syndicated programming. So take my advice and send that tape and résumé to New Orleans as soon as you can. And if you've got any close friends at the station, you might want to give them a heads-up.'* "

"Junior is putting this thing together?" Glory Lou was so engrossed in my recitation of the e-mails that she didn't notice the traffic signal at Sixteenth and H had turned green until the driver of the car behind us pounded the horn.

"So it would appear." I flipped to the next page. "Nothing else, really. Just Dr. Hipster thanking Lowenthal for thinking of him, and Lowenthal saying anytime, after he was so helpful to her when she was breaking into the business."

I shuffled the e-mails to the back of the pile of papers on my knees and studied the photograph, an eight-by-ten black-and-white glossy showing four men seated in a booth at a nightclub. They grinned jubilantly and raised their cocktail glasses in a toast. Judging from the clothing—wide ties and lapels—and the advertising posters for Old Gold cigarettes in the background, the photo dated to the mid-fifties. The corners were creased, but otherwise, the relic was bright and fresh.

I didn't need to read the black fountain pen signature in the bottom margin to identify one of the men making that long-ago toast. Cowboy hat and boots. And the hook. I wouldn't have recognized Neil Vermont, though, without the hand-lettered caption. The Neil Vermont who smiled at me across forty-plus years was slender, with a full head of dark hair styled in an elaborate pompadour. Today, he was bald and roly-poly.

The caption identified the remaining figures as Grant Simmerhorn and Wallace W. Wilson III.

The four original partners in Golden Empire Broadcasting. The Korean War buddies who pooled their savings to invest in a radio station.

The crisp, browned newspaper clipping bore a date in the mid-fifties. Kirt MacBride's column, from the old *Sacramento Union.* "Welcome to a newcomer on the Sacramento radio dial! Neil Vermont, T. R. O'Brien, Wally Wilson, and Grant Simmerhorn have emerged from their favorite booth at The Blue Door long enough to buy the Mutual Broadcasting affiliate. Warren Harriman will stay on as news director, but otherwise it promises to be a whole new sound. T. R. O'Brien will handle the day-by-day operation of the station, 'til further notice. . . ."

I fingered the three sheets of lined paper with the ragged top edges where they'd been torn from a spiral-bound notebook. Dr. Hipster's wispy handwriting, dated the day before his death and bearing the phone number and Capitol Mall address of Capital City Ventures.

The second sheet contained nothing but a column of numbers. The numbers varied, but always started with the same notation: 7:20 A.M.

Twenty minutes after seven in the morning. The moment when, according to the consultants who study such things, more folks are tuned to the radio than any other time of day. The golden moment for contests, promotional pitches, and can't-miss features like Paul Harvey. The first airing of the day for the Gold Rush Giveaway.

The fax had been sent from the station to Dr. Hipster's apartment and carried a date in early May.

" *'Thanks for sharing the shot of me and the boys from back in the Stone Age. It brought back a lot of memories. Stop by my office and I'll show you the original Blue Door contract. T. R.'* "

"Why did he send a fax, I wonder?" Glory Lou said as she accelerated onto Highway 160.

"You ever try calling Dr. Hipster at home in the middle of the day? Ninety percent of the time, he'd have the line tied up in one of his chat rooms on the Internet. Sometimes, I'd wait for hours to get through."

"Lordy. Hasn't T. R. ever heard of e-mail?"

I didn't answer. I was wondering about something else. What were T. R. O'Brien and Neil Vermont really doing when they were supposed to be fishing in Alaska?

Sacramento Talk Radio is hunkered down in a newish office complex off Highway 160, near Cal Expo and the Arden Faire shopping mall. Though it lacks the sex appeal of a Capitol Mall high-rise address, it's a perfect location for a broadcast news operation. Our reporters have a ten-minute drive, max, to the downtown government offices without the rest of the staff having to deal with the daily grind of downtown parking and traffic. Our broadcast tower and transmitter shack is maybe a quarter mile away, near the banks of the American River.

Glory Lou and I pulled into the almost-deserted station parking lot ten minutes after leaving Old Sacramento. A Volvo sedan that I didn't recognize as belonging to any of the station employees was the only other vehicle in the parking lot.

"Ms. Bogart? Shauna J.?"

I tensed, then recognized the voice of Lily McGovern. The environmental lobbyist emerged from the shade of a camellia bush next to· the front door and walked toward the news car. This morning, she wore a pantsuit the color of orange sherbet. A shade darker, and she risked being mistaken for an escapee from the Sacramento County lockup.

She carried a nine-and-a-half-by-eleven brown envelope.

"I waited for you as long as I could last night," I said. It was all I could do to keep from snatching the envelope out of her hand and tearing it open.

"I got trapped in an important hearing of the Senate Natural Resources Committee and then got stuck in traffic. I didn't get here 'til six-thirty. I waited a half hour until it became obvious you'd already left. I'm so sorry."

"Hey, no worries." This could work out to my advantage. If Lily McGovern's envelope contained what I hoped it did,

I'd have fresh ammunition to use in the interview with Greene this afternoon.

I got rid of McGovern as tactfully as I could, making one more promise to keep Earth Guardians out of the picture, then rushed into the station. I didn't even bother going all the way to my desk. Just plopped down on the rust-colored vinyl couch in the lobby, ripped open one end of the envelope, and poured the contents out onto the couch.

After five minutes of scanning, I knew McGovern had come through. It was all here: faxes, e-mails, letters, phone message slips. All from Senator Greene's office, all urging Earth Guardians' cooperation in allowing a glitzy high-rise casino on an achingly beautiful rocky point along the rugged and pristine Big Sur coastline.

I might be filing for unemployment insurance and sending out tapes and résumés by Tuesday morning, but in the meantime, I was going to have one helluva last show.

As long as the station signed back on the air by three.

I shoved McGovern's documents back into the envelope and stuffed it into my backpack. Glory Lou and I piled back into News Unit 5. I directed her to the back of the building, to a dirt road. She ground it into second as the news car clambered slowly over a packed earth berm protecting the station from the American River floodplain.

"I can't believe you've never been out to the transmitter," I said. "How long have you worked here?"

"Too busy getting out the news. Anyway, I'm not fascinated by all that techie stuff like you are, hon."

The news car crunched over gravel and came to a stop in front of a gunmetal-gray Quonset hut with an air-conditioning unit chugging away on top. It was raised on blocks to protect it from the floodwaters that swept the banks of the American River every decade or so. The shack didn't look like much, but inside I knew I'd find the five-thousand kilowatt transmitter that amped our air sound and sent it to hundreds of thousands of listeners from the Oregon border and beyond, depending on the skip. Our three-hundred-foot tower loomed behind the Quonset hut, a giant-sized Erector set of gray-and-orange steel girders and guy wires. It was the tallest structure within the city limits.

Terrence O'Brien emerged from the Quonset hut and blocked the door. An on-call engineer, even younger than Brandon Nguyen, tagged at his heels. Luke something-or-other. I'd met him once when he was helping out the broadcast engineering staff at a Sacramento Kings game. He looked uncomfortable, ill at ease. So did Terrence O'Brien.

Junior smoothed a scowl into something slightly more welcoming. "This isn't a good time to talk. We've got big trouble."

"That's why I'm here." I stepped out of the car and shut the door. "I thought you guys might need an extra hand."

"Thanks, but Luke and I are pretty close to getting the situation under control."

"I'm worried, too, about your father. I thought he was supposed to be back by this morning."

Junior shook his head. "What a comedy of errors. He finally gets a flight out of Seattle to San Francisco last night. Then SFO is fogged in and they land in San Jose. By now it's midnight. Father decided to stay the night in San Jose. The airline offered to fly him to Sacramento today, but he's ready to mutilate anyone connected with the airline industry at this point."

"I can well imagine." I could just picture T. R., red-faced, shaking his hook at some poor schmo behind the ticket counter.

"He rented a car and is driving back home this morning. I talked to him about an hour ago. He was just leaving San Jose."

I waved my arm at the tower. "Why are we off the air?"

Luke looked like he wanted to say something, but Junior cut him off. "Nothing major. Just blew a capacitor, that's all."

"When do you think you'll have us back up?"

"I was just on my way to go out and pick up a new part. Early afternoon at the latest, I would think. So you see," Junior said, smiling and stretching out his arms, "you have nothing to worry about."

"Yeah." I turned and opened the passenger door to the news

vehicle. Out of the corner of my eye, I watched Junior and Luke reenter the Quonset hut. They didn't lock the door.

I crept inside. It was eerie, without the flashing red lights, dancing meters, and electronic hum. I got as far as the front office before Luke spotted me and escorted me out, locking the door behind him.

But I did get a chance to watch Terrence O'Brien Jr. pick up the telephone, apparently continuing a conversation that Glory Lou and I had interrupted.

I could have sworn I heard him say something like ". . . hasn't a clue as to what this is really all about."

Glory Lou wanted to head back to Old Sacramento, just in case we were back on the air in time for live coverage of the Jazz Jubilee parade during the noon newscast. I couldn't think of anything better to do, so I tagged along, pretending to listen to the Limbaugh show on KFBK while sorting out my thoughts. Putting two and two together from what I'd already observed and discovered and getting not five, but a possible deadly scenario.

Dr. Hipster has visitors at the station after his show a week ago Tuesday evening. Edward Glott for sure. Wolinsky? I wasn't sure. They're wearing either real cop uniforms or the almost-identical garb of the Capital Square private security force. Didn't really matter. Dr. Hipster had seen them and their outfits often enough around his apartment building, so his guard is down.

The thugs demand Dr. Hipster turn over all his background material about the Greene campaign and agree to kill the story. Dr. Hipster stalls for time, records the promotional announcement with the coded message. "Don't touch that dial." He tells them the material they want is at his home, and agrees to turn it over the following morning. Knowing he's being watched, Dr. Hipster returns to his apartment and manages to stash The Blue Door file in the one place he hopes they'll never look: Bialystock's litter box.

Glott already knows Dr. Hipster kept a pistol inside his desk drawer. Probably let himself in with the passkey the pre-

vious evening, while Dr. Hipster was on the air, and conducted a quiet search. He takes the gun, fires a shot, places the gun in Dr. Hipster's right hand, and plants the phony note in the left.

Monty Rio's handiwork, at T. R.'s direction, to destroy the tapes with the promotional announcement, after it airs just once, guarantees that no one will be able to recall with any certainty Dr. Hipster's coded cry for help.

Until Rudy from West Sacramento screws things up for them by calling my show.

Why the hell would he call my show and blow the whole carefully constructed cover?

Who is Rudy from West Sacramento?

And, more to the point: What the hell does the stuff in The Blue Door file—an old picture and newspaper clipping and some e-mails of interest only to those in the industry—have to do with the election for governor?

What had I just overheard Junior saying? ". . . hasn't a clue as to what this is really all about"?

We drove past a Nadine Bostwick billboard as Highway 160 funneled into Twelfth Street, back into the downtown core. A melting pot of happy kids surrounded the silver-haired candidate. "A Vote for Your Future. And Theirs." The mid-morning temperature had already hit the high eighties. I could feel sweat trickling inside my borrowed jeans and sweatshirt. My hair, which I'd allowed to drip dry *au natural*, had started its little routine of simultaneously frizzing and matting.

I asked Glory Lou to drop me off at Downtown Plaza. "Thanks, I owe you one," I told her. "Oh, yeah. Could you stop by Pete's store and pick up my dress and take it back to your pals at the Music Circus?"

"Who was your slave before I came along, sweetie?" she said good-naturedly, pulling over into a red zone at Fifth and I Streets. "Go for it, girlfriend!"

I charged up a pair of tan cotton shorts, a teal-blue T-shirt, and—at last!—fresh underwear. I carted the shopping bag through the pedestrian tunnel under I-5, back to Old Sacramento, and elbowed my way through knots of T-shirted traditional jazz fans. A teenager toting a tuba and riding a skateboard almost knocked me down. At the Old Sacramento exit to the tunnel, a trio wearing knickers, argyle socks, striped shirts, and soft cloth newsboy caps played "Margie" on washboard, tuba, and banjo. They sounded peppy and cheerful, but they must have been sweltering in all that flannel and wool.

Mimi Blitzer had flung open the side doors of the Sacramento Talk Radio van. I spotted her pressing her precious sun visors into the hands of passersby. With the heat rising from the cobblestone street and wooden boardwalk, she didn't have trouble drumming up customers.

She frowned when she noticed me. "You're supposed to be wearing a station T-shirt. Didn't you read my memo?"

The promotion director was not only wearing the regulation T-shirt and sun visor, so help me, she even sported a pair of socks embroidered with the station call letters.

I spoke slowly and with great patience. "In case you haven't noticed, we're off the air."

"We'll be back soon, and meanwhile, the show must go on. We're still going to be in the parade. I went to a lot of trouble to borrow an antique flatbed truck. All of the rest of the air talent will be riding in the parade. I expect you to be there too."

"Sure thing, Mimi." Just to placate her, I grabbed one of the sun visors from the box. As I reached my hand into the van, I noticed a handful of white number ten envelopes rubberbanded and stashed in a corner of the box. The liner cards with the lucky numbers for today's Gold Rush Giveaway.

I snapped the elastic cord of the sun visor around my head and saluted Blitzer from the brim.

Back to the musty, cluttered confines of Retro Alley. I convinced Pete Kovacs's assistant to let me climb the stairs to the second floor. I was secretly glad to discover she was sixtyish and frumpy, sporting narrow reading glasses, hair styled in a short salt-and-pepper mop, and wearing a lumpy purple polyester jogging suit.

I found a steak knife in the top drawer of Kovacs's kitchenette, cut off the plastic price tags to my new duds, and changed quickly. I folded Kovacs's sweatshirt and jeans and left them in a neat pile on the futon. I sifted through my backpack and pulled out two eight-by-ten black-and-white photographs. T. R. O'Brien and his partners, back in the 1950s. Jeff Greene, Terrence O'Brien Jr., and the rest of The Farm Team graduates from eight years ago. I placed the two photos side by side on Kovacs's dining table.

Two different pictures, two different decades, two different sets of people. Connections? There was the father-and-son thing, of course. T. R. O'Brien and Terrence. I gazed at the father, grinning broadly and hoisting a cocktail glass from within a dimly lit booth in a 1950s nightclub. Then at the son, just another clean-cut yuppie in a double line of twenty or so similar young professionals.

Father and son. The father jubilant, celebrating the birth of his career. The son, cynical, going through the motions just to please the old man. Frozen in time, silently begging me to understand.

I slowly and carefully slid both photographs into my backpack and went out to find the one person who might have some answers.

26

"Where did you get this?"

Warren Harriman held the photo of the Golden Empire Broadcasting founders in both hands. His usual cheerful countenance remained unperturbed, but I could see two lines beginning to freeze around his mouth.

I stood inside the Jazz Jubilee media trailer. Outside, the temperature climbed and the crowds continued to pour into Old Sacramento, clogging the sidewalks in anticipation of the noon-hour parade that would mark the official opening of the four-day festival. Inside, an electric fan whirred and a radio blurted out the last hour of Rush Limbaugh. A portable television was tuned to Channel 3 with the sound off. Even with Limbaugh's nattering, the media trailer was a relatively cool and calm eye of the storm.

I'd run into Pete Kovacs on my half-block walk from Retro Alley to the media trailer. He wore jeans and his Hot Times Jazz Band T-shirt. The Panama hat with the Red Sox patch stitched to the band was back atop his long dark hair.

"Look for me and the band in the parade, okay?" he said with a wave. "We'll be riding in the Steve's Pizza truck."

"You said something to me last night about being the station's original news director," I said to Warren Harriman.

The Jubilee media coordinator rubbed his shiny round forehead. "I took this picture. How did you end up with it?"

I gave Warren Harriman the sanitized version: I was helping to clean out Dr. Hipster's apartment and found the photograph in his desk. I didn't say anything about finding the file hidden in the kitty litter box.

"Was this yours too?" I showed Harriman the *Sacramento Union* clipping.

Harriman carefully took the fragile browned piece of newsprint from my hands. "Kirt MacBride and I used to hang out at The Blue Door."

"What was The Blue Door contract, exactly?"

Harriman seated himself in a folding chair and gestured for me to do the same. "I was the news director at the station back when O'Brien, Vermont, Wilson, and Simmerhorn bought it. I was the only member of the original staff they kept on. They got the station for practically nothing, you understand, just chump change. TV was the new big thing back then and radio was dying."

"Or so everyone thought."

"You understand, the Korean War had just ended and these were four fellows in their early twenties, just glad to be alive and back in the states. No families, no responsibilities. I know. I felt exactly the same way when I came home from Guam back in '46. They used to get together almost every evening that summer at The Blue Door, just to drink a little, play some cards, listen to jazz."

"Then there really was a Blue Door!" I leaned forward in anticipation.

"Of course." Harriman smiled and closed his eyes, basking in the memory. "It started out as a speakeasy. In the thirties and forties, The Blue Door was one of the major jazz clubs on the West Coast. I saw Louis Armstrong there, Duke Ellington, Dinah Washington, Ella Fitzgerald, you name it, they all played The Blue Door."

"What happened?"

"Times change, neighborhoods change. They tore it down in 1968, to make way for I-5."

I briefly pictured my meeting with Dr. Hipster's son in front of a tract house in San Jose, and his comment that his dad had been curious about the legality of a contract signed some forty or fifty years ago. The Blue Door contract. "You were there the night T. R. O'Brien and his partners signed the Blue Door contract," I said to Harriman.

"They asked me to come over and take their picture. You have these four young men, their futures are ahead of them. They all had some savings. They figured, what the hell, let's pool our money and buy this little radio station, see if we can get rich. It was just a lark."

From outside, I heard the whup-whup of the TV news helicopters, getting in position for their live shots for the noon newscast.

"First they decide to buy the radio station. Then they have to find someone to actually run it."

"I think I've heard this part," I interrupted. "Didn't they cut the cards, with the guy holding the high card becoming the president and C.E.O.? T. R. O'Brien supposedly drew the ace of clubs with his hook."

"I don't know if that's exactly how it happened," Harriman said with a smile. "But basically you're correct. They cut the cards and T. R. O'Brien came out the winner. A couple of nights later, they put their agreement in writing. They got together with a lawyer, back at their favorite booth in The Blue Door. When they had it all signed and sealed, they called me to come down and take their picture."

"So you got to read the actual contract?" I tried to sound casual, to keep the anticipation out of my voice.

"No, I just heard rumors."

"I know T. R. O'Brien and Neil Vermont are still around." At least, I hoped so. "How about Wallace Wilson and Grant Simmerhorn?"

Harriman's cheery blue eyes grew somber. "We lost Grant Simmerhorn about ten years ago. Prostate cancer. Wally Wilson, now he got lucky. He invested in a ski resort up at Donner Summit, just before I-80 went through."

"Smart man."

"Wally always had good timing. He sold out at the right time, took the money and retired to Maui. Last I heard, he was playing golf every day."

"What's Neil Vermont's story, exactly? I know he's on the board of CalFac."

"He and Stas Kostantin grew up next door to each other. After Korea, when Vermont didn't have a whole lot of prospects, Kostantin gave him a job with his construction company. He rose within the ranks."

I picked up the photograph from Harriman's desk. "You say this is your stuff. Do you have any idea how Dr. Hipster might have ended up with it?"

Harriman scratched the soft white fuzz ringing his head. "I haven't actually looked at that picture in years. Or the Kirt MacBride clipping, for that matter. It must have been in that box of photographs I sold to Pete Kovacs."

I tensed at the mention of the name. "What box of photographs?"

"I used to collect autographed eight-by-tens. Back when I was news director, we used to have a lot of celebrities coming through the station. I ended up with some good stuff. Sinatra, Rosemary Clooney, Louis Armstrong, even Elvis. Politicians too, Nixon, Adlai Stevenson, LBJ, JFK when he was just a senator."

"Cool!"

"A couple of months ago, I decided to sell the collection. It really didn't mean that much to me personally these days, and I could use the money. So I took the whole box over to Pete Kovacs."

Warren Harriman sells a box of autographed photographs of entertainers and political figures to Pete Kovacs. Maybe he didn't go through the box too carefully before he handed it over to Kovacs. Maybe, stuck between Jack Paar and Pier Angeli, Kovacs finds the eight-by-ten of T. R. O'Brien, Neil Vermont, and their partners inside The Blue Door nightclub. Along with the Kirt MacBride clipping.

A month or so later, Kovacs has an appointment to appraise Dr. Hipster's collection of rock memorabilia. Maybe he recognizes the names on the photograph and newspaper clipping as having something to do with Dr. Hipster's radio station and takes them along. Maybe he figures Dr. Hipster might have some idea if it held any historic significance.

"Listen, I know you're busy," I said to Harriman, "but do you have any idea whether there's anyone around who might have read that contract they signed at The Blue Door?"

Harriman contemplated my question for a long moment. "Have you checked with Mrs. Yanamoto?"

At this moment, she was probably tooling along I-80, on her way to Silicon Valley to visit her grandchildren.

"Look," I said, "I know this stuff really belongs to you. But do you mind if I hang on to it for a few more days?"

Harriman stood and began pacing. "I don't see why not. After all, I haven't looked at it in about twenty years. I don't think I'll miss it for at least another twenty."

I could tell that Warren Harriman, for all his cheery graciousness, was growing impatient. I checked my watch. Almost noon. I carefully slipped the photograph and clipping into my backpack and shook hands with Harriman. "You've been very helpful."

Harriman smiled and covered my right hand with his left. "It was my pleasure. I'll be here all weekend, so come back anytime if I can be of assistance. It was fun, talking about the old times." He carted a folding chair out to a stoop formed by the wooden stairway leading to the media trailer door. "You're welcome to grab a chair and watch the parade with me. View's pretty good from here."

"I may do just that."

I stood next to Harriman on the stoop and shaded my eyes with my arm. Old Sacramento was bustin' at its seams, boardwalk and balconies choked with fans waiting for the parade to begin. The AARP crowd was well represented, but I spotted a fair number of folks my age, as well as kids and teens. Police officers on bikes and horseback kept the cobblestone streets clear. Channel 10 had set up their live truck directly across Second Street. Banners stretched across the midpoint of Second Street and above it all, the bright red Retro Alley balloon bobbed on its tether.

At the I Street end of Second Street, the staging area for the parade, I could see a color guard, several Keystone Kops, and an antique fire truck overflowing with gals in Gay Nineties floozy attire. I didn't see anything of Pete Kovacs or the Steve's Pizza truck. Or the flatbed truck where I was supposed to be riding with the rest of the radio station staff, for that matter.

A week ago, this entire wholesome, gee-whiz, good-old-days scene would have set Shauna J. Bogart's teeth on edge. Today I found myself tapping my toes with the rest of them.

I heard a drumroll and roar of applause from the crowd closest to the staging area. Warren Harriman was right. The stoop was a perfect spot for watching the parade. I turned and entered the trailer to help myself to a folding chair.

The radio was still tuned to the tail end of the Rush Limbaugh show. The KFBK announcer broke in at the end of the stop-set.

"Gubernatorial candidate Jeff Greene calls a news conference at noon at the State Capitol and promises a major announcement. Stay with us for live coverage."

27

If I'd been a guy, I would have thrown something.

I'd have picked up the TV set and hurled it out the door, sailing past Warren Harriman's innocent bald head, crashing into the middle of the parade on the hot asphalt of Second Street, smashing Jeff Greene's smug face into smithereens.

But being a gal, I could only scream and yell. I used most of the infamous seven naughty words we can't say on the radio. I combined cuss words with "mother" and "low-down."

Luckily for my dignity, it was a loud, noisy parade. I was able to explode without anyone hearing. Not even Warren Harriman, right outside.

I seethed as I forced myself to focus on Greene's handsome face and oh-so-sincere voice coming from the tiny screen.

"I want to thank all of you in the media for coming today on such short notice. With the election coming soon, I felt it was time to clear the air, once and for all, about the stories that are circulating about the involvement of my office with questionable land use dealings in southern Monterey County."

All three network affiliates carried the news conference live from Room 1190, the State Capitol press room, at the top of their noon newscasts. Jeff Greene stood at a podium, flanked on one side by his two trusty aids, Lucille Benson and Will Tucker.

On the other side, looking uncomfortable in an orange pant-suit, stood Lily McGovern.

"I want to state unequivocally and for the record that I had nothing to do with any backroom deals," Greene said. "It has come to my attention that a former member of my staff may have sent unauthorized letters on my office stationery, and used my office e-mail account without my knowledge."

I cursed the TV screen.

The soft *click-whir-click* of the newspaper photographers' cameras filled the background as Greene continued. "That staff member shall remain unnamed. However, I will state for the record that I accepted his resignation as soon as I became aware of this unauthorized and unethical use of my name."

"Slimy bastard!"

"I have never done anything except uphold the principles for which I am known. That includes protection and preservation of our state's precious natural resources, for our children and future generations."

"Double-crossing weasel!"

"With me today is Lily McGovern, legislative analyst for Earth Guardians, one of the largest and most respected environmental groups in the state. Ms. McGovern would like to say a few words."

I watched as Greene and McGovern traded places at the podium. McGovern hesitated for a second, then faced the camera, the light glancing off the lenses of her secretary glasses. She spoke with professional confidence. "I come before you today to announce the endorsement of Earth Guardians of Jeff Greene. Senator Greene has an impressive record when it comes to the issues of vital importance to our organization: protection of our natural resources, controlled and sensible growth, and preservation of the jewels of nature like the Big Sur coast. Earth Guardians urges all citizens who care about the environment to elect Jeff Greene the next governor of California."

Will Tucker allowed as how the candidate would be willing to take a few questions from the press. Good ol' Aggie Tarbell from the *Davis Daily Delineator* was first out of the box. I wondered if the CHP made her put out her cigarette, and if she'd managed to hurt any of them in the process. "How about your ties with The Farm Team and the corporations that fund the Foundation for Progressive Public Policy?"

"I'm proud of the year I spent with The Farm Team. It was a crucial experience in shaping my political career. As for the donors whose generosity makes possible the good work of The Farm Team, I can only say that I believe in maintaining cordial ties and open lines of communication with all factions in the state, including the business community."

I flipped back and forth among the newscasts until all three broke away for commercials. I cursed one more time and flicked off the TV.

No wonder Jeff Greene had been so accommodating last night. He knew he'd never have to make good on his promise to come on my show this afternoon to tell the voters of this state the truth about his sleazy deals with CalFac. Whatever agreement he made with the O'Briens to yank the station off the air made certain I wouldn't have a show. I wondered how much dough had actually changed hands. Maybe none. Greene could have just promised them something really juicy if elected. Like father-and-son judgeships. I had to admit, Junior would look stunning in black robes.

It went without saying I wouldn't be doing a show this afternoon, or ever, at least not on the O'Briens' radio station. Not if those e-mails between Dr. Hipster and Judith Lowenthal about an impending format change were accurate.

The only thing I didn't get was how The Blue Door fit into the scenario. Why would a contract signed by four war buddies back in the fifties have anything to do with the outcome of an election today?

I toyed briefly with the idea of going to KFBK with the story. But this business is so cutthroat, I'd probably be black-listed for life if word got out I'd consorted with the enemy while still under contract with Sacramento Talk Radio. The newspapers? Nah. Why would they believe me instead of the candidate and his retinue of consultants and handlers and multimillion-dollar advertising budget? Greene's people had already managed to get to Lily McGovern, and convince her to throw the endorsement of Earth Guardians to their side.

What could one lone radio talk show host hope to do?

I left the trailer and sliced my way through the crowd, stepping on a toe or two as I craned my neck in the searing heat. The grassy square surrounding the Pony Express statue where I'd sat in solitude two hours ago was packed cheek-by-jowl with cheering, applauding traditional jazz fans. I walked past the bronze horse and rider and bumped boobs to belly with Edward Glott.

"Afternoon, Ms. Bogart." Even though he was in plain-clothes, he tipped the brim of a nonexistent hat. "Nice day for a parade."

I nodded speechlessly. Heart pounding, I turned and bolted for the nearest hiding place I could find. A Porta Potti. Just like the Jubilee PR promised, they really were conveniently located everywhere.

The gleeful parade racket echoed inside the tiny green plastic box. Thank God, it was still early and hadn't been used much. I'd hate to imagine what one of these things would be like after four days in ninety-degree heat. I timed five minutes on my watch, then eased the door open. No heavyset figure in the vicinity or Smokey Bear hats bobbing above the sea of people. I slipped out of the loo and dove into the crowd.

Best to keep moving. I darted and wove my way through the merry mob. Uniforms everywhere. Sacramento PeeDee on horseback at every street corner kept the crowd from surging onto the parade route. Cops on bicycles, state park rangers patrolling on foot. I didn't see any CHP, but I would have bet money they'd be setting up a DUI checkpoint on the streets leading out of Old Sacramento as the day wore on.

I passed the Channel 10 live truck at Second and J and flinched when a carload of Keystone Kops careened by. Maybe I was becoming a tad paranoid.

"Shauna J. Bogart!" A pair of strong arms grabbed my shoulders. "You are Shauna J. Bogart, right?"

I gasped and stared back into the nervously grinning face of a man in his thirties. Thick hair covered his arms and legs, and poured over the top of his Jazz Jubilee volunteer T-shirt. A woman about his age, dressed in an identical T-shirt but without the hair, bubbled at his side. Jeez, lady, has anyone ever told you you're married to a human chia pet?

"We saw you last night at the Jazz Band Ball," the woman gushed.

"You probably don't recognize us," her hairy companion said. "We were dressed as Bonnie and Clyde."

The woman gave me a hug. "We thought you were wonderful. Do you think you'll be appearing with the band again? We listen to your show every day."

Clyde joined her in a group hug. "But you don't look anything like we thought you would."

I wasn't sure who scared me most, crooked cops or clingy fans.

"Shauna J.! I'm all looking everywhere for you."

Josh Friedman, out of breath, sweat trickling down the side of his face.

"Aren't you supposed to be in class?"

Josh dropped his head, staring at the boardwalk at our feet. "I almost wish I hadn't found you first. Glory Lou's looking for you too."

"What's going on?" I raised my voice to be heard above the din of a New Orleans street band.

Josh rocked back in his tennis shoes and shrugged awkwardly. "I've got some bad news."

"If it's about us being off the air, I know that."

Josh shook his head.

"And if it's about Jeff Greene and the news conference, I know about that too."

The intern pressed his lips together and shook his head, still staring at the boardwalk. Out of the corner of my eyes, I saw the antique flatbed truck holding the Sacramento Talk Radio personalities—sans the star of the afternoon show— jolting slowly down Front Street.

I clutched Josh gently by the shoulders and forced him to look at me. "Look, whatever it is, it can't be as bad as us being off the air, or Greene double-crossing me. Just tell me. I can take it."

I had to lean closer to hear what Josh was trying to say. I made him repeat it, just to make sure I hadn't heard him wrong.

"Monty Rio didn't make it."

· · ·

I finally stopped running when I found myself inside Freeway Gardens.

There were no gardens.

But there most definitely was a freeway.

Freeway Gardens, one of the major concert sites at the Jazz Jubilee, stood directly underneath I-5 as it vaulted over downtown Sacramento. An asphalt floor, decorated with oil slicks and white lines, revealed its humble role as a parking lot the other fifty-one weekends of the year. The eight lanes of I-5 served as the ceiling. The acoustics must have been a nightmare for the musicians, but at least it was cool, a shady, dim, echoing cave filled with music and laughter.

The bartender's button read, "51-50 at Freeway Gardens."

Fifty-one fifty. Police radio slang for a person acting strange in public, out of control, a danger to herself or others. Perfect.

The bartender who exchanged my drink tickets for a gin and tonic gave me a strange look. I couldn't have blamed him. After running from the embarcadero to the freeway in the heat, I must have been a mess. He sized up the situation and filled a prescription that was ninety percent gin.

I found a seat on the aisle toward the back and wiped my eyes and nose with a paper napkin. I raised my drink in a silent toast to the anonymous Jubilee wag who came up with the Freeway Gardens name, and I wondered how many beers had been consumed in the process.

Josh Friedman, breathing heavily, surfaced in the murk and took the empty white plastic folding chair at my side.

"You gotta do something!" he said, still panting from running after me.

"I don't 'gotta' do anything," I replied, taking a stiff gulp.

Josh's voice rose. "I don't believe this. You're just going to let them get away with it?"

"Damn right." I turned away, so I wouldn't have to look at his troubled face.

"I can't believe you're just going to sit there."

"Show me where it's written in my contract that Shauna J. Bogart has to risk her life on lost causes. This isn't *Charlie's Angels*.

These guys play for keeps. They've already killed Dr. Hipster and Monty Rio, and they came damn close to doing the same to me." I'd put another bandage on my still-festering hand, and the ugly bruise on my thigh peeked out from my shorts.

Josh dropped his head and said softly, "I still can't believe you're not doing anything."

"Yeah, well, better get used to it."

Josh stared at the asphalt, shaking his head slowly.

I guess I'd been a bit harsh. I took another slug of my drink and put my arm around Josh's shoulders. "I'm sorry I've disappointed you. But it's simple, really. I happen to like being alive and in one piece. Is that so hard to understand?"

"I believed in you," Josh said to the pavement. "I thought you stood for something. I thought you were different from all the rest."

"So you fell for the Shauna J. Bogart hype, just like everyone else," I said. "She's history."

"I believed in you," Josh repeated.

"Don't you get it? If I hadn't made a big deal about Dr. Hipster's death, if I hadn't kept poking around and stirring things up, maybe Monty Rio would still be alive."

Josh raised his head. "What do you plan to do, then?"

"I don't know." I took another generous sip.

The Holiday Inn probably had a car rental counter. Maybe I'd drive to Monterey, find a beach shack, lay low until the election was over and forgotten. Before splitting town, I'd leave a note for Pete Kovacs, asking him to take care of Bialystock. I pictured myself lying on the beach, reading trashy paperbacks. It felt good.

Eventually, I'd have to start sending out tapes and résumés. But no talk radio. I'll happily spin disks and read liner cards until the day I die a natural death, thank you very much.

"I'm not sure," I told Josh. "But I do know that just for today, I'm going to drink up all these tickets and listen to some music."

The emcee asked us to give a warm Jubilee welcome to a band called Blue Street. "The bad boys of Dixieland, all the way from Fresno, California."

I'd promised myself I wouldn't ever again think about the death of Dr. Hipster, the election, The Blue Door, or anything else that had happened to me the past ten days.

Maybe it was because of the name of the band.

Maybe it was hearing the same tunes that had been playing in the background when Rudy from West Sacramento first called my show.

Maybe it was because I sat at the exact spot where The Blue Door nightclub had stood forty years ago, before they tore it down to put in the freeway. If you really wanted to get cosmic, I could have been parked at the very spot of T. R. O'Brien's favorite booth. Or right in the space where Helen Hudson had leaned against an upright piano and recorded a live album. I could almost smell the whiskey and cigarette smoke and hear the clink of glasses raised in a toast over the notes of a sultry torch singer.

Maybe it was just all that gin.

Dr. Hipster's son, in front of his mother's house in San Jose, describing his last meeting with his father: "He wanted to know if a contract signed maybe like forty, fifty years ago was still valid."

Warren Harriman had been there the night they signed The Blue Door contract.

Terrence O'Brien Jr.: ". . . hasn't a clue as to what this is really all about."

But I did.

I turned to Josh. "We've got to get out of here."

"What for? You're history, remember?"

"A gal can change her mind, can't she? We've got to find a copy of The Blue Door contract. I'm almost positive I know why we're off the air."

I was also pretty sure I knew the true identity of Rudy from West Sacramento.

28

I knew T. R. O'Brien had a copy of the contract in his office.
He'd said so in his fax of two weeks ago to Dr. Hipster. All
I needed to do was to get back to the station, sneak in without
Junior spotting me, break into T. R.'s locked office, and search
through almost fifty years' worth of files.

But first I had to figure out a way to escape from Freeway
Gardens.

The familiar pear-shaped figure of Edward Glott, in plain-
clothes, filled one of the exits. The two female cops—the
short, bulked African-American and the tall, pumped Cauca-
sian—blocked another way out.

I was about to make a mad dash for the third and last exit
when a uniform I'd not seen before—gray slacks, white shirt,
radio clipped to his shoulder—appeared in the doorway,
framed in the sunlight of Old Sacramento. He spoke briefly to
the Jubilee volunteer on duty, then said something into his
two-way. For all I knew, he could have been the fire marshal.
At this point, I didn't trust anything in a uniform, not even a
meter maid.

Even if I could climb over the cyclone fence separating
Freeway Gardens from the I-5 off-ramp without anyone notic-
ing me, I'd probably get slammed by an eighteen-wheeler barreling off the interstate.

I could try to get in back of the stage with no one in the
audience of twelve hundred seeing me. But then I'd have to

scramble over the twelve-foot cement wall of the pedestrian tunnel.

That left the back wall, and the bar.

The crowd clapped in time as Blue Street launched into the old Dixie Cups hit "Iko Iko." A couple dozen women bobbing brightly colored parasols formed a mosh pit in front of the bandstand. Dozens in the audience leaped to their feet and started a conga line, snaking their way through the aisles separating the forest of white folding chairs.

"Remember *The Blues Brothers*?" I said to Josh.

The kid gave me a blank look. I felt about a thousand years old.

"How about *The Sound of Music*?"

"I love that movie! I cry every time they do the Edelweiss song."

"Yeah, well, get a grip. Remember the part at the music festival, where they escape from the Nazis?"

I drained the rest of my drink, slung my backpack over my shoulders, clutched Josh's hand, and spliced myself into the middle of the conga line. I even blew a kiss to Edward Glott when we passed by the exit.

We'd just reached the bar that formed the back boundary of Freeway Gardens.

"Now!" I shouted above the echoing din and grabbed Josh's arm. I dove underneath one of the folding banquet tables that formed the makeshift bar and duck-walked to the other side.

"Hey, you can't come back here!" Just my luck, a volunteer bartender who took his duties seriously.

When in doubt, act dumb. I gave the bartender a goofy grin. "Sorry, we were just leaving."

Sheets of plywood covered with posters from liquor and beer companies created a solid back wall for the bar area. Still clutching Josh's hand, I plunged through a gap between two sheets of plywood.

We were still under the freeway. But instead of an enclosed area filled with bands, fans, and booze, we were in a maze of trailers, golf carts, and more blue-and-white volunteer T-shirts. A Loomis truck was backed up to the entrance to one of the trailers.

"Can I help you?" One of the blue shirts confronted Josh and me.

The dopey smile worked again. "Sorry, we were just leaving." Josh and I darted around trailers and golf carts until we emerged into the bright streets of Old Sacramento.

I seized Josh's arm to slow his gallop into a more sedate canter. "Keep moving, but no running," I whispered. "Don't do anything to attract attention."

We slipped into Retro Alley and pretended to be interested in the binders of celebrity autographed eight-by-tens. Leonard Nimoy as Spock for $80, the entire original *Star Trek* cast at $235. Pete Kovacs's frumpy assistant pretty much ignored us, nodding her gray head once, then returning to what looked like a bookkeeper's ledger.

"Where's your car?" I whispered to Josh.

"I knew traffic and parking down here would be impossible, so Android dropped me off."

"Great. Take a look outside, see if you can find the news car."

Josh returned maybe two minutes later, shaking his head. "The station van's still parked in front of the ice-cream parlor next door. But no news car. The last time I saw Glory Lou, she's telling me she's driving over to your apartment. To tell you about Monty Rio."

If we could somehow manage to get out of Old Sacramento and into downtown without getting nabbed, we could catch a city bus. But I didn't want to be trapped in the bowels of the K Street pedestrian tunnel, like a rat in a sewer, with Edward Glott at one end and those two gals in uniform at the other.

I could always flee into West Sacramento. If I could just figure out a way across the river.

Margaret Hamilton as the Wicked Witch of the West ($300) leered at me from the pages of the Retro Alley autograph album. What I needed now was Dorothy's ruby-red slippers, to whisk me from Old Sacramento to Highway 160 and the radio station. I'd even settle for the Winged Monkeys, even though they gave me horrendous nightmares when I was a kid.

Josh tugged at my arm, leading me to the front window. He pointed to the store directly across the street.

Different Spokes For Different Folks Bicycle Rentals.

I saw a T-shirt once that said something about old age and cunning being able to triumph over youth and beauty. I thought about that slogan as Josh and I pedaled in the midday heat. For even though I was old enough to be the kid's mother, he had to puff and pant to keep up with me. The pedals seemed to fly effortlessly under my feet, fueled by the furies of anger, revenge, grief, and fear. For once, I barely noticed the searing heat, nor the brown smudge on the horizon from the forest fire in the foothills as we sailed under cottonwoods, sycamores, and valley oaks on the narrow ribbon of asphalt.

"I'm all wondering why you changed your mind," Josh shouted between gasps for air.

I slowed slightly so he could catch up and we could ride two abreast. "No election is worth risking my butt. Or the safety of people I care about. But when he starts messing with the radio station and my show, I can't let him get away with it."

We left the bike trail when it dipped under Highway 160 and cycled along the frontage road, past body shops, a printer, and a party rentals place. As we approached the tan stucco low-rise housing Sacramento Talk Radio, I guided Josh to the wooden fence that enclosed the satellite dishes. A perfect place to stash the bicycles.

The parking lot was empty, heat radiating off the expanse of black asphalt. Junior had apparently even sent home the board operator. I'd already pretty much concluded the O'Briens planned to keep the station off the air for the rest of the day, at least. The absence of the board operator confirmed my suspicion.

Even though the place looked deserted, I crossed the parking lot as fast as I could.

Getting in was easy. My passkey still worked. Our footsteps echoed through the silent hallways of the business office. On a normal Friday afternoon, the sales bullpen would have made the pit of the Chicago Board of Trade seem tame, what with salespeople writing up last-minute orders, closing deals, and jockeying for position on the weekend program log. This afternoon, even the hum of the computers was missing.

We reached the heavy oak door leading to T. R. O'Brien's office. Locked.

"Now what?" Josh asked.

"Easy. You're going to break in."

The intern looked at me blankly.

"Don't give me that innocent look. You broke into Monty Rio's office last weekend, remember? To get fax paper? I know you can do it."

"What if I get in trouble?"

"I'm your supervisor. I'll take the heat if we get caught."

Josh pointed to the ceiling, which consisted of squares of acoustic tile suspended from a grid of thin metal strips. He told me how, last Saturday, he borrowed a ladder from the engineering shop, pushed up one of the ceiling tiles, squeezed into the crawl space, and slithered over the wall separating Monty's office from the newsroom. Then he popped up another ceiling tile on the other side of the door and let himself drop to the floor of Monty's office.

"Think you could do it again?"

"Let's go find that ladder."

Less than five minutes later, Josh opened the door to T. R.'s office, made an exaggerated bow, and ushered me in.

T. R.'s filing cabinet was, of course, locked. That was no problem. I'd once watched Mrs. Yanamoto hide the keys inside an empty Tupperware container in her desk.

Josh began riffling through the debris on T. R.'s desk. "Take a look at this." He handed the bottom half of a box of file folders to me.

Instead of manila folders, the box held publicity photos, news clippings, and fan letters, all related to the career and the death of Dr. Hipster. The tape cartridge with his last promotional announcement sat on top, along with a note to Mrs.

Yanamoto instructing her to send it to Dr. Hipster's children in another week.

Josh breathed a sigh of relief. "I just knew I didn't accidentally put that cart in the stack to be bulked and stripped. I just knew it!"

"I never doubted you for a minute. I just wonder why T. R. didn't turn this stuff over to the family during the services."

"Maybe he wanted to wait until he was sure all of the fan mail had come in, so he could send it all in one package instead of piecemeal."

I returned my attention to T. R.'s files. In the top drawer, I found a stack of white number ten envelopes rubber-banded together and bearing this day's date. I stashed them in my backpack. Josh, meanwhile, began rooting around the stack of computer printouts from the Gold Rush Giveaway on T. R.'s desk. A moment later, he held up a length of brown reel-to-reel recording tape, no reel, just a string of tape with one end dangling to the floor. "Is this weird or what?"

"Lemme see that." I took the tape carefully from Josh's fingers. Josh was right, it was weird, or what. No one saves chunks of spliced tape. It's usually tossed as soon as the editing session is over.

From my practiced eye, this strand of tape looked like just about one hour's worth from the logger reel.

I took the tape to the production room and spliced leader—clear plastic nonrecording tape—to either end. I threaded one end into the hub of an empty plastic reel and slowly wound the reel until all of the tape had coiled onto the reel, then tucked the tail end into a take-up reel. I pressed the PLAY button.

"At six minutes after four on a Wednesday afternoon, you're tuned to the Shauna J. Bogart Show. We'll open the lines to your calls in a minute, but first, it's time to find another lucky winner in the Gold Rush Giveaway . . ."

I fast-forwarded what I estimated was fifteen minutes. "The lady told me to call. I'm all so excited!" The winner in the Gold Rush Giveaway. Tiffany? Something like that. I pressed the REWIND button and found what I was looking for.

Killer show tonight . . . biggest thing since this so-called election for governor ... gonna blow this town sky-high ... don't touch that dial ... The Hipster's tipsters have the score, the skinny, and the straight dope ...

I rewound the tape, removed it from the reel machine, placed it in my backpack between the envelope of documents from Lily McGovern and Dr. Hipster's Blue Door file, and headed back to T. R.'s office, Josh dogging my heels.

A minute or two later, I pulled four pages of onionskin paper from a folder marked "Golden Empire Broadcasting, pre-1960" from T. R.'s file drawer. No title, just a date, then long blocks of single-spaced type from a manual typewriter badly in need of a fresh ribbon. The final page bore the right signatures: T. R. O'Brien, Neil Vermont, Wallace W. Wilson III, and Grant Simmerhorn.

"I think this is it," I said softly, holding the four delicate sheets as carefully as if I'd just unearthed them from an ancient archaeological dig. I read rapidly. "It's just like Warren Harriman told me. They agreed to split the profits generated by the radio station in four equal parts. T. R. O'Brien came in first in the cut of the cards, so he gets to actually run the station. If he can't do it, then control of the station goes to the next partner in line. Look at this: He gets a salary, based on a percentage of the profits, in addition to his share of the overall profits."

I sat cross-legged on T. R.'s carpet and quoted from the actual text.

> *"If T. R. O'Brien should become unwilling or unable to fulfill his obligations, the title of Chief Executive Officer, and all privileges and compensation thereof, shall pass on to Neil Vermont, followed by Grant Simmerhorn and Wallace W. Wilson III.*
>
> *"The following shall be considered immediate forfeiture of the title of Chief Executive Officer, and all privileges and compensation thereof:*
>
> *"1. Failure to return a profit for at least six consecutive quarters,*
>
> *"2. Willfully and deliberately causing the station to*

lose its license to operate from the Federal Communications Commission,

"3. Failure to keep the station's ratings in the market's top ten for adults 18–54 for three consecutive ratings periods."

"Only three books?" Josh interrupted. "That seems tough."

"They only had two books a year, the fall and spring, back then," I said. "So three books would have given him a year and a half, instead of only nine months like today. That was fair."

I turned the thin, yellowed sheet and read the fourth and final condition to myself and then to Josh.

"We've got to get the station back on the air." I glanced at my watch and did some quick figuring in my head. "And we've got less than five hours."

29

"That contract can't possibly be legal, can it?"

Josh and I stood at the copy machine in the sales pit. I had to push the COPY DARKER button as far as it would go to get the faint typewritten lines of The Blue Door contract to come out. "The lawyer who put this together back in the fifties obviously thought so. And I'll bet Neil Vermont ran it by his attorney just this past month or so."

I read the original copy of the contract one last time before I returned it to the file drawer. I lingered over the fourth and final condition.

4. Failure to keep the station on the air for more than twelve consecutive hours for any reason, with the exception of acts of God, nuclear war, or orders of the FCC.

"T. R. could take it to court, of course," I said. Assuming we ever hear from him again. "But you know how long those things take. It could be months, years. Meanwhile, Junior's won. He's silenced the station, right before the election."

"I don't get it. So let's say this contract is legal, and Neil Vermont gets to take over. What's so bad about that?"

"They fire all the local air talent, put a bunch of syndicated hate-mongers on the air. They trade integrity for profits. Damn straight, that's bad."

We were surrounded by some of the best broadcast equipment in the business. Microphones, tape decks, mixing boards, telephone interfaces. Useless without a transmitter and tower.

I ushered Josh out the back door of the station and up and

over the packed earthen berm protecting the building from the
American River floodplain. We'd be conspicuous walking or
cycling on the dirt road leading to the Quonset hut housing
the transmitter, so we hacked our way cross-country, through
weeds and blackberry bushes. My feet and ankles soon wore
a coat of dirt and my legs bore dozens of tiny scratches. I
didn't even want to think about the bugs, mice, and God
knows what else living in this field.

Josh and I crouched behind one of the giant cement blocks
anchoring the tower's guy wires. The Quonset hut loomed
only a few yards away. Junior's BMW was pulled up to the
door, along with a red pickup truck that I figured belonged to
the on-call engineer, and a plain white sedan.

Two men stood on either side of the door. Wearing the
uniform of the Capital Square private security force.

"We need to return those bicycles or we'll have to pay for an
extra hour," Josh said. We were back in the deserted newsroom.

"Cool your jets. I'll just put it on my expense account. Go
find a plain white envelope."

The police scanner provided the only background noise in
the empty news pit. "Ten ten." Off duty. "Ten twenty-one b."
Phone home. "Code four." No assistance needed.

I chuckled to myself as I composed a string of numbers
from the keyboard of the newsroom computer and ran a three-
by-five card through the printer. When Josh returned with the
envelope, I sealed the card inside and printed today's date and
a time of 8:00 P.M. on the front. I placed it in my backpack
next to the other sealed envelopes with the Gold Rush Giveaway liner cards.

Forty minutes later we wheeled the bicycles into the Different
Spokes rental shop. "We had fun," Josh told the kid behind
the counter. "We'll do it again next year."

Glory Lou waved at us from across Second Street. "Sugar,
I've been looking all over for you."

You and everyone else. I took her by one arm and hustled her into the sanctuary of Retro Alley.

"What's up?" Glory Lou whispered as we huddled over the binders of autographed eight-by-tens.

"Simple. We're going to put the station back on the air. All we need are some wheels. Where'd you park the news car?"

Glory Lou made a face. "I'm driving back into Old Sacramento about an hour ago, okay? I've got all the passes stuck to the windshield, just like they told us. This sweet young officer controlling the traffic at the I Street entrance stops me and tells me I can't drive into Old Sacramento. I pointed to the credentials. He tells me all the vehicle passes for Sacramento Talk Radio have been canceled."

"No way!"

"And after all the positive coverage I gave the Sac PeeDee during their last bout of blue flu."

"What did you do?"

"Hon, what choice did I have? Traffic is backed up down to Fifth Street and these officers are ordering me to leave. So I parked under Downtown Plaza and hoofed it."

Terrific. Three licensed drivers, three owners of vehicles with up-to-date tags, and we had no transportation. This was not a mission that could be accomplished on bikes. Even if we could coax Glory Lou's hefty frame, turned out today in a white linen suit, blue silk blouse, and blue pumps, onto a two-wheeler.

"Let's go," I said. "I know someone who's got wheels and all the parking credentials we'll ever need."

I sent Josh to check out the radio station van and the remote broadcast setup on the balcony next door. Before he left, I pressed the Gold Rush Giveaway envelope for tonight's eight o'clock hour into his hand. "Blitzer's got the rest of the envelopes with the liner cards in the van. Pull out the envelope for the eight o'clock hour and substitute this one."

"What's this about?"

"Just having a little fun, that's all."

Josh came back into Retro Alley talking so rapidly I could hardly understand him.

"Brandon's all got the remote torn down and packed up in

the van. I'm all telling him to stop, but he's all Terrence O'Brien ordering him to return the van and the equipment to the station ASAP. I'm all . . ."

"Slow down. Did you do the thing with the contest envelope like I asked you?"

"Yeah, but I'm all . . ."

"For God's sake, stop saying 'I'm all.' Did you see any cops?"

Josh shook his head. I shot out of the door of Retro Alley before he could hit me with another "I'm all." I caught up with Brandon Nguyen, keys in hand, as he was putting the last box of Mimi Blitzer's sun visors into the back door of the station van. I glanced at the balcony. Empty, except for a few dangling telephone wires and the abandoned pink donut box.

"What do you think you're doing?" I asked the young engineering assistant.

"Haven't you heard? There's some part they can't get until tomorrow at the earliest. We're off the air 'til then." He turned away from the door of the van and faced me. "Too bad about your remote."

"Terrence O'Brien called you and ordered you to pack up everything and go back to the station?"

"Uh-huh."

"Get this," I said, doing my best to sound authoritative. "I hold a First Class Radio Telephone License with a Broadcast Endorsement. Therefore, I outrank you and I outrank Terrence O'Brien. Under the authority vested in me by the Federal Communications Commission, I am ordering you to put that equipment back on the balcony and set us up to sign back on the air."

I was bluffing shamelessly. But I placed my hopes on Brandon Nguyen being green enough to buy it.

"Furthermore, if Terrence O'Brien Jr. or anyone other than Gloria Louise Montalvo, Joshua Friedman, or myself attempts to call you, either by telephone, pager, or two-way, I am ordering you not to respond. Do you understand?"

Pete Kovacs had said something about a four o'clock gig at Turntable Junction. By my watch, it was a little after five,

meaning the Hot Times Dixieland Band should be winding
down the set.

Only three and a half hours left.

Turntable Junction turned out to be another cute Jubilee
name for the big tent in front of the State Railroad Museum.
I wasn't too keen on being trapped once again in an enclosed
area with only one way out. But the boys in the band had
saved my butt last night, and I figured I could count on them.
Plus, I now had Glory Lou as well as Josh as bodyguards.

The three of us slipped into the tent. I waited for the band
to finish "Sweet Georgia Brown" and for the applause to die
down. Then I approached the roped-off area in back of the
stage.

"Sorry, musicians only." Another in the legion of Jubilee
volunteers attempted to block my path. I swear, those people
were everywhere.

"I'm with the band." God, I've always wanted to use that
line.

I waved at Kovacs, who jumped to his feet from behind
the upright piano and beckoned the three of us to the backstage
area.

He gave me a hug scented with beer and sweat. "Great to
see you! I hope you're having a good time at your first Jubilee."

"Yeah. It's been swell." I gave him a quick peck on the
cheek. "You haven't lived until you've danced in a conga line
at Freeway Gardens."

"I'm just glad you're having fun. Any chance we can coax
you into making an appearance with the band again?"

"I'm going to have to sit this one out. Could I talk about
something important for a few minutes?"

Kovacs took off his Panama hat and wiped the sweat from
his forehead with a bandanna from the pocket of his jeans. He
glanced up to the stage, where the banjo player was vamping,
drawing out the introduction to "Copenhagen" over the impatient stirring of the audience. "Can it wait 'til we're finished
with this set?"

"It's really important, and I don't have much time."

Kovacs was already halfway up the wooden steps to the

stage. "Let me just get through this next number. I'll see what I can do."

A few hours ago, I would have relished the chance to cash in more of my drink tickets, relax in a seat on the aisle, and listen to Kovacs's band. But instead of the infectious beat of "Copenhagen" I heard only the ticking of the clock, leading inevitably toward eight-thirty.

Kovacs told the audience the next number would be Duke Ellington's "Don't Get Around Much Anymore," featuring a solo by the sax player. Then he jumped off the stage onto the dirt floor.

We stood in a tight knot backstage, Kovacs, Josh, Glory Lou, and me. Out of the corner of my eye, I saw two Sacramento cops talking to the bartender. Their posture was relaxed, and I saw one of the cops throw back his head and laugh. They didn't seem menacing, but still, I shuffled a couple of feet toward the center of the backstage area, where the plywood backing of the stage would hide me.

I knew Kovacs didn't have much time, so I gave him the three-and-a-half-minute, edited-for-Top-40-radio version.

Kovacs folded his arms. "You're saying your boss signed some sort of contract back in the fifties." He sounded skeptical.

"Yeah."

"This contract says if the station is off the air for twelve consecutive hours, Neil Vermont gets to take over. The station went off the air at eight-thirty this morning, so you and your friends have 'til eight-thirty tonight to get it back on the air."

"Correct."

"Say Neil Vermont gets the station. You're saying he'll let this Junior person actually call the shots when it comes to running the station."

I tried not to sound impatient. "We know what Junior will do. He'll fire me, and all of the rest of the local air talent. He'll put on a bunch of right-wing syndicated hate-mongers."

"And you can't go to the cops, because Junior has access to a private security force through the Capital City Ventures apartment complexes. His mother is on the board of the parent company. The head of this private security squad is retired from the Sacramento Police Department and still has friends on the force."

I nodded.

"You think Dr. Hipster was killed because he figured out what Junior was going to do."

Josh drew in a sharp breath and tugged at my T-shirt. I followed his pointed finger to the entrance to Turntable Junction. My two new gal pals in their Sac PeeDee uniforms had just strolled in.

"Look, you don't have to believe me," I told Kovacs. "Just let me borrow your van for an hour or so. I promise to be careful."

"Parnassus is a mite particular about who drives her." He glanced at the stage, where the sax player was just finishing his solo, then back to me. "I'd better go with you."

30

"Hon, there's something I've been wondering about," Glory Lou said. "Vivienne Kostantin and Neil Vermont. Are you absolutely sure that they're part of this?"

"Are they cold-blooded killers, you mean?" I said.

Glory Lou and Josh both nodded.

We leaned against the side of Kovacs's van. An SUV parked in the next slot helped shield us from any cops or rangers who might happen to walk by. The solid redbrick citadel of the State Railroad Museum sealed off the small parking lot from the rest of Old Sacramento. Overhead towered the on-ramp to the I Street Bridge across the Sacramento River. The grids of steel and cement provided welcome shade to the parking lot, but I still felt as if I'd gone from Main Street at Disneyland to the set of *Blade Runner*.

Josh, Glory Lou, and I had fled Turntable Junction after Kovacs agreed to meet us at the van as soon as the band finished the set. The Jubilee volunteer who'd let us into the backstage area obligingly pushed open a gap in the walls of the tent. The three of us squeezed through the gap and sprinted across the lawn in front of the Railroad Museum, Glory Lou cussing when one of her pumps got sucked into a muddy patch of grass.

Glory Lou tucked her blue silk blouse back into the waistband of her white linen skirt and shifted her weight against the side of the van. "I met Vivienne Kostantin once. We were both modeling in a celebrity fashion show to raise money for

Mercy Hospital. She was warm, charming, and just as gracious as she could be."

"You know what they say about those types," I said. "The steel hand in the velvet glove."

I gazed up at the crisscross of steel girders. "I don't think Vivienne Kostantin or Neil Vermont are killers, nor do I think they know the extent of Junior's plan." I was operating on sheer instinct. "I would guess Kostantin just told the chief of security for the Capital City Ventures apartment complexes to do whatever Junior instructed him to do."

"And I'll just bet Kostantin made it worth his while to do so," Glory Lou said. "She can afford it. Lordy, she's one of the richest women in California."

"But I would guess she believed all Junior wanted was to have Edward Glott do a little breaking-and-entering. Maybe rough up someone who hadn't been nice to her little boy."

"How about Neil Vermont?" Josh asked.

"I'm just guessing, but I'd bet Neil Vermont thinks all that's happening is that he's creating some sort of delay on the fishing trip to Alaska so T. R. doesn't get home in time to stop Junior. I wouldn't want him for my business partner. But I don't think he's a killer."

At least, I hoped not. I prayed that T. R. O'Brien was trapped at some bush pilot's airstrip, fuming and stewing. I could hardly bear to picture the alternative: sinking hook first into the frigid waters off some remote Alaskan island.

It was almost five-thirty before Kovacs rounded the corner of the Railroad Museum. "Sorry, but the audience demanded an encore."

Kovacs unlocked Parnassus. I directed Josh and Glory Lou to the cargo area. "Keep down until we get to Josh's house," I said as I followed the pair into the back of the van.

Parnassus must have been between antique shows and book fairs, because the cargo area wasn't filled with merchandise, just a half dozen or so empty cardboard boxes. I shoved the boxes to one side, picked a spot behind the passenger seat, and sat with my knees hunched in front of me. Josh assumed a similar pose, while Glory Lou demurely sat on her knees, her lower legs wrapped behind her. We could have been a trio

of illegal aliens being smuggled across the border. Well, Glory
Lou, maybe.

Parnassus started on the first try and Kovacs got us out of
Old Sacramento without a hitch. I even saw him touch the
brim of his Panama hat as he drove past the officer on duty
at the I Street entrance.

Then we hit the mother of all traffic jams.

We could not, of course, tune in Captain Mikey in the traffic chopper to find out what was going on. Captain Mikey was
probably taking advantage of the four-day weekend by driving
the entire length of I-5, or whatever it is that traffic reporters
do on their days off. I heard Kovacs punch up KFBK. According to Commander Bill in Newsflight One, the downtown
snarl was due to a combination of the start of a major holiday
weekend, the Jazz Jubilee, and a jackknifed eighteen-wheeler
on Topple Alley, a notorious connector ramp between I-5 and
the W-X Freeway.

I didn't care about the start of some state worker drone's
three-day weekend, nor about the Dixieland fans who were
still trying to bully their way into Old Sacramento. I didn't
even care if the eighteen-wheeler was carrying the serum that
was going to save all the children in the village.

All I cared about was that it took Kovacs practically a half
hour to drive the twenty-some blocks between Old Sacramento
and the DX House.

"This isn't my equipment, you know," Josh said as we climbed
the rickety back stairs to the bungalow on Twenty-first Street.

"Bring those cardboard boxes with you, okay?" I hollered
to Kovacs as he helped Glory Lou scramble out the back door
of the van.

Josh continued to nip at my heels. "Really. This isn't my
stuff. It belongs to Android. He bought it with the money he
won on *Jeopardy!* I just helped him pick out what we needed,
and to get it set up."

I climbed the stairs two at a time to the stifling second floor.
Too bad Android hadn't invested some of his *Jeopardy!* win-

nings in central air. Josh's housemate looked up from his computer as we burst into the pirate radio den.

"Here's the deal," I told Andrew. "I need to borrow your radio equipment for a couple of hours. Not everything, just the transmitter, the telephone interface, and some copper wire. Oh, yeah. The Ampex," I added, gesturing to the reel-to-reel tape machine.

"I'm all, I don't know."

Josh gave his housemate a condensed version of The Blue Door contract. "If we don't get the station back on the air by eight-thirty, Mr. O'Brien loses the station and he has to give it to this other guy. And if this other guy messes up, then he has to turn it over to another one of the original partners. It's all part of a contract they signed, like, fifty years ago."

"You mean like a tontine?"

"A what?" I asked.

"A tontine," Andrew said patiently. "An annuity scheme in which the last survivor among the subscribers gets to keep all the benefits."

Enough of this whiz kid stuff. "Does that mean we can borrow your equipment? I promise we'll take good care of it."

If this kid had been as slow with the signaling button on *Jeopardy!* he'd never have won the teen tournament. "If you help us out, I'll see to it that you get to do a show on our station," I said. "Just a tryout."

He was way too cool to show excitement. "Whatever." But I caught Andrew and Josh exchanging high-fives when they thought I wasn't looking.

I let Andrew direct the dismantling of the ham radio transmitter, the amplifier, the reel machine, and the telephone interface. It was, after all, his equipment. "Put everything in boxes," I said. "And be sure to fold in the tops. I don't want anyone seeing us carrying this stuff around Old Sacramento."

Just for fun, I stacked some of the boys' tape cartridges into one of the boxes. For fun, and for protection. Without access to the network, nor to the commercials back at the station, I was going to have a lot of airtime to fill. The boys and their TV theme music, their sound effects, and their parodies of commercials could come in handy.

"Don't forget the copper wire," I said.

Andrew pulled a large spool from the bottom of the metal shelving unit. "Think you'll need all this?"

"Everything you've got."

Andrew wanted to go with us back to Old Sacramento, but I wouldn't hear of it. "Sorry, but things could get a little dicey tonight." I had misgivings about letting Josh tag along, but he'd been through so much with me. No way I could make him stay home without a major struggle.

Josh's housemate couldn't have looked more crestfallen if he'd flubbed an easy Daily Double after betting a bundle. "Someone's got to stay home and monitor the frequency," I told him. "I'm counting on you to aircheck us at eight-thirty tonight."

"I've been thinking, hon," Glory Lou said. She shifted her white linen-encased thighs on the thinly carpeted metal floor of the van, trying to find a more comfortable position. "Let's say everything you say is true about T. R. losing the station and having to turn it over to Neil Vermont if we're off the air for more than twelve consecutive hours."

"Yeah?" I winced as Parnassus jolted over the railroad tracks between Nineteenth and Twentieth on the ride back to Old Sacramento. Jeez, why didn't Kovacs get some new shocks?

"Why did Junior wait so long to put his plan into action? T. R. left for Alaska last Friday. Wouldn't it have made more sense to do it last weekend?"

"I've thought about that too. But what I'm thinking is, Junior didn't totally have his plan together a week ago. He needed to have Monty Rio meet with the consultant from Triple R, and that didn't happen until Monday. And he probably needed to get contracts signed with all of the syndicators, stuff he couldn't do until his father was out of the picture."

I glimpsed the palms of Capitol Park out the left side of the front window. Why was Kovacs going up L Street? We'd run into gridlock for sure when we hit the Greyhound station and Downtown Plaza.

"And another thing," I said. "Junior needed to get everyone out of town. The chief engineer, absolutely, also Mrs. Yana-moto. The Memorial Day weekend gave him the perfect ex-cuse to give the staff a day off. Who's going to complain?"

Glory Lou said, "Vivienne Kostantin is loaded. If her little boy wanted a radio station so badly, why not just buy one for him?"

"Because he doesn't want just any radio station. He wants this one. T. R. O'Brien's station. Junior's waited a long time for this chance."

"Hey, you can't park here!" I couldn't see the owner of the voice, but I could picture her. Stationed with arms folded on a junior high school playground with a whistle around her neck.

Kovacs had just parked Parnassus in the alley next to the back door to Retro Alley and was lifting the first cardboard box of equipment out the back door. Damn! Josh, Glory Lou, and I scrunched as tightly as we could on the floor of the van behind the remaining boxes.

"Elmarie!" I heard Pete say. "Good to see you again."

"Pete Kovacs, you play a mean piano and you look mighty fine up there onstage, but I'm sorry, I can't let you park your van here. You're blocking a fire exit." But the woman's voice softened from a bark to a friendly yelp.

"I won't be more than five minutes, promise. Just got to unload these boxes. And I do have a delivery permit."

"Well, I don't know . . ."

"See, Elmarie, here's the thing. I just bought a terrific col-lection of vintage 78s. Sinatra, Ellington, Count Basie, Louis Armstrong. Great stuff! I know I'll be able to sell a ton this weekend. But I can't sell it unless I can get it out of the van and into the store. Okay?"

I could just picture Kovacs giving Elmarie his aw-shucks grin. I just hoped he wasn't telling her too good of a story, and that she'd ask to take a look at the record by Ol' Blue Eyes.

By this time, Elmarie was positively purring. "Shoot, I

never could say no to you. Okay, you've got five minutes."

Kovacs finished unloading the boxes, then signaled the coast was clear. Just in time, because my legs were starting to fall asleep. I heard a tearing sound and Glory Lou moaning, "Lordy, there goes another pair of panty hose," as we scooted out of the van and into the back door to Retro Alley.

"Who was that?" I asked Kovacs as we lugged the boxes to the front of the store.

"Who, Elmarie?"

"Of course, Elmarie."

Kovacs balanced his box on the piano bench. "Elmarie Flagg has been doing parking control for the Jubilee since this thing first got started back in 1972. Right after she retired from teaching girls' P.E. at Sutter Middle School."

Josh and Glory Lou made for the front door with their boxes. "Hold on, you guys," I said. "Let's make sure we're not walking into a trap."

I sent Kovacs out for reconnaissance. "I didn't see any cops," he reported. "But there is a guy standing at the front door to the ice-cream parlor. I think he may be the same fellow who was hanging around your apartment complex last night. Big, jowly. No uniform."

"Rolls of fat around the middle? Big butt?"

Kovacs nodded.

I peered out the front window. From my angle, I couldn't see the front door of the ice-cream parlor, but I did have a clear shot at the radio station van, still parked in front. Brandon Nguyen, leaning against the driver's side door, smiled and waved when he saw me. I shook my head violently and put my finger to my lips. He got the drift and assumed his bored slouch.

The bell on the front door tinkled as a trio wearing Jubilee badges entered the store and began exploring the rack with the old bowling shirts. I motioned Kovacs, Josh, and Glory Lou to a corner. "Glott's back," I said in a whisper. "We've got to figure out a way to get the equipment out of Retro Alley, into the ice-cream parlor, and up the stairs to the balcony without him seeing us."

"Why don't we take it out our back door and into the back door of the ice-cream joint?" Josh suggested.

"Great idea," Kovacs said. "Except the ice-cream parlor doesn't have a back door. They bricked it in when they did the historic restoration. Follow me."

We each hoisted a box and, as instructed, followed Kovacs as he led us behind the counter. His gray-headed assistant looked up once, adjusted her reading glasses, and returned to her ledger, apparently used to her boss's eccentricities.

Kovacs took a flashlight hanging from a hook on the wall and opened a trapdoor, revealing a set of tumbledown stairs leading to a basement. I must have looked dubious, because he said, "Don't worry. I fixed all the loose boards just last month."

We landed in the gloomy cavern of the basement. "This used to be the first floor," Kovacs said. He arced the flashlight over crumbling brick walls and gaping doorways leading into dark emptiness. "Sacramento is built on floodplain. The first few years in the city's history, the pioneers got washed out pretty regular. Then in 1863 someone got the idea to raise the city by ten feet, above the high water mark."

"Epic!" Josh said, while I did my best to resist the urge to scamper back up the stairs.

"It was a massive engineering feat," Kovacs continued. Here he was being The History Channel while all I wanted to do was get the hell out. "They carted in literally tons of dirt by wagon and wheelbarrow. Some of the owners jacked up their buildings and filled the space underneath with dirt. Others—like the owner of this place—just turned the first floor into a basement. The second story became the new ground-level floor."

"Could we just move along?" I asked.

I followed Kovacs's flashlight through the dank tomb. I was disoriented, but I was pretty sure we were heading toward what would be the front of Retro Alley, toward Second Street.

"Here's the interesting part," Kovacs said. "When they were busy raising the city, most of the building owners didn't bother to fill in the space between the old sidewalks and the new ones."

"The underground passages," Glory Lou said in awe. "I'd heard about them. But as I live and breathe, I didn't think they still existed."

Three years I lived in Seattle, and never once did I take in the Underground Seattle tour, even though it's supposed to be one of the city's better attractions. Right up there with the Space Needle and the Pike Place Market. I almost had to walk out of *Les Miz*, when they got to the scene where Valjean is in the Paris sewer. I'm not claustrophobic. Just something about tiny, dark, damp underground spaces.

But I was damned if I was going to wuss out now, when we were so close. I tightened my grip on the cardboard box holding the precious transmitting equipment and followed the bobbing circle of yellow light. A blast of icy, foul-smelling air assaulted me as we rounded a corner. Somewhere in the blackness, I swear I could hear a faint clink of metal hitting metal, like the rattle of a chain.

"There're all sorts of legends about the underground passages." I could hear Kovacs's voice in the darkness, but I could barely make out his figure as we entered the narrow subterranean tunnel. "Supposedly they run all the way to the river. They used them for smuggling illegal Chinese immigrants into the city. Back during Prohibition, they were perfect for bootlegging. Course, I don't know how much of this is true."

"But it sure does make a good story," Glory Lou said.

I shushed them as we made our way through the tunnel. We could be passing directly underneath Edward Glott.

Up another flight of flimsy wooden stairs, through another trapdoor, and up we popped in the back storage room of the ice-cream parlor. Freezers and cardboard cartons of cones, napkins, cups, and straws never looked so good.

The owners were busy scooping out cones for a line of heat-crazed jazz fans that stretched out the door. They never noticed the four of us schlepping boxes up their stairs to the second-floor party room.

A slight breeze blew in from the Delta, providing a smidgen of relief to the relentless Sacramento sun when we finally parked our boxes on the balcony. The folding table and chairs were back in place, along with the console, mikes, head-phones, and cart machines. Brandon Nguyen had even draped the station banner over the balcony. So far, so good.

I looked over the front edge of the balcony. From that angle I could see the station van parked directly below. But not the front door of the ice-cream parlor. I tried peering over the side edge, into the two-foot gap that separated the creamery from Pete Kovacs's store.

There he slouched, Edward Glott, chomping on a burrito and reading a copy of *Town and Country* magazine. Probably picking out the dream house—and the trophy wife—he'd buy with all the loot Vivienne Kostantin was giving him to help out her little boy.

I assembled the troops. "Here's the deal," I told them. "We've got to work quiet, and we've got to work fast." I glanced at my watch. Seven on the dot.

"I'm wondering about something," Josh said.

I nodded at him to continue. "Okay, you've got a trans-mitter and all the other equipment. At the DX House, we don't have a tower, just a length of copper wire hanging out the window."

"You could hardly build a three-hundred foot tower in your backyard without drawing some attention to yourselves," I agreed.

"But we weren't interested in covering the whole city. We just wanted to reach the frat houses on Twenty-first Street, and your place, of course. But to really have the station back on the air, and to meet the terms of the contract, don't you have to cover the whole metropolitan area?"

"The contract is vague on a lot of things. But yes, that would be nice."

Josh fidgeted nervously. "That's what I'm trying to say. We don't have a tower."

I looked up at the Retro Alley advertising balloon, wafting peacefully in the Delta breeze. "Yes we do."

31

"I don't mean to burst your balloon, so to speak," Kovacs said. "But this is going to be more trouble than you may think."

"What's the big deal?" I asked. "You go over to your balcony and reel in your cute little red balloon. You let out all the air. If anyone sees you, just tell 'em you're fixing a leak."

Kovacs folded his arms and nodded.

"Then you take the balloon and the helium tank through the basement and back up the stairs to me. We attach copper wire instead of rope, give the balloon another shot of helium, and it's up, up, and away."

"That balloon is bigger than it looks from here. It takes a long time to let all the air out. I'd say at least fifteen minutes, maybe twenty. Then you've got to fold it up. And have you ever tried lifting one of those helium tanks?"

Josh raised his hand. "Wouldn't it be easier to keep the balloon over on Mr. Kovacs's balcony? We could drape the copper wire from the transmitter over the railing to his balcony and then attach it to the balloon. All Mr. Kovacs would have to do is lower the balloon, get rid of the rope, and attach the copper wire."

I gave Josh a quick thumbs-up. "Now, what are we standing around for?"

Josh took charge of hooking up the ham radio transmitter, since he'd done it before with Android. "Just don't forget to change the frequency from 1620 AM to the Sacramento Talk Radio frequency." Kovacs, of course, had the task of diving back into the catacombs under Old Sacramento and surfacing on his balcony to wrestle with the balloon. I assigned Glory Lou the job of helping Kovacs attach the copper wire from this side of the balcony, since she had the longest arms of the crew.

Me, I tinkered with the telephone interface and the reel-to-reel machine.

"I wondered what you had planned for phone lines," Josh said as he watched me prepare to clip a Pac Bell cable onto the Gentner telephone interface box.

"Obviously, we can't use the regular talk lines, since they go into the station. But that's okay. We've got phone lines here."

I held four telephone cables in my left hand. "This line," I said, grabbing one of the wires with my right hand, "originally hooked up the laptops with the computer system back in the newsroom. This"—transferring a second line—"was the IFB line."

"What you guys use so you can listen in your headphones to the air sound from back at the station, right?"

"Correct." I took the third phone wire. "This was our broadcast loop. It carried our air sound from the remote back to the station. And this fourth line"—I made one last hand-to-hand transfer—"was our emergency land line between the remote and the station. If anyone at the station needed to reach us, they'd call us on this line. Now we don't need any of these phone lines hooking us up to the station."

"Yeah, we are the station," Josh said. Then he added, "How will you know what phone numbers to give out when we go back on the air?"

I picked up a discarded beige plastic telephone from the floor and showed him four phone numbers written on cart labels and stuck to the bottom. "It's SOP when we go on remotes. The engineer on duty writes down the phone numbers we've been assigned by Pac Bell and sticks them on the receiver."

Pete Kovacs was right. The balloon was a bigger hassle than I'd thought. Josh and I had finished hooking up all the gear while Kovacs and Glory Lou still struggled with the

torpedo-shaped floating billboard. Kovacs had pulled his hair
back, only a few short tufts of gray showing from underneath
the Panama hat, while Glory Lou had doffed her white linen
jacket.

Kovacs had been right, too, about how big that sucker was.
Reeled in, the balloon filled the Retro Alley balcony and
threatened to pitch him overboard.

"Yo, Pete! Need any help up there?"

Not Elmarie Flagg!

Josh and Glory Lou immediately dropped to the balcony
floor, while I backed through the door into the birthday party
room. I located the owner of the bellow, a rawboned, leather-
skinned woman with hair an unnatural color of yellow. She
stood on the boardwalk across the street, carried a clipboard,
and wore white shorts that drooped past her knees, sneakers,
white socks, and a blue-and-white Jazz Jubilee volunteer T-
shirt.

Kovacs struggled alone with the bobbing oversize beach
toy. One false move and the balloon would break free, launch-
ing untethered into the skies. As Kovacs grasped both hands
around the bottom of the balloon, I watched helplessly as the
end of the copper wire slipped between the antique millwork
of the railing into the gap separating the Retro Alley balcony
from the ice-cream parlor.

"No problem, Elmarie." Kovacs did his best to sound casual. "Just checking her for leaks, that's all. But thanks for
asking."

Elmarie and her clipboard loped south on Second Street,
no doubt searching for parking permit scofflaws. Josh and
Glory Lou stood slowly, while I peered cautiously into the gap
between the two balconies. The end of the copper wire dangled
not two feet from Edward Glott's head. Brandon Nguyen
watched in fascination, but Glott never looked up from his
magazine.

Josh joined Glory Lou in helping Kovacs detach the nylon
rope from the balloon and attach the copper wire. The cooling
breeze from the Delta, normally so welcome, set the miniature
dirigible bouncing and bobbing on the balcony.

Hard to believe almost thirty years earlier, I'd spent a few moments of a summer evening on this very balcony with Dr. Hipster, watching him smoke pot, drink tequila, and hide the empties under the floorboards. If there'd been a joint and a fifth of tequila on the balcony on this warm evening in the dawn of the twenty-first century, I'd have gladly partaken.

The washboard trio wearing the flannel knickers and diamond-patterned wool vests had taken position on the board-walk across Second Street, filling the air with a peppy version of "Down in Honky-Tonk Town." I tried to picture my gen-eration's great-grandchildren attending festivals where bell bottoms, platform shoes, and the music of Steely Dan would seem equally quaint.

Josh's and Glory Lou's jubilant whispers jolted me back to reality. I inspected the copper wire attached securely to the loop at the bottom of the balloon. The other end of the wire wound around the top rail of Kovacs's balcony, then stretched across the gap, where Josh had clipped it to the back of the transmitter. "We're clear for takeoff."

Kovacs loosened his grip on the balloon. The four of us watched in awe as she rose slowly, proudly, into the sky. If I'd had a bottle of champagne, I'd have cracked it against the balcony, no doubt baptizing Edward Glott.

"Will this really work?" Kovacs asked as I stretched across the gap to give him a hug.

"It worked for Marconi. It's almost as good as having a fifty-foot tower. I cut a length of wire exactly one-quarter length of our frequency in meters. Our signal will radiate out from the wire. Everyone in the whole metro area will be able to tune us in, loud and clear."

Kovacs, panting from his run through the underground passage and up the stairs, joined us for a last-minute briefing in the birthday party room.

"Glory Lou, you've still got your field deck, right?"

She nodded, hefting her shoulder bag.

"Go out and get me some sound. Crowd sounds, vendors, anything. Do MOS"—man-on-the-street interviews—"or see if you can get some music on tape. One of the foreign bands, maybe."

"The New Bohemia Jazz Orchestra has a gig at eight at Riverfront Refuge," Kovacs suggested.

I turned to Josh. "Line up some callers. See if you can get the executive director of the Jubilee. Roger what's-his-name. Roger Krum. If you can't get him, then try Warren Harriman in the media trailer. Any celebrities you can find. Shoot, I'll even put Elmarie Flagg on the air."

Josh copied the four phone numbers onto one of my business cards and followed Glory Lou down the stairs.

"You've already done way too much already," I said to Kovacs. "But I have one more favor to ask."

"Here," he said, handing me the Celtics sweatshirt I'd worn this morning. "I picked this up for you on my way back. It'll cool down fast up here once the sun goes down." He'd already donned a similar Red Sox sweatshirt.

I pulled the thick, warm cotton cloth over my head. "I need someone to stay with me and produce the show. It's easy, really. Just someone to help me get the callers on the air, and to pass messages back and forth to Josh and Glory Lou."

"Sounds like fun!"

Kovacs and I seated ourselves side by side on the folding chairs at the table with the remote console and mikes. The sun slipped behind the buildings on Second Street, sending long shadows slanting across the bricks and cobblestones. The music and applause from a half-dozen different concert sites filled the air, while a siren blared in the distance. A stiff gust of wind whipped through the newspapers, paper cups, and stale pastries left over by the morning team. I was thankful Kovacs had thought of the sweatshirt.

One final check. The cartridge holding our station's legal ID positioned in the cart deck. The reel with that missing hour of my show threaded onto the Ampex and cued up to Dr. Hipster's promotional announcement. Microphone positioned directly in front. Headphones, pens, yellow legal pad, envelope full of documents from Lily McGovern.

7:51:15, according to the two-inch-high LED numerals on the digital clock.

I leaned across the table to flip the switch that would start the heterodynes humming, the needles dancing, and the sound of my voice racing up the copper wire and out to the radios of the capital city.

Two sets of footsteps.

One belonging to a smooth, self-assured pair of Gucci loafers. The other, a plodding, size-twelve set of Florsheims.

I twisted in the metal folding chair so I could see the door leading from the balcony back into the birthday party room just as Terrence O'Brien Jr. burst through, followed by Edward Glott.

Glott had a gun.

32

Junior and Glott squeezed their way around the table to the front of the balcony, Glott keeping me firmly covered with the pistol. As soon as they cleared the doorway, I grasped Kovacs's hand under the table and poised to flee.

Go for it!

I turned and rose halfway out of the chair, ready to bolt into the party room.

Until I saw the tall, hefty blonde and the short, stocky African-American in the city police uniforms, guns drawn, crouching in the shadows. The blonde slid behind one of the video games, while the African-American dove under a banquet table, dragging with her the tail end of a tablecloth covered with clown faces.

I sagged. Glott alone, Kovacs and I might have been able to disarm. But not Glott plus two cops, all packing heat.

"You shouldn't have told that kid in engineering not to answer the two-way," Junior said. "I smelled a rat when he didn't return to the station and he didn't respond to my calls. Then Glott here forgot to wear his pager." Junior shot his gluttonous partner a disgusted look. "So I had to come down to Old Sacramento to see what was going on."

Keep him talking. Isn't that what they always advise in those TV shows about psycho kidnappings and hostage situations? The longer Kovacs and I stayed up on the balcony, the better chance we had. I gambled that not even Junior would be rash enough to order Glott to execute us with a potential

audience of thousands. There was always the chance that
Glory Lou or Josh or even Elmarie Flagg would cruise by on
Second Street and spot a man with a gun on the balcony.

Kovacs must have watched the same made-for-TV movie.
"You realize you can't do anything to us," he said. "Too many
people know what's going on. Take my band, for instance.
The boys are going to stop by any minute. We're booked to
perform on her show this evening."

Swear to God, if I get out of this alive, I'll bulk erase every
single one of my rock 'n' roll themes and hire Hot Times as
the new house band.

"You couldn't wait for the old man to retire, could you?"
I said to Junior. "You had to take over now."

The muscle in Junior's left cheek pulsated, but he kept his
cool. "You can't prove a thing."

"T. R. was willing to give you everything. A good education, a salary to support your expensive tastes, access to the
right people and the finest things in life. Except for the one
thing that you really wanted."

Junior replied by jerking the cord of the mult box—the
multiple outlet box into which all of our electrical gear was
plugged—from the orange extension cord leading into the
party room and our source of juice.

"Dr. Hipster figured out what you were up to," I said. "So
you enlisted the help of Glott here and one of his cohorts to
eliminate him. But what they didn't know is, Dr. Hipster had
a visitor, someone whom he was expecting for an appointment
he'd set up earlier. Maybe the visitor's in the john, maybe he's
out on the balcony playing with the cat while all of this is
going down. The point is, the guy sees something that he
shouldn't, realizes something's off, and he scrams."

Glott grunted.

"You or your underling—maybe Wolinsky—spot this mys-
terious visitor when he leaves Dr. Hipster's apartment. My
guess is, he gets into someone's car at Twelfth and N. Probably had prearranged to get picked up after he finishes his
meeting with Dr. Hipster. You follow him around town all
day, until that afternoon, when they drive to the Raley's in
West Sacramento to listen to a band."

Another grunt from Glott. Neither affirmative nor negative, just my cue to continue.

"You see him at the pay phone. He's calling my show as Rudy from West Sacramento. You hear the band, make note of the name of the band and some of their tunes. After he finishes calling my show, the guy boards a city bus or gets into a different vehicle. You lose him."

8:13:04.

Junior could no longer be contained. "He wasn't supposed to kill him, dammit!"

"Prove it."

"Glott had had specific instructions from me just to scare him, to convince him to give us his file and shut up about whatever he knew about the contract, and to agree not to tell the old man."

"Then how'd he end up with a bullet in his head?"

Junior looked at Glott. The hefty former cop said, "Things get outta hand sometimes. One of the hazards of the business."

"You whipped together a cover-up until you could figure out what to do next," I said to Junior. "You were the one who searched Dr. Hipster's desk drawer. You hoped to find his file on the Blue Door contract. Instead, you ran across the fan letters, and realized you'd stumbled across something that might work as a suicide note. You put Dr. Hipster's letter to that gal up in Placerville in an envelope with my name on it, gave it to Glott and told him to plant it in Dr. Hipster's apartment where the police would find it."

"I don't know what you're talking about."

"Monty Rio was no accident," I said. "You were afraid he knew too much about the missing tapes with Dr. Hipster's last promotional announcement. He was in on the meeting with the guys from Triple R so he had to have known what you were planning to do with the station. You saw Monty and me together at the Salt Shaker the other night when you showed up with the sales guys to celebrate making your May budget, remember? You couldn't risk Monty and me sharing information and figuring out what you were really up to, and what had really happened to Dr. Hipster. So you get Glott to arrange for one of his thugs on the security force to try to run over me while I'm out riding my bike, and to force Monty's car off the Garden Highway."

"Those levee roads are dangerous, especially when a man's been drinking and driving a car with faulty brakes," Glott said. "Accidents happen all the time."

"It's really too bad," Junior said. The setting sun at his back created an evil halo around his handsome body. "I had plans for you. You know my new morning show? O.B. in the A.M.? O'Brien and Bogart. We would have made a great team."

"Sidekick to a psycho. Sounds tempting, but I think I'll pass."

Glott and Junior put their heads together for a few moments. For all my flippancy, I writhed inwardly in agony. 8:15:12. Then Glott nodded slowly and gestured toward the door with the pistol. "Let's go."

My entire life did not flash before my eyes. It was not a cosmic moment. It wasn't even a Kodak moment. I could hardly bear to look at Kovacs as he clutched my hand under the table. He was a nice guy, just trying to help. Why did I have to drag him into this mess? Looked like I'd never win a Marconi Award, or be inducted into the Broadcasting Hall of Fame. Except maybe posthumously.

A silly thought kept running through my mind. The poem from *Off Mike and Outta Sight* that Junior had copied into Dr. Hipster's suicide note. What was it, exactly? Something about all is useless without love? I always hated sappy sentimentality. Funny that I would think of it at a moment like this.

"Get moving," Glott ordered.

"Not so fast, fatso!" The voice: high-pitched, gritty, a dentist's drill skittering across a blackboard. Two streaks of silver darted from the balcony door. One gun. And one hook.

I fought back the urge to fling myself into T. R. O'Brien's arms. He positioned his cowboy-booted feet next to my folding chair, his pistol squared off against Edward Glott. Junior's eyes grew larger, but other than that, I had to give him points for coolness under pressure.

"My boy, you should have known I'd take a radio with me to Alaska," T. R. said. "I was able to pull in the station at night. The skip, you know."

Junior stood next to Glott between the table and the balcony railing. "How very interesting."

"You should have made sure we had the right winner in the Gold Rush Giveaway Monday night. As soon as I heard another Sac State student winning the contest, I knew something was seriously wrong back at the station."

Junior folded his arms.

"Neil Vermont never was able to shut up once he started drinking. Something the two of you have in common, I believe. He let spill about paying off the bush pilot not to pick us up like he was supposed to."

The fingers of Junior's right hand began to pull and dig at the skin on the back of his left hand.

"The next morning I radioed the bush pilot and told him I'd double whatever Vermont had offered to pick me up ASAP and fly me into Ketchikan."

T. R. paused and handed me the gun. Jeez! What did he expect me to do? I hefted the thing in shaking hands, both fists wrapped around the part with the trigger. I did my best to keep it aimed at the general direction of Edward Glott.

My boss dug into his shirt pocket, pulled out a package of unfiltered Camels and a Bic lighter, shook out one cigarette, placed it between his lips and lit up, all with one hand. He inhaled deeply, then transferred the cigarette to the hook. Then—thank God—he took back the gun.

"I took a few spare parts out of the CB radio before I left camp," T. R. continued. "Don't worry, the rest of the guys have got plenty of food and beer. I instructed the pilot to pick them up tomorrow morning. Neil Vermont should be limping home sometime Sunday afternoon."

"How very clever of you, Father." But his bravado was starting to crumble. His hands trembled and spittle was gathering at the corner of his mouth.

"My boy, the thing I don't understand is why you had to go through all this plotting just to get your hands on the radio station. You're my only child, my sole heir. I'm a tough old bird, but someday I'm going to wear out. Sonny, it all would have been yours."

"You were never willing to give me the one thing I really wanted."

For the first time T. R.'s voice faltered. "What?"

"I never really wanted all this other stuff, the money and the power. I just wanted to be Terry Tiger."

"Son, we've been through this before," T. R. said gently. "You're destined for much bigger things."

"You never really gave me a chance."

"I had no idea it meant so much to you. I am sorry. I truly am."

8:23:46.

Two things were possible.

One, Junior and T. R. would hug, cry, and promise to make it up to each other. Glott would surrender and Junior would spend a few years in a Club Fed–type facility.

But Junior opted for the second possibility.

His eyes got a scary, glazed look. Lawrence Harvey, being slowly driven mad by the Commies and Angela Lansbury in *The Manchurian Candidate*.

"Screw you." A spray of saliva. He nodded to Glott.

Glott reached across the corner of the table and yanked me out of the folding chair. Fast for someone so hefty. Glott held me against his massive gut, a meaty arm across my throat. I felt the icy steel of the pistol against my forehead.

I am proud to report that I did not scream. I did, however, come close to requiring my second set of fresh undies of the day.

Kovacs leaped out of the chair next to me.

"No!" I shouted. As in: Don't be a hero! As in: Don't shoot!

Glott smashed the butt of the pistol against Kovacs's forehead. Blood gushed down the side of his face and he crashed back into the folding chair, collapsing onto the wooden floor of the balcony. His Panama hat flew off and his graying brown hair fell over his bleeding forehead.

This time I screamed.

Then a lot of stuff happened at once.

The two female cops burst into the balcony, crouched in the classic marksman's pose, guns pointed at Edward Glott. "Freeze, sucker!"

My captor dropped the pistol and shifted his 250-plus pounds, landing on a loose floorboard. The board collapsed with a crunch of old, dry wood. Glott's huge arm relaxed its hold around my neck. I dropped to the floor and rolled to the balcony railing.

Glott lost his balance and toppled like a bowling pin, caroming into Junior. The younger O'Brien pitched ass-over-teakettle and crashed into the reproduction Victorian woodwork that formed the railing. More crunching, splintering, and thuds as a three-foot chunk of railing broke away and landed on the cobblestones one story below.

Junior let out a sickening cry and slid over the edge.

His arms flailed and he frantically grabbed hold of my right leg as he plunged into space.

I desperately grappled at one of the railing posts that still appeared to be intact. The post shook, but it held.

Junior's hands slid to my foot. I could feel his fingers scrabbling at my sandals.

The post I clutched so desperately began to splinter and tear.

A ripping sound as the Velcro strap to my sandal separated. Another agonized cry.

From my spot on the floor of the balcony, I had a perfect view. Junior, still clutching my Teva, plummeting into the air, heading straight for the harsh cobblestone street.

He landed butt-first on the roof of the radio station van, bounced once, then slid down the side of the van to the street. His elegant suit jacket had torn at the shoulder, and he clasped his right ankle, rocking in pain, but otherwise it looked like he'd survive to stand trial.

I was also in the ideal position to peer past Glott, into the hole in the floorboard, where the ex-cop's massive foot still thrashed.

When they rehabbed the old Golden Empire Broadcasting building and restored it to its nineteenth-century splendor, they never bothered to redo the balcony floor.

Just past Glott's cheap shoe I saw something smooth and shiny.

A tequila bottle.

33

"You okay?" Kovacs held his left hand out to help me up. His right hand pressed a bandanna against the cut on his forehead.

Blood oozed from the scrape on my hand from two nights ago, and my legs quivered when I tried to stand. But it looked like I was going to make it. "I think so. How about you?"

"Only a scratch. I jumped back before Glott was able to hit me full-on. Pretty good reflexes for an old guy."

The blonde in the city police uniform was busy putting cuffs around the wrists of the beached whale that was Edward Glott, while T. R. covered him with his gun.

"Who's she?" I asked Kovacs. He shook his head and raised his free hand, palm up.

T. R. kept his eyes and gun trained on Glott, but spoke to me. "The Sac PeeDee chief 'n' me go way back. I called him from Portland last night and asked him to keep an eye on you. I understand you gave his finest quite a chase."

O'Brien paused to chuckle. "Meet Officer Melody Van Pelt," he said, indicating the Amazon. "Sergeant Donette Mitchell is on her way downstairs to cover Junior until the paramedics arrive."

I gave Officer Van Pelt a quick nod, then hobbled with my one bare foot to the table.

8:29:14.

I inserted the plug to the mult box. Lights glowed and needles popped to attention. I flicked the switch to the transmitter, then punched up the cart with our legal ID, the call letters, and city of license. I started my theme music, cleared my throat, and opened the mike.

The last rays of the setting sun sparkled and glistened off the copper wire leading to the big red balloon suspended over Old Sacramento. I could almost see the electrons dancing as my words raced up the wire and radiated out into car radios, boom boxes, and Walkmans all over the capital city.

"At 8:29 on a Friday evening, live from Old Sacramento, Shauna J. Bogart is back on the air!"

I welcomed my listeners to the show and gave out the phone numbers. Then I closed the mike and played the *Jeopardy!* theme music that I'd filched from Josh's collection to give myself time to figure out what I'd do next.

"What the hell took you so long?" I asked T. R.

"Cora 'n' me met up at SeaTac Wednesday afternoon. I didn't know exactly what was going down, but I figured Junior must have some help from the cops. I didn't know who to trust."

"I know the feeling."

"I had a bad feeling Junior or his pals might be watching the airport. Cora rented a car and we took turns driving. Damn piece of junk broke a fan belt outside of Yreka. We hit town around six."

"Why'd you make me sweat for so long out here on the balcony?"

"We figured it'd be safer to grab you and your friend after Glott brought you back into the building. Anyway, I knew you could take care of yourself."

"You really had me going there about the missing hour of tape on the logger reel. For the longest time, I thought you were trying to get rid of any recorded evidence of Dr. Hipster's danger message."

"That young gal, that Tiffany, she was the first bogus winner in the Gold Rush Giveaway. I had to make sure there wasn't the slightest hint the contest might not be on the level. I told Monty Rio to pull off the entire hour from the logger reel so's I could keep it under lock and key."

"Yeah, when she said that bit about 'the lady told me to

call' I assumed she was referring to me when I announced the winning numbers on the air."

I was about to continue that thought when the *Jeopardy!* theme ended on three bouncy notes.

"A lot of you saw or heard Jeff Greene's news conference earlier today," I said into the mike. "If you did, you know he told us he never made any questionable deals with major developers. Stay tuned, because we have exclusive evidence linking Senator Greene to a deal that threatens to destroy the last major stretch of undeveloped coastland in the state." I glanced next to the mike, where a brown envelope held Lily McGovern's paper trail.

"But first, as you may know, this station was off the air for nearly twelve hours today. It wasn't due to technical difficulties, the weather, or your radio. I went to a lot of trouble to get this station back on the air. Me and my colleagues. We didn't do it just so we could break a story about one of the candidates for governor. If this station didn't do it, someone else would."

I was winging it totally. "It doesn't matter to me who wins the election. What's important is that this radio station stays on the air. It's a local, independent voice. Do you have any idea how few of us are left in this country? Time was, every city this size or larger had at least a dozen stations like this one, either locally owned or owned by a small chain, with local announcers and local DJs.

"Nowadays, they're almost all controlled by two major corporations, with syndicated talk hosts, or canned music off the satellite. Folks, this station came very, very close to joining those ranks today. Shauna J. Bogart, for one, wasn't going to sit by and let it happen."

I thought about urging my listeners to support businesses that advertise on local, independent radio stations. To fill out a ratings diary, even if it's a hassle, if Arbitron sends them one. To write to the FCC if their local, independent station gets swallowed up by a media giant.

But I didn't want to sound preachy. So I only said, "I just happen to think we're losing something precious and vital to

America when we lose our local, independent radio stations. But enough on that. Let's take some calls!"

A small crowd gathered in the darkness of Second Street to watch the show. Brandon Nguyen had hooked up the speakers on top of the station van. He'd also found a couple of theatrical spotlights in the party room, which provided much-needed light.

Josh and Glory Lou joined me around the makeshift radio station, Josh in his old position of call screener. Without access to the computer, he did it the old-fashioned way, slipping me pieces of paper from a yellow legal pad. Glory Lou, meanwhile, handed me a half-dozen cassette tapes, cued up to the start of interviews and music from Jubilee bands. From the edge of the balcony, I could see T. R. watching the paramedics tend to his son, while the two city cops stood guard.

Josh and Glory Lou and T. R., I wanted to gather them up and hold them close. They were the nearest thing I'd had to family in a long time. Hell, they *were* family.

If only Pete Kovacs were here with me. He'd figured maybe he'd better get that cut on his forehead checked out after all. He'd left to find the Jubilee first-aid tent shortly after I'd gotten the station back on the air.

I scanned Josh's list of callers.

On Line One, Marv from Rio Linda, saying the black helicopters had something to do with the station being off the air for most of the day.

On Line Two, Diane on a car phone, wanting to know if it's true Bill Gates is giving away his entire fortune, and all you need to do to get your share is to forward an e-mail to five friends.

On Line Three, Ferretman Bob, demanding to know what any of this has to do with Senator Greene's stand on legalization.

A familiar name on Line Four. I punched it up on the telephone interface.

"Miz Bogart. I am from offering to you congratulations."

I could hear Glory Lou's whisper and T. R.'s cackle as Josh pointed to something in the street.

I didn't really need to follow Josh's outstretched arm indicating a figure standing next to a lamppost. But I did anyway. In the glow of the artificial gaslight, I could just make out a man in jeans, black T-shirt, and a fringed jacket. Graying hair flowed from a Panama hat with a Red Sox logo on the band. A white bandage clung to his forehead. He held a cellular phone to his ear.

Rudy from West Sacramento.

"Aren't you forgetting something?" A familiar scrawny figure trotted from the party room onto the balcony. Mimi Blitzer paused to catch her breath from her run up the stairs. She held a white number ten envelope in her right hand.

"Of course. The Gold Rush Giveaway. How could I be so careless? Have a seat, Mimi." I offered the empty folding chair across from me.

"We guaranteed a winner every hour today," Blitzer said as she seated herself. "So you've got to read this number before nine o'clock."

"No problem. As soon as Glory Lou's interview with the manager of the Jubilee finishes, I'll get right on it." I glanced at the tape cassette deck and figured the interview had at least another two minutes to run.

"It's scary how expensive weddings have gotten these days, isn't it?" I said to Blitzer.

She ignored my comment and placed the envelope on the table with the hand wearing the engagement ring.

"Chateaubriand, a designer gown, a disc jockey. A money dance is hardly going to cover all that expense." Not to mention a fiancé who can't even get an offer from a big law firm after graduating from King Hall at UC Davis. That job with the state won't even come close to meeting the needs of a bride with expensive tastes.

"Just hurry up and read the numbers." Blitzer's voice took a desperate tone.

"Don't worry, I'll get to it." I clasped my hands behind my head and looked up at the strand of copper wire and the Retro Alley balloon wafting in the twilight breeze. "What did you and Alvin promise those Sac State students, anyway? I know you were making up a whole new batch of winning numbers and supplying them to the students, so don't try to deny it. A percentage of the winnings if they called the station at the prearranged time when we read their lucky numbers? Or just a flat fee?"

"I think you've been listening to your own airchecks too much," Biltzer said. "You're getting paranoid."

I smiled and reached across the table, took the envelope from Blitzer, slit it open, and removed the three-by-five card. The same card I'd prepared a few hours earlier. The very card that Josh, at my direction, had planted in Blitzer's stack of envelopes in the station van. Originally, before I was positive what she was up to, I'd dreamed up the stream of numbers as a gag. Now I figured I could tweak Blitzer's conscience by reading them with just the right inflection. Of course, I could always just expose her little scam over the air, or even call 9-1-1. But with all the cops roaming Old Sacramento and listening to their coded lingo over our loudspeakers, the plan simmering in my brain could prove to be much more fun.

"Ten-fourteen." Citizen holding a suspect.

"Fifty-one fifty." Out-of-control mental/emotional problem.

"Ten-zero." Use caution.

"Twelve." Code twelve, alert news media.

I held the three-by-five card and opened the mike. "Coming up next, another guaranteed winner in the Gold Rush Giveaway on the Shauna J. Bogart Show. So don't touch that dial!"

Keep Reading for an Excerpt

from Joyce Krieg's Next Mystery

SLIP CUE

Coming Soon

from St. Martin's/Minotaur!

The fact that she had local roots made the story all the juicier.

In the background, I could hear the thrum of afternoon traffic on Highway 160 beating its way past the bulletproof glass and through the walls of the on-air radio studio. Newspaper clippings and faxes cluttered the control console. The call-in lines blinked in two-beat harmony with a car dealer's jingle. "Save your dough, deal with Joe." A television monitor suspended over the console, the sound muted, carried the first game of the World Series.

"You're tuned to The Shauna J. Bogart Show," I said into the mike. "T-N-A—talk, news, and attitude—for Sacramento's drive home. We'll be right back after this."

I punched the button on the top cart deck, activating a promotional announcement for the sports talk show that followed my three hours of airtime. I handed the wire copy to my executive producer and gestured to the guest mike. "We'll break in with a bulletin soon as I finish this stop-set," I told him through the intercom.

A few months ago, I wouldn't have trusted Josh Friedman to nuke a bag of microwave popcorn without setting off a second-stage smog alert, let alone go on the air with a breaking news story. He was only a college intern, eager but green. That was before he proved to me how loyal and resourceful he could be. Okay, okay. The kid helped save my butt. Not only did Josh earn a fancy title for his efforts, but I wangled some money out of the boss to actually pay him to be my producer-slash-flunky.

"You're back with Shauna J. Bogart. Before we take your calls, Josh Friedman joins us in the Sacramento Talk Radio newsroom." I flipped the on-air switch to the guest mike and pointed a finger at Josh.

The student's voice was rapid but steady. "A spokesman for the Monterey County Sheriff has confirmed reports that the television star known as Jasmine has escaped from custody. She was being transported from a routine appearance in the courthouse in downtown Salinas back to the county jail when the escape occurred."

I picked up the remote and flicked the TV monitor to CNN. Even with the sound off, I could follow the story from the on-screen images: The '70s-era album cover, *Jasmine Soup*, the singer at the peak of her rock diva glory, an exotic nymph in flowing rich hippie garb, surrounded by the symbols of the zodiac. If you listen to oldies radio, you can undoubtedly recite all three verses to her one big Top 40 hit, "Meet Me at the Casbah." Next came footage from her more recent incarnation as a sitcom star, playing the middle-aged earth mother to a Partridge Family–style band. Then Jasmine in handcuffs and jail overalls, defiant in front of the TV cameras. The map of northern California, blinking buttons to indicate the Monterey peninsula, scene of the crime, and the county seat of Salinas some 20 miles to the east. The *People* magazine cover—From Songbird to Jailbird—and the gritty black-and-white of the tabloid headlines—Bad Trippin' with Jasmine.

Sex, drugs, and rock'n'roll. It always sells.

"Repeating our top story, officials in Salinas confirm Jasmine has escaped from custody. Keep it tuned to Sacramento Talk Radio for the latest." Josh pointed, throwing it back to me.

No matter what, stay with the story. If a quarter-century working behind the mike has taught me nothing else, I've learned the importance of never to letting anything stand in the way of a breaking news story. That, and never letting callers named for flowers or months get on the air.

"We'll go live to the network as soon as they have new

developments," I told my listeners. "In the meantime, we're lining up phoners from Salinas, so don't go away."

WHERE THE HELL IS SALINAS, ANYWAY? My executive producer, tapping a message on the computer linking his call screener booth with the on-air studio.

Jeez, don't they make college students read Steinbeck these days? *East of Eden, The Pastures of Heaven?*

SOUTH OF SILICON VALLEY, NORTH OF L.A. THE NATION'S SALAD BOWL. TRY DIRECTORY ASSISTANCE IN 831. I returned the message while keeping my ears tuned to Debbie from Carmichael on Line Two. Debbie claimed to have known Jasmine when she was just plain Cynthia Pepper, a B-plus average student at El Camino High School.

"She was just the sweetest thing," Debbie said. "There's no way she could have done all those horrible things you media people keep saying she did. Just no way."

"I'm not saying you're wrong," I replied. "And I believe in innocent until proven guilty in a court of law. But you've got to admit it looks bad."

"Who's to say someone else didn't kill Johnny Venture? Jasmine could have just been in the wrong place at the wrong time. How do we know for sure?"

"If she really didn't do it, why break out of jail? Why not wait for the verdict and walk away a free woman?"

The callers pretty much reflected the tabloid court of opinion. Take your pick. Jasmine was a victim of male aggression who finally fought back. Or she was an innocent waif who got into something way over her head. Or a ruthless diva who would stop at nothing to make sure she stayed in the national spotlight. My attention darted from the callers to CNN, the program log, the control board, back to the screener booth. Judging from the body language coming from the other side of the glass—lots of palm slaps to the forehead—things were not going well, telephone-wise, between Sacramento and Salinas.

"No luck?" I asked Josh on the intercom during a commercial break.

"The sheriff's holding a news conference at five, so no one's saying anything 'til then."

"Live at five. How convenient for the TV cameras."

"The AP stringer's in the field and I can't track her down. The local network affiliate's on deadline and won't help."

"You tried the courthouse, of course."

"Can't get through. Every line is busy."

Truth is, it doesn't mean squat whether we get anyone from Salinas to agree to talk to us on the air. We could simply have let the network run, any network, and the listeners would have known everything there was to know about Jasmine's jail escape. Or we could have kept reading wire service copy. But a live interview with someone on the scene creates the illusion our station is one-up on everyone else. Even if all the interviewee is doing is parroting Associated Press copy.

"AP just sent over a longer story," Josh said.

"I'll throw it to you cold coming out of the last spot."

A taped announcement ended with a caution that my actual mileage will vary. I played my theme music, reintroduced the Shauna J. Bogart show, announced the time and temperature, and let Josh take over.

"The escape apparently took place two hours ago," Josh read into the guest mike. "A van transporting Jasmine and four other female prisoners from the courthouse back to the correction facility was surrounded by armed men. Witnesses say the van was stopped at a traffic signal next to the Salinas rodeo grounds. The men forced the driver out of the van and took control. The van was last seen traveling at high speed on Highway 101 northbound onramp. It was followed by a vehicle described by witnesses as a late '70s Chevy Impala. The other prisoners in the van have been identified as Ofelia Hernandez of King City, and Irmalinda Guzman, Marcelina Villareal, and Bobette Dooley, all of Salinas."

The AP update ended by informing us Jasmine had been in court earlier in the day for all of five minutes on a reduction of bail motion. The DA asked for a continuance, which the judge granted.

Meanwhile, Captain Mikey in the traffic chopper had a particularly juicy tie-up on US 50 to warn us about, complete with alternate routes. That interruption gave me time to dash to my desk and pick up the latest *Broadcasting Yearbook*. I heaved the thick paperback through the door of the call screener booth. "Look up the jazz station in Monterey and see if you can track down Donovan Sinclair."

Josh gave me a quizzical look, but picked up the receiver and began flipping through the pages.

"Make sure he can go on the air with us before the sheriff's news conference," I added through the intercom as I popped the headphones over my ears and adjusted the mike.

Five minutes later, and a full fifteen minutes before the sheriff was due to face the press, Josh flashed a thumbs-up. SINCLAIR'S HOLDING ON THE HOTLINE. WHERE DO YOU KNOW THIS GUY FROM, ANYWAY?

JUST ONE OF THOSE RADIO THINGS.

One of the many things I love about this business is how everyone knows one another in the radio community. Go to any town in America and chances are you'll find a friend, someone you once worked with on the climb up or on the long slide down. Or at least someone who knows the same people you do, and shares your passion for and insider's knowledge of the most intimate of the communications media.

GOOD JOB, I added to my message to Josh.

"In case you've just joined us, repeating the hour's top story, the pop music star known as Jasmine, accused of homicide in the death of an elderly man in a Monterey peninsula hotel, has escaped from custody," I told my listeners. "The correction facility van carrying Jasmine and four other female prisoners was hijacked by armed men while she was being transported from an appearance at the Monterey County courthouse in Salinas back to the county jail.

"The Monterey County sheriff is holding a news conference at five. Of course, we'll be carrying it live. In the meantime, exclusively for Sacramento Talk Radio, we bring you a live interview with a Monterey County insider, an eyewitness to the local scene."

Well, I didn't actually say he was an eyewitness to the escape, did I?

"This isn't about Jasmine," Sinclair said in a radio announcer school baritone after I'd introduced the Monterey disk jockey to my listeners.

"Run that by us again," I said.

"The jailbreak. It doesn't have anything to do with Jasmine. She was just along for the ride."

"What makes you say that?"

"Look at the scenario," Donovan said. "Two of those young ladies in the van had connections with local Latino gangs. The men who surrounded the van have been described by witnesses as Hispanic. They were driving a low-rider vehicle. When this thing shakes out, it'll turn out one of those guys was trying to bust out his girlfriend. Or kidnap some rival's girlfriend. Everyone around here knows this had nothing to do with some out-of-town celebrity suspect."

"No way!" I knew I was gushing, but I couldn't help myself. This was great stuff! I just hoped the hosts at the other local news radio stations were tuned in. Not to mention the news directors of the TV stations and the editorial staff at the *Sacramento Bee.*

"You know, Jasmine wasn't even supposed to be in court today," Donovan continued.

"I thought it was some routine motion for reduction of bail."

"The hearing was calendared for tomorrow. They moved it up at the last minute because the judge had some sort of personal emergency."

I managed to squeeze in one last traffic update before the top of the hour and the start of the sheriff's news conference. Off mike, I told Donovan he'd been terrific. "No one else has the Latino gang angle."

"You're pretty terrific yourself," he replied. "You're the only media person who thought to call a local insider like me instead of dealing with that circus over at the courthouse."

"How do you know all this stuff, anyway? You can tell me and still protect your sources. We're off the air now."

"You know the sheriff? We're real close. In fact, we had a little thing going on a few years ago."

I don't know what I expected from the Monterey County sheriff when the law enforcement officer appeared on the network

TV screens at five. Typical small town cop, I suppose. But the chief law enforcement officer for Monterey County wasn't fat or grizzled, didn't wear a rumpled suit covered with doughnut crumbs, and didn't speak with a cracker twang.

Sheriff Maria Elena Perez smashed a lot of stereotypes when she made her live, coast-to-coast debut, that's for certain.

"We're following up on several leads linking the hijacking of the correction facility van with Latino gang activity," she told reporters. "One of the prisoners who escaped was a known associate of the leader of a major Salinas street gang."

Thank you, Donovan Sinclair.

I opened the network pot, allowing the satellite feed to air live without interruption, and left the air studio for the newsroom, where I could watch four TV monitors instead of just one. ABC, CBS, NBC, and CNN brought me Maria Elena Perez in quadruplet: an unsmiling woman in her 50s wearing a simple dark gray suit, blue silk blouse, masses of black hair shot with gray caught neatly in a silver comb above each ear.

She spoke forthrightly, directly into the cameras. "I pledge the full strength of my department in tracking down and recapturing the escaped inmates, including the suspect known as Jasmine. We take it seriously when a jailbreak happens in Monterey County on my watch."

If she could make good on her pledge, I had an idea we'd be seeing more of Maria Elena Perez on the political scene in the years to come.

Josh Friedman joined me under the bank of TV monitors and handed me a slick, four-color magazine. "It just came in today's mail." *Sacramento* magazine, folded open to the "Out and About in Sacramento" section, which had nothing to do with gay nightlife but instead chronicled the capital city's A-list social circuit. Photograph of a frizzy-haired woman in a slinky black dress standing next to a man in a tux. "Sacramento's celebrity couple to watch continues to be Shauna J. Bogart and Pete Kovacs. She's the top-rated afternoon radio talk show host, and he's the Old Sacramento antiques dealer and hot jazz pianist. We caught up with this busy pair at the opening night gala for the State Fair."

I reread the cutline and handed the magazine back to Josh.

Pete Kovacs. He'd called me just before the show, hoping we'd be able to get together this evening. He sounded serious, said he had something "important" to talk to me about, and something "interesting" to show me.

I was pretty sure I knew what Pete Kovacs wanted to talk about. And damned if I knew how I was going to let him down easy.

The networks cut away from the news conference and back to filler material: stand-ups in front of the courthouse and the jail, maps with dotted lines showing the getaway route, more Jasmine career highlights. ABC had dug up footage from a headline performance at the Fillmore, Jasmine crooning the opening lines to "Meet Me at the Casbah."

Meet me at the casbah
The incense will light our way
It's twelve steps over a light wave
Then mellow out in a bright cave . . .

Never did figure out what all that was supposed to mean.

I continued to stare at the bank of TV monitors and wondered, not for the first time, why none of the attention was focused on a meek man with a white beard, a quiet little fellow whom you'd never notice. Unless you listened to him, of course, and entered his private world. The man Jasmine was accused of smothering with a pillow in a cabin in a aged Monterey motor court.

An over-the-hill DJ named Johnny Venture.

I slashed my signature on the bottom of the program log and gathered up headphones, show notes, and news clipping file. The 6:00 P.M. network newscast sounder boomed across the airwaves. The Jasmine jail escape was, of course, the lead story. No surprise there. I waited until the network newscaster moved on to the next item—car bombing in the Middle East, no big surprise there either—and allowed myself to savor the memory of my performance for the past three hours, highlights playing back in my mind like a tape slowly unspooling.

". . . Monterey County authorities say they have found a correctional facility van used in today's daring escape of television star Jasmine and four other inmates. It was abandoned next to a lettuce field near the community of Spreckels southeast of Salinas. Still no sign of the suspect. . . ."

". . . Sacramento Talk Radio has located Brianna Burke, who plays the part of the oldest daughter on *Yo Mama*. She has agreed to talk exclusively on The Shauna J. Bogart Show, Ms. Burke, what was Jasmine like to work with on the set . . ."

". . . Okay, okay. I know Jasmine was overheard by a bunch of people in a hotel lobby telling Johnny Venture that she hoped he'd rot in hell just a few hours before she allegedly killed him. But that doesn't necessarily mean she was threatening him. It could have just been her way of flirting . . ."

". . . This just in to the Sacramento Talk Radio newsroom, our sources in Salinas say two of the women who escaped with Jasmine have been apprehended in the parking lot at a

Salinas shopping mall. Stay tuned for an exclusive report. . . ."

" . . . Monterey County Sheriff Maria Elena Perez has just confirmed earlier reports that two of the inmates who escaped with Jasmine have been apprehended. We go live to the sheriff's office in Salinas . . ."

" . . . You heard it here first on Sacramento Talk Radio. The Monterey County Sheriff has just revealed one of the inmates who escaped with Jasmine has strong ties with the so-called Mexican mafia. Ofelia Hernandez of King City, arrested on a charge of assault and battery, is still at large. So is Bobette Dooley of Salinas, who is facing charges of assault and disturbing the peace. . . ."

I heaved open the soundproof door of the on-air studio and did a little do-si-do around the sports talk guy whose show followed my three hours of airtime. Steve Garland was laden with headphones, notebooks, faxes, news clippings, stats books, and a super-size bucket of soda from the convenience mart.

"Killer show!" he said to me by way of greeting.

I was in junior high, a gawky loner who spent her after-school hours listening to the radio and re-reading back issues of *Mad* magazine, the year "Meet Me at the Casbah" charted as a Hitbound Sound on Top 40 radio. The seductive melody and enigmatic lyrics—what the hell was "twelve steps over a light wave" anyway?—made it one of those tunes that defined an era, just like "Stayin' Alive" time-stamps the disco era of a few years later. Or how all those "Yeah, Yeah, Yeah" Beatles tunes sum up 1964. I actually met Jasmine five or six years after "Meet Me" went platinum. By then, I had managed to parley my geek girl's knowledge of radio engineering, plus a naturally low-pitched voice and a talent for patter honed after all those countless hours glued to the radio, into a gig as the sole female DJ on the top-rated FM station in San Francisco. Jasmine dropped by the studio to plug the first of her many comeback attempts. I met a lot of stars on their way up and their way down in those days, and my memories are somewhat vague: a coked out, overly made-up, steel-edge woman old before her time. But that description could fit most of the rock'n'roll chicks back in the '70s.

Interesting, how people's lives intersect for a moment, a day, or a year, and then take widely-divergent paths, like two streams that flow together for a few miles, then split apart, one meandering through sunlit meadows and the other thundering down a rocky precipice. The gawky adolescent staring at the LP cover with its airbrushed photo of the rock star and dreaming of the day when she, too, would wear velvet, lace, and flowers in her hair, and be adored by millions, becomes, in 30 years, the trusted voice of authority, reporting the humiliating downfall of her one-time idol.

My musings came to a halt at the sight of a long-haired man wearing a Boston Celtics sweatshirt sitting on top of my desk, his jeans-clad legs swinging over the side.

"How'd you get in here?" I asked.

"Is that any way for Sacramento's hottest celebrity couple to greet each other?" Pete Kovacs smiled and opened his arms for an embrace.

Pete Kovacs and I had hooked up this past Memorial Day weekend, when we shared a moment of terror on a balcony in Old Sacramento and managed to stop the last remaining family-owned radio station in the Sacramento market from falling into the hands of a big corporate chain. By the time the Fourth of July fireworks had exploded in the sky over Cal Expo, we'd become an item, trading phone calls every evening, spending most weekends together, even exchanging keys to each other's cribs.

Now the Halloween decorations were up in all of the stores, and he was saying he had something "interesting" to show me and something "important" to talk about.

If this "interesting" and "important" thing involved a diamond ring, I had no idea how I would respond.

I mean, I liked the guy. We were of the same mind on all the important stuff: politics (progressive), money (moderate conservatism), kids (he'd been there, done that; if my biological clock was ticking, I couldn't hear it), and pizza (cheese plus one topping, two at the most, and no "garbage", i.e. no pineapple, artichoke hearts, or free-range mesquite-grilled chicken). Our ages were a good match-up, me in my thirties (okay, thirty-nine) and Pete in his mid-forties. We agreed that any *Cheers* rerun with Diane automatically trumped a Rebecca episode, and we didn't snarl at each other over petty annoyances like the toilet seat being left up or down. We had fun hangin' with each other, and, well, we just looked like we belonged together, like that photo in *Sacramento* magazine.

I just wasn't sure if I was ready to commit to the whole marriage *megillah*. We hadn't been together all that long, really. We'd yet to survive the emotional HazMat zone of the Terrible Trio of holidays: Thanksgiving, Christmas, and New Year's Eve. Age and experience had taught me the wisdom of caution when it came to personal relationships. Like the old song says, fools rush in.

And yet . . . he made me feel good. Very, very good.

"Your boss's secretary was just locking up when I pulled into the parking lot," Kovacs said. "She waited and held the door open for me. I think she likes me."

"A woman of excellent taste," I said as I disentangled myself from his hug.

A cardboard file storage container squatted on the desk next to Kovacs. Not exactly the blue box from Tiffany that I'd secretly anticipated. "I thought you might find this interesting." Kovacs slid off the desk, dug into the box, and pulled out a bubble-wrapped package. He undid the plastic and let slip out a thin, round disk roughly the size of a personal pizza. He held it reverently against the palms of both hands, careful not to let his fingers touch the surface.

"Gee, a 45," I said.

He peered at the words on the label. "The Dee Vines, recorded live at the El Jay studio on Stockton Boulevard in 1961."

"Isn't that interesting?" I said, trying to sound as if I cared. Sure, I remembered 45 RPM records. Even bought a few as a kid until my allowance grew big enough to cover the cost of LPs. In fact, *Jasmine Soup* was the first thirty-three-and-a-third in my collection.

Kovacs retrieved a cassette tape from the box. "I copied the 'Cruisin' on K Street' 45 onto tape. You've just got to hear this." He placed the casette in the deck in one of the newsroom's editing stations and pressed the play button. The sounds of four-part harmony crooning about the joys of teen-age cars and crushes poured from the speaker. I'd not even been born during the doo-wop era, but to my untrained ear, the Dee Vines sounded at least as harmonious as the Platters. I had to admit, "Cruisin' on K Street" boasted cute lyrics and a catchy beat. Like they say, you could dance to it.

"Aren't they just great?" Kovacs said when the last note faded. "The granddaughter of one of the Dee Vines came by the store with this box a couple of weeks ago. She's trying to decide what to do with the old demo tapes and disks Grandpa left her. Is it worth trying to sell them, or should she donate the whole box to the city archives and take the tax write-off?"

"You're asking the wrong person. This is way, way before my time. I never even heard of the Dee Vines or this El Jay recording studio."

"From what the granddaughter told me, El Jay provided an affordable way for local bands, black and white, to make re-cordings back in the fifties and sixties, when it was possible for a group to actually have a regional hit without being on a major label."

"Yeah, and actually get some airplay on the local radio station," I agreed. I couldn't fault Pete for his intentions. This stuff actually *was* intriguing. But when a gal's expecting a ring—or at least a tennis bracelet—it's a bit of a letdown to be presented with a box full of dusty garage band tapes and disks.

The newsroom was deserted, silent except for the chatter of the police scanners. There was still a chance of turning the situation around. I threaded the fingers of my right hand into Kovacs's left-hand digits. "You said you had something im-portant you wanted to tell me, remember?" I said in a seduc-tive whisper.

"Oh, that." Kovacs didn't look pleased. In fact, he looked like he would have taken a step back, if the heavy wooden desk hadn't blocked his way. "You know that thing we were doing in San Francisco next week?"

"What about it?" I detached my hand, focusing on his use

of past tense. *Were?* Yours truly was scheduled to be inducted into the Northern California Broadcast Legends Hall of Fame a week from Friday. Okay, it's not exactly winning a Peabody, but it meant a lot to me to get that kind of recognition from the radio personalities I'd idolized as a child.

"What if I have to cancel? It looks like something might be coming up."

I paused to remind myself that I was no longer fifteen, and this wasn't the Sophomore Sock Hop. "I can't pretend I'm not bummed," I said finally. "But I know you wouldn't bail out on me unless this 'something' really is important."

Kovacs let out a relieved sigh. "I'll make it up to you, I promise."

"I know you will, sweetie. In fact," I gave him a quick squeeze, "I'll let you start tonight."

I stuffed a couple of press kits that I meant to glance at later into my backpack, grabbed my car keys, made for the door, then stopped mid-stride. "Damn. Almost forgot to sign off the logs." I did a 180 and headed for the on-air studio, Kovacs following.

A foot-wide ditch ran down the middle of the on-air studio. The station had been in shambles for weeks now, ever since the owner decided he finally had enough money in the budget to go digital. It was a development to which I had decidedly mixed feelings. I could well understand the lure of digital: one tiny CD replacing miles of recording tape, laptops taking the place of piles of paper. But I wasn't sure if I was ready to give up tape for good. I already missed records, those magic platters. And turntables, the subtle *thonk* of the needle making first contact with vinyl.

Sometimes, I feel as if I'm the only person left in radio who still knows how to do a slip cue.

I peered into the cavity at a small portion of the miles and miles of cable crisscrossing the floor, walls, and ceiling of the station. There's an old truism in radio about the chief engineer being the one person with job security, because only he (it's almost always a he) knows where all those wires go, and how they're hooked up.

Kovacs caught up with me, stopping just short of the abyss.

He still carried the cardboard file box, his fingers wrapped into the holes on each side. "Thanks again for being such a good sport," he said as soon as Garland segued into a commercial break and closed the mike.

"I already told you not to worry." I turned my back to him so I could slash my signature onto the transmitter log. "It's no big deal."

"For real?"

I took the box from Kovacs's hands, placed it on the floor, backed him into a corner, put both hands around his neck and drew him close. The sports guy held his palm up for silence and flipped a switch. The red on-air light filled the control room with a warm glow.

"For real." I whispered so the mike wouldn't pick up my voice. I gave Kovacs a kiss, long and lingering. My plan was to snatch my stuff and race over his apartment, where we could start tearing each other's clothes off.

I would have made it, had it not been for the ringing phone.

Not the newsroom hotline, or one of the on-air lines. The phone on my desk, its line connected to the station switchboard, which had closed down at least an hour ago.

"Yeah?" I said cautiously into the receiver.

"Shauna J. Bogart. This is Shauna J. Bogart?" Male with an accent that sounded to me like it had had originated south of the border.

"Who wants to know?"

"This lady wants to set up a meeting with Shauna J. Bogart."

"Shauna J.'s gone for the day. Try calling back tomorrow during business hours and ask her executive producer to check her calendar. Depending on who this lady is, of course."

"You'll want to meet with her when you know who she is."

"Yeah, well, lots of people want to meet with Shauna J. Bogart. How'd you get through to this number, anyway?"

The caller ignored my last question. "The lady told me to tell you to meet her at the casbah."